The Contentious Business of Samuel Seabury

Lexie Conyngham

The Contentious Business of Samuel Seabury

Lexie Conyngham

ISBN: 978-1-910926-82-6

Cover illustration by Helen Braid at
www.ellieillustrates.co.uk

ACKNOWLEDGMENTS

With thanks to Richard Coleman, who came up with the idea.

Dramatis Personae

The Skinner household:
Bishop John Skinner,
His wife Mary
His children Jane, Margaret, Johnnie and William
His servants, Jean the cook and Charlie Rob

Guests of the Skinner household:
Dr. Samuel Seabury of Connecticut
Rev. Myles Cooper of Edinburgh
Bishop Arthur Petrie of Moray
Bishop Robert Kilgour of Aberdeen

The inhabitants of Longacre and Broad Street:
Luzie Rob, nee Gheertzoon
William Smith, architect, and his son John
Bodsy Bowers, teacher
George and Margaret Houstoun, merchants
Mennie, builder
Mrs. Gray, Superintendent of women's hospital on Queen Street

The Meston household:
Cuthbert Meston, merchant
His brother, Stephen
His stepson, Jeremiah Hosie
His warehouseman, Alan Beith
His maid, Minnie Towie

Mr. William Seller, retired teacher, Inverugie
Robert Shand, magistrate, and his henchman
Simmie, the Peterhead carrier

Prologue

Right, well, I'll warn you, straight off. This is a story with a great number of bishops in it.

I tell you now, for I know there are those who will not be doing with bishops - even, maybe, some who will have little to do with a church at all. But bishops, they're still a wee bittie controversial here in Scotland. But I can tell you - and I've kent a few - that there are bishops and there are bishops, and they're all as human as the next man, so there's no reason on God's good earth why a story about bishops might not be as interesting as any other.

When I say a great number, anyway, really what I mean is three. And a fellow, too, that wants to be a bishop. I canna say I'd want to myself, for there's a great deal of book-learning required, and a lot of running about the country, even on the winter roads, and there's no money in it at all. In England, I've heard tell, the bishops are grand folk in palaces - ha! That's no the case up here. No the case at all. Otherwise I doubt I would be able to say I know three bishops - maybe four. Not even working for one of them, for a palace is a gey big place, I should think, and I doubt any of yon English bishops ventures too far into the servants' quarters.

Anyway, this story happened a while ago, when the bishops in Scotland were in even worse state than they are now - the Penal Laws were still about, that stopped Episcopalians (that's the church that has the bishops, unless you count the Papists but they're a different thing altogether), the laws stopped Episcopalians meeting together more than four at a time, even in their own home, unless it was their own family, ken. In case they were Jacobites. And the Episcopalians had had a good deal to put up with, for every time one of the ministers would maybe hold a service or have a wee place folks could meet, some troublemakers would come and burn it down. This had happened a few times in Aberdeen, where I bide, but by 1784 which is the year of our story, here, things were a bit quieter and a man called John Skinner had come in from the country to be the minister to some of the town's Episcopalians, and he did that in a house he had built in the Longacre, next to Marischal College - he had his wee bit chapel upstairs and he and his family lived sort of around it, and as long as he kept his mouth mostly shut, he was allowed to get on with things. So much so that a few years syne he had been made - now, wait till I get it right - Co-Adjutant Bishop of Aberdeen. So there's the first of our bishops.

How do I ken all this? Well, my name's Charlie Rob. I live in Aberdeen with my wife Luzie, and I'm the manservant in the household of Bishop Skinner.

And what I'm about to tell you now - well, you can look up some of the people in books and find out all about them. If I tell you what was going on inside their heads you'll ken I'm making it up. But other folk here ... who am I to tell you what is true and what is not true? Some of that you will have to judge for yourself. But I'll start by saying that at the beginning of November in that year I mentioned, 1784, one of the bishops was quite excited, but all of them were just a wee bit afraid. As well they might be - even though they had no idea what was to happen next.

Chapter One

As if it were not quite bad enough, thought Myles Cooper, the woman next to him threw up.

She had every excuse. When Myles and Seabury had gone down to the harbour at Leith, Myles was convinced that the coastal packet to Aberdeen would be cancelled. The wind even there, in the shelter, jostled the wooden boats against each other like late-night drinkers trying to get into a howff before it closed. He was convinced they would not be leaving today - indeed, he offered up a prayer that they would not be leaving today. He was quite ready to turn around and hurry back to his little flat in the Cowgate, with its warmth and its comforts and its small but carefully chosen selection of fine wines, but the packet master was already taking their baggage from the porter they had hired, and urging them to get on board. And Seabury - Seabury, though he must have been exhausted, clutched at the master's offered arm with all the desperation of a man taking his last chance, and took a determined leap on to the deck. Myles could not be left behind. He reached out for the master's hand, closed his eyes, and swooped on to the boat in a heavy flutter of black coat tails, like a dying albatross.

Not a good omen, even for a religious man.

He thought of it now, as he clutched his carefully laundered handkerchief in trembling fingers and wiped his face and shoulder, and as an afterthought, offered the soiled cloth to the woman to clean herself, too. The fat man was still shouting at Seabury, oblivious. Every word hit Myles like a blow.

'As good as Papists but without the courage of your convictions! Trouble-making, treacherous trashtries!'

A neat bit of rhetoric, Myles thought as he clung to the pole that held up their meagre shelter. Seabury, despite the wind whipping his curling grey hair around his broad face – he had almost lost his hat, and now held it hard to his chest - managed a kind of smile which, knowing Seabury, was probably intended to be consolatory.

'Dinna you laugh at me, you prinked-up idolator!' bellowed the fat man.

Myles tried to move further away, but to leave the shelter was to be thrown across the deck. His back was stiff with panic. Was the man going to hit Seabury? Draw a blade? What would happen when they reached Aberdeen, if they ever did?

'Oh, aye, it'll be grand,' the packet master had said, without much hint of irony, as Myles gathered himself up off the deck. 'Just you hang on there, and dinna move about too much – I'm using your weight for balance. You and him.' He had nodded to a fat man in an expensive overcoat and fine, shiny boots, on which the splashing salt water had already made inroads. The man had nodded to them shortly. In any other circumstances Myles would just have nodded back and gone to sit elsewhere, but this was where the packet master had told them to stand. And so, with the passengers huddled under the beating shelter, they had set out, the wind lashing them sideways all the way up the coast, heedless of the packet master's manoeuvres. Crossing the Atlantic had not been worse than this.

They had known it was going to take a while for they had booked a cheap passage, one that called in several harbours along the way. One or two they were supposed to call into they skipped, with the packet master remarking casually that it was 'a bittie too brisk' to enter safely. They looked bleak, abandoned places, a few houses battened down against the storm, swiftly left behind as their own vessel ploughed on.

Conversation was not easy, but Myles was nervous, and could not seem to stop himself. And so it was that he had told the fat man that they were two Episcopal clergymen, heading for Aberdeen for a great and wonderful purpose. And that, somewhere about Montrose, had set the fat man off on his rant.

Myles felt sick, and he knew it was not the motion of the boat – though that continued bad enough, as they inched up the coastline of Forfarshire, towards Kincardineshire (he had looked on a map before they had set out, for he liked to be prepared). He hated quarrels, shouting, angry people. It made him shrink inside, made him shake, made him remember ...

It was already growing dark. If he squinted, he could see cliffs passing, with narrow beaches at their feet and hints of cottages on the top, green pastures, sprinkled with snow, folding and tilting with the cliffs' headlands and breaks. Then at last he saw the mouth of a broad river - they had passed the Esk at Montrose, so he was certain that this was the Dee - and beyond, emerging from the dusk, lights, more lights than in a village. And on the air, just now and then as the wind swerved about the land, the scent of wood fires, and cooking, and all the detritus of gathered human existence. This had to be Aberdeen.

A harbour about the size of Leith's own welcomed them in at the mouth of the river. Houses of all sizes waiting in lines, almost down to the shoreline, then stepping up quickly to some higher land beyond. Myles had never been here before and he knew Seabury had not, either. New territory, new people. And for Seabury at least, perhaps a new beginning.

The packet master wriggled his vessel through a mixture of shipping - whalers, Myles thought, as well as Dutchmen, fishing boats of all sizes, little local boats that probably took up shellfish. He focussed on each of them as the boards beneath his feet gradually steadied their movement and the crew busied themselves with sails and oars and preparation for docking. The passengers gradually let go of the shelter, wriggling stiffened fingers, brushing snow from their shoulders, trying a step or two to remind themselves about balance, or to get a better view, maybe see someone waiting for them. There would be no one waiting for Seabury, Myles thought. They were early.

The fat man's wrath seemed to have burned itself out. He stood, prosperous and dignified, in the bow, as if guiding his own merchantman back from the East Indies with all the gold and spices safe below. He did not spare a look for Seabury and Myles as they looked for their baggage, replaced their hats, and waited for the gangplank to be placed for disembarkation.

'Janie's got an admirer! Janie's got an admirer!'

Charlie Rob, who was cleaning the tappit hen in the chapel ready for Sunday, suppressed a grin. There was nothing, he had observed in his life, quite as annoying for a young lady as a little brother.

Jane Skinner, also at work dusting, turned a look of offended surprise at young John.

'Just the one, Johnnie?' she asked. 'Good heavens, I should have thought I merited more than that!'

Johnnie subsided, but he gave a little skip about the stone-flagged floor.

'I'm sure you have lots, Janie, honest. But there's one's been hanging about outside all day, and now he's standing in the snow, staring up at your window!'

'Really? All day?' Jane looked concerned now. 'Are you sure it's not a beggar waiting for alms? Someone with a stall?'

'He's not!'

'Then who is he? I'm sure it's nothing to do with me, but it's not the weather for anybody to be waiting all day outside. Do you know his name, Johnnie?'

Johnnie drew himself up to a height of some importance – after all, he was sixteen, and almost a young man.

'Aye, I do, for Stevie at school has a big brother who knows him. His name's Jeremiah Hosie.'

'Oh ... Jeremiah Hosie. Yes, I do know him.' Jane Skinner sighed, and Charlie gave her a quick look.

'Problems, Miss Jane?' he asked. He might have been a servant, but he was one of the family.

'I don't think it's anything to worry about, Charlie. Johnnie, if you're going to stay down here in the chapel you might as well start polishing the benches. Here's a cloth.'

'But I've got to go and do my schoolwork!' John objected.

'Oh, dear, that's a shame,' said Jane, as John scuttled off quickly. She looked at Charlie with a smile. 'I thought he wouldn't linger if there was work to be done!'

'He's keen enough on his schoolbooks,' said Charlie, in John's defence.

'But there is a deal of work to be done,' said Jane. 'If we are ever to be ready for this man Dr. Seabury coming on Wednesday. I think Papa does not quite know what to expect.'

'He's American, is he no?' asked Charlie. Dr. Seabury was the cause of endless household speculation, not just here, in the

Skinners' house, but at his own home, too. 'Will he speak Scots like us?'

'I think he speaks English, so we should be able to understand him,' said Jane. 'And I think Papa said he had studied in Edinburgh, so he's been in Scotland before.'

'And he's a clergyman.'

'That's right.'

'But your father's a Bishop,' Charlie pointed out. 'Why would a clergyman coming make him nervish? Even a foreign one.'

'It's ... it's a strange one, Charlie,' said Jane, frowning. 'I don't know that Papa has told me all the ins and outs, but Dr. Seabury wants to be a Bishop, too.'

'In Scotland? Don't we have all the Bishops we need?' Charlie stopped - that sounded a bit ungracious. He liked working for Bishop Skinner, and the other bishops he had met while he worked there were fine men.

'No, not in Scotland. In America.'

'Then why is he here?'

'To be a bishop, Charlie, you need at least two other bishops to consecrate you. And there aren't any other bishops in America. So he had to come here, to where there are other bishops.'

'I see,' said Charlie. It seemed simple. 'So why is Bishop Skinner not so sure about it?'

'I suppose,' said Jane, after a bit of thought, 'that not everyone who wants to be a bishop is really suitable. So Papa will want to talk with him, see what he's like. I suppose that happens with everyone who wants to be a bishop. But it just maybe seems like a bigger business, when it's the first bishop in America. Imagine! All that great country, and no bishops.'

A few years ago, that thought would not have bothered Charlie, brought up in the established Church with not a bishop to be seen. But he had brushed up against the Episcopalians, and liked them, and now here he was working for a bishop. Who knew what way life would go?

But he still thought that Jane had turned the subject when she had encouraged young Johnnie to leave the chapel, and being a dogged man, he went back to it.

'So is there a problem with this Jeremiah Hosie, then, miss?' he asked. He had a feeling he knew the name, but he could not quite place it in his head. Jane carried on rubbing at the bulbous base of a brass vase, making it catch the candlelight like gold.

'I think John might be right, and he is a kind of admirer,' she said. 'I met him at Miss Graham's - you know, at the school. It was all very correct! There were several young men there from respectable families around the town, and us, the older girls. He just seemed to latch on to me, unfortunately.'

'Do you no like the man, then?' Charlie asked.

'He's very handsome - *very* handsome,' Jane acknowledged.

'Would your father no approve?'

Jane did not respond for a moment, apparently working on putting an unheard-of shine on a small patch of brass.

'Well, no, I don't think he would. But more than that, I don't know that I approve. And yet I can't just put my finger on why I don't.'

'Well, then,' said Charlie. He set aside the tappit hen, and began to work on the benches that Johnnie had refused.

'Even so, what is he doing standing outside all day on a Friday? In the snow? He works for his stepfather, I believe: he should probably have been doing something more useful, somewhere.'

'Maybe Johnnie's mistaken,' said Charlie, trying to be reassuring. 'Or maybe Mr. Hosie has some business about the place. I mean, miss ...' he floundered a little, 'I mean, I'm sure he would acknowledge your ... um ... charms ... um ... as much as any other gentleman, but it might not be anything to concern yourself about.'

Jane Skinner laughed heartily.

'That's beautifully put, Charlie, but I am a bit concerned about him. He's - he's not what I would call steady.'

'Steady?'

'Stable. In his right wits.' She stopped rubbing, and stood straight for a moment. 'In fact, between you and me, I think he might be quite mad.'

Chapter Two

The fat man strode off the boat as if he owned it, the harbour, and the fine warehouses around it. Myles gestured to Seabury to follow, then put a tentative foot on the slippery wood himself. They must have looked odd, he thought, to anyone watching: all three men were broad, tall, and dressed in black, heavy overcoats. Even their hats looked similar, for the fat man favoured a broad brim against the snow, not unlike a cleric's hat. Myles angled his head to look about him, and the shape of his hat called to mind, almost, a bird's beak. He remembered hearing children in the Cowgate singing, 'Three craws, sitting on a wall ...' He almost laughed, though it was more nerves than anything.

Seabury stopped where their baggage had been piled by the packet's crew, and looked about him. If Myles was nervous, then Seabury must be. The last throw of the dice for him, or it would be back off to America, Myles supposed, with his tail between his legs. Or maybe he would stay in Scotland. Myles did not want to think of returning to America, not under any circumstances. Seabury was a brave man.

'I should have asked about inns when we were on the boat,' Seabury said. He had a rich, polished voice, full of authority - one of his best attributes, Myles had always thought, a little jealous. 'But I don't think that fellow was going to give us much of a recommendation, do you?' He laughed, nodding after the fat man as he made his way across the harbour's slippery cobbles, snapping at some miserable lad who had evidently come to meet him. The lad was covered in snow, and struggling with some package the fat man had almost thrown at him to carry. 'Poor fellow: he must have an unhappy life.' Myles thought Seabury meant the boy, but after a moment he thought perhaps he meant the fat man. Seabury's compassion sometimes fell on odd objects.

'You stay here with the baggage, and I'll go and ask over there,' said Seabury. 'No sense in carrying it any further than we have to.' He headed off tentatively to some low stone building. Myles watched him for a moment, then turned to see the fat man making for a warehouse. It looked like the kind of grand warehouse where the owner lived over it in some style, keeping a wary eye on the comings and goings of his own business and of the harbour. A merchant, then: Myles had thought as much.

'Excuse me, sir.'

Myles jumped, and tensed to run. But the man who had approached him looked harmless enough. He was elderly, and thin, but dressed well and warmly against the weather.

'Forgive me, sir,' said the newcomer, 'for I have startled you. Can you tell me, please, if you are Dr. Samuel Seabury?'

'No! No, I'm not,' said Myles at once. Then, feeling unaccountably like Peter denying Christ, he carried on over-hastily. 'But I do know him. I can point him out to you.'

'So he was on this boat, then? That's good to know.' He tilted his narrow head thoughtfully. 'A friend suggested he might be. And if you could indeed point him out? I should be most grateful.'

A friend? Myles was suspicious at once. What friend might have known that they were setting off early for Aberdeen? But he gathered his wits about him, trying to still his agitated heart.

'Of course,' he said. 'That's him, just over there. No doubt he'll be back here in a minute, but you could easily catch him up.' He took a deep breath, but the man was nodding in polite gratitude. He turned to look in the direction that Myles had indicated, and Myles saw that he had a sharp nose like the gnomon on a sundial, so thin he had barely noticed it when they stood face to face. The man turned back.

'Oh, I see he's busy just now. I'll catch up with him later, I'm sure. I too have an engagement. But it is good to know he is here, that he's arrived safely.' The thin man, unsmiling, bowed, and turned, and headed off, up the hill, away from the harbour.

'Who shall I say has been asking for him?' Myles belatedly called after the man, but the man apparently did not hear, stalking along on thin legs, pale stockings bright in the snowlight.

'Five days, Charlie! Will we be ready?'

Bishop Skinner was smiling his usual, gentle smile, but Charlie thought the twinkle in his eye had more to do with nerves than good humour today.

'It depends, sir, what else you want done.'

'Ha! Well, if I knew that, I would tell you! What has Mrs. Skinner asked you to do?'

'The mistress said to remember that Bishop Kilgour and Bishop Petrie would be coming, sir,' said Charlie helpfully. 'And to do what we would usually do for them. She said that none of them is staying here, is that right, sir?'

'I should have known my wife would be in control of the situation,' said Skinner with a sigh. He sank on to the chair at his desk. 'No, none of them is staying at Longacre, so far as I know. Bishop Kilgour will likely stay at the New Inn, as usual. Bishop Petrie ... I'm not sure. He's growing very frail, and he might have decided to stay with friends. As for Dr. Seabury and his companion, I have no idea. I have not offered accommodation. I thought it might be awkward, you know, Charlie, if we turned him down and still had to see him at breakfast.'

'Aye, sir.' It would be very awkward. 'Can I ask, sir, if you're likely to turn him down?'

Skinner sighed again, and leaned back in the chair, fidgeting with some papers on his desk.

'It's not straightforward, Charlie. From all I've heard, he's a good man - but I haven't heard that much, and I've never met him.'

'Aye, I can see you'd need to be careful, sir,' said Charlie. He had no idea how you might go about choosing a bishop. Mr. Skinner had only been bishop a couple of years himself, and he wasn't even a proper bishop, as Charlie understood it - he was a kind of helper to Bishop Kilgour. Bishop Kilgour was Bishop of Aberdeen, but he was Primus, too, the chief of the Scottish bishops, so he had appointed Mr. Skinner as - what was it again? A co-dodger? Co-adjutor, that was it - to look after Aberdeen while he was doing other things. And while he was getting older. Bishop Kilgour was a fair age, but still full of energy. Bishop Petrie was much younger, but you wouldn't have known it.

'It's worse than just choosing the right man, though, Charlie. That bit's not so much up to us – God chooses bishops – whether they like it or not!' he added with a laugh, a little wave of his hand excusing his own appointment. 'We just have to see if we can work out what God wants. But this case is a bit different. You see, Dr. Seabury has already been down in England, trying to be made bishop there.'

'Well, sir, if they turned him down in England ...'

'They turned him down in England because, now that America is independent, he could not swear allegiance to King George. And that's part of the English consecration ceremony, you see. So whether they liked him or not, and whether God wants it or not, they couldn't really consecrate him, not in England.'

'So now he's trying Scotland? But is King George not our king, too?'

'He is,' said Skinner, with what was almost a wink, 'but our bishops don't have to swear allegiance to him. So we can consecrate Dr. Seabury and he can go back to America without any problem. But if we do that, will it annoy the English?'

Charlie cleared his throat.

'There are some that say annoying the English is what we Scots do best, sir.'

'True!' Skinner laughed again. 'True, indeed. But I have a yearning, Charlie, that one day we'll get the Penal Laws repealed, and be allowed to worship freely again. I know, it almost feels as if we can, but those laws are still there, still tainting us, and I'd like to see them gone. And annoying the English is probably not the best way to start that process. Do you think?'

Charlie nodded. He liked the way Bishop Skinner explained things. Even difficult things usually made sense.

'But the thing is,' Skinner went on, 'it's possible that the English will be perfectly pleased if we consecrate Dr. Seabury. If they liked him, and wanted him to be a bishop, and felt that God wanted him to be a bishop, but couldn't consecrate him themselves, then perhaps we're the next best thing.'

'But do you know that, sir?' asked Charlie. Once again, Bishop Skinner sighed.

'No, Charlie, I don't. I don't even think that Bishop Kilgour knows that. Alas, I may save my breath to cool my porage – we'll likely know nothing at all until Dr. Seabury arrives. And that will be not be until Wednesday, so we can only speculate until then.'

Myles did not have long to wait, in anxious though, until Seabury returned to rescue him and the bags.

'There's somewhere called the New Inn,' said Seabury, rubbing his gloved hands together hard against the cold harbour air, 'but it sounds a bit much for my budget. There's another one somewhere called the Gallowgate that would be cheaper.'

Myles shuddered.

'I told you I would pay,' he said. 'If the New Inn is the best place, then let us by all means go there. Is it nearer by than the Gallowgate place?'

'It's up at the top of this hill, apparently. The Gallowgate is the same direction, but further.'

'Is there a porter here will carry our bags?'

'I'm sure there is, but Myles, I can carry my own bag. Most of my luggage is back in Edinburgh in your flat. Save your money!'

'I said I would meet the expenses,' said Myles, stubbornly. Something about the very word Gallowgate put him off the cheaper inn, and besides, he had been fortunate in taking his money out of America when he had fled. He was able to live very comfortably for now. Seabury, crossing the Atlantic at his own expense, had already been running short when he reached Edinburgh after so many months waiting in England, but that was no reason why Myles should suffer with him. Far better to pay for the finer, and closer, accommodation. 'Anyway, you don't want to go and see Bishop Skinner after a bad dinner, do you?'

Seabury's eyes widened in anxious anticipation.

'I have no intention of disturbing Bishop Skinner tonight,' he said quickly. 'I'll send him a note tomorrow and let him know we've arrived – and arrived early, too. He needs fair warning, I think.' He gave a little shiver. Myles could understand it. He needed to make no false steps here. He had to give himself the best possible chance.

'Then at least let us see if we can secure ourselves a good night's sleep,' Myles tried. 'Come on: I shall have frozen to the ground if we stay here much longer!'

Seabury called over a porter and Myles instructed him to take the bags to the New Inn. The porter dashed off more quickly than Myles liked, or could follow, on the steep hill.

'Do you think he was a trustworthy fellow?' he asked.

'I think so,' said Seabury. 'I'm sure the bags will be there on our arrival. We'd better get on and follow, though!'

Their road led them up past the warehouses by the quay, to judge by the directions Seabury had received. Even at this time of day there was plenty of toing and froing about them, and as they approached one doorway, the door shot open.

'Out you go, miss! I'll not have your kind around here!'

And almost across their feet as they staggered back out of the way, a small figure birled, all legs and arms. Just before the door slammed shut, Myles recognised the person there, even if he had not already known the voice. It was the fat man from the boat.

Chapter Three

The child was on her feet before they could even move. Seabury called out to her but she was already away up an alley, vanishing into the dusk. Myles reckoned he could not be paid enough to follow her up there, whatever the problem, and fortunately Seabury seemed to agree.

'She didn't seem to be hurt, anyway,' he murmured. They still stood by the warehouse door, and from inside they could hear shouting – the fat man's overbearing voice, altogether too familiar from the boat journey, and two other men, perhaps remonstrating with him over the girl. Myles was not sure: they could hear no words, and one voice was much softer than the other. In any case, he was cold and hungry, and the raised voices made him nervous.

'Let's go and find this inn, and see if our bags are safely arrived,' he said.

'Well, I don't think there's much we can do here,' Seabury agreed. 'For all we know she was a thief.'

But he looked uneasy as he turned away. Myles decided to say no more, and followed his friend up the hill to where, he hoped, a good meal awaited, with a bottle of wine and a comfortable bed for the night. And no shouting.

'And where do you think she's going to go, at this time of the night?'

The young man was breathless, and his eyes burned bright with passion.

'No doubt she'll find her own kind.' The fat man managed to combine anger with a smirk.

'What's that supposed to mean?' the young man snapped.

'Oh, you're gey ready to defend the fair sex! You should be out trying to find a suitable wife for yourself, instead of crawling around after the servants.' The young man flinched, but even as he opened his mouth to respond, he frowned, concerned. His stepfather must be tired after his journey: the shouting had died down more easily than usual. The fat man eased himself into the only armchair in the room, leaving the other two, the young man and a middle-aged man in a decent coat, to perch on a bench by the table. The young man flung himself back to lean on the table, but his companion nudged him and pointed to the spilled broth, the tipped pot. There was no one to clear it up unless one of them set to: the maid was gone.

'I'll do it, Jem,' said the other man. He had the anxious, watchful face of a perpetual peacemaker. The young man stood in one dramatic movement.

'No,' he said, 'you sit there, Uncle. I'll fetch a cloth. Minnie always leaves everything in good order – it should be easy enough to find.'

That was a side-swipe at the fat man, but all he did was growl in response.

'Are you well, Cuthbert?' asked the man at the table. 'You look weary.'

'Well enough, Stephen,' muttered the fat man. 'Well enough to deal with that kind of business in my own house, though it was not a good thing to come home to.'

'You could maybe have left it till the morning,' said Stephen gently. 'It's no kind of a night to be out.'

'Like I say, she'll find her place – someone to keep her warm, no doubt.'

'She's not like that, Cuthbert, and you know it,' said Stephen.

'Then what way is she expecting a bairn?' the fat man demanded, and Stephen shuffled a little as his brother's voice rose again. Jem came back from rooting in the press in the corner, and for a moment Stephen braced himself in case Jem responded to his stepfather's question. But Jem, for once, started in to wipe up the spilled broth, and once it was cleared he set the pot back over the fire in a manner that suggested he had some idea what he was doing. And before Cuthbert could fire his temper up again, a small, sandy man entered the room and bowed.

'Aye, take your seat, Alan. Minnie's left us, so Jem will be serving tonight. And he'd better not be slow, for I have business to be about.' Cuthbert's lips stretched into the semblance of a smile as he watched Jem tend the pot. He did not, therefore, notice the look of astonishment and concern that passed over the face of the small sandy man, as he took his place on the bench by the table.

Charlie was awake before light on Saturday morning, though in Aberdeen in November that almost went without saying. He did not live in the Skinners' house in Longacre, as he had lived in his employers' houses when he was younger. Now that he was a married man, with bairns (though they had grown and moved), he lived out – not least because his wife had her own business, and they had a small property of their own.

It was not, he thought, quite time to be out of bed. Years of being in service had given him a keen sense of when to rise, and when he could have another five minutes with his arms around his wife. Yet when he reached out for her, he found that she was already awake, too, and lying flat on her back, staring up at the dark ceiling.

'You all right, dearie?' he asked her, concerned.

She sighed.

'I think so.'

'Oh, aye, well, that would stop me worrying, right enough.'

She gave a short laugh.

'Nearly time to get up.'

'We have a mintie or two. Tell me what's wrong.'

She paused, as if trying to find the words. Her Scots was fine, so he knew it must be a difficult subject.

'I had a visit last night from Cuthbert Meston.'

'Well, there's an honour!' Charlie propped himself up on his elbow, surprised that Luzie was not more pleased than she sounded. 'You've been trying for years to come under his notice!'

'Aye,' said Luzie, 'but not in this way. He was – well, he was no very pleasant.'

'What way?'

'Well,' she amended, 'he was at first. He said he'd been hearing great things about our coffee. All his customers, he said, wanted to know about Luzie Rob's coffee, and whether he stocked anything like it, and if not, why not?'

'That's good ...' Charlie was cautious.

'Aye, well. So he asked me to get him some, so he could stock it, too.'

'Oh, aye?'

'I said I'd have to think about it, that I didna have a big supply myself. You ken, my father imports it, and passes some on to us.'

'I ken, aye.'

'So he said he'd pay me for it, and I said it didna matter, for it wasna there to be paid for. Then he said he'd pay me to stop selling it.'

'He what?'

'He said I could just tell my customers I couldna get it any more.'

'But it's one of your best sellers, is it no?'

'It is. So I said I wouldna, for it was a question of looking after my customers, as much as making money out of it. Which it is, in a way. Anyway, I didna like the way he was looking at me, and I wanted him out of the warehouse.'

'And what did he say to that?'

'He said he'd made me a good offer - though he hadna, for no price had been mentioned - and given me fair warning. And he had his walking stick with him, and he birled it about a bit and I thought maybe he was going to break something, for he had a bad look in his eye. Real nasty, ken?'

'Worse than some of the others? Adams, maybe? He wasna friendly during the Dutch war. Or Houstoun?'

'Houstoun doesna like a woman in trade, but he resents me having the best coffee in the town when he won't let himself buy it from me. And when he did condescend to ask, I turned him down. No - not like those foolish men. Meston was much worse.' She shivered.

Charlie slid his arm around Luzie's waist, holding her close.

'Tell me he didna hit you,' he whispered.

She shook her head, and he felt the shift of her braided hair against his face.

'He didna hit me, no, nor any of the stock. But he knew I thought he was going to, for he leaned over towards me, sudden, and said, 'Fair warning,' in a real mean wee voice. Then he stood up and said 'It's a grand wee business you've had here. But I think your time is over, Mistress Rob.' And he went off into the dark and that was that. But I'm just wondering ... what if he comes back today?'

Not long after, Luzie was up and had the fire lit, and a kettle swung over it. Charlie had his own duties, heavy-hearted though he was, and brought in more firewood to keep the fire going for the day. Even in the cold morning air the house was heavily scented with fresh coffee and the lingering odour of – was it nutmeg? Probably. Last week it had been cinnamon. Charlie kissed his wife, wrapped a shawl about his neck, and headed out to fetch water.

What was he to do? Once she had told him, Luzie herself clearly felt better, and said there was no need for him to stay at home to protect her. She was a tough woman, no doubt about it.

Luzie was Dutch, the daughter of a merchant, and saw no reason why she should not be a merchant herself. Using her father's connexions in Amsterdam, she imported coffee, tea and spices from the Low Countries into Aberdeen, selling them on to tradesmen inland. It was not a large business, but that did not mean she did not have ambition. She had begun with a few packets of tea her father had sent her, and within a couple of years had been able, in Charlie's name, to rent a small warehouse with living quarters behind in the prominent Broad Street, near the Marischal College. Charlie had occasionally caught her eyeing the shop next door, as if planning further expansion. Intermittent hostilities with Holland had caused her to name the business 'L. Rob', rather than to use her more exotic surname, Gheertzoon, but she had tricked out the establishment with blue and white tiles and the dark wood that reminded Charlie of her father's house in Amsterdam. Occasionally Charlie wondered if she had married him simply to make inroads into Aberdeen markets.

Nevertheless, he did want to protect her. He knew he was far from being a brave man – the thought of any threat from Cuthbert Meston made his stomach shrink inside him – but he loved Luzie, loved her determination, her drive, her spark. The thought that some great bully could come and damp that spark pushed him as close to anger as he ever went. But he was nervous, too. Cuthbert Meston had done no damage yesterday, but he had threatened – what might he do today? What was he planning? Could he be nearby already, watching the warehouse, waiting for him to go out?

The nearest well was at the mouth of Longacre, just beyond where the tenements made a dark tunnel into it from Broad Street, and within clear view of Bishop Skinner's house. Despite the early hour there was already a queue formed, drowsy neighbours nodding greetings in the uncertain light of occasional street lamps. A light or two flickered in the windows of the College, where Charlie pictured some reluctant student huddled over his books. Not the life for him, though Bishop Skinner had been to college and had upwards of fifty books. He glanced over at the Skinner house. Downstairs was in darkness, at the front, anyway. Upstairs a light shone in the chapel – one candle, he thought. Bishop Skinner was saying his morning prayers. A quick look back at his own house, through the tunnel: it seemed quiet.

'Aye, Charlie,' a neighbour, Mennie, greeted him. 'How's the day looking?'

Charlie grinned.

'I'll tell you when it's light enough to see,' he said. 'What about yourself?'

'No so bad, aye? Could be worse.' He nodded, as if pleased with himself for being so positive. 'Do you think that fellow over yonder is waiting for water like the rest of us, or is he looking to break into a house?'

Chapter Four

'What fellow?' Charlie squinted across the dark street. A tall, slim figure stood propped in a doorway. 'He has no bucket that I can see.'

'No ... and he seems well enough dressed to be out for a sup from the common well.'

'I dinna ken how you can tell that in this light,' Charlie objected. 'I couldn't swear to you that he was young or old, rich or poor, fair or black or red. In fact, it's that dark over yonder if the man only had the one leg I couldn't tell.'

His neighbour gave a rich chuckle.

'Aye, you're right, there.'

'It could even be a woman,' Charlie added, 'for all that I can see.'

'That'd be a gey tall woman, Charlie – I dinna ken where you've been courting!'

The man behind them in the queue made an unnecessary remark about all women looking tall to a man on his knees, and for a moment the conversation darted among subjects of which bishops would not approve. Charlie's neighbour cuffed the newcomer's ear, not hard, and turned back to Charlie.

'But it's the fellow's clothes, see? The outline of him. The rest of us is just in whatever was to hand – see your old shawl, that you always throw on on a cold morning to come here? And I'm in my short jacket. But yon fellow's in a good long cloak and a hat.'

'Aye, you're right,' said Charlie, studying the man more

closely. It was too slim to be Cuthbert Meston looking for trouble, was his first thought. Then it crossed his mind, briefly, that this might be the mysterious Dr. Seabury, waiting to call on Bishop Skinner. He did seem to have his gaze fixed, as far as Charlie could tell from here, on Skinner's upstairs flat. But he really could not see any details of the man, except the outline that his neighbour had pointed out and the merest pale blot of what was presumably the man's face.

'Come on, whose turn is it?' called someone behind them, and Charlie seized his turn at the pump, filling his neighbour's buckets before his own.

There were probably not many in Aberdeen who began their day with a cup of fine, freshly ground and prepared coffee, but Luzie insisted on it.

'We can call it making sure the goods are the very best,' she always said with a brisk nod. 'And it brightens the mind for a day of trade.'

'Or a day of service,' Charlie agreed, now that he had grown to appreciate the bitter taste. Cuthbert Meston's customers were right to be interested. The children, once they were past their tenth birthdays, had it with lots of milk and sugar, and Luzie claimed that that was why they were the brightest bairns in the town. Charlie thought that any child of Luzie's was almost obliged to be bright, or she would simply have chivvied them into it.

Thus invigorated, he was at the door of Bishop Skinner's flat at his usual time, carrying more water, and ready to help with whatever was required. The maid Jean, who was missing an arm, took the buckets, one by one, and let Charlie receive his orders from the Bishop's wife. Mrs. Skinner was counting pots of jam in the pantry.

'Saturday,' said Mrs. Skinner, as if the world had been waiting for her to decide what day it was. 'The Bishop will want to write his sermon for tomorrow, so as usual he should be left in peace until noon. If at all possible,' she added with a weary smile. Charlie smiled back. Even those church members who most appreciated the sermon on a Sunday forgot, often, that it had to be written. Mrs. Skinner was most protective of her husband, but there were times when even she could not persuade visitors that this was not the most appropriate time for a call. 'So if you can answer the door, Charlie, I'd be very grateful. Let me see ... we need coals in the parlour and the bedrooms – the children are all up, I believe, so whatever time you can manage – and then if you could give the windows a wash, particularly in the chapel and in Bishop Skinner's bookroom when he's finished there – I don't want Dr. Seabury thinking the house even darker than it already is in November. I wonder what America is like at this time of year?'

'Mrs. Skinner, will you no take the weight off your feet?' put in the maid. Mrs. Skinner sighed, placed a hand irresistibly on her stomach, and sank on to a stool by the kitchen fire that the maid was bringing to life. Charlie was not sure how many pregnancies she had gone through, but she had certainly lost a child or two before now. Luzie said it was because she did not rest enough. Charlie could well believe it. Jean brought Mrs. Skinner a cup of chocolate, and went through what she was expected to buy at market today. Charlie was just taking off his coat when there was a chapping at the front door. He replaced his coat, and went to see who it was.

'Aye, aye,' said the man.

'Who is it?' called Mrs. Skinner.

'The Peterhead carrier,' said Charlie, grinning at the man. He was a well-kent face at their door.

'Oh, no – is it a letter from Bishop Kilgour?' Mrs. Skinner asked.

'Aye, mistress,' the carrier shouted past Charlie. 'He asked me to take it straight here.' He handed a crisp letter to Charlie, the wrapper directed in Bishop Kilgour's business-like hand. 'He's paid,' he added quickly to Charlie.

'Urgent, then?'

The carrier nodded.

'I'll see you later,' he said, and returned to his cart. In any other place he would have gone to the back door, but the houses here were hard up against the college wall.

Mrs. Skinner sighed.

'You'd better take it up, then,' she said. 'So much for peace until noon!'

Charlie straightened his coat and headed up the narrow stair to the floor where the chapel was – just the front room, really, decorated plainly enough for any parish minister. It was brave, he thought, of Bishop Skinner to have the place of worship in his house, for several other chapels used by the Episcopalians during the years when the Penal Laws were at their harshest had been burned down. Changing times.

Bishop Skinner's bookroom door was a little ajar, despite his wife's thoughts on peace till noon. Charlie pushed it open.

'A letter from Bishop Kilgour, sir. The carrier says it's urgent.'

Bishop Skinner was at his desk, leaning back in his chair with his hands folded in front of him. He was either seeking inspiration or praying for support. He sat forward, and reached out a hand for the letter.

'Stay, Charlie, in case I need to send a reply.' He thumbed open the letter, tearing neatly around Kilgour's seal, and unfolded it. There seemed to be more than one piece of paper inside, and, as far as Charlie could see without being overly curious, in two different hands. Bishop Skinner flicked between them, then began to read. Only a few words in, and he stopped.

'I knew there would be trouble,' he said softly, and pressed his thumb and forefinger to his temples. He held it there for a moment, then slid his full hand down his face, revealing a worried expression.

'What is it, sir?' asked Charlie, after a moment.

'Some helpful person ...' he looked to the foot of the letter, 'a Mr. Seller, has sent a letter to Bishop Kilgour - oh, and that letter is reporting information from some school friend living in London - it's a long chain of who knows how reputable gossip! Let me see ...

'"He says" - that is, this Mr. Seller's friend says - "Sunday last a Dr. Seabury an American clergyman set out from London to Aberdeen with expectation of being consecrated by Bishops Kilgour, Petrie & Skinner ... against the earnest and sound advice of the Archbishops of Canterbury and York, to whom his design was communicated, they not thinking him a fit person, especially as he was active and deeply engaged against Congress, that he would by this forward step render Episcopacy suspected there." Well, that's no good! That's exactly what I was worried about. If the Archbishops don't think Dr. Seabury is a fit person, going against America's new government ... but then who does this person think he is, to know the minds of the Archbishops?' Skinner read on in silence for a moment, then emitted a little puff of frustration.

'There's some more stuff about American politics, and then

he says, "If you value your own peace and advantage as a Christian Society see that your Bishops meddle not in this Consecration, till they have Corresponded upon it with the Archbishop of Canterbury, who will take it as an instance of great condescension of brotherly love, which on this occasion they will have a very favourable opportunity to show." Good heavens!' Another minute or two of silent reading. 'Then he has the gall to suggest we might like to send one of our bishops over to America instead, because it would pay him well! If we were in it for the money ... Here's an interesting bit: "My bosom friend your Cousin Dr. Smith" - now I'm losing track. Is this Mr. Seller's cousin? Bishop Kilgour's? The school friend's? I think it must be Seller's. "Your cousin Dr. Smith is deeply interested in this affair. I expect him here after the Autumn meeting of the American clergy, with recommendations from the States of America to be consecrated a Bishop, but all his designs will be frustrated in case your Bishops consecrate Seabury, a man of strong passions and resentments and Dr. Smith's avowed enemy." What think you of that, Charlie?' Bishop Skinner shot him an assessing look.

'I think it sounds like something I would step far away from, sir,' said Charlie firmly.

'I'm inclined to agree ... let's see what Bishop Kilgour has to say. He'll have an opinion - he'll probably have decided exactly what to do. I'm glad I'm not in his shoes, but I'm very glad that he is! Oh.' Skinner made a face at Kilgour's covering letter, and began to read from it.

'"... I know not what to make of it; whether matters be as there represented; or if this be a manoeuvre to answer some View of Dr. Smith, who has the Character of a very ambitious, designing Man. If Dr. Seabury has applied to us contrary to the Advice of the two Archbishops; and if they are likely to take umbrage at us, I do not think that the people who approached us on Dr. Seabury's behalf act either friendly or fair. However this Remonstrance, though from a yet unknown hand, makes caution necessary; and I have sent it you, that you may the better know, how to deal with Dr. Seabury; to enquire of him what Recommendations he has from America, how Matters stand between him and the Archbishops, and what else appears to You necessary from the inclosed Information." Oh. Well, that's not entirely helpful.'

'So you have to decide?'

'I have to decide, and write back to Bishop Kilgour by return of post. Well, that won't be till Monday now - but even by then I still won't know what Dr. Seabury is like. And who is this Dr. Smith? And who is Mr. Seller, and why is it his business?' Skinner sank back in his chair again, and stared past Charlie at some point in the distance. His long face was always rather pale, but Charlie thought it had taken on an unhealthy tinge in the last few minutes. He wished he could do something to help, but what did he know about bishops? He knew a little of America, for an old master of his had fought there in the seven years' war, but that was from twenty years ago and no use whatsoever in the present instance. All he could do was to frown sympathetically, and await orders.

At last Bishop Skinner drew up his shoulders and shook his head vigorously.

'Sermon first,' he said, and managed a smile. 'Sermon first, and then I'll consider the rest. Thank you, Charlie: would you mind bringing me a glass of brandy in about an hour?'

'Of course, sir,' said Charlie, and left him to it.

Chapter Five

'Where's that lad? Swooning around again, I suppose?'

Cuthbert Meston had not stayed very late in his bed, considering how fatigued he had seemed the previous evening. It was a mystery why he had bothered heading out again into the night, but he had come back looking pleased with himself. This morning, however, he had made his feelings known by stamping around the cold kitchen, complaining at the lack of fire, hot water, and porage. In the warehouse his brother Stephen and the warehouseman, Alan, looked pointedly away from each other and made sure they were labouring away, or at least looking like it, when Cuthbert finally beat the door open and strode into the store.

'I said, where's that lad?'

'If you mean Alan, brother ...' Stephen suggested, 'he's working hard just over there.'

'I don't need to be told that he's working hard. I only need to be told if he isn't,' Cuthbert informed Stephen briskly. 'But it's Jem I'm looking for. You can tell me if you ever see him working hard. I'll know to look out for the sun rising in the west the same day.'

Stephen tried a little laugh, but it did not get far. He watched Alan go past, effortlessly hefting a barrel on one shoulder, making his escape.

'I think he went out early,' he said. 'Perhaps to see to some cargo arriving?' It was highly unlikely, but Stephen liked to make an effort to restore peace.

'There's no cargo due today,' said Cuthbert, but the mention of cargoes seemed to divert his mind a little. He went to the sloping stand that served as a desk – it allowed ledgers and accounts to be consulted while reducing the temptation of wasting time by sitting down - and pulled out one of the daybooks, muttering to himself as he drew one damp finger down the lines of writing. Stephen edged over to young Alan as he returned to the warehouse, noting his blotchy face and tired eyes. No one slept very well when Cuthbert Meston was in a temper.

'Any idea where Jem went?' he asked quietly.

'I don't know, sir,' said Alan, just as softly. 'But he did say something last night about visiting a lady.'

'He didn't go out last night, did he?' asked Stephen in alarm. If Jem had spent the night with a lady the repercussions could be grim. Bad enough some girl from the streets.

'No, sir, I heard him head out before dawn. He had his best boots on, I think, because he left his second best ones for polishing.'

'Some hope of that, with Minnie gone,' muttered Stephen, and Alan nodded. 'Any idea who the lady is? Did he say?'

Alan shook his head, then half-shrugged.

'I'm not sure,' he said, 'but I believe she bides near Broad Street. And her faither's something to do with the church.'

'Something to do with the church? You mean a minister?' He glanced quickly across at Cuthbert, but his brother's attention was fully on the daybook.

'Not a minister exactly. Och, look, sir, I don't really know at all. It's just a few things he's said and I've maybe put them together all wrong.'

'Aye, well,' Stephen admitted, 'you're a bright lad, but it could easily be that Jem is visiting more than one female, couldn't it?'

'Wouldn't be the first time, sir, no,' Alan agreed.

'Where's the fourth barrel of cloves?' Cuthbert suddenly demanded from across the warehouse.

'The fourth? Ah, now,' said Stephen, hurrying over to placate his brother, 'that's something I meant to tell you. It's coming on Monday. Some problem with loading at Veere, I believe. They're doing their best, but they had no wish to bring you something that was not up to standard ...' What else could he say? He tried to think.

'Veere?'

Stephen waited for the explosion, holding his breath.

'Aye, well, I suppose Monday's time enough.'

'It's ... is it?' Stephen felt his head reel. Cuthbert seemed quite happy with the arrangement.

'They're not urgent – I'd rather have them right than on time. Within reason. Now, can either of you tell me truly where Jem has gone?'

Stephen and Alan took a look at each other, and shook their heads. Stephen could see the same wary shock on Alan's face. Strictly speaking, no, they could not.

Cuthbert sighed weightily, and folded away the daybook.

'I'm going out to look for him,' he announced, and tramped back out of the warehouse towards their house.

'Why?' Stephen asked, when his brother was out of earshot. 'Why on earth would he go to the trouble?'

But Alan had no more idea than Stephen had, and they went back to work among the sharp scents of spices, teas and coffees.

Cuthbert Meston assumed his outdoor clothing with all the grandeur of a magistrate taking on his robes of office. His waistcoat and coat were in complementary shades of blue with touches of pink, his breeches were yellow, and his boots a pleasing chestnut. His overcoat was in a green so dark it could be mistaken for black – a fresh one, not the genuine black one he had worn for his journey to and from Edinburgh. At the thought of Edinburgh, his shoulders slumped and the fine line of his upper garments was creased and dejected.

For as long as he could remember, Cuthbert Meston had had no moment of doubt. He had always known what to do – what to buy, what to sell, what friends to make, whom to ignore. Who to marry, of course. When he had received the letter from Edinburgh, there had been no hesitation. He had made arrangements at once to head south, and was at the harbour promptly on the scheduled day of departure to catch the coastal packet.

By the time he had returned yesterday evening, tired but still determined to get on, face all that had to be faced, he had felt he was a changed man.

He had picked a quarrel on the boat, with complete strangers. It was true his temper was legendary, but strangers? Who had done their best to cause him no offence? Well, if you discounted the mention of religion, of course. But really, apart from that ...

And the girl – where had she gone, when she had fled? He had barely paused when she had broken the news. He had simply thrown her out. He had always thought she was a humble, respectable girl – perhaps it was the shock. But he had not considered what might happen to her, not thought of where she might go now. Not even thought who might clear up after dinner. Not even thought who might light the fire for his breakfast.

And Jem ...

He had to find Jem.

Charlie had no sooner reached the kitchen again when there was a rattle at the front door's risp. He hurried to answer it, but Mrs. Skinner, coming down the stairs far too fast for a woman in her condition, reached it at the same time. She paused and smoothed her skirts, catching her breath, as Charlie opened the door.

'It's a note for Bishop Skinner,' said the lad on the doorstep.

'Well, of course,' said Mrs. Skinner, seizing the paper from Charlie's hand.

'Address the mistress properly,' said Charlie, who liked things to be done correctly for his employers. 'Mistress, or madam.'

'My, is that no fine?' asked the lad, pretending to be impressed.

Mrs. Skinner had torn the note open, and was reading it quickly. 'Oh, my word!' she gasped. 'It's Dr. Seabury – he's here already! Oh, goodness!' She sank back against the wall, but Charlie could see she was not going to faint. She was simply allowing her mind space to rush ahead. 'Coals, windows, fires lit and settled ... kettle boiled, bread fetched ... there's butter and jam aplenty to greet him and then dinner ... what? Fowls, yes, for there are pickled walnuts and some late cabbage. Gooseberries ... a custard, if we have enough eggs ... Right, young man.' Her eyes focussed sharply again as she addressed the boy who had brought the message. 'Bid Dr. Seabury and his companion most welcome to Aberdeen, and ask if they will be good enough to join us for a dish of tea in two hours – ten o'clock. Can you remember that, or do you want me to write it down?'

'I do this every day, Missus,' retorted the boy. 'Most welcome, and come for tea at ten. Can I say they're expected to dinner? Or are they fowls for some other party?'

'Don't be cheeky!' Mrs. Skinner waved a finger at him. 'I can see you're clever. Now, away back with you.' She found a coin in the pocket at her waist, and he grinned as he loped off.

'Which first now, then, mistress?' asked Charlie.

'The fowls, I think, in case they run out. Then the coal, so that Jean can set the fires. Then the windows, if there's still time and it isn't raining. Oh, and if you see eggs about the place get - maybe two dozen, if they have them? We can always pickle them if there are too many.'

The pantry was full of pickles. An Episcopal clergyman, even a Bishop, could rarely afford fresh out of season, and a clergyman's wife had to be a fine economist. Charlie fetched his coat from the kitchen, and headed off to find a couple of reasonably fed fowls for roasting, carrying a basket in case of eggs.

It was Charlie, too, who with hands still pink and damp from washing the windows headed out just before ten to fetch Dr. Seabury and whoever was with him. He was to guide them the short distance from the New Inn, in the Castlegate - not a happy place for Charlie, though a busy and prosperous part of the town - back to Longacre. He headed out towards Broad Street, a cleaner route underfoot than some of the lanes he could have used as shortcuts. The queue at the well was shorter now and less urgent, more of an excuse for a news with the neighbours. Some of the older folk perched on the edge of the horse trough, taking the weight off their feet, though they might not linger so long today in the bitter cold as they would in the warmer months. Charlie looked around to see if the tall man was still in the doorway - as if he would be, hours later - but the doorway was empty. Instead he noticed someone much more alarming. Cuthbert Meston, broad and prosperous, was striding up Broad Street in the direction of the college.

Charlie studied him, discreetly, for a long moment, as if he could perhaps find a weakness he could use for Luzie's preservation. Meston was a thickset, powerful-looking man, with a history of good eating behind him. He had removed his hat, as if he required something to fidget with. Looked at sideways, his head seemed elongated, almost fish-like: his eyes, nose and mouth crowded together at the front, his tiny ears, like gills, punctuated each side and his hair, which was powdered grey, had receded into a kind of pad at the back. A fish, then. Could Charlie think of that, and fear him less? But he was a powerful fish, all the same.

Even as he neared him, feeling his hands shake, Charlie saw Meston hesitate, glancing down Longacre, then stop altogether and give the short street a hard stare. Charlie, relieved that the man's focus did not seem to be on Luzie's warehouse, came slowly closer, but did not approach him: he would not expect a merchant of Meston's stature to recognise him, or to acknowledge him if he did remember his face, even if he had not just threatened Charlie's wife. Meston's well-booted foot tapped the cassies briefly, irritably, as if he could not quite make up his mind. Then he turned and strode off without a backward glance. Charlie watched him go, gradually relaxing, then shrugged and headed in the other direction, towards the Castlegate and the New Inn.

Chapter Six

'Will we be quite safe, do you think?'

Charlie sighed. He had been admitted to the over-warm parlour used by Dr. Seabury and his companion, a Mr. Myles Cooper from Edinburgh. Dr. Seabury seemed a sensible man, but then, almost anyone might beside Mr. Cooper.

'I dinna think that Bishop Skinner would invite us to go anywhere that was not safe, Myles,' said Dr. Seabury. He spoke oddly, Charlie thought: it must be an American way of speaking, but he had picked up odd bits of Scots, too. The combination made Charlie's ears itch. 'And presumably his wife and children live there. He'd no risk them, surely.'

Myles Cooper's hands wriggled together.

'I just think we should be careful. I heard one of the maids say that Longacre was rough at night.' His hands, spread briefly and apologetically, shot back together again as if scared of losing each other. Dr. Seabury, who was poised and ready in hat and coat when Charlie arrived, was clearly anxious to be off. He smoothed his gloves between his fingers, as if smoothing out his own impatience.

'Well, it isn't night time, Myles. But if you're not happy, then by all means stay here where it's safe. I'm sure this fellow will escort me there without any problem.'

'Aye, sir,' said Charlie, trying his best to look like an effective, but reassuring, bodyguard. Myles Cooper looked him up and down, clearly unimpressed. The feeling was mutual: Charlie might not, as a servant, have been able to stare quite so directly, but he had been able to take in the soft, overfed face with its high colour, the anxious eyes, the fluttering lips. If they were attacked in Longacre, he knew which of these men would stay and fight beside him, and which would be running for cover like a frightened hen. Mind, thought Charlie reasonably, sometimes running was the most sensible thing to do.

'We must not do Bishop Skinner the discourtesy of being late, Myles – I'm afeart you'll have to make your mind up fast!'

Myles' shoulders shrank up into his neck, but he seemed even more reluctant to be left on his own.

'I'll come,' he said, almost firmly, and then made a great fuss of finding his coat and his hat and his gloves so that Charlie's own fingers were twitching with impatience by the time the two visitors were finally ready, and he could lead them out into the fresh air. Myles yelped at the cold, but then, the parlour had been very warm. Dr. Seabury looked about him with interest.

'I went for a short walk this morning – what's your name, forgive me?'

'Charlie, sir.'

'I walked down along this street here, which seemed respectable enough,' Seabury gestured west, towards St. Nicholas' Kirk. 'That's a fine church, but I gather it is for the established kirk?'

'Aye, sir. Though it's an old one, they tell me, older than the Kirk itself.'

'Like St. Giles in Edinburgh.' Seabury nodded. 'And how many congregations of Episcopalians are there here in Aberdeen?'

'Three, sir. There's Bishop Skinner's congregation and Mr. Aitken's, which is over that way. And then there's a Qualified chapel, sir.'

'And you can worship now freely?'

Charlie thought back to Bishop Skinner's comments yesterday about the Penal Laws.

'Mostly, aye, sir. The Episcopalians were always strong up here in the north-east, so I'm told.'

'Hm,' said Seabury, 'that is not always to one's advantage. Strength can be interpreted as threat, don't you think?'

'I suppose, sir.'

He checked to see that Myles Cooper was not lost as they rounded the corner into Broad Street.

'Myles, is this not a fine street?' Seabury called out to his friend. 'And books! See? Book warehouses.'

'I smell some fine coffee,' Myles responded, sniffing the air, more impressed by that than by the street. He looked more cheerful than Charlie had yet seen him. 'That is well worth investigating, going by that scent.'

'It could be coming from my wife's warehouse, sir,' Charlie could not resist telling him, unable to conceal the pride in his voice. 'It's just along here.'

'Your wife's warehouse?' Seabury looked bewildered.

'Aye, sir. She imports tea, coffee and spices from Amsterdam, and sells them on into the country. But she always has some for the town trade, for particular customers.'

'But you don't work with her in this? It's her own business?'

'She tells me I couldna sell water to a parched man, sir,' said Charlie with a chuckle. 'I keep away and leave her to her own work.'

Seabury laughed.

'There are certainly those who can sell and those who cannot,' he agreed. 'One of my slaves is an excellent marketer, and the other, like you, alas. But we each have our own skills, don't we?'

Slaves? Charlie felt his jaw drop. Both Dr. Seabury and Myles were diverted by the quality of the warehouses on Broad Street, and Charlie was spared any further conversation as they approached Longacre. Reaching the corner, he was surprised to notice, in the same doorway as this morning, what seemed to be the same figure – a tall, slim man with a long cloak and a broad-brimmed hat, under which his long, reddish brown hair was unpowdered. Charlie thought he might never have noticed him but for the intense expression on the man's face: his eyes seemed to burn. Charlie shivered. Was it his imagination that the man seemed focussed on the Skinners' house? Even if it were not, it was not comfortable to see a man like that anywhere near.

Dr. Seabury and Myles Cooper were still lingering around the corner of Longacre, and Charlie dismissed thoughts of the young man and went back a few steps to fetch them.

'Come along, Myles: I'm sure you can call in later and buy whatever it is.'

'But that smell is enchanting!' Myles exclaimed. 'I simply must – oh, no!'

And the big man shrank suddenly into the warehouse

doorway. Charlie could see even from here that he was trembling, while Dr. Seabury stared about him, then seemed to spot someone he knew. For a moment Charlie thought that Seabury was going to duck into the doorway with his friend, but despite a look of intense uneasiness Seabury stood his ground. Charlie swung round to try to work out who it was they knew. After all, they had only just arrived in Aberdeen. Had someone followed them from Edinburgh? Someone to do with ... who was it, Mr. Seller, who had written that very odd letter?

'It's all right, Charlie,' said Seabury, from behind him. 'I dinna think he would honestly do anything to harm us. We just don't particularly want to meet him. But thank you!'

Charlie realised he had unconsciously spread his arms, protective of his charges, as he scanned the crowds.

'Who's the problem, then, sir? Maybe I can make sure he doesna come near you.'

'It's that man there!' squeaked Myles. 'That man in the greeny black coat. He's terrible! I'm not,' he said suddenly sideways to Charlie, 'I'm not an angry person, but that man made me – so frustrated! He shouts, you see. Shouts very loudly.' And Myles Cooper's eyes closed in pain, as though he could hear the shouting even now. Charlie, frowning, looked back to where Myles had pointed. There was only one man whose coat could be described as greeny black. To Charlie's surprise, he recognised him once again. It was Cuthbert Meston.

'He's a merchant in the town,' he explained, as if that would somehow help. 'Spices and teas and coffees, like my wife.'

'He's a friend of yours, then?' Dr. Seabury asked quickly, a hand out to Myles to stop him from commenting.

'Oh, no, sir, not him.' Charlie swallowed. Meston's threats were no concern of Dr. Seabury's, who had enough to worry about. 'He's – he's too grand for the likes of us!'

'I see.' Dr. Seabury cast a cautious look at Cuthbert Meston, and Charlie glanced back, too.

Odd. Once again, Cuthbert Meston seemed to find Longacre unusually fascinating. He stood motionless at the end of the side street, oblivious to the Saturday morning crowds parting about him, and gazed down it, as if he might find something there he needed.

Charlie looked back down Longacre, at the well, the horse

trough, the door of Bishop Skinner's house and chapel, the high wall of Marischal College above them. The people in the short street were just the usual neighbours one would expect.

At the far end of the street, though, his eye was caught by a slight movement. Round the corner of one of the less salubrious lanes, half-hidden by a stack of fragmentary crates, Charlie could just see an almost familiar face. But even as he watched, the young man with the fiery gaze turned back to the dark lane, took to his heels, and vanished.

It might not have been the best of weather for a brisk walk, but at least it was not raining. Jane Skinner preferred daily exercise to fretting herself over a perfect complexion, and she was persuasive enough that an old school friend, Miss Canon, was prepared to accompany her for respectability and gossip and a turn around the Castlegate, where the market stalls made a good enough excuse for two young women to be out and about. Miss Canon was liable to make the walk twice the length it could be, as she would stop at every stall, but Jane was a patient girl and pleased enough with her company that she did not mind at all.

'And so your visitor from America is coming today?' Miss Canon asked, between passing judgement on a string of sausages on one stall and giggling at a love token brooch with a fat dove on it at the next. As she had also linked arms firmly with Jane, this meant a deal of being tugged about as if by an ill-disciplined dog. Fortunately neither of them favoured very wide hoops on their skirts, or they would never have fitted through the narrow spaces between stalls.

'He is now, yes. We had not expected him until Wednesday.'

'How exciting! What do you think an American gentleman looks like?'

'Much like a Scottish one, I should think,' said Jane. 'I don't remember hearing anyone who fought there ever mentioning that they looked any different. And they speak a form of English, not unlike Scots.'

'Is he married?' Miss Canon's mind was clearly lingering on the love token.

'I think he's widowed. With grown up children.'

'Oh. Wealthy?'

'He's a clergyman. It's not likely.'

'Oh, dear. Is he on his own?'

'I think he has a companion with him, a friend he's been staying with in Edinburgh.'

'And is he married?'

'I had not thought to enquire.'

'Oh.' Miss Canon paced thoughtfully for a moment, eyes withdrawn from the market's attractions. 'Well, that is a good thing, then,' she said. 'I should not like to think of you being whisked away to America. Or even to Edinburgh.'

Jane smiled.

'That is very kind of you! I should miss you, too!'

'I should like to think,' said Miss Canon warmly, 'that we shall both marry good, kind, Aberdeen men, and be able to visit each other and be friends still when we have our grandchildren at our knees. Would not that be the perfect thing?'

'It's a very appealing idea,' said Jane dutifully. She would like to travel a little, she thought - maybe not as far as America, but Edinburgh or London would be interesting. Ho, ho, she thought: maybe one day. 'But I should like to hear what this gentleman has to say of America, all the same. And he has been in England, too, before he came up to Edinburgh. So this should be a very interesting visit, I believe.'

'You will be all wrapped up with them and never have time to see me!' said Miss Canon, with unseemly petulance. Then she brightened - Miss Canon was never dull for long. 'And then when we do meet you will be bursting with all you have heard! What fun that will be, to hear all about it!'

'Oh! Eggs,' said Jane suddenly. 'My mother sent Charlie out for eggs earlier but he was only able to find a dozen. There are some on that stand, beside the kale. I have left room in my basket, just in case.'

They crossed over to the stall and were intent on the stall holder's demonstration that the eggs were not stale, when Jane felt a hand on her arm. She spun to see the newcomer, heart beating like a drum.

Chapter Seven

'Miss Skinner,' said Jeremiah Hosie, bowing. 'Forgive me for disturbing you – I see you are fixed on your purchase.'

Tall, thin, intense, with hair neither dyed nor powdered but clothes at the very apex of the mode – Jane had not yet found much to admire here. Miss Canon, however, clearly had other opinions.

'Oh, Mr. Hosie!' fluttered Miss Canon. 'How charming! I hope you are quite well?'

'Miss Canon.' Hosie made a slightly less elaborate bow. 'I am quite well, thank you. And you?'

'Oh, yes, yes! Very well indeed. Oh, Jane, now we have a man to escort us we could walk a little further, could we not? I'm sure Mr. Hosie would keep us very safe indeed!'

'Alas,' said Jane firmly, 'I must not be gone too much longer from home. My mother will need me. It was good of her to let me out for some exercise.'

'She is well, too, I trust?' asked Jeremiah Hosie, his gaze fixed on Jane. She had the uneasy feeling that she was the mouse to his cat, and that if she made a bid for freedom she might be pounced on.

'She is quite well, thank you. It is only that we have visitors arriving, and there is a great deal to be done.' She bit her tongue. There was surely no harm to him knowing about their visitors – indeed, in a place the size of Aberdeen he might well know about them already – but for some reason she felt that any information she gave him about herself, or her circumstances, might be used somehow against her. Yet how?

'Then please allow me to escort you home.'

'I have no wish to take you out of your way, Mr. Hosie.'

'Indeed you will not. I have business in Broad Street anyway.'

'I live in the Upperkirkgate, Mr. Hosie,' put in Miss Canon. 'I wonder if you would be good enough to walk me to my door? It is only a little further – if you have business in Broad Street anyway.' Her eyes widened, teasing a little, but Jeremiah Hosie was immune.

'What's that?'

'I live in the Upperkirkgate,' Miss Canon repeated, managing to maintain her smile.

'Yes, yes, I know.' He considered. 'We could go that way first, then come back to Longacre.'

'Well, whatever way we are to go,' said Jane, seeing herself fated to be escorted home by him, no matter what she said, 'let us go now. I have paid for my eggs, and it is growing cold again.' She might as well get it over with. And anyway, at least Miss Canon seemed likely to enjoy the walk.

They saw Miss Canon to the door of her tenement, Jane hugging her while Jem made an absent-minded bow. Then he offered his arm to Jane as he turned away almost at once. It would have been a clear snub if she had not taken it, though she found herself glancing around to make sure no one she knew was watching. There would be somebody, no doubt, ready to report back that the Bishop's daughter had been seen in the company of – well, a respectable merchant's son. Stepson. But reports led to gossip, and gossip led to assumptions, and assumptions, if they were not watched, could lead to misunderstandings, and anger, and resentment ... She had seen it with other girls, once or twice, and she did not want to be part of it herself. She had no intention of encouraging Jeremiah Hosie, but at the same time she had no wish to see him embarrassed.

She was inclined to walk quickly, but he had set a slow, almost solemn pace, and she could not seem to shift him to make short work of the distance between the Upperkirkgate, past the gate of the College to the entry to Longacre. At least he was not one of those men who bombard with chatter, too nervous to take a breath between words. Instead he seemed to be on the brink of saying something, but not quite ready to say it. She wished he would get on with it, but at the same time she prayed it would not be some kind of proposal. Surely it was too early for that? But Jeremiah Hosie was an impetuous man. If he thought something, he said it - or that was her impression. And if he could say it dramatically, all the better. She sighed, a little louder than she had intended.

'Are you all right?' he asked at once. 'Is our pace fatiguing you?'

'No, no,' she said politely. 'Only that I do need to be home ...'

'Is all well with your family? Is it that? Is there some trouble?'

'No - as I said, we are expecting visitors. Quite, um, significant visitors, and we are a little ... excited over it. So I really need to be home to help my mother ...'

'Ah, to have a mother!'

Jane was taken aback. Of course, she knew that Jeremiah had lost his mother quite young, and she should perhaps have been more sensitive in talking about her own mother ... surely people talked about their mothers in front of him all the time? She fell silent, and they walked another slow pace or two.

'Do you not think it a wonder?'

'I'm sorry?' Having a mother? She wished he would walk faster.

'Motherhood. Bringing a child into this world of pain, to nurture it and care for it.'

'Well, yes,' she conceded. 'It is a remarkable thing. And God's own Son ...' Could she divert him into religious talk? She felt on safer ground there.

'An extraordinary thing. The fragility of woman, to bear so much. To undergo such suffering -'

'As Mary did,' she put in. Otherwise the conversation was growing somewhat indelicate.

'Last night,' he spoke across her, 'last night my abhorrent stepfather returned from his journey to Edinburgh and discovered that our maid was with child. What do you think he did, to this delicate bearer of another soul?'

Jane knew Cuthbert Meston's reputation for foul temper and arrogance. She thought she could probably guess, but after a dramatic pause, Jeremiah did not give her a chance.

'He cast her out into the night! In the cold, and the snow! A lost creature, to find warmth and comfort where she could!'

His voice had risen: people were stopping and staring. Once again, Jane prayed no one she knew would happen to pass by. Or could someone rescue her?

'Oh, dear,' said Jane helplessly. 'That is very bad of him. Do you know where she went? There are places that can offer shelter, if she can be found. My father will know.'

'She is gone! Vanished into the night!'

'Well, she can't have gone very far,' said Jane, brisk now. 'Did you go after her?'

For a moment the expression on Jeremiah's handsome face flitted from outrage to mild embarrassment.

'I was prevented,' he said.

Jane pictured for a moment Cuthbert Meston in the indignity of a physical struggle with his stepson. It seemed unlikely, somehow.

'Perhaps you could prevail upon the father? Is his name known?'

'Alas, no. She is a poor little thing, Minnie. It is possible that she fell into bad company.'

'While staying in your home?'

'Our home – Cuthbert Meston's house – is by the harbour. You may have heard what such places are like.'

'Of course,' she said. They were edging towards the entry to Longacre. If she could have done so with decorum, she would have sprinted for it. She tried to think of a different tack. 'Have you other servants? Might they know where she has gone?'

'There is a warehouseman, Alan Beith. A quiet fellow. I cannot see that she would have confided in him: he is only in the house for his meals. My uncle and my father – that is my step-uncle and my stepfather, of course - manage the rest of the business between them. My stepfather does not like to spend money unnecessarily, and he does not trust servants.' He sighed. 'It may be weeks before he looks for someone to replace Minnie. And she was a very fair cook and laundress.'

Jane suppressed a smile. Was this his main concern? Jeremiah's clothing was always a little flamboyant – take the apple green gloves he was so elegantly carrying in his left hand, despite the cold - but it was expensive and well cared for, and he gave the impression of a man who wanted for nothing – except perhaps reason and common sense. He would not like to be seen, she fancied, with dirty cuffs or an unbrushed coat. Well, she thought, as they finally reached Longacre, perhaps he would have to develop some of those skills himself.

Charlie, turning at Bishop Skinner's front door to allow the two visitors to pass inside before him, noticed Jane Skinner coming along the entrance to Longacre escorted by a tall young man, though they were both still in the shadow of the entrance and he could not see the man's face clearly. He hoped it was someone she liked. He was very fond of Jane, thinking her a sensible girl, and he was keen to see her happily settled.

He followed the visitors into the narrow hallway, and took their coats. Myles gave him a suspicious look as though believing Charlie might go through the pockets for loose change the moment Myles' back was turned, but Charlie looked blandly past him and hung the coat on a one of the hooks along the hall. Dr. Seabury, a little shaky, handed over his gloves and hat but his gaze was fixed on the door next to them.

'If you'll please follow me, sirs,' said Charlie, and Seabury waved him ahead with a nervous grin.

The family was waiting in the parlour: not Jane, of course, but Margaret, who was sixteen and freckled more than she would like, Johnnie, the naughty one, and little William, who was just starting school and seemed set to be a bright lad. And Mrs. Skinner, settled comfortably in the corner of a sopha with her children beside her, and a healthy colour, Charlie was pleased to note. And of course, rising to greet the visitors with a welcoming smile and an outstretched hand, Bishop Skinner himself. Charlie was proud of him: the visitors would never guess from his expression the worries he had over this arrival and its consequences.

'Welcome to Aberdeen, Dr. Seabury! And Mr. Cooper, though you are a near neighbour in Edinburgh. I hope your passage was a calm one?'

'Very tolerable, I thank you, my lord,' said Seabury, but Bishop Skinner quickly shook his head, still smiling.

'Bishop Skinner, or Mr. Skinner, if you like,' he said, 'but not my lord! Not in Scotland. I thought it would be pleasant if we sat, all of us, and took some tea before any more serious conversation. I should not like to think that I was interrogating you like a prisoner before you had even sat down!'

'You are most kind, sir, and thoughtful,' said Seabury.

'May I present my family?' Bishop Skinner introduced them, nodding approval as Margaret curtseyed and the boys made very proper bows. 'We have all been most excited over your arrival, and after so long a journey, so many delays!'

'It was hardly Dr. Seabury's fault – the delays were entirely the responsibility of –'

'Thank you, Myles: the delays are behind us, anyway. I'm delighted to be here.'

Myles' shoulders worked, and Charlie noticed his hands once again clutching at each other. The meeting, which had been going along very amiably, was suddenly tense. But before Bishop Skinner could do anything about it, they were interrupted.

'Are you going to be the Bishop of America?' demanded little William.

Everybody laughed, half in relief.

'I don't know yet if I am to be Bishop of anywhere!' Dr. Seabury said, bending down to William's level as best he could – he was not a slim man. 'But the purpose for which I am here is to ask to be consecrated as Bishop of Connecticut, which is a small – but I think very beautiful and important – part of America. To be Bishop of all America – that would be an extraordinary thing. It is a vast country!'

William's mouth made an O.

'May I go and look again at the map book, Father?' he asked. 'I had not thought it so big on the page!'

Bishop Skinner smiled.

'You may take the map book out of the bookroom as Dr. Seabury and I retire there, and look at it then. For now, it is your place to sit quietly and be an ornament to the room, and not a burden to your poor mother.'

William, content, squirmed back against Mrs. Skinner, and settled down to watch proceedings. Charlie thought he would not be quite so resigned had he not seen that there were two plates of cake on the table, and had named one of the pieces for himself.

'Now, do sit yourselves, gentlemen. The tea is already here and fit to be poured, I believe.' Mrs. Skinner was able to reach the urn from her seat, by design, and Margaret helped Charlie to distribute the cups and plates as Bishop Skinner carried on. 'So you arrived yesterday?'

'Last evening, sir,' said Seabury. 'Through Myles' generosity we are staying at the New Inn.'

So that was Myles Cooper's role in this, Charlie thought: he holds the purse strings.

'You'll not have seen much of Aberdeen, then,' Bishop Skinner was saying.

'Not much yet, no. From what I saw on a short stroll this morning, it is a fine place altogether. I had not imagined so many great buildings!'

'It is not so fine as Edinburgh, perhaps,' Bishop Skinner acknowledged, 'but it serves a good purpose, between the country and the sea. And there are, of course, two universities, where I believe Edinburgh has still only one!'

'Ah, but a very fine one, sir!' Seabury rose willingly to the challenge. 'I much enjoyed my time there.'

'Where did you go on your stroll?'

'Towards St. Nicholas' Kirk and round a hill ... and somewhere called the Green? Though there was no green that I could see. The buildings around the Castlegate are also much to be admired. There is one by the inn that seems very venerable.'

'The magistrates' offices,' said Myles Cooper, then blushed. Charlie did not think he looked a well man.

'The magistrates? Oh, yes, well, the Town House and the tolbooth, that's right. I suppose that is where the magistrates are to be found.' Bishop Skinner looked slightly perplexed. 'Well, if the weather improves, perhaps we shall have time for some walks while you are here, to see further afield.'

Bishop Skinner was doing his best, but the tension in the air was still tangible. Dr. Seabury was anxious to start the real conversation – the one where Bishop Skinner would begin to discern whether or not he was fit to be a Bishop, whether or not it was God's plan. Of course he was nervous – Charlie would have been terrified.

At last, Mrs. Skinner nodded to her husband and rose, taking the children with her.

'I shall leave you gentlemen to your talk,' she said pleasantly. 'William, run and fetch the map book and let your father have his bookroom.'

Seabury scrambled to his feet to bow to her, followed more slowly by Myles, wiping cake crumbs from his generous lips.

'I hope you will both stay to dinner?' she asked.

'You're very kind, ma'am!'

'Then I shall look forward to seeing you later.'

Charlie held the door for her as she left.

'Come, then, gentlemen,' said Bishop Skinner, 'let us discuss more weighty matters. Charlie, some brandy to the bookroom, please.'

Chapter Eight

On reflection, the brandy may have been a mistake.

The bottle was empty when the three men emerged for dinner: that laid the foundation. Bishop Skinner was quite sober, and Dr. Seabury seemed, if anything, a little calmer than he had before. Myles Cooper, on the other hand, was alarmingly cheerful.

'Do you think that dinner will calm him down?' Mrs. Skinner muttered to Charlie on the landing.

'I'll make sure he has good helpings, mistress.'

Dinner did help, though it was clear that Myles could pack away more food than any other man at the table. Charlie met Mrs. Skinner's uneasy gaze once or twice as Myles helped himself to more pie, and another glass of claret, without needing Charlie's assistance. In conversation, too, he was quite independent – by the end of the main course Charlie felt he was entirely up to the moment with any gossip Edinburgh could provide. After dinner, Bishop Skinner had a quiet word with Seabury, and they left Myles to snore on the sopha at his leisure while they disappeared once more into the bookroom, this time with some of Luzie's coffee to enliven their minds.

Myles required no further attention, waking with remarkable promptness in time for supper. Bishop Skinner emerged once again from the bookroom, and met Charlie in the parlour.

'He's having a moment of quiet prayer,' he explained, nodding at the bookroom door. 'He'll be out shortly.'

'Can I ask if everything is going well, sir?'

Bishop Skinner hesitated, then smiled.

'I think so, Charlie. But we'll see. Early days.'

The atmosphere at Cuthbert Meston's house was no less tense. Jeremiah returned, warily, for his dinner, to find that his uncle – step-uncle – Stephen had sent Alan the warehouseman out for some hot pies and a couple of roasted fowl, and was sitting by the fire trying to make something that resembled gravy. The smell was not encouraging.

'Where's my father?' Jeremiah asked, throwing down his gloves on the table. His glove, he noted, with an oath. 'Damn, I must have dropped one. Where is he?' He picked up the lone glove and stroked it, as if it could tell him where the other one was.

'He's gone out looking for you.' Stephen ran a hand through his tousled hair. He never looked quite at ease: it was as if he was constantly poised to apologise for his brother. Jeremiah, despite himself, was fond of Stephen.

'For me?' Jeremiah turned in surprise, forgetting the glove. 'That's strange. Usually he waits.'

'Aye,' said Stephen with a smile. 'Stoking his anger here, ready to pounce on you when you get back!'

Jeremiah frowned.

'Do you think going out to look for me is worse or better?'

Stephen Meston sat back from the hearth, abandoning the gravy.

'I don't know, Jem. I'm worried, to be honest. He's been back since for a lantern, but he went straight back out again. He didna look angry, for once. He looked as if he had something big on his mind.'

'About me?'

Stephen shrugged.

'I'd say it was something to do with his visit to Edinburgh. Whether that's about you or not, I have no idea. But it was you he went out looking for.'

If that had been intended to reassure Jeremiah, it failed almost as badly as the gravy.

'You keep a most excellent table, Mrs. Skinner,' Myles Cooper declared at supper. The words were a little indistinct, but Mrs. Skinner smiled politely.

'I'm glad you're enjoying it, Mr. Cooper. Jane, will you pass

Mr. Cooper a clean napkin?'

Jane, with a very straight face, handed over a clean napkin while Charlie deftly whisked away the one on which Myles had spilled half a boat of white sauce, without seeming to notice. Seabury, eating neatly and steadily, caught the end of the manoeuvre and blinked, a little cross, Charlie thought.

'Dr. Seabury has been telling me all about his time as a student in Edinburgh,' said Bishop Skinner smoothly. 'What a fine town it is! Though times are a little calmer now, of course.'

Conversation turned neatly to Edinburgh and its attractions, Myles continued to make inroads into every plate of food on the table, and Dr. Seabury, Charlie saw, relaxed, just a little.

'It has been more than good of you to welcome us into your home, Mrs. Skinner,' said Seabury at the top of the stairs. 'It is rare that Myles is at ease outside his own flat: you have made him very comfortable.' It might have been an apology, thought Charlie, holding their coats ready at the bottom of the stairs. It took both him and Seabury to get Myles into his and buttoned up, and then they had to manhandle him through the door.

'Oh! Look at that!' Jane Skinner had come down to go to the kitchen. She stooped and plucked something from the doorstep. 'Oh, no.'

'What's that, miss?'

She held out something in a sickly shade of green, and turned confidentially to Charlie.

'One of Jeremiah Hosie's gloves. Oh, no – I don't want him to have an excuse to come back!'

'I'll take it to him, miss. Where does he live?'

'With Cuthbert Meston – you know. His stepfather. In the big spice warehouse down by the harbour.'

Charlie's heart sank. Had he known that Cuthbert Meston had a stepson? Had he put two and two together? If he ever had, he had forgotten. And Jeremiah Hosie had been hanging about Broad Street and Longacre an awful lot recently – Jane's suitor, if her little brother was to be believed, but not a welcome one, if Jane herself was to be believed. Charlie cast a look at Myles, being propped up by Seabury outside. He tucked the glove into his coat, and took a deep breath.

'I'll take it there when I've seen them to the inn. Dinna worry, miss.'

'Thank you, Charlie. If you're sure it won't keep you up too late?'

'Och, no, miss. And I wouldna like you to lose any sleep over it.' He heard himself say the words, but he felt like Daniel taking an evening stroll down to the lion's den.

Oblivious, Jane smiled and patted him on the arm, and he turned away to deal with their visitors.

Myles had looked on the point of sleep all the way along Longacre and round by Broad Street to the Castlegate: only the firm pressure from Dr. Seabury and Charlie seemed to keep him going. But as soon as they had him up to his room, he brightened, flung off his coat, and called the servant to bring more wine. Charlie glanced at Dr. Seabury.

'Do you need any help, sir?'

Seabury shook his head, resigned.

'There is little to be done. He'll settle in now and drink till he falls asleep – by which time, if I am blessed, I shall be long asleep myself. I'm in the room next door, and I believe the walls are thick.' Seabury eyed Charlie and drew breath. 'I hope we have done nothing to offend your master the Bishop, or good Mrs. Skinner?'

'I don't believe so, sir.' The Skinners were steady people.

'Then that is a relief. Tomorrow no doubt he will sleep late, and the Bishop and I can speak undisturbed. It gives me great joy to be in conversation with him: you are truly blessed in your employer, Charlie.'

'I've been very fortunate, sir,' Charlie agreed.

'Where's that wine?' Myles demanded. 'A man could die of thirst here!'

Seabury watched him without responding for a moment, then turned back to Charlie.

'My family has slaves, you know.'

Charlie, taken aback, said nothing. But slaves?

'I think we could not do that in Scotland, could we?'

'No, sir, you could not. Not since six years ago.'

'Hm.'

Charlie wondered if he were dismissed, but he waited just a

moment.

'The Romans had slaves. They are mentioned in the Bible.'

'There's lots of things mentioned in the Bible, sir, that we might not like,' said Charlie, surprising himself. Dr. Seabury smiled.

'I think your wife would struggle to find goods to sell in her warehouse were it not for the armies of slaves working on the plantations - coffee and sugar and even the cotton bags she packs it in.'

Charlie's head struggled. He knew it, of course, bu tit was so far away - like Dr. Seabury's slaves. Was there a difference between farm slaves and household slaves? Farm labourers here could be badly treated. But so could household servants, by some masters.

As if he could read Charlie's thoughts, Dr. Seabury said,

'I try to treat my own slaves well. Would you rather, Charlie, be a free man treated badly, or a slave treated well?'

Charlie frowned, too many thoughts whirring about him.

'As a free man, sir, I could walk away.'

'Hm. Could you, Charlie?'

And now he knew he was dismissed, and he bowed, and left, puzzled at Dr. Seabury's words.

Once outside, he checked to see he had not dropped Jeremiah Hosie's skyrie green glove, and headed across the Castlegate to Marischal Street, which would take him down to the harbour. He knew the Meston warehouse, having been there once or twice to take a message for Luzie to do with trade: he had forgotten that Jane's unwanted suitor was Meston's stepson. He turned the corner at the foot of the street and hurried along to the door that led to both warehouse and dwelling house, but the place was in darkness. Could they have retired for the night already?

He rattled at the risp, noting that it was well painted against the sea air. The whole place looked well turned out - Charlie was sure that Luzie would aspire to a place this size, this grand and prominent, proud as she was of the warehouse on Broad Street. Knowing Luzie, she would get it one day. He had every faith in her.

No answer. He rattled again, and stood back to look up at the windows. None was shuttered, which implied that the family was still out, and not settled in for the night. He paused, wondering what to do with the glove. It was late to be disturbing a neighbour for such an apparently trivial thing, but he did not want to let Jane down. He wondered if there was a side door that might have been left unlocked, though it seemed unlikely. Was there even a way round the side of the building? There seemed to be a lane, anyway.

A lane with someone in it.

Someone who appeared to be engaged in punching a barrel, with regular, hard thuds and muttering.

'Um, hello?' said Charlie, braced to run in case the man wanted a substitute for the barrel. The man jumped.

'Hello?' he repeated, after a breath. 'Who's that?'

'I'm looking for Jeremiah Hosie. I have something to return to him.' There was silence. 'Are you all right, there? Only you seem a bit ...'

'I'm fine,' said the man, coming now to the mouth of the lane. He was small and sandy – it was just possible that Charlie could have beaten him in a fight, if need be. His face, by the light of the lamps that lit this part of the harbour, was pale, his eyes distracted. 'What did you say you were here for?'

'I think I have something of Mr. Hosie's. Do you know him?'

The man's sigh must have emptied his lungs.

'Aye. Sorry, who did you say you were?'

Charlie had not told him, but he was not sure that the man would have taken it in if he had. His mind was clearly elsewhere.

'I'm a servant at the house of Bishop Skinner in Longacre.'

'A bishop? I doubt Jeremiah Hosie was there. Mr. Meston does not hold with bishops.'

Charlie tried to work out how to avoid involving Jane.

'Someone happened to see Mr. Hosie in – er, these green gloves, or something similar, and then one was found almost on our doorstep. I offered to bring it back.' He tentatively showed the man the glove. Was it really green? Or yellow? It was hard to tell.

'Aye, it looks a bit like one of Mr. Hosie's – or it's the like of thing he would wear, anyway. Do you want –'

'Alan! What are you doing out here? Is there a problem?'

Chapter Nine

Charlie turned – was this Jeremiah Hosie? But the man who was approaching was not as young as he had assumed Mr. Hosie would be – nor as well-turned out.

'No, it's fine, Mr. Stephen. This man's just come back with what looks like one of Mr. Jeremiah's gloves.'

'Oh, he was missing one earlier – it probably is.' He peered at the offending object. 'Aye, that's the colour. I wouldna wear it myself, but I daresay it cost a bit. He'll be pleased to get it back.' He nodded. 'But why are you out here in the cold, Alan? Is my brother back?' he added, in an odd tone that made Charlie give him a sharp look. Was he pleased? Wary? It was very hard to tell.

'No, sir, Mr. Meston's still away out, Mr. Stephen. And Mr. Jeremiah went out again not long after you and he hasna returned yet, either. I was just out putting the rubbish for the scaffies.'

He did not look at Charlie when he said this. Charlie had put rubbish out for the scaffies many times, and it had never involved punching a barrel with slow, determined anger.

'Well, I've been near as far as the Stocket Lands looking for my brother, and never a sign of him anywhere.' Stephen Meston took off his hat, which had been sitting crooked anyway, and scrubbed at his untidy hair as if perhaps he could discover his brother there. He had the same odd-shaped head as his brother, long front to back with all his features close together, but in his case there was a larger cap of hair at the back and it was dyed a fashionable jet black. But his face was friendly. He looked more closely at Charlie. 'You wouldna happen to know my brother, would you? His name's Cuthbert Meston – big fellow, well dressed. Where have you been? Have you seen anyone like that?'

'I know him to see, and I did see him earlier today, as it so happens,' said Charlie. It was hard to believe that this approachable man could be Cuthbert Meston's brother. 'Along Broad Street, about the entry to Longacre. Twice, in fact,' he remembered. 'But that was well before dinner time.'

'Longacre? Who was he after there? Or what?' Stephen scratched his head again, looking lost. 'Where could he be?'

'Well, my master lives there, but he was not visiting him,' said Charlie, trying to be helpful. 'There's the Methodist meeting house, and the Quaker burying ground down the far end. And then there's the Berean meeting house, too. He's no a Berean, is he?'

Stephen Meston gave him a quizzical look.

'No, he's not a Berean. Nor a Methodist nor yet a Quaker. Who's your master?'

'Bishop Skinner.'

Stephen almost burst out laughing.

'That least of all! No wonder he is not visiting there. But it looks strange that he had any interest in Longacre at all, if it is that full of meeting houses and ministers. My brother has little sympathy for the church.'

Charlie wondered how he got away with that. It was hard enough to be an Episcopalian without the local minister wanting to know why you hadn't been to the kirk.

'Well, I cannot think of anywhere else to look tonight. And I am not going out again after Jeremiah: if he was fool enough to go wandering off in the night, he's big enough to look after himself.'

'Is Mr. Meston not?' asked Charlie. Apologetically, he added, 'He always looks a powerful kind of a man to me.'

'Powerful? Oh, aye, yes, I suppose,' Stephen Meston agreed. 'And normally ... But he wasna himself this morning. Not himself at all. Maybe,' he went on, with a slightly forced grin, 'maybe that's why he's looking for a meeting house in Longacre! Here,' he added, fishing a couple of coins out of his pocket, 'here's for your trouble, and maybe for letting me know, if you can, if you do see my brother? I'd not – I'd not like harm to come to him, all the same.'

'Thank you, sir.' Charlie bowed, and turned to go.

All the same - what did Stephen Meston mean by that?

Charlie had never been fond of the harbour, or the sea, and it was even colder down here by the water than it had felt up in the town, particularly when he had been standing outside for so long. In fact, he seemed to be shivering even in the warmth of his coat and muffler. He hoped he was not coming down with something. He hurried back up the hill, feeling the slushy ground starting to freeze under his boots.

Broad Street was quiet, most people by now in their beds ready for the Sabbath. He almost made straight for home himself, but he lingered for a moment at the entry to Longacre. Had he fastened the front door behind him as he came out? It was usually his job as he left at night, but with looking after Dr. Seabury - and Myles - he had a niggling feeling he might have forgotten. And it would be the work of a few moments only to nip down the lane and try the front door. He had his key in his pocket.

This was about the only time on the clock's face when there was no one queuing at the well. The street had an empty look, too, but some late drinker was propping up the horse trough beyond the well. Charlie tutted. That was a good way to being found dead in the morning, lying out in this weather. He supposed he ought to go and rouse the fellow, send him on his way.

He headed for the trough, more confused the closer he came. The man - if it was a man - seemed to be leaning over the low trough - leaning, even, into the water. He really would be frozen. Was he trying to take a drink?

Charlie, a growing sense of dread coming over him, approached with caution.

'Hi there!' he tried. And a little louder 'Hey, are you all right?'

The person did not move. Charlie edged closer, reached out, touched the man's back. Surely a man - he was a good size, in a dark coat. Oh, no - not Myles Cooper? Had he staggered out of the inn again and come here?

Charlie shook the man as best he could, but to no avail, and now he knew there was little hope. The man's head was submerged in the water, which was starting to freeze. He must have drowned.

Charlie angled round him until he could grab his shoulders and, with a mighty effort, push him back, free of the water. Was it Myles Cooper?

His feelings on that, even as he struggled, were mixed. Myles Cooper was not particularly appealing, but at the same time Charlie felt some responsibility for him, and for Dr. Seabury, who would no doubt miss his companion. But the build, and the circumstances, did make Charlie wonder ...

The body overbalanced, slid from Charlie's frozen fingers, and fell slowly backward, landing with a dreadful thud on the cassies. Charlie winced, feeling the man's pain for him, then peered at the face in the street's miserable light.

It was not Myles Cooper. It was Cuthbert Meston.

Chapter Ten

Charlie sat back for a moment, against the edge of the horse trough, heedless of the cold water soaking his arms, the fronts of his legs, and now his behouchie. Where should he go? Or rather, where should he go first? Back to Meston's warehouse to break the bad news, tell them the search was over? But that would mean leaving the dead man here. It would not be respectful, and if he did not feel inclined to be that respectful to Meston, it would not be fair on some other passerby, finding the body sprawled out like that. Raising the neighbours? They wouldn't thank him, he was sure. To the magistrates, then, to report a death? But would they be interested in a man who had tipped himself into a horse trough? Or should he just go to Bishop Skinner? He would know what to do - but would he already be in his bed?

Charlie glanced up at the Skinner house. Perhaps it was not as late as he thought, for there was a light on still slipping through the shutters of the parlour, and a fainter but closer one somewhere back in the upstairs chapel. That was his decision made. With an apologetic nod at Meston's body, Charlie hopped off the trough, wriggled at the cold wet of his breeches, and hurried across to the Skinners' front door.

'Cuthbert Meston? The merchant?' Bishop Skinner scrambled to his feet from his interrupted prayers.

'I think so,' said Charlie, 'and I ken he's missing from his home this evening.'

'That makes it more likely, indeed,' said Skinner thoughtfully.

'And he's just outside? Hm.' He glanced about the chapel. 'We should bring him in. Help me move these benches, Charlie, and we'll make a kind of bier for him. Cuthbert Meston ... I doubt the two of us could lift him between us, could we? You'd maybe better go and waken a few of the neighbours to help.'

So Charlie did end up rousing those he thought would be fittest, and least likely to refuse. Half a dozen of them lifted Meston, cracking the ice on his hair and his coat, slid a ladder under him, and carried him with various levels of respect and difficulty up into the chapel. A local lad followed bearing Meston's wide-brimmed hat, like a religious relic.

'He'll no melt in here, onywyes,' remarked one man, with a shiver. Charlie knew the man from the well queues – his name was Mennie.

'The chapel is only heated for services,' Charlie explained.

'Then you'll want him out by the morn, nae doubt,' said the man sensibly. 'And I'll be wanting my ladder back. I'll send my lad down to Meston's warehouse, get them to fetch him home.'

'Charlie, do you know the Mestons? Know something about them?' Bishop Skinner was delicately trying to tidy Cuthbert Meston's collar and muffler. 'I'll place his hat beside him,' he murmured to himself. Charlie thought about Luzie, and swallowed.

'I was down there this evening, sir, returning a glove. They said he was missing.'

'A glove?' Skinner touched Meston's gloved hands, and glanced up at Charlie.

'His stepson's, not his, sir.'

'Oh. Can you bring a couple of lamps over?'

The more fatigued neighbours were retreating to their beds, but Mennie and his lad, more curious, remained, waiting to see what might happen next. Charlie lit two lamps and carried them closer to the makeshift bier. There was a collective gasp. Charlie looked more closely.

The expression on Meston's half-frozen face was clearer now than it had been in the dark street. This was not a man who had been knocked cold before sinking oblivious into the water. This was a man who had known he was drowning, and despite his fear and wrath could do nothing to prevent it. The look on his face was going to linger at the back of Charlie's nightmares for a long time to come.

'Does a'body else think that doesna look like a man that died by accident?' asked Mennie, clutching at the foot of his ladder for support.

'It could have been an accident,' said Bishop Skinner, more in hope than expectation. 'He could have fallen and then, for some reason, not been able to ...'

'How so?' asked Mennie. 'Was there a'thing on top of him when he was found?'

All eyes turned to Charlie, who felt himself go scarlet.

'Nothing, sir,' he said nervously, though already his imagination was trying to trick him, telling him there had been beams, or rocks, or barrels, stopping him from shifting the bulky corpse. If they knew what Meston had been threatening against Luzie, would they suspect him of holding Meston down in the water?

'Had he been drinking?' asked Mennie's lad.

'You'll hae to sniff at him,' said another man, laughing, then subsided at a look from the Bishop. 'Aye, sorry.' But Bishop Skinner did lower his long nose over Meston's drawn lips.

'I can't smell anything much,' he said.

'We'll maybe hae to get the magistrate,' said Mennie, not looking that pleased at the prospect.

'I was just thinking that,' said the Bishop, and he, too, did not rush to send Charlie for him. Instead, he said, 'Charlie, if you've been down there already this evening, maybe you should go and break the bad news to them. Tell them they are most welcome to come here and sit with him tonight, or make arrangements straight away to take him home, whichever they desire. I shall stay with him in any case until they arrive.'

The frost was setting in hard outside, and Charlie heard the town kirk's bell toll midnight as he slithered over lumps of what had been slush earlier, clutching the railings as he descended Marischal Street once more to the harbour. If he kept moving, he told himself, he would barely feel the icy wet chafing of his breeches. Most of the lamps were out now, so the railings were also helpful in telling him where the street was: the rest fell to chance. He could see very little here, even in the crisp starlight. His feet and hands worked without direction: his mind was busy with all that had happened.

It did not sit well with him to rejoice in any man's death, but if someone had had to die that night, then the fact that it was a man who had threatened his wife gave Charlie some satisfaction, guilty though he might feel at it. And he was relieved, after all, that the body had not been Myles Cooper's, though he had no great love for him, either.

But what had Cuthbert Meston been doing in Longacre?

Charlie thought back. Since Luzie had told him about Meston's threats, Charlie reckoned he had seen Meston twice, at least, around Broad Street and the mouth of Longacre. Yet before that he was not sure that he had seen him near Longacre at all, and certainly Luzie would have mentioned it if he had ventured before into her warehouse. It was just not a part of the town that Meston frequented, as far as Charlie knew. Certainly not Longacre. There were not many customers for the best spices and teas in Longacre. And his family had not known of a good reason for Meston to be there, either.

His family ... Charlie's feet went from under him and he sat down suddenly on the bridge over Jamaica Street. Winded, he took a moment to catch his breath before he could stand again, brush off the muck and check himself for breakages. No, he was fine, or he would be, if he kept moving before the bruises settled in.

But Meston's family – that was a thought. Just because Meston was dead, did that mean that Luzie was now free from any threat? Stephen Meston was involved in the business, even if Jeremiah Hosie were not – and there was the man Alan, too. And Jeremiah Hosie had been in Longacre, too, today. Jane Skinner must have seen him, for she had known that the skyrie green glove belonged to him. In fact, probably the tall man he had seen her with when he reached the Skinners' house with Dr. Seabury and Myles Cooper – the one whose face he had not clearly seen – could that have been Jeremiah Hosie? Quite possibly. Not that Charlie would know him again if he saw him.

He skidded round the corner of the Meston warehouse, and made his way once again to the front door of the house. Before he rattled the risp, he took a quick look round into the lanie where he had seen the man Alan before, but the lane seemed this time to contain only barrels.

Not surprisingly, it took a few risp rattles before Charlie heard some faint movement from within the house. At last he heard a lock click – no bolts, though, he noted, for presumably they were still waiting for Cuthbert Meston to return home. He stepped back a little as the door inched open.

'Who is it? Is that you, Cuthbert? Did you forget your key?'

'It's not Mr. Meston,' said Charlie. 'It's Charlie Rob – I was here earlier, with Mr. Hosie's glove.'

'You again? What do you want?' The door had not budged. Clearly Stephen Meston's hospitality had a line drawn under it about here.

'Could I maybe come in, please, sir?' asked Charlie, trying to convey something of his errand just by his tone of voice.

'Why would you want to do that at this time of the night?' Stephen's candle appeared in the narrow opening. Presumably behind it he was examining the face of this eccentric on his doorstep.

'I have some bad news, sir,' said Charlie, keeping his voice low. 'It might be better given you indoors.'

'Bad news?' There was a moment's hesitation, but Charlie had the feeling that Stephen's mind was working quickly, listing possibilities, rather than keeping him out. He was right. 'Come on in, then. It's late, but there might still be some heat in the kitchen.'

He led the way back up the stairs to the flat above the warehouse. There was indeed a dim, promising glow in the kitchen fire, and Stephen gave it a poke and a few twigs to consider, leaving the candle on the table for both of them. Then he turned, his face set.

'Which of them is it? And how bad?'

'It's bad, sir. Cuthbert Meston was found dead in Longacre this evening. Head down in a horse trough.'

'In a ... was he drowned?'

'I don't know, sir. He might have knocked his head or something.' It had seemed unlikely, but Charlie supposed it was possible.

'Is he still there? In Longacre? Was it an accident?' He turned towards the door. 'Jem! Jem, are you back?'

There was no reply, and the flat echoed empty.

'I had feared it might be Jem,' said Stephen Meston quietly. 'I mean – not that it isn't bad enough. My brother, dead, I mean ... Are they sure it's him? Was it an accident?'

'As to the accident, I don't know, sir. I'm fairly sure it's him. And yes, he's still in Longacre. The neighbours carried him indoors, not to have him lying frozen in the street. He's in Bishop Skinner's chapel.'

'He's in – in what?'

'The Episcopal chapel, sir.'

Stephen stared at him, mouth open. Then he threw back his head, and laughed and laughed.

He laughed so helplessly, propped, wobbling, against the table, that neither of them heard the door downstairs open and close. The first they knew anyone had come in was when a tall young man paused in the kitchen doorway, staring in bewilderment at Stephen, a half-smile on his face as if ready to join in with the joke. His hair was reddish brown, lying straight and longish on either side of a face with dark brows, full lips and eyes that burned, even at rest. Not an easy face, Charlie thought.

Stephen saw him, and the laughter died in an instant.

'Jem!'

Charlie stared at the young man. Jeremiah Hosie – this must be him. But Charlie knew his face, now that he could see it clearly. It was the man who had been lingering in doorways in Longacre – just across from where his stepfather had died.

Chapter Eleven

'Jem, it's bad news,' said Stephen Meston quickly. 'Really bad news. Your stepfather is dead.'

Charlie could swear Stephen was holding his breath as a range of expressions twisted Jeremiah's face from shock to dismay to curiosity to – what was that last one? Satisfaction? None settled for more than an instant, before he tilted his chin up and opted for a kind of defiance.

'Is he, indeed? Who killed him?'

Charlie gaped.

'What?' Stephen seemed as taken aback as Charlie. 'What makes you say that, Jem? It was an accident!'

'Was it?' Jeremiah, who was, Charlie realised now, really very young, flicked off his gloves – a different pair, not the lurid green ones – and flung them on the table. 'That will be a great disappointment for many people. I'm sure there was a list of those who would have liked to kill him.'

'Jem, you can't say that! Your own stepfather!'

'Stepfather, yes,' said Jeremiah. 'Not father. My father I lost a long time ago.' Now he had assumed an air of tragedy. Charlie reflected that he himself could barely remember his own parents. Perhaps that was easier than loving them and losing them. 'Anyway,' said Jem, arranging himself by the table, 'you were laughing, Uncle Stephen.'

'I was,' said Stephen, shamefaced. 'I was – upset.'

'By his death? You know what he was like.'

'Jem, he died in the street. The neighbours who found him have taken him into – into an Episcopal chapel.'

If Stephen expected Jem to laugh, too, he was to be disappointed.

'An Episcopal chapel?' Jem breathed, his burning eyes suddenly intense. 'What street? Where did he die?'

'In Longacre. What does it matter?'

'In Longacre,' Jem repeated. 'In Longacre. Bishop Skinner's chapel?' He seemed to be struggling with the words.

'That's right, yes,' said Charlie. 'I work for the Bishop.'

Jem sank on to the bench beside the table, staring past Charlie and Stephen. Charlie could not read his face at all now. And at last, Jem did not seem to be play acting.

'See, thing is,' said Charlie, breaking the silence, 'tomorrow's the Sabbath –'

'Oh,' Jem groaned.

'And my master the Bishop could do with the chapel for the morning service. I mean, if it's really not possible ...' He was not quite sure what he did mean. But he did think that Bishop Skinner would be accommodating if necessary – though with the chapel all beautifully cleaned and polished for Dr. Seabury coming, it seemed a shame not to be able to use it.

'We'll need to get him out of there,' said Stephen, nodding. 'Can you imagine? Cuthbert in a chapel!'

'It's ... it's incredible,' said Jem softly. 'What was he doing up there, anyway? Why was he in Longacre?' He leapt to his feet suddenly, making the other two jump. 'How did he die?'

'He was drowned in the horse trough,' said Charlie, swallowing hard. 'He may have stumbled and fallen.' Or maybe not.

'The horse trough ... That is not far at all from – from the chapel, is it?'

'No, Mr. Hosie. It's only a step or two.' Jem would know: he had spent enough time recently standing in that doorway.

'We'll take the cart,' said Stephen at last. 'Jem, go and rouse Alan and get him to fetch out the cart. I'll get dressed. And I'll find a decent blanket.'

'He'll not be feeling the cold,' said Jem, a bit waspish.

'We dinna want the whole world staring at him,' said Stephen flatly, and lit a second candle from his first before taking his own one away. Jem and Charlie were left in the kitchen.

'I'll go ahead and tell them you're coming just the now,' Charlie offered. 'Bishop Skinner's sitting with him.'

'You work for him, you say?' Jem snatched up the second candle, and leaned over Charlie, holding the light near his face. Charlie edged away.

'I do, aye.'

'Then you'll know ... you'll know Miss Skinner.'

'Of course.'

'Tell me,' said Jem, 'have you seen her this evening? When the body was found, when it was brought into your chapel?'

Charlie thought back, but he was fairly sure that Jane had not been around. She would know by now, of course.

'I dinna think she was about, no.'

'Right.' Jem nodded, though whether he was pleased or displeased it was hard to tell.

'I'll get going then,' said Charlie. He did not mind Stephen Meston much - at least he was more polite than his brother - but Jeremiah Hosie's company was like lying in a bed of thistles and hoping to get a good night's sleep. He could do with being out of it for a while.

On his way back along Broad Street, he called in to the warehouse. Luzie was at the table, the candle burning low as she worked at her accounts.

'You'll spoil your eyes,' said Charlie, kissing the back of her neck. She pressed back against him, then turned into the embrace of his arms.

'Is that you back, then?'

'No, I've more to do.' Luzie was used to it: clergy could not always keep regular hours. 'But I've some news.'

'Good, I hope?'

'Not for everyone. Cuthbert Meston is dead.'

'What? Not Cuthbert Meston?'

'Why not? No one's immortal.'

'No, of course not, but I'd have thought Cuthbert Meston wouldn't allow anything that didn't fit in with his plans.' She pulled back from him for a moment, taking it in. 'How did he die? A seizure?'

'Oh,' said Charlie, 'well, it might have been, I suppose. He was found in the horse trough on Longacre. I thought he had drowned.'

'In Longacre? What on earth was he doing there?' He could see Luzie felt that was a bit too close for comfort.

'I don't know.'

'Was it the Bishop that found him?'

'No ...' Charlie heard himself hesitating. 'No, it was me.'

'You?' She eyed him for a moment. He heard her swallow. 'Charlie, you didna – quarrel with him, or anything?'

'Me? No! I mean –' He did not want it to sound as if he had not thought to defend her against Meston's threats, all the same. 'I would have gone to talk to him, but there hasna been time. I saw him twa, three times today, but I was always busy. See, the American gentleman has arrived.'

'Already? I thought he wasna expected till Wednesday.'

'He wasna – he's come early. With his pal. And neither of them liked Meston, either – they met him on the boat from Edinburgh.' He had just remembered that. At the back of his mind had been the thought of telling Dr. Seabury and Myles Cooper about the death, and how they – particularly Myles – might react to a sudden death in the street outside Bishop Skinner's house, but now he thought that Myles, at least, might be quite pleased that Meston was dead.

'Anyway, I have to go back, as soon as I've found some dry breeks,' he said, as Luzie assimilated all the news. 'Meston's brother and stepson are bringing a cart for him so he's clear for tomorrow – the Bishop had the body taken into the chapel – and I'd better go and see if the Bishop needs any help. Then that should be me.' He was already at the kist that held their spare clothes, digging for a spare pair.

'I'll see you when you're done,' said Luzie, still frowning. 'Cuthbert Meston dead, though. I shouldn't say it, not so soon, but I wonder who'll take over his business?'

Bishop Skinner was on his knees again when Charlie quietly made his way into the chapel. The neighbours had left. Charlie waited a moment before the Bishop grabbed a chair to pull himself up, and sat on it, looking tired.

'Well, Charlie? What news?'

'Mr. Stephen Meston and Mr. Jeremiah Hosie are coming up with a cart, sir. I came ahead.'

'That's good. I don't want to seem inhospitable, but this is not a large space, and Cuthbert Meston is quite a large man.'

Charlie glanced over at the makeshift bier, covered now with a sheet.

'How do you think it happened, sir?'

Bishop Skinner shifted slightly in his seat.

'I want to say it was an accident,' he said. 'I do. I don't think he was stunned, though. Either something prevented him, despite his being conscious, from pushing himself out, or ...'

'Or maybe he had a seizure, sir?'

The Bishop turned to him gratefully.

'A seizure! Of course – that would be it. That would explain the expression on his face, and his powerlessness to help himself. And he was a big man, and highly coloured – a stroke, perhaps, or a heart attack?' He sat back, looking mightily relieved. Charlie was pleased to have given him some comfort. Yet in the back of his mind, he still felt uneasy. Why was that? A seizure was the perfect explanation, and the Bishop was right: Cuthbert Meston was a heavy, angry man, and just the kind to die that way.

He was still trying to puzzle out his misgivings when they heard voices outside, and wheels grating on the icy cassies. Charlie jumped up to open the front door.

You would have thought the chapel was some kind of trap, he reckoned, looking at their faces as they came in. Stephen edged in first, eyes wide and wary, followed by Jeremiah Hosie, his every movement considered, and at the back the sandy man – Alan Beith, wasn't it? – that Charlie had seen when he first went to return Jeremiah's glove. It seemed like days ago. Alan seemed just as bothered at the situation as the other two. Charlie showed them up into the chapel, and Bishop Skinner rose to greet them.

'I am so sorry for your loss,' he said. 'You must be Stephen Meston.' He bowed to Stephen, who returned the bow uneasily. 'And Mr. Hosie?'

'Sir.' Jeremiah's bow was more elegant, and he bestowed a smile on the Bishop. Charlie wondered at it for a moment, then remembered Jane. Jeremiah Hosie was probably trying, amidst everything else, to make a good impression on Jane's father. Charlie felt a little sorry for him.

The Bishop was explaining about the service in the morning, and expressing his gratitude that they had come so promptly to fetch the body home.

'It's a small place,' he said apologetically, 'but we have tried to make him welcome.'

'Aye,' said Stephen. 'Thank you. I can see that, sir.'

'Have you told the magistrates, sir?' Jeremiah Hosie asked, with an air of humble wisdom. This time Charlie tried not to laugh. Jeremiah could play three parts in a minute. Was any of them real?

'The magistrates? No,' said Bishop Skinner. 'I assume it was an accident.'

Jem nodded sagely. Stephen glared at him, and turned back to the Bishop.

'Quite right, sir. An accident.'

'In fact,' said the Bishop, 'we thought it might have been a seizure. The expression on his face ... well, prepare yourselves.'

At once Jeremiah stepped over to the covered corpse and pulled back the sheet. He gasped, in spite of himself. Stephen was by his side in an instant, and gave a little, anguished cry.

'Aye, not a peaceful death, I'm afraid,' said the Bishop gently.

'Told you,' said Jem, so softly Charlie was not sure that the Bishop would have heard. But Bishop Skinner paused.

'Do you think it likely that he was killed deliberately?' he asked. When they did not answer at once, he added, 'Have you some suspicion of a particular person?'

'You mean had he quarrelled with anyone? Ha!' Jem could not restrain himself for long. 'My stepfather was forever quarrelling. With all kinds of people.'

'Badly enough for this?' asked Bishop Skinner. 'And recently enough?'

'Nae doubt,' said Stephen with a heavy sigh. 'Though he has been away in Edinburgh recently.'

'That might just mean that someone was biding their time till he got back,' said Jem.

'Maybe so,' said the Bishop. 'What was he doing in Longacre, do you know? Was he visiting someone here? Someone who could perhaps tell you more about his evening, his mood, his health?'

Stephen and Jem looked at each other, and shrugged.

'We wondered that, sir,' said Stephen, 'but there's nobody we can think of. He had no business nor acquaintance here that we know of.'

'Or in Broad Street?'

'He must know someone in Broad Street,' Stephen admitted, 'for it is mostly tradesmen. But no one I can think of that he would have been visiting. So late on a Saturday, too.'

Well, there was one business that Cuthbert Meston had visited since he had returned from Edinburgh, thought Charlie. But if no one else was going to mention the warehouse of L. Rob, née Gheertzoon, he was not going to, either.

Chapter Twelve

Charlie helped Alan load Cuthbert Meston's stiffening corpse on to the Mestons' cart, avoiding as much as possible looking at the dead man's face. Alan took the bulk of the dead man's weight, clearly used to warehouse work. The Skinners' spare sheet was replaced with the Mestons' blanket, and Bishop Skinner and Charlie watched solemnly from the door as Stephen, Jeremiah and Alan, feet slithering, tried to keep the cart on a straight route up Longacre and towards their warehouse by the harbour. As they vanished into the darkness of the passage back to Broad Street, Bishop Skinner sighed, and turned away.

'I note that it did not occur to any of them to ask for a prayer over the dead man,' he remarked.

'I dinna think that was uppermost in any of their minds,' Charlie acknowledged.

'Well,' said the Bishop, and hesitated. 'It's past bed time, certainly, and Sabbath tomorrow - well, today. I'd like to hear more from you of what you think of the Mestons - or, well, Mr. Stephen Meston and Mr. Hosie and - was it Alan? But it's late. We can talk tomorrow, if you will.'

'Aye, sir.' Charlie had not realised till now how tired he was. It had certainly been a long day. Threats and Americans and a dead body - that was enough. He bade the Bishop good night, leaving him to lock his own door, and headed home in the wake of the Mestons.

Sunday morning proper was crisp and biting cold, with air that numbed your ears and nose in a moment and dulled your eyes with water the minute you opened the door. Charlie took his coffee quickly - Sunday meant an earlier start than week days - and hurried off to the Skinner house to get the fire lit in the chapel. Once it was going, he cleared away the makeshift bier of benches and made sure the place was as free of dust and as well polished as it was ever likely to be. The chapel was new and had as yet, amongst its congregation, had no call for a coffin table. Charlie wondered what Dr. Seabury would think of the place. What were chapels like in America? He could not begin to imagine.

'Dr. Seabury wants to join us early,' said Mrs. Skinner, meeting Charlie and the maid Jean in the kitchen. 'He will help the Bishop with the service, but will not preach this morning. I daresay Mr. Cooper will arrive with Dr. Seabury.' Her face remained entirely blank at this observation. Charlie was sure she was reckoning how bad Myles Cooper's head might be this morning. 'Then they will dine with us, of course. I should think that Dr. Seabury at least will spend the rest of the day here again. It's hardly the weather for a pleasant walk about the town, and he might preach this afternoon.'

Charlie and Jean nodded obediently. Mrs. Skinner was a good mistress and a sensible one: there was no use in telling servants the absolute basics of what was needed from them. The more a servant knew about the household's intended business, the better able he or she would be to change horses in midstream, or prepare for eventualities.

'When's Bishop Kilgour and Bishop Petrie coming, mistress?' asked Jean.

'They'll be here on Friday, I believe,' said Mrs. Skinner, 'so we don't need to worry about them yet. And we're well used to them, aren't we? Have you parsnips in, Jean, for soup for Bishop Petrie? You ken he's fond of something sweet.'

'Aye, mistress.' Charlie noted the indulgent glance that passed between them. Bishop Petrie did not enjoy good health, but he was a delight to look after.

'Charlie, you'd better go and fetch Dr. Seabury - and Mr. Cooper - and bring them here if they're ready. You've the coals upstairs?'

'Aye, mistress,' Charlie echoed Jean.

'Then Jean, you can do the fires up there. Is there anything else you need Charlie to lift for you before he heads off again?'

There was nothing, and in a few minutes Charlie was making for Broad Street again, casting, as he had earlier, a wary glance towards the horse trough. One of the neighbours was watering his horse there, jagged edges of ice scattered on the cassies on either side. It was Mennie: he nodded to Charlie and waved him over.

'Any more about yon fellow Meston?' he asked.

'His brother came to fetch him home last night.'

'Aye, I thought I heard wheels late on. Have they sent for the magistrate?'

'No idea. It's out of our hands now.'

Mennie shook his head gravely, and leaned in, confidential.

'No out of yours, Charlie, my man. If they go to the magistrates, first thing they'll ask is who found him, and how. And then they'll want to know when you last saw him alive, and how long he'd been dead, and who and what you saw round about him – oh, aye, it'll be a long time before you're done with the magistrates, Charlie. But I suppose,' he added, distancing himself again, 'you've no control over all that now. It'll be them that decides, the Mestons. You'll maybe be all right, maybe no. But it's a fine thing for you that there's no enmity between you and Cuthbert Meston, no reason for you to wish him any harm. I mean, you and him?' Mennie gave a raw chuckle, coughed, and turned back to his horse. 'Good luck, Charlie, my man.'

No enmity, only that Meston had threated Luzie. No, no enmity at all.

Charlie had trouble breathing as he headed off to Broad Street. He wanted to go and tell Luzie not to speak to anyone of what had happened between her and Meston. He wanted to hide her away, safe. But if he were to be suspected of anything to do with Meston's death, surely he should not be seen running to Luzie when he should be fetching Dr. Seabury?

'Are you all right, there? What way are you peching?'

He jumped, and spun about. Next to him was the small, sandy-haired servant of the Mestons – what was his name again? Alan, that was it. If he had not spoken, Charlie was not sure he would have noticed the man at all.

'Peching? Oh,' said Charlie, trying to find a reason for his breathlessness. 'Oh, I'm just in a hurry. A task for my master.'

'Oh, aye, I'll no keep you then,' said Alan. He was paler than Charlie had seen him before, this morning: the pinching cold seemed unable to redden his freckled cheeks, and there were dark circles under his eyes. No doubt Charlie looked much the same. Servants had to rise early, however late the night.

'Were you heading for my master's house? Something to do with last night?' Charlie asked, and the pause helped him to catch his breath and calm himself. Unless, he thought suddenly, Alan was here to warn Bishop Skinner that Meston's family had sent for the magistrates.

'I was. Mr. Stephen - well, I suppose he's Mr. Meston now, but that's a hard thing to call him - he wasna sure he had made his thanks to the Bishop last night, not properly, and he had little recollection of anything he might have been told about where Mr. Meston's body was found, or the circumstances. Should I just go on and see the Bishop? No doubt there's a maid can take this in - Mr. Stephen has written a letter, since it's awkward for him to leave the house, with the corpse and all there.' His mouth made a little, wry smile, which did not reach his eyes. Charlie thought he sounded stiff, his speech disjointed, as though he were not used to much of it. But perhaps it was the shock. 'Mr. Meston would have said it was gey bad for business. Funny how it's him that's the cause.'

Charlie drew breath, still feeling a bit light-headed.

'It was I who found him,' he said, 'so there's no need for you to disturb the Bishop - and I can take him the letter, if you'd like.'

'Oh, aye? That would be good of you, though it's fine to be out of the house.' For a moment he seemed to consider something, then nodded minutely and carried on. 'So could you tell me more about last night, then?'

'I could - will you walk along a bit with me? I'm going to the New Inn.'

'To the New Inn? Aye, that's - that's the direction I was going to head in.'

He turned that way, but Charlie was forced to walk slowly beside him. As they crossed Queen Street, which ran parallel to Longacre but in a grander, less secretive manner, Alan cast a quick look down it, as if debating that route to wherever he was going next, but this time he shook his head slightly, and carried on beside Charlie.

'So what can you tell me, if you don't mind?' he asked.

'I was on my way home - from your place, as it happens, when I went to return Mr. Hosie's glove. I came into Longacre the usual way, by the passage under the tenements. It was shadowy - you can imagine, it's no a wide street - and I looked over to the well and the horse trough because ... I dinna ken. They're just there, ken?'

Alan nodded politely, happy to accept such an explanation, apparently.

'I saw there was someone leaning against the trough, and I was worried in case it was someone drunk. Because it was that cold, you see, and I thought if he dozed off there he could be dead by the morning. Then when I came closer, I saw the fellow - sorry, but I thought it must be someone from nearby - I saw he had his head in the water. Well, when I think about it now I suppose it made sense that he was dead, for he must have been there for a while - I hadna heard a splash, at all - but of course at the time I panicked and tried to get him out.'

'And you managed? All by yourself?' Alan stopped in surprise. 'He was no a small man.'

'No ... it took a whilie, but I managed in the end. And then of course I saw he really was dead, and I went to get Bishop Skinner, who was still up, and we roused a few neighbours to bring him into the chapel.'

'I see,' said Alan. 'So he must have been there a bittie?'

'I suppose so, aye.'

'Was there a'body else about at all?'

As soon as he heard the question, Charlie knew he had missed something. It had not even occurred to him to look around. He had been intent on shifting the man from the water. Yet ...

'I didna see a'body,' he said, slowly, 'nobody at all. But I had the notion, ken, that there was somebody about the place. That's ... when I went through the passage into Longacre, that's when I thought there was someone about. I looked over at a doorway where there had been someone waiting in the morning, but the doorway was empty. Then I saw - Mr. Meston - at the horse trough, and I suppose I thought that was who I thought was there, if you see what I mean.'

'I think so,' said Alan.

'Does it make any sense to you? Was he ailing, at all? Could he have had a fit?'

Alan shrugged.

'He never said a'thing about being ill, but I dinna think he would have. He was tired, right enough – o'er tired when he arrived back from Edinburgh on the boat. I was surprised when he said he was heading out again. And he was up bright and early yesterday, and away out. But he never said where he was going, and I never thought he was a'thing but just tired. But a fit – well, that could happen to a'body, could it no?'

'That's very true,' Charlie agreed, relieved. A seizure would be the best answer. No tragic accident, to make the people of Longacre feart that something might happen again – a loose stone, or a ... he was not even sure he could think of some other way for Cuthbert Meston to have fallen accidentally into the trough. No ghosts, nor murderers. Just a bit of ill health, a moment's pain, and then death.

'Of course,' Alan went on, 'it could just as well be murder, could it no?'

Chapter Thirteen

Alan left him at the foot of Lodge Walk, that headed under the stern façade of the Tolbooth and made – not entirely to Charlie's surprise – for Queen Street. Charlie wondered idly what his errand there might be, on a Sabbath when his master lay dead at home. The poorhouse was through that way, and the Methodist meeting house, and the Quakers. Was Alan a Methodist? Maybe so. Charlie was not one to hold a man's beliefs against him: he had had enough of that when he began attending Episcopalian services.

Dr. Seabury and Myles Cooper were ready and waiting when he arrived to collect them.

'I thought perhaps we should begin to make our own way,' said Dr. Seabury, as friendly as ever, 'but then I realised there are probably several routes, and I had no idea which one you might pick when you were on your own. And it would have caused so much more inconvenience to miss you on the way.'

'I said we should wait,' put in Myles. 'It's barely even daylight out there. Are you sure the family will be up?'

'They're definitely up, sir,' said Charlie. 'Bishop Skinner is expecting you, and asks you both, sirs, to be their guests for the rest of the day.'

'Most kind! Most kind,' said Dr. Seabury. 'Then if you are quite ready, Myles, shall we allow Charlie to lead us back to Bishop Skinner's charming home?'

Despite his consumption of both food and wine the previous evening, Myles seemed unscathed as Charlie led the men downstairs and out of the inn. They both, however, shivered in the sharp cold, and huddled into their dark coats. From the back, Charlie thought, as he ushered them into the street, they looked very similar, particularly when they clamped their hats down over their hair, for Myles' was a dark fair colour, while Dr. Seabury's was already quite grey - natural, not powdered.

'And is all well in the Skinner household today, Charlie?' Dr. Seabury asked.

'Fairly well, thank you, sir,' said Charlie. Should he mention Meston's death? He was not sure. If he did it would probably send Myles into some kind of seizure, too.

He decided to let Bishop Skinner tell them the news if he thought it wise, and escorted the two men along the icy street and back to Longacre. Bishop Skinner was waiting for them in the parlour.

'Before we go up to the chapel, gentlemen,' he said, 'I have some unpleasant news to impart, which we may wish to reflect upon in our prayers. Charlie here found a dead man outside last night. We brought him into the chapel to rest, but his family have since taken him home. I would not like you to have heard about it casually, though of course your acquaintance in this town is still small.'

Dr. Seabury frowned.

'That is very sad,' he said, 'though no doubt in this cold weather it is not uncommon for the poor and homeless to find themselves without shelter. Is there a poorhouse in the town?'

'There is, but of course it cannot take in everyone. And in any case, that is not relevant here, for this man was not fit material for the poorhouse. He was a well-to-do merchant, who drowned in the horse trough outside.'

'In the horse trough!' squeaked Myles. 'How could that happen?'

Charlie imagined that in Myles' inner gaze horse troughs had now taken on a new guise, rearing up to swallow innocent passersby.

'An accident, we think,' said Bishop Skinner smoothly. 'Possibly a seizure.'

'How tragic,' said Dr. Seabury. 'Again, perhaps the cold ...?'

'Perhaps.'

'Perhaps he was attacked by robbers!' said Myles, a hand pressed to his own chest.

Bishop Skinner blinked.

'It had not occurred to me to ask if there was anything missing,' he said, surprised. 'Charlie, did you notice? Had he a watch, or a pocket book?'

'I don't know what was in his pockets, sir, and his coat was buttoned up.'

'That's true,' said Bishop Skinner. 'And he had warm gloves on, so I could not see any rings. Though I suppose the fact that he had his gloves on shows no one tried to steal any rings, either, wouldn't you say?'

'A political attack, perhaps?' Myles was not to be placated.

'It seems unlikely.' Bishop Skinner's voice was soothing. 'There is very little of that kind of thing here. Not these days.'

'You have no idea how fortunate you are,' said Myles. 'The least thing ... the threat to innocent people ... the ideas people have ...'

'My dear Mr. Cooper,' said the Bishop, 'please, sit down! Charlie, will you fetch over some brandy? Mr. Cooper is not at all well, I fear.'

'I am – I am quite well, thank you! I am quite recovered. Quite recovered.'

Nevertheless he seized the brandy glass offered by Charlie, and downed half the tawny liquid in one go. With a glance at the Bishop, Charlie topped it up just a little.

'I'm afraid Mr. Cooper had a very bad experience during our, ah, little revolution,' said Dr. Seabury. 'The people of his sympathies in New York – Tory loyalists, you see – were all told, on several occasions, to flee for their lives, or anticipate their doom.'

'They hated me,' Myles whispered. 'Me, in particular. They sent me all kinds of threats, you know. I could not sleep safe. Do you know what they said? They said they would seize me in my bed, and shave my head, and cut off my ears!' His voice rose perilously. 'And slit my nose! And strip me naked! And then they were going to set me adrift on the sea!' The words wailed about the room, as Myles' fat fingers tightened on the glass. Charlie hoped he would not break it. 'Then a mob attacked me! A mob! I thought I would be dragged to my death! But I escaped!' A cunning look danced quickly over his face. 'I had friends, you know. Friends of whom they knew nothing. I had ...' He trailed off, as if he had said too much.

'And that is why he came over to Edinburgh,' Dr. Seabury

finished gently, 'leaving a great deal of his worth behind him.'

'And they still owe me money,' snapped Myles. 'King's College still owes me money. How hard I worked there! I was the principal, you know.'

Charlie was confused. King's College was in Aberdeen's Aulton, but perhaps the King had more than one college – and until recently it would have been quite acceptable for him to have one in America, presumably.

'Well,' said Bishop Skinner, clearly a little shaken by all of this, 'I can assure you that whatever killed Cuthbert Meston, it was unlikely to be a politically-minded mob. We would have heard it, for one thing.'

'Who did you say?' asked Dr. Seabury suddenly.

'Cuthbert Meston. That was the merchant's name.'

Dr. Seabury looked at Charlie.

'Is that not the man we saw in the street? The one we told you we had encountered on the boat?'

'Aye, sir,' said Charlie reluctantly. Thing were beginning to look messy. 'That was the man.'

'You didn't say – but then why would you?' said Bishop Skinner. 'You met him on the boat from Edinburgh?'

'He attacked us!' Myles breathed.

'He hardly attacked us,' said Dr. Seabury, more reasonably, though Charlie could see he was disturbed by the news. 'He was angry, but it seemed to me he was angry at religion generally, and at Episcopalians in particular. He was not a happy man.'

'He was certainly an angry man,' Bishop Skinner agreed, 'and not a religious one. I am sorry you should have encountered him on your journey.'

'It was nothing,' said Dr. Seabury with a smile. The look on Myles' face said otherwise, but he managed to remain silent.

'Let us go downstairs to the chapel and pray,' said Bishop Skinner. 'It seems to me that we all need a little spiritual refreshment.'

'Perfect,' said Dr. Seabury. 'Come, Myles, let us go up.'

It took Myles a moment to relinquish his brandy glass, draining it before he was willing to let it go. Then Bishop Skinner graciously led the way from the parlour, and Charlie was left to tidy the brandy away.

For a moment he had a little peace to himself, while he saw

to the fire, opened the shutters to the beginnings of daylight, listened to the chapel door open and shut downstairs. Myles' behaviour was astonishing, though if he really had been threatened like that – that would be horrible. It seemed that Scotland was not the only country where the people fought amongst themselves when there was no one else to fight. But there had been little trouble in Scotland now for years – Charlie prayed it would never again come to threats or dangers, families broken, friends divided. It was bad enough when individuals were killed, through greed or hatred or fear or love. He wondered which of these, if any, had killed Cuthbert Meston.

He stopped for a moment and stared out at the street, at the innocent horse trough, the icy snow around it, the queue of neighbours at the well as usual, even on the Sabbath. Not everyone was organised enough, or lucky enough, to take in all the water they needed on a Saturday night, and he was sure there were a few there now who had gone out only to hear if there was any further gossip about Cuthbert Meston and his mysterious death. One or two had been here last night, helping bring the body into the chapel. No doubt they had well-embellished stories to tell.

As he watched, he saw some of the people outside turn to look over at the passage that led to Broad Street. Something seemed to interest them – a man, no, two men, striding with purpose into the narrow street, then pausing to look about them. It was hard, with the people in between, for Charlie to see them clearly: all he could really see was the tops of their hats. One of the men seemed to glance over at the well and its queue, then approached, apparently to ask for directions, for there was waving of hands and nodding, and in a moment he saw faces he knew, neighbours at the well, looking over at him, at the Skinners' house, while the two strangers made their way across the slithery street towards their front door.

Fighting a sudden keen desire to flee, Charlie made for the hall, and was already halfway there when he heard the risp rattled in a most unSabbath-like manner. He hurried down the last few steps and paused, listening. From the chapel upstairs, he heard Bishop Skinner's faint voice, calmly leading their prayers, as if nothing were happening. From outside he heard nothing. He drew a deep breath, and opened the door.

He knew at once it was the magistrate.

'Is this Bishop Skinner's house?' the man asked, peering

beyond Charlie as though trying to find any distinguishing features about the place.

'It is, sir,' said Charlie. 'The Bishop is at prayer just now. Who shall I say?'

'Robert Shand,' said the man, drawing himself up. He was thin, with particularly sharp looking ears. Charlie almost expected them to pierce the brim of his hat.

'Aye, sir. My master will be an hour or so. Would you care to wait in the parlour?'

'In the parlour? No! I should not care to wait in the parlour,' snapped the man. 'I'm expected at my own kirk in an hour. I have no time to wait. And the matter is an urgent one.'

'Charlie?'

Charlie turned at the welcome interruption. Bishop Skinner had emerged from the chapel to his rescue.

'This gentleman is looking for you, sir,' said Charlie. 'Mr. Robert Shand.'

'From the magistrate,' said Shand confidently. 'Are you Bishop Skinner?'

'I am, sir,' said the Bishop mildly. 'Would you come into the parlour, anyway? I trust we shall not detain you long.'

'It is not you I seek,' said Shand sharply. 'I am here in connexion with the death of Cuthbert Meston, merchant. I seek to speak with a Dr. Samuel Seabury.'

Chapter Fourteen

Bishop Skinner took an involuntary step backwards, his head on one side in confusion. A squawk of dismay came from the chapel - Myles, of course, Charlie thought. And why not? If the magistrates were looking for Dr. Seabury in connexion with Cuthbert Meston, they were bound to look for Myles next. Not that Charlie could understand really why the magistrates should be looking for either of them.

For a moment, nobody moved. Bishop Skinner, his head no doubt spinning with memories of hostile powers, hastily concealed church services, arrests and betrayals, stretched out a protective hand as if to stop Robert Shand going up to the chapel. The look on Robert Shand's face was enough to remind anyone of hostile powers: he clearly had little sympathy for Episcopalians, an expression of distaste hovering over his honed features as he contemplated the Bishop. But the silence was broken by the sound of footsteps on a stone floor, and then Dr. Seabury appeared at the top of the stairs

'Good morning,' he said, his serious eyes with their heavy brows tempered by a look that spoke of a readiness to do his duty. 'I am Samuel Seabury. May I be of assistance?'

Bishop Skinner, with an admixture of charm and determination, managed to move the conversation out of the cold hallway and into the parlour, where he sent Charlie for wine for Robert Shand, and ale for his companion, some kind of sergeant, at Charlie's guess. The sergeant followed Charlie down to the kitchen, and stood there, a little awkward, as Charlie poured ale for him and Jean carried glasses, one-handed, back up to the parlour.

'That's a strange thing,' said Charlie companionably, when Jean had gone. 'How did Mr. Shand even know that Dr. Seabury was here?'

'Asked at the New Inn, aye?' said the sergeant, or whatever he was. 'Asked there, was told he was likely round at Bishop Skinner's. Doesna like bishops, Mr. Shand. Swore a bit at that. But he had to come looking, aye?'

'And why's that?' Charlie asked. 'Your good health, sir.'

'And yours too, sir.' The man slapped ale down his throat, and sat back with a satisfied sigh. 'It's a case of murder, aye? Cuthbert Meston, yon merchant Mr. Shand named, he was murdered!'

'My!' said Charlie, trying to look suitably impressed. 'Are they sure?'

'What way sure?' the man asked. A constable, perhaps: Charlie modified his opinions based on the man's apparent intelligence. But Charlie was never that sure that he himself was bright, so he still proceeded with caution.

'I mean,' he said, 'I heard tell that Mr. Meston was dead, but what way do they think it's murder? The way I heard it, he took a fit and fell into a horse trough. The one outside there, in fact.' He gestured to the street, not wishing to seem to distance the household from the event.

The constable - or was he something even more lowly? - frowned, and drank more ale.

'I canna mind ... would it be his wifie or whatever? Some person in his family, his wife or maybe his father - or would it be his brother?' He stopped a moment, and rubbed very comprehensively at his left ear, as if it might stimulate a slowing brain into action. It met with limited success. 'Onyhow, somebody said they thought there would be good reason for somebody - somebody else, that is, not the first somebody - to kill Mr. Meston. Said he was affa fine at making enemies. So they wanted the magistrate to look into the matter, and see, that's where I come in.'

'You help the magistrate to investigate?' asked Charlie, hoping he was wrong.

'Investigate? Me?' asked the man. 'Naw. It's just where I come in - into the house, ken. And find out what I can, to help Mr.

Shand. Aye?'

'Aye,' said Charlie, hoping Mr. Shand was not depending too heavily on the man. 'Well, anyway, that explains why you're looking in to Mr. Meston's death. And how he found Dr. Seabury. But why did he want to find Dr. Seabury? What's the connexion between Mr. Meston and Dr. Seabury?'

The man scowled again, and the ear underwent another alarming massage. By the time he stopped, the whole left side of his face was bright red. Charlie hoped he was not going to do himself some damage.

'Well,' he said, 'Mr. Shand kens that Mr. Meston and your man Dr. Seabury was on the same boatie coming in frae Edinburgh on Friday, and a mannie cried ... what was it now? Mr. Cowper?'

'Mr. Cooper,' Charlie told him, resignedly.

'Aye, that's the fellow. The three of them was on the same boatie, and they had words.'

'Did they, now?' said Charlie, with what he felt was a passable imitation of surprise.

'They did. Giving it laldy, that's what I heard. The ither passengers too feart to go near them. It's a wonder there weren't more injuries. Is the fellow Cooper here, too?'

It was hardly a secret.

'Aye, he is,' said Charlie. 'That was him heading down the stair after Dr. Seabury and the Bishop. Your Mr. Shand will be talking to him now, no doubt.'

'Oh.' The man looked disappointed, and Charlie wondered if that was the bit of information he had hoped to prise out of Charlie over a mug of ale. Then he wondered what time it was. People would soon be starting to arrive for the morning service, surely? And that would be awkward. As the Bishop had said, the Penal Laws were relaxed but they had not been repealed, and if twenty or thirty worshippers began to turn up for a service that should not, by law, have more than four at it, and there was an unsympathetic magistrate actually downstairs in the same house ... Charlie wondered if he should go out into the street and try to stop people coming in, or if he should slip them in quietly one by one and lock the chapel door behind them, hoping that Mr. Shand would not think to investigate.

Jean returned to the kitchen, met Charlie's eye with a look of disgust at the whole situation, and set to to prepare dinner for after the morning service. She pointedly ignored the magistrate's henchman, stepping around him as if he had been a piece of unwanted furniture unaccountably dumped in her kitchen. Charlie wondered if the rest of the household was poised somewhere waiting to hear what had happened, what was happening, wary of becoming involved. The boys, John and William, would be being scrubbed within an inch of their lives and their hair brushed damp and flat for the Sabbath. John relished the day away from his studies, but William could usually find a Sunday excuse to read something improving. The girls, Jane and Margaret, and their mother, would be laced into their Sunday best gowns, particularly with their important guests here. Jean, with her one arm, was not much use at helping with lacing, so the family had to help each other. Then it would not be long before –

'What is happening?' Mrs. Skinner exclaimed as she came into the kitchen. 'Who do we have in the parlour now? Is it another for dinner?'

Then she saw the magistrate's henchman, and gave a little 'Oh!' of surprise.

'It's Robert Shand, the magistrate, mistress,' Charlie explained, 'and this is his man. He's wanting to talk to Dr. Seabury about Cuthbert Meston.'

'Aye,' said the man, no respecter of persons, with a gleam in his eye, 'for the pair of them had a stushie on the boat, afore Mr. Meston was killed dead, and my master wants to know the whys and wherefores of it.'

'Dr. Seabury? In a stushie?' Mrs. Skinner's hand fluttered protectively about her stomach.

'Fists flying, they tell me,' said the man with satisfaction. 'A'body terrified.'

'Good – good heavens!' She turned to Charlie. 'Is the Bishop in there with them?'

'Aye, mistress.'

'Hm. Have they any refreshments?'

'Jean took them in some wine.'

'They'll need sustenance, no doubt, too – wine at this hour and no food! Charlie, take them some of that cake that's in the kitchen.' She met Charlie's eye.

'Aye, mistress,' said Charlie without expression. He knew what she meant.

Who had told the magistrate that Dr. Seabury and Cuthbert Meston had quarrelled on the boat? Or was someone trying to get Dr. Seabury into trouble? As Charlie paused outside the parlour door, he remembered the letter sent to the Bishop telling him not to get involved with Dr. Seabury. Maybe the writer had been quite correct: perhaps Dr. Seabury was not the suitable person he appeared. Would this do harm to Bishop Skinner? Charlie hoped not.

There was no stushie going on in the parlour, anyway. The room had a chill to it: Charlie thought to tend the fire, but it was blazing nicely. Robert Shand was perched, sharp as a shard of ice, on the edge of an upright chair, hands folded calmly on his lap. Opposite him, Dr. Seabury had taken a lower seat and was leaning forward, earnestly talking to him. To one side Bishop Skinner watched intently, his long face paler than usual, while Myles Cooper, shoulders drawn in to make himself as small as possible, was standing by the window, staring out. Charlie could just see his lips working as if he were going over to himself all that was happening. The man had been upset enough earlier. How was he feeling now, with the authorities questioning his friend – and no doubt ready to question him, too?

Charlie took his time serving the cake – declined by both Shand and Seabury but pounced on by Cooper – and topping up the wine glasses. Robert Shand and Dr. Seabury were oblivious to him, he was sure.

'We noticed him when we all boarded the packet in Edinburgh,' Dr. Seabury was explaining. 'I don't believe I had ever seen him before that – I had not spent many days in Edinburgh on this occasion.'

'On this occasion?'

'I studied there some years ago.'

'Never mind that: did you know who he was?'

'No, not at all. I only discovered his name yesterday, when we saw him in the street here and Charlie – that servant there – told us who he was.'

'I see.'

Charlie's hands clamped briefly on the empty bottle. Would Robert Shand want to question him, too? He should not have ventured near the parlour.

'So you knew his name, and no doubt it would then have been an easy step to find out where he lived. Is that what you did?'

'Not at all!' Dr. Seabury shook his heavy head. 'I had no wish for further conversation with him. If he had approached me, of course,' he added quickly, with a glance at Bishop Skinner, 'if he had sent me any communication, in the spirit of reconciliation, then of course I should have spoken with him. But even so, the business on the boat hardly justified such a thing. He was angry – I believe not even angry with us, but with some circumstance he did not disclose – and we happened to represent something he did not like.'

'He was a horrid man!' Myles spun abruptly. 'Horrid. He shouted and shouted. He frightened – other passengers.'

Robert Shand, hands still folded neatly, considered.

'Where were you last night?' he asked. 'Did you stay here?'

'We left here at ... about eleven, was it not, Bishop?'

'I believe so.'

'Charlie walked us to our inn. We went straight there, and did not stir again until this morning.'

'Can you prove that?'

For a moment, the room seemed even colder.

'Prove it?' Dr. Seabury repeated. Myles, breathless, met his eye. 'No, Mr. Shand, I don't believe I can. We are in two separate rooms.'

'Then that is very unfortunate, Dr. Seabury,' said Mr. Shand.

Chapter Fifteen

Charlie managed to report back to Mrs. Skinner just after Robert Shand had left, taking his unimpressive henchman with him. She drummed her thimble finger on the kitchen table; she had been sewing vests for the new baby.

'Where is the Bishop?' she asked.

'I think he's in the chapel, mistress,' said Charlie.

'Alone?'

'That I could not say.'

She frowned, staring down at the needlework on the table. Then she rose with some effort, spreading her heavy skirts around her, and gestured to Charlie to follow her. In the hallway she mounted the stairs slowly and was about to push open the chapel door when Bishop Skinner appeared in the doorway, matching her concerned expression on his own face.

'My dear,' she said, 'is all well?'

He took her hands in his.

'I have no idea. The magistrate has allowed Dr. Seabury to remain free for now, but with an undertaking on all our parts that he will not leave the town. Mr. Cooper is weeping in the parlour.'

'Why Dr. Seabury, and not Mr. Cooper?' Mrs. Skinner asked.

'There you have me. I don't know that either. Perhaps Mr. Cooper did not argue so loudly with Cuthbert Meston on the boat.'

'You don't believe that Dr. Seabury has done anything wrong, do you?' she asked, though Charlie was not sure what she expected the answer to be. The Bishop squeezed her hands more closely.

'In my heart I am sure he has not. He seems a good man. But we barely know him, do we? And we do know – only too well – what extremes men can be driven to when frightened or threatened. He and Mr. Cooper have had a bad time of it, these last few years. And that can harm a man, too.'

'My dear,' said Mrs. Skinner, 'let me know what I can do.'

'Talk with me – that is the best thing you can do.' He glanced past her at Charlie. 'Do not think yourself a silent attendant here, Charlie. You have almost seen more of Dr. Seabury and Mr. Cooper than we have, and you have lived in this town longer than I. Come, let us go into the chapel – it wants half an hour to the service still, and we can talk privately.'

He ushered them past him into the chapel where the candles were as yet unlit, except for one by the reading desk. The Bishop began to light others from it with a spill. Mrs. Skinner sat carefully on a stool.

'I don't understand,' the Bishop said over his shoulder, 'how they discovered that Dr. Seabury and Cuthbert Meston quarrelled on the boat – that baffles me. Just luck, coming upon gossip? Did Meston mention it at home? Or was it some deliberate attempt to harm Dr. Seabury?'

'You think someone is trying to discredit him further? After that letter?' asked Mrs. Skinner.

'Yet they did quarrel on the boat, apparently. Neither Dr. Seabury nor Mr. Cooper denies that.'

'From all I hear, Cuthbert Meston would have quarrelled with his own reflection,' said Mrs. Skinner. Charlie nodded agreement.

'It's true,' the Bishop sighed. 'I don't know whether to be glad or not that this has happened before we have made any decision on a consecration. It's certainly best that it happens now, and can be cleared up or not as the case may be. But if it had happened after we had consecrated him, the whole matter would be out of our hands. I mean, in a church sense. We'd still be held responsible, I suppose, if he has done anything wrong.' He screwed up his face in a frown, and rubbed his eyes with finger and thumb. 'What on earth am I to say to Bishop Kilgour? Or Bishop Petrie? They made me responsible for taking care of Dr. Seabury until they arrived. What will they say if he has been arrested for murder? Bishop Kilgour has worked very hard as the foremost bishop to make people think better of our church. This will not please him at all!'

'Well,' said Mrs. Skinner after a moment, 'could Dr. Seabury have done it, or not?'

They both looked at Charlie, who blinked.

'You're asking me?'

'You were the last to see Dr. Seabury and Mr. Cooper last night, and the first to find Mr. Meston's body. What do you think? Could either of them have killed him?'

Charlie thought over the events of the previous evening. When he had seen the body, his first fear was that it had been Myles Cooper. He had not been entirely surprised at the thought that Mr. Cooper might have left the inn in the middle of the night and ventured into the terrifying Aberdeen streets, buoyed up by the courage of alcohol.

'I think either of them could have, sir. Mr. Cooper was fou, if I can say that –'

'There's no argument there, Charlie. Mr. Cooper was indeed very drunk.'

Charlie nodded.

'So Dr. Seabury - with no disrespect intended, sir - Dr. Seabury could have crept out without Mr. Cooper knowing anything about it, even if they had shared a room, which I believe they did not. And there would have been time, I suppose, before I found the body, for Mr. Cooper to sober up a bit and be capable of going out. But sir, why would they? How could they have known that Mr. Meston was going to be there? Even his brother didn't know where he was, and if he had had to guess he would not have chosen Longacre.'

'Yes, fairly said.' The Bishop waved a long finger at Charlie. 'What on earth was Cuthbert Meston doing here in Longacre? I don't believe I had ever seen him around here before.'

'He had been around here a few times since Friday,' said Charlie. 'He was even here - or in Broad Street, anyway - on Friday evening, after he returned from Edinburgh.'

'You saw him?'

Charlie hesitated. He had said too much in his effort to be helpful: he had not intended to bring Luzie into this.

'Somebody mentioned they'd seen him,' he said. 'And then I saw him myself, too, yesterday.'

'When you told Dr. Seabury his name?'

'That and another time.' Charlie was happy now to be away from Friday night. 'I saw him twa-three times on Broad Street yesterday, and it seemed to me he was taking an awful interest in Longacre. He was just standing at the entrance, staring down this way. When I mentioned that to his brother Mr. Stephen Meston, he was that surprised, for he could think of nothing that would take him this way at all.'

'Perhaps he was feeling a call to the Church,' said Bishop Skinner, managing a smile even in the circumstances.

'Aye, that'd be likely,' said his wife drily. 'I could just see him at the Berean Meeting House.'

'Well,' said the Bishop, 'at least Bishop Kilgour and Bishop Petrie won't be arriving before Friday, according to their arrangements - since Dr. Seabury wasn't expected till Wednesday anyway. I'll write to Bishop Kilgour in the morning, tell him I've looked at that strange letter, and reassure him that everything is going well. No sense in alarming him before there's something definite to alarm him about. By Friday, with God's blessing, perhaps everything will be clear. Wouldn't you say?'

'If this hadn't happened,' said Mrs. Skinner thoughtfully, 'how would you say things are progressing?'

'You mean with Dr. Seabury? Very well, I should have said. He has answered the allegations in that letter with great conviction, directing me to evidence for the friendliness with which the English bishops treated him, short of agreeing to consecrate him. He is sure it was only the matter of the oath of allegiance that prevented them, but he is quite happy for Bishop Kilgour to write to Canterbury or York and ask them to confirm that. The man Smith, who apparently instigated the letter, does not, he says, have the support of the American clergy and is an ambitious, grasping individual who wishes himself to become the first bishop in America. Of course this could all be words, but I found him very convincing - and I know Bishop Kilgour is indeed looking into all of this. And aside from that - and suspicions of murder - I find him, so well as I can so far judge, to be a sober, sensible, and sincere man, with a deep spiritual conviction and a proper humility in all of this.'

'He'll not be pleased, I should say, if more happens to delay him,' said Mrs. Skinner.

'You're right there. He knows we are his last hope in this endeavour, and I should say, though he has not stated it clearly, that his funding is running low. Mr. Cooper is supporting him at his own expense.'

It occurred to Charlie that whatever money Myles still felt he was owed in America, he must have managed to bring plenty home with him if he could support both himself and Dr. Seabury in the manner in which Myles seemed to enjoy. Either that, or he made a habit of visiting other clergy and eating and drinking his fill. It was an uncharitable thought, and he felt some shame even as he smiled to himself at it.

'What do you think of him, Charlie?' The Bishop took him by surprise. 'For a servant often sees a side of a man that his peers do not see.'

Charlie ducked his head in acknowledgement of the fact.

'But he seems much as you've said, sir. Of course, I've had no great conversation with him about spiritual matters, but he has been kindly enough, worried, if anything, that he might cause inconvenience or offence. There is one thing, though, sir, which caused me some thought.'

'What's that?'

'He tells me he owns slaves.'

'Ah ...' Bishop Skinner's gaze sank to the floor, and he drummed his long fingers on the side of a chair. 'Slaves ... Truly, America is a strange place. And yet, there have been slaves here, too, over the centuries. The Romans, I believe, took many British people away and sold them into slavery. Abraham had slaves ... And yet, and yet. The Quakers, I believe, are petitioning Parliament on the matter. I shall speak with Dr. Seabury about his slaves, and see what he has to say.'

'He asked if I would rather be a well-treated slave or a badly-treated free man, sir.'

'And what did you say?'

'I said if I were free I could leave a bad master. But he said it was not always that easy.'

'I hope you do not think yourself ill-treated here, Charlie!' said Mrs. Skinner, half-humorous, half-anxious.

'No, indeed, mistress, not at all.'

'Thank goodness for that! John, my dear, we must ready the

chapel for the service.'

'Yes, indeed. I shall talk on with Dr. Seabury after that, and see what transpires.'

The congregation gathered for Morning Prayer. There were more of them than usual, Charlie thought, curious to see the mysterious Dr. Seabury. He and Myles Cooper stood and sat and knelt with the rest of the worshippers while Bishop Skinner, in his Geneva gown and teaching bands, led the service, preached gently, set the note for the Tate & Brady psalms, and prayed fervently.

The Bishop was closeted with Dr. Seabury for the bulk of the day. Mrs. Skinner offered Myles Cooper any number of books to read to pass the time as he waited, but it seemed that Mr. Cooper was not particularly interested in books, and he preferred to sleep the day away in the parlour, gradually spreading himself over the sopha so that no one else could fit on to it. Charlie spent the day in the kitchen, helping Jean carry and chop and shift things that she could not manage herself with one arm, and at last, when it came time for dinner, he went up to Bishop Skinner's bookroom to let the two interlocutors know.

'You'll want to stretch your legs, no doubt,' the Bishop said to Dr. Seabury, ushering him out of the room. 'I shall see you at the table. Charlie, a word, if you would?'

Charlie squeezed past the door and into the cramped room.

'Shut the door for a moment, eh?'

'Is something the matter, sir?'

'Not as such, no,' said the Bishop, leaning against his desk, arms folded. 'I've been talking with Dr. Seabury, as you know, and I've been doing some thinking. He told me, as I said, that this fellow Dr. Smith is against his consecration, and then there's the matter of someone spreading gossip about that quarrel on the boat. What if – now, tell me truly what you think, Charlie, for I know you've a little experience in this kind of thing – what if someone, walking about Longacre late at night, saw a largish man in a wide-brimmed hat and a dark coat, and attacked him – believing not that it was Cuthbert Meston, but that it was Samuel Seabury?'

Chapter Sixteen

Charlie was taken aback. Of course he had started by wondering if the body was that of Myles Cooper, but it had not occurred to him that any mistake had been made but his own. It took a moment for him to picture the situation as the Bishop had suggested it.

'I suppose,' he said at last, 'that it's more likely that someone was looking for Dr. Seabury out there, than looking for Mr. Meston. But are they even sure yet that Mr. Meston was killed? I mean murdered?'

'That's not very clear, I have to say. It seemed to me that Robert Shand was speculating, based not so much on what they could tell had happened to Cuthbert Meston and more on the fact that someone had the shadow of a reason to kill him.'

Charlie pondered for another long minute. He wondered why Bishop Skinner had asked him for his opinion. It was true that when Charlie had been a young man his then master had been killed in a duel, but that was hardly the same thing, and Charlie was sure that the Bishop's mind worked twenty times as fast as his own.

'But who in Aberdeen would want to kill Dr. Seabury? He's hardly been here two days. He canna know many people.'

'Yet someone told the magistrate that he had quarrelled with Meston.'

'Aye, but that's no killing him, is it, sir?'

'No, true, but it shows that someone knows him, to some extent. And knew where he was staying.'

'The man that letter mentioned, that Dr. Seabury said was against him - was it Smith? He's in America, is he no?'

'I suppose so. But what about the man who sent the letter? William Seller, in Inverugie. Inverugie's only up by Peterhead, where Bishop Kilgour lives. He could easily be in Aberdeen.'

'I suppose so, sir.' It was thirty odd miles to Peterhead. Charlie had no idea how far it was from there to Inverugie, but maybe not far.

'Do you think you could find out a bit more about him, Charlie? Have you any acquaintances that direction?'

'I canna call one to mind, sir, but I can ask about, certainly. I think Luzie has a customer that direction. I'll ask her.'

'You do that: thank you, Charlie. Are you going home after dinner as usual?'

'If that's all right, sir.'

'Of course – as long as you can come back later to take Dr. Seabury and Mr. Cooper back safely to the inn. I think Mr. Cooper will be even more reluctant to venture out tonight.'

'Aye, sir, I'll do that.'

It was only as Charlie trotted along to the kitchen to help Jean carry in the dinner that it occurred to him that if someone had tried to kill Dr. Seabury last night, and realised they had failed, they might well try again tonight.

Dr. Seabury preached at the afternoon service, and the little chapel was packed. He had a trick of emphasising his points by waving his handkerchief like a flag. He could be allowed his eccentricities, though, Charlie thought: he could see from Bishop Skinner's face that the sermon was meeting with his approval. Another test passed.

'No,' said Luzie, as they sat at their own table to eat later, 'I've never heard of anyone called Seller. I could write to the man I sell coffee to in Peterhead, but I don't know when he might reply.' She lifted the heavy dish of beef and gravy with the ease born of working in her own warehouse. The meal itself was rather more gravy than beef – they might drink the finest coffee in the north east, but they were not rich enough to afford slabs of meat.

'I might just go and talk to the carrier,' said Charlie.

'What do you need to find out about this Seller for, anyway?'

It was good to have something like her full attention, her sharp blue eyes taking him in. On any day but Sunday, she often had her business books open at the table, one eye on them even as she talked with him. She said she could do both things at once, but Charlie was never quite convinced, maybe because he knew it would be beyond his own powers.

'It's an idea the Bishop has,' he began. 'He wondered if maybe Cuthbert Meston had been killed by mistake, and that whoever it was really meant to kill Dr. Seabury.'

Luzie looked at him in astonishment.

'You said Dr. Seabury seems a nice man. Why would anyone want to kill him?' She considered, then added, 'And why not Cuthbert Meston? Lots of people must have wanted to kill him! You must have lists of them, without looking for people who might have wanted to kill a stranger from America.'

'I don't know. They would have looked a bit alike from the back, particularly in the dark. And when I saw the body, I thought it might be Myles Cooper.'

'This friend of Dr. Seabury's? But why did you think that?'

Charlie shrugged.

'I didna realise at first the man was dead: I thought he was drunk, and the last drunk I'd seen had been Mr. Cooper. And it struck me as, well, Mr. Cooper was that drunk he could well have wandered out of the inn again and got confused. And he's the kind of person that things happen to, I think: he's the kind that bullies pick on. Or stupid accidents happen to. And I really didn't want it to be him, because I felt responsible, ken?'

Luzie put a hand out and laid it on Charlie's arm, giving him an understanding smile. She knew how he could take things on, even when he didn't have to.

'So all that went through my head before I had even thought it might be someone else entirely, or even someone dead.'

'So, three men who all looked a bit alike. From the back, in the dark.' She wiped gravy delicately from her lips as she thought about it. 'I wonder how many other men in Aberdeen might also look much the same?'

'The thing is, someone might have expected to see Dr. Seabury in Longacre. They would be less likely to expect to see Mr. Meston.'

'They could have been following him, or have arranged to meet him. Or picked on him randomly to rob him. Was he robbed?'

'That's another thing I dinna ken.' He sighed. 'There's lots of them.'

'Well, there you are, then. That's probably what happened: wealthy looking man out late, dark street, not the best street, either. No lantern – did you find a lantern?'

'No,' said Charlie, sitting up, 'no, I didn't, and none of the neighbours mentioned finding one, either.'

'Wealthy looking, foolish man with no lantern, then. He was bound to be robbed.'

'Poor man.' He saw the expression on Luzie's face. 'I mean, I ken he was no the nicest of men, and you could well have done without him taking any notice of your business, but you wouldna wish that on him, would you?'

'I just wonder,' said Luzie, neatly avoiding the question, 'if that's really the end of it. His family will take over his business, no doubt. Will I find one of them at the door, telling me the same thing?'

Charlie made a face at the thought, but remembered Stephen Meston, Jem Hosie, and Alan the warehouseman.

'I've only met his brother and his stepson, but they don't seem so aggressive as Cuthbert Meston,' he told her. 'Maybe it was just him doing it.'

'Maybe ...'

It was his turn to squeeze her hand. Luzie was always so strong and determined: he did not like to see her even a wee bit cowed. She smiled at him, but he could see the anxiety in her eyes.

'Anyway, even if they appear both of them at the door,' she said, showing more of her usual spirit, 'I shall not submit! They will see how a woman from Amsterdam runs her business!'

'That's you, Luzie!' said Charlie proudly. 'And I'll be right beside you.'

They grinned at each other before returning to their dinner. But Charlie could not yet quell the worry he felt. How like his brother was Stephen Meston?

Myles Cooper was not quite so drunk that night: at both dinner and supper the supply of wine had been more judiciously controlled, something with which Charlie noted Dr. Seabury seemed to co-operate entirely. He could tell the two of them were nervous going back to the New Inn, though he had taken the precaution of bringing a large stick with him, leaving the carrying of the lantern to Dr. Seabury.

Lantern ... how had Mr. Meston ventured into Longacre after dark without a lantern? Had not someone at the Meston warehouse mentioned a lantern?

Charlie saw the two clergy to their rooms, and bade them good night, returning to Longacre only to make sure the house was properly locked up. Then, finding no further bodies, he went home to his wife and his bed.

On Monday morning, a fortuitous coincidence occurred. Charlie called at the Skinner house to make sure all was in order and he was not needed urgently, and found that Bishop Skinner, up early as usual, had already written his intended letter to the Primus, Bishop Kilgour, reassuring him about Samuel Seabury.

'Will you take this to the Peterhead carrier, Charlie?' he asked.

'Aye, sir - and I'll ask him about Mr. Seller when I'm there.'

Bishop Skinner grinned.

'Perfect!'

So Charlie made his way back to Broad Street again and across the Castlegate to an inn, respectable enough, despite backing nearly into St. Ninian's Chapel where the soldiers were barracked. In the yard at the back, where the small stables were, he found a man with a striking head of spiky tow-fair hair, scrubbing down a hand cart with a bucket of hot water and a look of resignation. It was indeed the Peterhead carrier.

'I should have done this on Saturday when I got here,' he sighed, seeing Charlie approach, 'but man, it was freezing, and the mud on the wheels was something terrible. So of course I could do nothing yesterday on the Sabbath, and now it's that caked on the cart is twice the weight. Have you something there for me to take for your wifie?'

'No, Simmie, I've nothing the day for her, but I've a letter for Bishop Kilgour from my master,' said Charlie. 'But if you're there for a whilie anyway I'll give you a hand with that. I wouldna mind a word with you while I'm here.'

'A word? Here, here's another clout.' He handed Charlie a slightly cleaner cloth and set to on his own side of the cart with a hard brush. For a moment Charlie did not even try to make himself heard, and started soaking the mud on his side to soften it. His fingers were quickly cold but the work was satisfying, and it took a bit of time before he tried again to ask Simmie what he wanted to know.

'I'm seeking news of a Mr. William Seller, who I believe bides in Inverugie. Do you ken him?'

'Aye, I do,' said Simmie, now wiping his side of the cart. 'Man, look at the state of this. I'll no get home the night at this rate.'

'What can you tell me about him?'

'About Seller?' Simmie reflected for a moment. Charlie sloshed a bit of water over where he had loosened the mud, and was pleased to see plenty of it running off and into the slush of the stableyard. 'He bides on his own, barring an auld maid that attended his mother. His wife's dead these long years. I think he reads a lot,' he added, apologetically. 'I dinna go often to his place unless something needs a reply – he comes into Peterhead to pick up his letters and so on.'

'Aye, well. Look, is that any good?'

Simmie came round and gazed at Charlie's work, nodding approval.

'Aye, man, that'll help well enough!'

'If I wanted to go and see Mr. Seller, do you think he would talk to me?'

Simmie looked at him in surprise.

'You want to go to talk to Mr. Seller? All the way up to Inverugie? What for would you do that? Does he owe you money?'

'No!' Charlie laughed. 'No, I just want – well, my master might just want – to ask him something.'

'Oh, aye, I could see William Seller just fancying being pals with a bishop, ken,' said Simmie, nodding to himself. 'That would be the like of him. But you canna go and see him in Inverugie, mind, Charlie, not now.'

'Why not? He's not dead, is he?' asked Charlie, in sudden alarm.

'Dead? No, not when I last heard. Though he's a fair age, right enough. No, he's no in Inverugie just the now.'

'Then where is he? Could my master maybe write to him?'

'He could if he likes,' Simmie acknowledged. 'Or he could go and see him for himself. Mr. Seller told me last week he was heading for Aberdeen, to stay a wee whilie.'

'In Aberdeen?' Then, thought Charlie, what had there been to stop him attacking someone in the street that he might have thought was Dr. Seabury?

Chapter Seventeen

'Have you any notion where he might stay when he's in Aberdeen?'

The carrier made a face expressive of having been asked for too much information, and shrugged.

'I dinna deliver a'thing to him here,' he said. 'I've no call to ken where he might be.'

Charlie reckoned he still had enough credit from helping clean the cart to ask one more question, though.

'What does he look like?'

'Like the better sort of dominie.'

Charlie frowned – he could not go about Aberdeen looking for someone like a schoolmaster. There would be dozens of them.

'An idea of his build? The colour of his hair? His age?'

'Are you looking a portrait of the fellow? For goodness' sake,' said the carrier in disgust, but he set his cloth down, folded his arms, and thought hard. 'He's a wainisht-like person, not much flesh on his bones. I'd say he's mebbe in his sixties, and his hair's grey, tied back in a black velvet ribbon. Gentlemanly, and well mannered, and his clothes are good. What else?' He sucked at his teeth, concentrating, eyes half-closed. 'I'd say he's tall, but it's maybe just that he's so thin. Thin, aye! Even his nose is thin: it's like a wee sail on his face to catch the wind.'

Charlie saw that was all he was to get, but he was grateful for it.

'Thanks, my friend.'

'Aye, well, thank you for helping with the cart, and all. Mind, I tell you, I've paid for it!'

'So you have!' said Charlie, and they shook hands to confirm it.

Back at the Skinners' house, Charlie found that Dr. Seabury had already arrived with an anxious Myles Cooper. They were in the hall.

'I hope you don't mind that we didn't wait for you this morning, Charlie,' said Dr. Seabury with a smile. 'I felt we knew our way well enough now.'

'Nevertheless ...' put in Myles.

'And it is perfectly safe in daylight, is it not?' Dr. Seabury carried on, giving Myles a mildly reproving look. 'Perfectly safe. I see Bishop Skinner's daughters and sons going about in the street in a respectable and secure manner, so why should not we, two braw grown-up men?'

Charlie nodded, wincing again at Dr. Seabury's use of Scots, but as he showed the men to Bishop Skinner's bookroom again, he wondered if Dr. Seabury was right. Presumably Bishop Skinner had not mentioned to them his theory that it was in fact Dr. Seabury who had been the murderer's intended target. If indeed there had been a murderer.

He found Mrs. Skinner in the kitchen, with her feet up before the stove, talking over the day's plans with Jean. She continued to work at her sewing.

'I told her to sit down,' said Jean to Charlie. 'She's got too much to bother her at the minute: she needs to take it easy.'

'And so I am taking it easy,' said Mrs. Skinner. 'Look at me! Lazing my time away.' Her open gown was lightly laced for her swelling stomach – she was indeed relaxed.

Charlie grinned.

'That'll be the day, mistress.'

'It looks as if Dr. Seabury and Mr. Cooper are here for the day again,' said Mrs. Skinner. 'If it stays fine, my husband means to take them out for a walk over to the Loch lands and Spring Garden, show them Gordon's Hospital and the Town Kirk, that kind of thing. Then they could have dinner somewhere over there: he has great hopes that Mr. Aitken of St. John's Chapel would feed them.' She sighed. 'I don't want to sound inhospitable, but that Mr. Cooper puts away more food and drink than our whole family at one meal.'

'Mainly the drink, from all I've seen,' Jean remarked, at a volume which might have been intended to make you think she had meant it only for herself. Mrs. Skinner made a face.

'Aye, maybe so. Well, anyway, it would be a relief if they spent one day away, just to allow us to catch up with ourselves. Not that I have anything against Dr. Seabury: he seems a very pleasant gentleman.'

'If they're heading out, mistress,' said Charlie, 'do you think they'll need me?'

'Why, Charlie? Did you want to do something else?'

'It's just that Luzie feels she should go down to pay her respects at Cuthbert Meston's house, being in the same trade.' That was what Luzie had given as her excuse, anyway. 'And she wants me to go with her, ken, in case there's any problem with her being a woman in trade on her own.'

'There can be, sometimes, can't there?' Mrs. Skinner acknowledged. 'Well, Charlie, I'd recommend you go and do that before my husband thinks up some reason that he wants an escort. It's possible they will not even venture out this morning, so if you're quick you'll maybe not be missed at all.'

Charlie took her at her word, and as soon as he had helped Jean with preparing some vegetables he hurried home.

'Have you been to his warehouse before?' he asked Luzie as they walked down Marischal Street to the harbour. Luzie had a scarf tied about her best bonnet, but still had to clutch it against the wind nipping up from the sea. She changed hands so she could take Charlie's arm and more easily see his face.

'I went there once when I first came here,' she said. 'Before I talked to you about opening my own warehouse, I wanted to see who else was trading in the same things, and how they did it. So I went round all of them. Cuthbert Meston's was the best, I thought: the others are much smaller, and only do a little trade alongside other things. He and I are the only ones to specialise. I of course have a much smaller business. At present, anyway.'

'I didn't know you'd done that. What did he say to you?'

'Well,' said Luzie, 'obviously I did not go in and say I intend to set up in competition with you, can you give me any advice? No, I go in and pretend I am looking for a special spice – I think I called it Tobagona – and asked him if he stocked it. I probably said something like I have heard you are the best spice merchant in the town, so I knew you would have it if anyone had.'

Charlie laughed, picturing it.

'And maybe I pretended to be a little dim, you know? So that he would not think of me as any kind of threat. I let him talk about all the spices he had – I was impressed, so I had no need to pretend at that – and then he gave me a dish of his coffee, and that showed me that I could do better than he in coffee, anyway. And he was most charming, though I could see he was wondering what on earth Tobagona was, and in the end he promised me that he would import it and named me a price, which, if I had ever thought I might have to pay it for this mythical spice, might have caused me to faint there and then. But I agreed that if he managed to import it I would buy it. I said I would return, as I was in the process of finding a good house in the area and could not give him an address, and I have not been back since.'

'Do you think he suspected anything?'

'From a woman? I doubt it. That only came when people started to tell him there was better coffee in Aberdeen than the adequate stuff he was selling. That, of course, could not be tolerated, from man or woman, and so he comes to visit me.'

'I wonder where he heard that, and when?' Charlie mused.

'I don't know. It could have been any number of people. My customers are growing, and of course I do not know to whom they supply coffee, or to what guests they might offer it. Why should you care? It's not as if anyone was maligning me.'

'No ... But Cuthbert Meston was just back from Edinburgh, and by the accounts of his brother he was very tired, and a bit quiet. But he made the effort then to go out again, saying he had to. And the only thing I know he did that evening was to visit your warehouse and threaten you.'

Luzie stopped, and looked at him.

'You're right,' she said, after a moment's thought, 'that seems excessive. He could have threatened me any time.'

'So did he go out specifically to do that? Or did his business take him up our direction and it occurred to him he could just call in on his way, or on his way back? Had he already heard about your coffee, or was it that whoever he had just met mentioned it to him, and it was therefore on his mind?'

'Well, I don't know,' said Luzie, turning to continue down the street. 'It seems to make little difference to me.'

But it might, thought Charlie: it might indicate what kind of business Cuthbert Meston was doing that night, or at least with whom he was doing it. And that might tell them more about his state of mind - and why he was lingering about Longacre.

They were not the only visitors at the flat by the warehouse. A number of the town's better class of merchant were there, or appeared behind them, or were just leaving as they arrived, all paying their respects at the decease of one of their own. It was not the funeral proper yet and they discovered that Cuthbert Meston had not been kisted: he still lay, coffinless, on his bed, a fresh nightshirt crisp about him and a bandage circling jaw and head to keep his mouth closed. The mourners, if mourning was what they were doing, did not linger in there but moved in and out of the room quickly, so that it seemed death had had little effect on Cuthbert Meston's popularity.

Charlie and Luzie followed the little procession into the deadroom and out again. Charlie noted that someone had done their best to soften the expression on Meston's face, though it still looked uncomfortable. Not much else could be seen of his flesh for Charlie to judge whether or not he had been murdered, but he hoped he was right in thinking that indeed the man had just had a seizure. It must be so, surely.

But what was he doing in Longacre, and without a lantern? The questions would not go away, no matter how much he told himself that there were bound to be perfectly innocent answers. But if he had been visiting someone in Longacre, someone of whom Stephen Meston and the rest of the household seemed to know nothing, why had they not come forward and said anything? Longacre's gossips were not known for their reticence, around the well of a morning. Surely someone knew something about him?

One or two of the other merchants were accompanied by their wives, and Luzie seemed to spy some acquaintance amongst them. She darted off to a spot by the kitchen window where no doubt the gossip was just as thorough as the well claik. Charlie smiled, and looked about to see where Stephen Meston was, or Jeremiah Hosie, or, nearer his own level, Alan Beith the warehouseman. The kitchen was crowded, but he just managed to spot Stephen by the table and went to pay his respects.

'Aye, good of you to come,' said Stephen Meston. His face was pale in the hot room, and had a clammy, worried look to it. 'Have a bit of bread. I'm sorry the food's not very ... we lost our maid, just the other day.'

'Lost her?' Charlie glanced at the bread but decided he was not hungry. 'That's unfortunate.'

'I mean my brother ... got rid of her. We've no one new yet.' He seemed flustered. Charlie hoped he had not tried baking the bread himself, but it certainly had an inexpert look to it. Stephen Meston glanced past him. 'Oh, Mr. Adams! Good of you to come. Here, have some bread.'

Charlie shifted out of the way, duty done, and looked about the kitchen, but he scarcely had time to see if there was anyone he could talk to when he felt a tug on his elbow. Turning, he found the warehouseman, Alan, behind him.

'Have you a mintie?' Alan asked. 'Come away into the warehouse, would you?'

Curious, Charlie followed the sandy man down the stairs and through a door into a large space redolent of his wife's own warehouse. Coffee, tea, cinnamon, nutmeg, cloves ... the air was golden with the scents, heavy with flavour. He breathed in steadily, trying to avoid coughing.

Alan scuttled in behind him, and shut the door into the passage.

'Have you heard?' he said. 'Have the magistrates been to see you?'

'To see me?' asked Charlie, and felt his heart race. 'No: they've been to see a guest of my master's.'

'Aye, aye, no doubt there'll be others, too, that they'll want to talk to.'

'What do you mean?' asked Charlie, but at once he knew, even before Alan said it.

'When we brought him home, we found a big bruise on the back of his neck. Where he must have been held under the water, see?'

'Oh, my ...'

'So there's no doubt at all. The man was murdered.'

Chapter Eighteen

'That's no good,' said Charlie after a minute.

'No,' Alan agreed. He had a mild, gentle voice, and it seemed to make what they were talking about all the more threatening. 'I think you need to watch out. That was my first thought, anyway.'

'Me?' Charlie found himself looking round quickly, to see if anyone was listening, but they were alone in the warehouse. 'What for should I be watching out?' Did Alan know that his late master had threatened Luzie? But Alan raised a placating hand.

'I mean because you were the one to find him, ken? And you were around the place that evening – who's to say you hadna been looking for him? And him killed just outside your master's house?' Alan sighed, and shook his head. 'It just seemed to me you needed warning. Before the magistrate turns up on your doorstep.'

'That's ... that's awfa good of you,' Charlie forced himself to say. Alan did seem to mean it kindly, after all. But it was a shock: who else would put together all those things just like that? 'I suppose the magistrates have been here?'

'Aye,' said Alan, 'they came to see the body. I went up for them myself, see, yesterday morning, when Mr. Stephen found that bruise.'

'But there must be other people who might have wanted to kill Cuthbert Meston!' Charlie's voice rose as the enormity of the situation hit him. Alan backed off slightly, edging around a barrel to put it between him and Charlie. Charlie tried to bring his own breathing back to normal. 'I'm sorry, sorry about that. But I mean –

I ken he was your master and all, but he wasna that popular!'

'He was a very good master to me,' said Alan solemnly.

'But there could be a wheen of reasons why he was killed. I mean, was he robbed, for instance?'

'He wasna. He had a purse with coin in it still at his belt.'

'Well ... maybe someone meant to rob him, but when they'd pushed him into the trough they couldn't shift him, and ran off? Or panicked when they saw they'd killed him?'

'I'm not saying that's not true, or not possible,' said Alan, his voice still soft even with an edge of worry. 'But I'm just saying nobody knows. And you've just got all these connexions. I mean, anyway, why are you here today?'

'I brought my wife, who's in the same trade,' said Charlie, without thinking.

'Your wife's in the same trade?' Alan looked almost surprised. 'What's her name, then?'

'Luzie Rob,' Charlie mumbled the words. It was no use hiding them now: it would have been easy for Alan to work it out, no doubt, if he remembered or could find out Charlie's surname.

'L. Rob? In Broad Street?'

'That's right, aye.'

'Very fine coffee?' asked Alan.

There was silence for a moment. Then Charlie drew himself up – to a height that was a few inches more than Alan's.

'Aye,' he said, 'very fine coffee. No doubt about that.'

He met Alan's eye. He knew that whatever had happened on Saturday night, more than just Cuthbert Meston knew that he had had dealings with Luzie.

Finding the body, living near the scene, visiting the man's house earlier in the evening – and now a motive, too. If Charlie could have done it at that very minute, he would have started running, and not stopped till he was in Timbucktoo. Somehow he found his way back out of the warehouse, though, and instead wriggled his way through the queue of mourners and back up to the kitchen of Meston's flat to find Luzie, and take her away from here.

But before he could even see Luzie, he was stopped in his tracks by Jeremiah Hosie, whose dramatic gestures seemed even more emphatic than usual. He swung a long arm about and seized Charlie by the lapel of his coat, leaning close to Charlie's face.

'The man that works for the Skinners, are you not?' he asked. His breath explained some of his wild movements: he had clearly been drinking.

'I am, sir,' said Charlie moderately.

'How fortunate.' The long fingers slid down his lapel, then Jem leaned back dangerously and ran both hands through his wild hair, pressing his temples with the heels of his thumbs as if to ease a chronic ache. He frowned, and shook his head. 'How fortunate for you to work in such a place.'

'Bishop Skinner is a kind master, that's very true,' Charlie agreed.

'A kind master! A devoted husband! A devout priest! A doting father too, no doubt!' Elaborate hand gestures accompanied each point. In the crowded kitchen, people had to squeeze away so as not to be poked or slapped, but no one came to interrupt. 'Not unlike my own dear, departed stepfather.' His face slid easily into deep mourning, dark eyes sagging like an ancient hound.

'I believe he is all those things, yes,' said Charlie.

'A doting father ... of a most beautiful daughter.' Jem leaned close again, his tone confidential. At least he had the decency not to go bandying her name about at the top of his voice. 'Tell me,' Jem went on, 'are there plans for her betrothal? For a jewel like that will no doubt marry soon.'

'I don't know of any, sir,' said Charlie, 'and even if I did it would not be my place to speak of them outside the family.'

'Of course not! The loyal servant.' Jem swung round as if he wanted to bring Charlie's loyalty to the attention of the whole room. Charlie ducked, but fortunately Jem was much more interested in Jane Skinner. 'She is – is she not? – everything that is wise, witty and lovely.'

'I am sure she is much valued, sir,' said Charlie.

'She is undoubtedly valued by me.' His arms swooped again, and he stared for a moment at the ceiling, as if seeking further inspiration there. Then he spun back to Charlie. 'Do you think her father would entertain my suit? Do you think there's a chance for me? Tell me truly – what's your name again?'

'Charlie, sir.'

'Tell me truly, Charlie. Would Bishop Skinner consent to his daughter becoming my wife?'

'I don't know, sir. He has not mentioned such a thing.'

'Then perhaps I have a chance!' Jem pressed the back of his hand to his forehead and closed his dark eyes. Then he flung both hands in the air and tossed his head back. 'May the Lord be praised!' he cried, and the kitchen fell silent.

'Jem,' said his uncle, suddenly beside them, 'could you maybe go and see if Longmuir's has any more of that ale? Another barrel should be enough.'

'Of course,' said Jem, from ardent lover to obedient nephew in a moment. 'At once.' He made a bow to Charlie that was more fit for King George, and set off like a hero going in to battle. Stephen Meston puffed out a sigh, and turned to Charlie.

'I'm sorry, Charlie,' he said, valiantly remembering the name. 'I'm afraid he's – um, well, he's young.'

'Aye, sir, it happens to us all,' Charlie agreed mildly, though he thought that having plenty of work to do at that age tended to cure such a disposition quite quickly.

'It's good of you to come and pay your respects,' said Meston. 'Are you here on the Bishop's behalf?'

'No, I'm sure he'll come later,' said Charlie. There was no sense in hiding it from Stephen Meston if his warehouseman already knew. 'My wife is in the same line of business. L. Rob, in Broad Street. I came with her.'

'That's your wife!' Stephen's surprise looked genuine for a moment, then he frowned. 'I had no idea.'

'Why would you, sir? It's a small concern, compared with this,' he gestured towards the warehouse. 'And I doubt we would have met before yesterday. Not to know each other, anyway.' Cuthbert Meston had certainly not been the kind to converse with servants, but Stephen Meston seemed to have a more common touch. And a merchant's attitude towards his customers might sometimes seem like that of a servant towards a master. It was not always clear where one stood, particularly when one's wife was a merchant, too.

'I wonder if my brother knew her, then?'

'I don't think so,' said Charlie, as smoothly as he could manage.

'He would have been happy to help her, you know, provide her with any advice or acquaintance she might have found helpful. It cannot be easy for a woman in the merchant trade. Tell me, is she from a merchant family? Is her father local?'

'No, not really, but yes, he is a merchant,' said Charlie.

'That might explain, then, why the name is unfamiliar. But the offer is there: if she is in need of any assistance. Is it spices and teas, too?'

'Aye, sir, and coffee.' Charlie was watching Stephen. At the word 'coffee', there was – or did he imagine it? – the least twitch around Stephen's left eye.

'And you are in service ...' Stephen may have been trying to change the subject. 'I mentioned, I think, that we have lost our maid. If you happen to know of anyone seeking a position I'd be very grateful if you would mention us. The conditions are good, as you see, and the wages not ungenerous.'

Charlie nodded.

'And could I say, sir, how the last maid lost her place?'

Stephen frowned.

'She fell pregnant, that is how. I think any respectable girl would understand that that is not acceptable behaviour in a good household.'

'Oh, aye, indeed, sir. Any respectable girl would.'

'My brother was annoyed, of course,' Stephen Meston went on. 'It brings down the character of a household, something like that. He was a generous man, as I've said, but you would not expect him to keep a girl on who behaves like that.' He paused, tapping his fingers against the side of his glass, a little flurry of agitation. Charlie stayed quiet. 'My brother had a – a reputation, you know, for ill temper. You may have heard, or perhaps not, if your wife is only a small merchant. Anyway,' he pressed on without waiting for a response, 'it was ill founded, of course. My brother was a man who liked to maintain high standards, in his home and in his business. You know? High standards. And it – it caused him *concern*' – having struggled to find the word he gave it some emphasis – 'to see standards allowed to slip. You understand?'

'Aye, sir, I do.' Well, he understood the words. But Stephen Meston seemed to be trying to tell him something, and he was not at all sure what that was. He had a sudden desire to find Luzie and go home: he was out of his depth here, he knew that.

For all their determination that Cuthbert Meston had been a generous man, a good master, a beloved stepfather, Charlie could not quite believe any of it. Was the household trying to make amends for not having been very fond of Meston before his death, avoiding speaking ill of the dead? Or were they, he wondered, building some kind of united front, a defence against – against what? Accusations of murder?

Charlie was beginning to doubt Bishop Skinner's theory that Samuel Seabury had been the intended victim. It seemed much more likely that someone had killed Cuthbert Meston exactly because he had been Cuthbert Meston – not generous and devoted, but bullying and bad-tempered. And if his brother, his stepson and his warehouseman were so determined not to be accused – so determined, in fact, in the case of Alan the warehouseman, as to try to throw suspicion on Charlie himself, did that mean that the murderer was one of these three men?

Chapter Nineteen

In the end it was Luzie who rescued him. With a sweet and noncommittal smile at Stephen Meston she interrupted their conversation and before Stephen might have asked for an introduction, or Charlie thought of it, she had disengaged him and whisked him off down the stairs and out again into the bright, sharp air of the harbour.

'That's enough business time wasted,' she said briskly, 'and you did not look as if you were enjoying yourself. Thank you for coming with me.'

'I was happy to,' said Charlie, though his thoughts were still back in the house with Stephen Meston and Jem Hosie and Alan Beith.

'It was good to meet those women and talk. But it is never quite easy: they are not comfortable that I have my own business, though some of them are so involved in their husband's affairs that they might as well own the place for themselves.'

'Some women do,' Charlie said.

'But they are milliners and corsetmakers.'

'And lodging house keepers,' Charlie put in. It was an old conversation for them and fitted them well. 'And ale house keepers.'

'Aye, well, I am none of those,' said Luzie, with just a hint of superiority. They grinned at each other.

'No, indeed not!' said Charlie. 'Aye, well, I suppose I'd best get back to my work.'

'Yes, you had!' They had reached Broad Street, and home. Charlie had no need to go in, but slipped after her through the doorway to embrace her. He left for Longacre with a smile on his face, and only as the distance lengthened between him and Luzie did the smile fade and the thoughts of his various conversations down at the harbour start to play through his mind again. Stephen's steadfast defence of his brother, which had not been wholly convincing. Jem's intense interest in Jane Skinner - should he tell the Bishop? And Alan's warnings ... he should probably not mention those to Luzie, not until he had to, anyway. But what about the Bishop's theory? Had Meston been killed for himself or in mistake for Samuel Seabury? Charlie kept coming back to the question of why Cuthbert Meston had been in Longacre, and why anyone else should look for him there. Whereas anyone looking for Dr. Seabury, halfway between the Skinner house and the New Inn, might well look for him in Longacre. And that Mr. Seller, writer of that strange letter, was now in Aberdeen ... Charlie scowled as he reached the Skinners' door. If he were a gambling man, he would not bet on either answer yet.

'They've gone to Mr. Aitken's for dinner!' said Mrs. Skinner as soon as Charlie appeared in the kitchen. 'God forgive me, but it has given me enormous pleasure to say good bye to them for the day. Charlie, could you take a brush to the bookroom floor while you have the chance? I'm sure there's clart all over it.'

Charlie would have liked something more challenging to distract his mind for a while, but he took the usual accoutrements upstairs and began work, carrying on from the bookroom and sweeping the bedrooms and the stairs. Mrs. Skinner was right: the wooden floors had attracted a deal of mud and dirt over the last couple of days, and it was a satisfying job in the end. He was just reaching the foot of the stair when he heard a step behind him. It was Jane Skinner.

'Hello, there, Charlie. That's a fine bucket of muck you've collected!'

'Aye, makes it worthwhile. Miss Jane, can I have a word?' Best, at least, to get this simpler matter sorted out. Forewarned was forearmed.

'What is it, Charlie?'

And he told her what Jeremiah Hosie had said to him earlier, about asking her father for her hand. Jane's eyes widened and she gulped.

'Thank you, Charlie! Goodness - I have to warn Papa. He might just mistake Mr. Hosie for a normal person and say yes. Was he rolling his eyes and waving his hands about?'

'A bittie more than I've seen before, aye,' Charlie agreed. 'But then he had drink taken.'

'He was drunk?'

'Not entirely.'

'Oh! It's quite enough to deal with Mr. Cooper. Is Papa in, do you know?'

'The mistress says the Bishop and Dr. Seabury and Mr. Cooper are all off to Mr. Aitken's at St. John's for dinner.'

'Oh, that's a pity. The sooner I have the chance to tell him, the better ...'

'I'll try and help if I can, miss.'

'Thank you, Charlie. And at least they are all out and away and leaving us in peace for a few hours. Mamma could do with a rest!'

'Aye, miss. I'd say she's enjoying it.'

'Good!'

After dinner, a simple affair with Jane and Margaret and the boys home from school, and Mrs. Skinner being waited on hand and foot by her family, as well as by Jean and Charlie, the house grew wonderfully quiet. The boys had gone back to their dominie, Margaret and Jane were doing their sewing by the parlour window, and Mrs. Skinner lay on the sopha with her feet properly up, sewing to hand. With everything cleared in the kitchen, Jean too settled down to a bit of needlework – her one-hand-and-teeth technique meant she was only trusted with the roughest of mending – and Charlie sat at the kitchen fire, polishing the household's boots. With the door open into the hall, they could hear the great clock tick thoughtfully, the faint sound of occasional words in the parlour, odd steps and voices from the street beyond the front door. Occasionally wheels rolled past, but usually nothing heavier than a handcart: Longacre was not a very busy street. The whole house seemed to take a deep breath, and relax. Charlie did his best not to think about everything that had happened since last Friday, not to worry about Luzie in the shop with only the shop boy to help her, not to find himself listening for the arrival of the magistrates, looking for him. He was still trying this when his attention was caught by something heavier than the average handcart, drawing to a halt just outside the front door.

He was on his feet, exchanging a puzzled frown with Jean, before any other sound came.

'D'you think they've had to hire someone to wheel yon fellow Cooper home?' asked Jean. 'If so, I wish they'd taken him straight to the inn.'

'Maybe there's been an accident,' said Charlie anxiously. He headed for the door before the risp could be rattled, and opened it, holding his breath.

Outside there was indeed a handcart, guided by a youngish lad and containing, in no apparent order of importance, a willow kist, a cheery-looking lap dog, and a small, wizened and equally cheery Bishop. It was not Bishop Skinner.

'Bishop Petrie!' cried Charlie.

'Ah! Charlie!' Bishop Petrie waved a tiny gloved hand, and did his best to pull himself up out of the cart. It seemed, however, that he had been tipped in there in such a way that his legs were higher than the rest of him, and though he waved his feet in the air energetically he could not extract himself. Charlie and the cart boy went to help him, while the lap dog danced in circles around them, offering advice in the form of sharp, high-pitched barks.

It took some time until Bishop Arthur Petrie was upright and on the doorstep, and Charlie took charge of the willow kist. By then Mrs. Skinner, Jane and Margaret were all in the hall, ready to welcome him in.

'Bishop Petrie! Surely you haven't come all the way from Meiklefolla in a handcart!' cried Mrs. Skinner, appalled. Charlie had been told that Meiklefolla, near Fyvie, was about twenty miles north west of Aberdeen. If the little bishop had come all that way in a hand cart it was a wonder he could still stand.

'I couldn't have walked it, Mrs. Skinner!'

'Well, no, but I mean ...'

'I was quite comfortable, and of course Jamie here had to take a rest every now and again so I was able to stretch my legs.' Bishop Petrie beamed, his pink cheeks flushed with the cold and his eyes bright. 'And it is so good to see you all, and looking so well! Is my brother bishop within? Is John Skinner here?'

'He is out, sir! But you must come in straight away and get warmed up! Jane, go and poke the fire. Margaret, tell Jean to bring a toddy, and some cake. Charlie, you know where Bishop Petrie is to sleep, do you not? Make sure Jean airs the bed when she's made the toddy. Oh, goodness, Bishop, you have us all alarmed at such an arrival!'

Mrs. Skinner was polite enough not to point out that Bishop Petrie was also two days early, as everyone sorted themselves out and the little man was hurried out of his coat and upstairs to the warm parlour. The little lap dog (Hepzibah, apparently) hopped on to his knee as soon as he sat down, turned round three times and went instantly to sleep.

'I hope you'll forgive me for arriving early, Mrs. Skinner,' said Petrie, 'but I was quite sure that the journey would exhaust me, and I wanted to be fresh and ready when Dr. Seabury arrives! What excitement!'

'But Dr. Seabury is already arrived,' said Mrs. Skinner. 'He came early, too – he arrived on Friday evening, and came to see my husband on Saturday. With his friend, Mr. Cooper, from Edinburgh.'

'Oh!' Petrie's face fell in dismay. 'Oh, dear – but then, perhaps I should let poor John be with his conversations? Or could I be of assistance, do you think?'

'Dear Bishop Petrie,' said Mrs. Skinner warmly, 'I know very well that my husband values any conversation he has with you, and if you are here to help with Dr. Seabury, he will be delighted. As are we all.'

When Bishop Skinner came back with the others, the party was a very happy one. Petrie and the newcomers were introduced with great cordiality – there could be nothing else with Arthur Petrie – and only Bishop Skinner himself, pleased as he clearly was to see his brother bishop, seemed concerned. He drew Charlie aside on to the landing outside the parlour.

'You have not heard anyone tell Bishop Petrie about the murder, have you?'

'No, sir, I have not. I'm sure Mrs. Skinner would be more careful than that.'

'I'm not so worried that he should hear about the murder itself, only that he should not know, yet, that the magistrate questioned Dr. Seabury.' He sighed, rubbing his high forehead with the tips of his fingers. 'And I'm not sure I want Dr. Seabury to know what you and I discussed yesterday. Have you made any headway there?'

Charlie took a moment to make sure he knew what Bishop Skinner was talking about.

'I spoke to the Peterhead carrier, sir. He knows the gentleman in question, and gave me a description, but says he is from home at present.'

'Oh, well, then –'

'Sir, he is said to be in Aberdeen.'

'Oh! Oh, dear me, that is not good, is it?' He seemed on the point of saying something else, but at that Dr. Seabury, followed as night the day by Mr. Cooper, came out on to the landing, smiling.

'I hope all is well?' asked Dr. Seabury. 'I wondered if there had been any news? You'll forgive my interest, I hope!'

'Of course – very natural in the circumstances,' said Bishop Skinner at once. 'I was just asking Charlie the same question. Charlie, have you been back to the Meston household today?'

'Aye, sir. I went there with my wife to pay our respects.'

'Your wife the merchant, eh?' Mr. Cooper put in, looking pleased with himself, and Charlie wondered how many wives the man thought he had.

'Of course,' said Bishop Skinner. 'Did you learn anything new, at all?'

'Well, sir,' Charlie took a deep breath. 'It seems they're quite sure now – because of a bruise on the back of Cuthbert Meston's neck – that he was definitely murdered.'

There was a little gasp from Myles Cooper, of course. Bishop Skinner nodded, quite prepared for the news.

'And did they know if the magistrates had anyone in mind? Aside from their interview with our friends here.' He smiled, making it something like a joke, but Myles was already flapping his hands.

'Such a horrid man. Such a horrid, horrid man!'

'Myles, you can hardly say that, just because he shouted at us on the boat!' Seabury objected. 'You must have seen how unhappy he was. We were simply the nearest people to take the brunt.'

'No, no, there's more than that. Surely you remember, Samuel?' Myles' hands drew apart then snapped together again, irresistibly. 'Don't you remember the girl?'

'Oh!' Samuel Seabury's eyes widened, and self-reproach flooded his face. 'Oh, my goodness, the girl! I had entirely forgotten.'

Chapter Twenty

'What girl?' asked Bishop Skinner.

'As we were passing Mr. Meston's warehouse, I suppose it was, down by the harbour, the night we arrived,' said Myles Cooper in some excitement, 'we saw him throw a girl out into the street!'

Bishop Skinner looked as if he would have liked to rub his forehead again.

'I'm sorry, I don't understand, Mr. Cooper. What girl?'

'A very small, young girl,' said Dr. Seabury. 'I went to see if she was all right, but she sprang up and ran off.'

'Straight up an alley!' agreed Myles Cooper. His cheeks were glowing with excitement at the story – or it could have been that Mr. Aitken of St. John's also needed to replenish his wine cellar after Myles Cooper's visit.

'And the door was slammed shut. It was such a cold night, and the poor little thing – her clothes, what one could see, seemed very thin. But she was away before we could help her.'

'So what was she? Who was she? Do you know?'

'Excuse me, sirs,' said Charlie, 'but Mr. Stephen Meston mentioned to me today that Mr. Meston had thrown out their maid recently. Could this be the same girl?'

'It seems more than likely,' said Cooper at once. 'What other girls would they have about the place?'

There was a pause while they all failed to say what they were thinking.

'Did Mr. Stephen Meston say why the maid had been thrown out?' Bishop Skinner asked at last.

'He said she had fallen pregnant, and that his brother had had every right, keeping the household to a high standard, to throw her out.'

'I suppose he had,' said the Bishop. 'Whether or not he should is another matter. I wonder where the poor girl went?'

'This girl was tiny,' said Myles. 'Surely not old enough to be pregnant.'

'I'm not so sure,' said Dr. Seabury. 'She might have been small for her age. I wonder where she went, in the cold? I'm ashamed to say that with everything that has happened I had not thought about her since that night.'

'I wonder who the father is?' asked the Bishop, his tone even more sombre. 'Who lives in the house, Charlie?'

'I don't believe there are any women, sir, not now. Mrs. Meston has been dead for years, and there are only the two brothers, and Cuthbert Meston's stepson, Jeremiah Hosie.' He would say nothing about Jem in front of Dr. Seabury and Mr. Cooper unless he had to. That was Jane's business.

'Hm,' said Bishop Skinner. 'What if the child's father, hearing of what had happened, followed Cuthbert Meston and took his revenge?'

'Or a member of the maid's family?' Dr. Seabury nodded sadly. 'Yes, that is possible. Perhaps they only meant to hold his head in the trough to punish him, but the cold killed him, or they held him down longer than they had intended?'

'Perhaps ... we may never know. But it is a line of enquiry that the magistrates might find it useful to follow, do you not think? Charlie, do you think you could go down to the Mestons' warehouse again, and see if you can find out more about this girl?'

Charlie's heart sank. Again?

But even if Bishop Skinner did go down to pay his respects to a man who had lain dead in his chapel, it would be much harder for him to ask questions about a missing servant than it would for Charlie.

He nodded.

'Aye, sir, I'll do my best.'

In fact Charlie went and sat in the kitchen again, just for a little, before he felt equal to venturing out. Yes, he was reluctant to go, but he also wanted to sort some things out in his head, before he had a conversation with anyone else. Jean in the kitchen was not a chatty woman, and was happy enough to let him sit there and ponder in peace.

Right, he thought, he was not to mention anything about Cuthbert Meston, or his death, to Bishop Petrie. That could be difficult because Bishop Petrie was always enquiring after people, and knew all kinds of folks that Charlie would assume he had never heard of, so he had to keep on his toes there. He wondered if Bishop Skinner was right not to tell Bishop Petrie: it was true that Arthur Petrie was physically frail, but Charlie always thought he was a wise man, and perhaps Bishop Skinner was taking too much on himself in order to protect Bishop Petrie when he did not need protecting. Bishop Petrie must have helped to interview prospective bishops before, and would probably know what he was doing. Well, that was for Bishop Skinner to decide – what did Charlie really know of such things?

Then, he thought, he was not to mention to Dr. Seabury or Mr. Cooper – particularly not Mr. Cooper, who would probably have a fit – Bishop Skinner's theory that Dr. Seabury had been the intended victim, and not Mr. Meston at all. As far as Charlie was concerned, the theory had yet to be proved, but it was not to be mentioned, nevertheless.

Then he was not to mention Jeremiah Hosie to Bishop Skinner, whatever his own misgivings about the man, until Jane herself had had the chance to talk to her father about him. What good that would do he was not sure, but if Jane needed his help in any way he would give it, and if that included not mentioning Jeremiah Hosie – or not with regard to Jane, anyway – then that was what he would do.

And then lastly, he thought about his conversation with Alan, the Mestons' warehouseman. Were the magistrates going to come for him? Charlie had been down at the Mestons' warehouse, and could be thought to have been looking for Cuthbert Meston; he had had the opportunity to kill him, right outside where Charlie worked – it struck him that a sensible man, planning to kill another man, would not do it on his own doorstep, but perhaps that was not the way that the magistrates thought – and he had some reason to kill him, perhaps, if they took into account what Meston had said to Luzie, and what Alan had hinted that he knew about that. But would Alan tell the magistrate about Luzie? Alan seemed a pleasant man, if a little quiet. But if he thought, too, that Charlie had done it – but then would he warn him off? Charlie sighed. In any case, he did not want to mention any of that to Luzie. She would feel guilty, and worry, and there was, at least for now, no need.

So armed with a clearer idea in his head of the people to whom he was not to say things, if not necessarily with a reason why, he stood and pulled on his coat and muffler, and began his reluctant trudge back towards Marischal Street.

The day was still fine, though the sun, never very high anyway at this time of year, was already skimming down towards the horizon behind the town. Its warmth, such as it was, had melted the top layer of slushy snow which was now starting to freeze again, and folk were slithering and sliding in the streets where the sun's rays no longer reached. Towards the harbour the traffic had worn much of the melted snow away in the course of the day, and it was easier walking, even down the hill – the salty air, too, seemed to limit the same build-up of snow here as there was elsewhere in the town.

Charlie stopped for a moment at the foot of the hill to look about the harbour, telling himself he might see something relevant to the Mestons, but really trying to postpone as long as possible his latest visit to their house. What on earth was he going to say? How could he justify his interest in a missing maid, whose name he did not even know? He meandered to his right, away from the Meston warehouse, and eyed the ships in the harbour with his usual distrust.

Against his wishes, and completely to his surprise, Charlie had ended up on a ship twenty years ago from Leith to Amsterdam. Of course he had had to return to Scotland after that, but had sworn that he would never go near the sea again, for to chance one's luck on it twice might have been necessary, but to try it again and again was just foolish.

Yet friendship, and later love, had drawn him back to Amsterdam several more times over the years, until he brought Luzie home with him. Now she was the one who concerned herself with boats and ships and cargoes, sailings and arrivals, and he for the most part was able to ignore the sea, except when she was able to draw him again to go and visit her father and sister. He knew where the Dutchmen tended to dock, even knew the names of some of the ships and their masters, and occasionally had to come down here and supervise an unloading on Luzie's behalf, though he did his best not to go on board anything that lay on the water. He supposed that this was also the part of the quay that Cuthbert Meston and his associates would frequent. Would Luzie's cargoes be vulnerable, if, say, Stephen Meston could get to them before Luzie did? Charlie was still not sure how he felt about Stephen Meston. He had done his best – as had Alan and Jeremiah Hosie – to give out that they all missed Cuthbert Meston, that he was a good man and a decent employer. But that was not what gossip said, and in this case Charlie was inclined to believe gossip. And if Stephen Meston was prepared to lie to defend his brother, was he trustworthy in other respects? Would he, now, threaten Luzie's business?

He was staring at one particular Dutchman, his eyes trying to sort out what always looked to him like a complete guddle of ropes and spars and sheets of canvas, while his mind tried to sort out everything else, when a familiar figure swaggered past, trailing one hand on the top of a black cane and tossing back a headful of red-brown hair. It was Jeremiah Hosie.

Before Charlie could decide if tackling him on his own might be easier than facing the whole household, Jeremiah turned with a swoop of his shoulders and saw him. At once he headed for Charlie, who, though he found the man alarming, stood his ground.

'You there! It's ...' He flung out a hand – gloved today in deepest black, Charlie noted – and pressed one finger against his temple, screwing his eyes closed, the model of intense concentration. 'Charlie!'

'Aye, sir.'

'We must talk, you and I, Charlie,' said Jem, seizing Charlie's arm and linking his own hand into it.

'Must we, sir?'

'Indeed we must, Charlie! For you, and you alone – for the moment, anyway – you are the all too human bridge that forms the link between me and Paradise.'

Charlie said nothing.

'You, and you alone, until of course I obtain her revered – and reverend – father's consent, are my point of contact with that angel bending low from Heaven, bestowing her grace on an unworthy world, and descending, on the breath of clouds, to set foot in Aberdeen.' He stopped, clearly dissatisfied with how his poetry had concluded, and released Charlie from his grasp. 'But stay, worthy serf – are you perchance here at the harbour to bear a message from her? Could she be so merciful? Could you sustain so joyous a burden?'

'I'm sure I could, sir, if asked, but I don't. I mean, I'm not – I have no such message.'

'Alas!' Jeremiah smote his forehead, then had to straighten his hat. 'Then what are you here for?'

'I'm here,' said Charlie, stumbling over words he had not quite prepared, 'to ask about the maid you had.'

'The maid?'

'Aye, the one who left.'

'What, Minnie?' Jem stopped, and for once offered no dramatic gesture.

'Was that her name, sir?'

'Minnie.' Jem nodded, and finding himself beside a stone bollard, he sank on to it. 'Aye, Minnie. That was bad.'

Chapter Twenty-One

'So what happened, sir?' Charlie asked after a moment.

'It was last Friday. My stepfather had just returned from a visit to Edinburgh – he had been away for two or three weeks.'

Charlie noted that – no one had thought to ask before, but it might be a useful piece of information.

'What was he away doing?' He thought he might as well ask. Jem cast a displeased look at him and for a moment he thought he had gone too far.

'Who knows?' said Jem. 'My stepfather did not often tell us what he was doing. I suppose it was trade. It almost always is. What else is there?'

'So what happened with Minnie, then, sir?'

'Oh, she must have decided to wait and tell my stepfather when he came home, for she was in the middle of making the supper, ready for when he appeared – you have no idea how much he insisted on that, and how is a servant supposed to know if a packet is delayed or a horse casts a shoe?'

Charlie nodded. His masters had always been a little more reasonable, but he knew there were some who thought their servants could work miracles.

'She told him, very respectfully – as she always was – that she was expecting a child.'

'Did she say whose the child was?'

Jem looked at him quickly, and away. Did he think Charlie might be asking because it was his child? Charlie felt himself blush at the thought.

'She had no chance. No sooner were the words out of her mouth than he had her by the back of her neck, marched her down the stairs and threw her out of the door.'

'Where did he think she would go?'

'Go?' Jem pondered, as if the question had not struck him before. 'I don't know that he thought about it at all. He simply got rid of the problem.'

'Do you know where she might have gone, then?' Charlie wondered how much more he could press on here before Jem came to the realisation that he was telling a strange servant quite a bit about his household.

'I don't know. I don't think she had any family in the town. She was from somewhere in the country ... where, now? Newmachar? Newburgh? I always muddle them. Is Miss Skinner concerned? I daresay with her father a clergyman she knows places that maybe take in girls like – like Minnie.'

'She probably does, sir.' Charlie had no idea. 'If only we could track her down for Miss Skinner to make sure she's all right.' It felt a bit wrong, using Jane like that, but he told himself that she would not mind, really. If it helped her father, and perhaps even helped the girl to a better life, then no doubt Jane would be well pleased. But he was still uncomfortable.

'Come, then,' said Jem, rising to his feet. 'Let us go and see if my uncle knows more about little Minnie than I do. We were very fond of her, you know, as a servant. She was one of the family.'

So much so that you cannot remember where she came from, or tell me the name of any of her friends, or guess where she might be now. Or tell me the father of her bairn. Well, it was not unusual, Charlie thought. He had been lucky, but many were not.

But as he followed Jem across the quay, it occurred to him that Stephen Meston might not be very sympathetic to any enquiries about Minnie. He had asked Charlie to help him look out for a new maid. How would he feel to find out that Charlie had told the Skinners about the old one, to the extent that they wanted to go looking for her to see she was all right? He began to drag his feet, trying to think of some way of working it out, but as they arrived, far too soon, at the Meston warehouse, he was saved. Mourners who had not managed to visit earlier in the day were now around the doorway and in the hall, and Jem, suddenly reluctant to be seen, ducked straight in through the warehouse door, dragging Charlie behind him.

'Uncle Stephen only sent me out to fetch something,' he explained. 'I cannot bear being cooped up in there with all those gossiping ull-fashent folks, coming to see who's what and hear the latest claik about what is supposed to have happened. I'm not going back in until they've all gone away,' he finished petulantly. He looked around 'Oh, Alan! What are you doing in here? I thought my uncle said the warehouse was to be closed for the days until the burial.'

'Aye, that was before an order came in for a grocer in Inverurie,' Alan said bleakly. 'He dithered a bit, then said he didna think his brother could rest easy knowing business was being allowed to suffer, and so here I am.' He gestured to the table in front of him, where he was making up parcels of tea with brown paper, string and sealing wax. Then he frowned at Charlie. 'What are you doing back?'

'Charlie's here to find out what happened to Minnie. I don't suppose you know, do you? You barely knew her, did you? Nothing much between the warehouse and the flat.'

'That's right,' Alan agreed, though for a moment his fingers fumbled the string, making a knot that was unlikely to hold. He pulled it out and started again. 'What for are you looking her?' he asked. 'She's no like to be ready to work for a whilie.'

'Miss Skinner is concerned for her welfare,' said Jem, luxuriating in the name. 'Miss Skinner wants to know how to find her, to look after her. Miss Skinner is an angel.'

Charlie tried not to meet Alan's pale eyes, but he was sure he saw them roll.

'I see,' he said. 'Well, if I should happen to hear a'thing from her - not that it's likely, mind - I'll be sure to pass it on.'

'Well, then,' said Jem. 'That's the best we can do. Now, I'm off before Uncle Stephen finds me and pins my wings upstairs again. Charlie, remember that you're my bridge! I depend upon you! Alan, adieu.'

He swept from the warehouse, pausing at the door to check that his way was safe, and vanished. Charlie raised his eyebrows at Alan.

'Want a hand? I've done a few of those packets myself in the past.'

'Aye, I suppose. The sooner I get it done ...'

Charlie took up string and paper, and began to form neat parcels for Alan to seal.

'How well did you know Minnie?' he asked after a while.

'When you work in a place ...' said Alan, but did not expand. Charlie nodded.

'Did she mention family? Friends? Somewhere she might have gone?'

Alan dropped the parcel he was sealing, and the wax smeared. He swore.

'Are you sure you're trying to help her? Not try to fine her for fornication, or the like?'

'I don't suppose Miss Skinner has even thought of it,' said Charlie, which was true, as far as it went.

Alan looked down at the wax, and picked at the hardening edges with a fingernail.

'She's in the hospital in Lodge Walk, by Queen Street. I went to see her but they wouldna let me in.'

Charlie remembered now seeing Alan up on Broad Street yesterday morning, and how the small man had trotted off down Lodge Walk, by the Tolbooth.

'Then you were friendly?'

'Friendly enough that I was happy to try to take her her things. I've gathered them up for her. She didna have much, but Cuthbert Meston threw her out without anything but her shawl and the clothes she was standing in.'

'You said this morning he was a good master.'

'To me, aye. To her, no. He didna even ask - find out what the story was - let her explain - a'thing at all.'

'What was the story?'

Alan turned away.

'What way should I know? They wouldna let me see her.'

It was dark by the time Charlie left the Meston warehouse, and he hurried back up the hill to the town, anxious in case he was late to help with supper. He was sure that the whole errand had taken much longer than Bishop Skinner had expected, but when he arrived back at Longacre the family and their guests were still arranged about bookroom and parlour, and Jean was concocting soup in the kitchen. The Bishop must have been looking out for him, though, for Charlie had not done more than lift out a stack of clean plates to be heated when Skinner appeared in the kitchen doorway, eager for news.

'Her name is Minnie, sir, and I'm told she's in the hospital along the way – the one at the corner of Lodge Walk and Queen Street .'

'So near us?' The Bishop thrummed his fingers on the doorpost. 'Could that be the reason that Cuthbert Meston was in this area? Could he have had second thoughts, and be making arrangements to take her back into his household?'

'The warehouseman, Alan, he says he tried to get to see her, for he had gathered up her stuff to take her, but they wouldna let him in.'

'No, I think they're quite strict there. In fact, I'm a wee bit surprised they let her in at all. I thought that women in her condition – sorry, Jean – were not allowed.'

Jean jerked her shoulder, acknowledging the apology.

'I heard the new superintendent there's a gey soft-hearted quine,' she said in return. 'If there's someone on her doorstep in dire need, she canna turn them away. Aye,' she said, returning to her soup, 'she'll no keep her job long, doing that like of a thing.'

'Sadly, you could be right. Anything else, Charlie? Any word on who the father might be?'

'It could be this warehouseman,' Charlie admitted, 'for he was more friendly with her than the family seemed to know. But then there would be no reason for them not to marry, for I dinna think Alan's got a wife. It could be the stepson, Jem, for he seemed upset right enough at the way she had been treated.'

'Or it could be someone from outside the household altogether,' said the Bishop. 'The harbour is not a safe place for a woman on her own, and I daresay she had errands to do without anyone escorting her.' He sighed. 'The poor child - she might not even bear any blame in this situation, and yet she is the one to suffer.'

Something that sounded like a snort from Jean made the Bishop pause.

'Will you step into the dining room, Charlie? I don't want to distract Jean when she's busy.'

Charlie followed him into the dining room and saw that Jean had the table ready for supper, all on her own, which was probably why she was cross. He would have to be particularly helpful for the rest of the evening.

'What do you think, Charlie? You've been involved in something like this before. I know I took you by surprise with my idea that it might be Dr. Seabury they intended to kill, but now you've had time to think about it, what's your mind?'

'My mind, sir?' Charlie did not like questions like that. He had to have thoughts for a while, be familiar with them, turn them over and look at them from many different angles, before he was happy letting them out to meet other people. 'Well ... I can see what you mean, I suppose. And Mr. Seller is supposed to be in Aberdeen. But if he is, then where is he? I havena seen a'body hanging around here to keep an eye out for Dr. Seabury.' Except Jem Hosie, he reminded himself, but his motives were entirely different. 'Or maybe it's someone else wanting to stop Dr. Seabury being a bishop, but I canna see a'thing to tell me who, or where they are, or why. Sorry, sir. But I can see all kinds of people who didna like Mr. Meston at all.'

'And I should be reassured by that, Charlie, I really should, for I respect your opinion.' That was another sentence that Charlie did not like. It seemed to place an awful lot of responsibility on him. 'Nevertheless, there is something about what happened the other night, and something about that letter, that I do not like at all. I hope you are right, Charlie, but I'm terribly afraid you are not.'

Chapter Twenty-Two

'Sir,' said Charlie, whose mind had been dotting around all they had just been saying, 'what about the girl? I mean, she had a good reason to hate Mr. Meston, did she no?'

'We did wonder about an angry father, or brother, didn't we? But if she's gone to the hospital, it seems she has nowhere else to go. She may have no family to take that kind of revenge. Not that it should be condoned,' the Bishop added hurriedly, 'but it's at least understandable.'

'But if not family, what about the girl herself?' asked Charlie again.

Bishop Skinner frowned.

'He was a big man,' he objected. 'Could she actually have done it?'

'If maybe she had taken him by surprise,' said Charlie. 'And we know she was nearby, if she's in the hospital. She could maybe have seen him going by, and gone out after him.'

'It was dark ... But he'd have had a lantern, of course. Maybe she could.'

'The lantern's missing, if he had one,' said Charlie suddenly, remembering again. 'I dinna think there was one near him when I found him.'

'That's odd. A man like that, respectable, going about without a lantern? Most decent men going about at that time of night would at least have a servant with them, wouldn't they? That had not occurred to me.'

'Whoever killed him might have taken the lantern, sir,' Charlie put in. 'As to the servant ... I think Mr. Meston liked to go off and do things on his own, with no one else knowing. He certainly seemed to on Friday and Saturday last, and his family don't even seem very clear what he was doing down in Edinburgh. A servant might have got in his way, sir.'

Bishop Skinner smiled.

'You're growing awful cynical, Charlie. What do you think he was up to?'

'Me?' Charlie winced. How could he tell the Bishop what Meston had said to Luzie? He thought as fast as he could. 'I doubt he had some business dealings he wanted kept quiet, that's all. What else could draw him out when he was tired after his journey, on a Friday night?'

'Business certainly seems to have been the centre of his life,' the Bishop sighed. 'Poor fellow. He'll know better now.'

He had been leaning against the dining table, arms folded, trying not to disarrange any of Jean's work with the cutlery and plates. Now he pushed himself upright.

'Would you go and see if you can visit the girl at the hospital, Charlie? Even if she does not confess all to you, perhaps she knows something that will help us. For I cannot see Bishop Kilgour and Bishop Petrie wanting this hanging over them when Bishop Kilgour comes on Friday, and if it's not cleared up by then I shall have to tell them.'

'Why not tell them now, sir? Bishop Petrie, anyway. He's bound to be able to help somehow.'

Skinner's long face turned even more anxious.

'I should, Charlie, yes. I probably should. But – and I know it's my pride – I'm not that long a bishop myself, and I want them to think I can cope. I really do. But if I can't sort it out soon I'll have to tell them, I know. A candidate for consecration being questioned by the magistrate for murder? Aye, I'll have to tell them.'

Charlie did not want Bishop Skinner to have to wait any longer than necessary for answers to his questions, so after supper, when the two bishops had settled down in the parlour with Dr. Seabury, and Mr. Cooper dozed comfortably in an easy chair, Charlie asked Mrs. Skinner if he could go on an errand, to be back before the visitors needed to be escorted to their inn.

'Of course, Charlie, as long as you are not too long. For myself, I am making my excuses and retiring for the night. If they require my opinion on Dr. Seabury's suitability for consecration, they will have to wait until tomorrow at least.' They exchanged a grin. It might have sounded daft, a woman helping to choose a bishop, but Charlie knew that Bishop Skinner was a great respecter of his wife's opinions. He bowed goodnight to her, fetched his muffler, and took a lantern - like a respectable person - before heading out into the darkened Longacre. He had helped Jean clear up enough to placate her, but his fingers were damp from the dishes and now chilled fast in the cold air.

For once he headed down Longacre, passing the neighbours' houses rather than going under the tenement to Broad Street. A few late or desperate women on the same side as the Skinners' house were taking in their frozen washing - the houses on that side ran back against the college wall and there were no back greens for drying in private. Some thought Longacre a rough place, but in that house was Bodsy Bowers, a handsome Master of Arts from the college who taught small boys and girls the rudiments of their letters, and down there was William Smith, an architect, with his family. He often worked with Mennie, the builder who had lent his ladder to carry Cuthbert Meston into the chapel. Houstoun's, the small grocer near the end of the street, was decent enough and more than respectable, even if he and Luzie were mutually reluctant to do business. Aye, there were rougher places by far in Aberdeen. At the foot of Longacre Charlie turned right into broad North Street, where the scents of the mealmarket made the air feel warmer, briefly. Then he turned right again and into the wide entrance of Queen Street, less savoury with the slaughterhouse halfway along it. Beyond that, at the turning into Lodge Walk, was the hospital, a grand name for a small enough building.

It was a two-storey house, really, a little wider than those on either side but lower, too. A token slice of land at the front had been given over to something like a garden, but if it was intended as a place for recuperating women to sit out and watch the world go by, they might have had to take their turns. Charlie had probably passed the building a hundred times before without paying it much attention, and it was hard to scrutinise it now in the dark. But the lantern light reflected a well-polished front door and its bright handle and risp, and clean windows shuttered on the inside, and the path had been swept clear of snow. A light shone in the hall, evidently, for the transom over the front door glowed faintly golden. The matrons and old maids who lived out their days here would be used to a certain quality of existence. How had Minnie felt, turning up here? Had she expected to be taken in, or only hoped? Jean was quite right: women expecting children outside wedlock would not normally be welcomed here, or in many other places, either. The better class of woman might be hidden and protected by their families, husbands found for them, marriages arranged, whether wanted or not. But a maid thrown out by her employer, one without a family of her own nearby, she had little resource to depend on. Would that drive her to rage enough to take her revenge on her old master? Was she that kind of girl?

If Alan had not been allowed in to see the girl – Minnie – then Charlie wondered if he would be, either. He would have to call on some of the dignity of working for Bishop Skinner to try to carry him over the threshold. He paused at the end of the path to rearrange his muffler, brush down his coat and kick the snow off his boots, then straightened his shoulders, lifted his lantern to light his own face for whoever opened the door, and strode forward confidently to rattle the risp.

In only a moment a maid, in her middle years and nearly as broad as she was tall, opened the door with a snap, scowling. Charlie was half-backed down the path but as soon as she saw him clearly, the scowl faded, to be replaced by a suspicious look.

'Aye, what's your will?'

'I'm here on Bishop Skinner's orders,' said Charlie, making sure he was standing straight again. 'He's enquiring for the welfare of a girl named Minnie, who came here, he believes, on Friday night or not much after.'

'Bishop Skinner? Is he the young fellow?'

'Well ...' said Charlie, 'I suppose so. For a bishop, onywye.' Bishops Kilgour and Petrie were both a fair bit older.

The maid gave him an up and down look that took in, Charlie was sure, what he had had for breakfast and who had made his boots.

'Aye, well,' she said, 'you'd better come in, then.'

One step further than Alan, Charlie thought, edging past the maid to gain the narrow hallway.

'You can wait in there,' said the maid, an elbow pointing into a parlour. 'Wipe your boots afore you do.'

Charlie did his best to wipe them again, and went to stand in the parlour. There were three chairs inside, and a long bench. All were occupied.

'Is it supper time?' demanded the woman on the nearest end of the bench.

'It's a stranger,' said one in a chair, in a prime position near the small fire. 'He'll no ken.'

'He might be new,' said the bench woman. Her clothes spoke of a decayed finery, her face a cobweb of wrinkles.

'He's no old, that's for sure,' said the chair woman, with a sharp look at Charlie. He glanced at the others around the room. None was young enough to be Minnie, anyway: they all seemed ancient. 'I dinna ken fit he's after.'

'After?' echoed bench woman in mild alarm. 'Fit is he after? It had better no be me!'

'Hush, now, Ellie, I doubt he's after any of us.'

'I'm looking for a girl called Minnie,' said Charlie, brave enough to interrupt at last.

There was silence.

'Minnie?' asked bench woman, at last. 'She's no here.'

'Aye, I can see that,' said Charlie, intending to sound encouraging. 'But I'm here in the hope of seeing her.'

'Aye, well,' said chair woman. 'Hope maketh not ashamed.'

Wise nods accompanied this remark, and the room fell silent. But in a moment there were footsteps in the hall outside, and another woman entered, this time a clever, kindly-looking individual around the age of forty. She wore a spotless apron over a dark, practical dress, and greeted Charlie in a friendly fashion.

'Would you come through to my private parlour, please? I'm Mrs. Gray. I gather you're enquiring about one of our inmates.' She turned briskly and Charlie had to trot to keep up. 'So much to do,' she said, 'and then this on top of everything!'

'I'm very sorry,' said Charlie. 'I don't want to take up too much of your time, but the Bishop ...'

'Yes, I've heard he's a very good man,' she said. She ushered Charlie into a room that was scarcely more than a large press, containing a small table serving as a desk and two upright chairs. She gestured to him to take one, and she sat carefully on the other, as if her back were paining her. 'What is his interest in this girl Minnie?'

'He's concerned for her welfare, that's all,' said Charlie. 'He's never met her, to the best of my knowledge. He heard that she had been thrown out of her place because – '

'Because she was expecting a child out of wedlock, yes.' The woman frowned, and rubbed her forehead. 'It's against the regulations. I should never have taken her in.'

'Then why did you, mistress? Did you know her?'

'No, I ... I found her on the doorstep, on Friday night. Whether it was chance, or whether she had some hopes of gaining admittance here, I don't know – I never asked her. I was returning from supper at a friend's house, well fed, warm, escorted by a reliable manservant - and there she was, so thin and pale I thought she was already dead. When she moved I thought I should faint.' She did not look the fainting kind. 'I brought her in, and found her somewhere to sleep. When the managers found out on Saturday, they were not at all pleased.'

'Did they send her away?' he asked, suddenly anxious.

'No, they did not, to my surprise. But they told me she would have to be gone soon. I told them she was not well.' She gave a little shudder, and he wondered what it had taken to convince the managers.

'Then may I see her? So that I can reassure the Bishop.'

'No, I'm afraid you can't.' She brought herself back from whatever memory she had of the trustees. 'Not now.'

'Then when?'

'No, you misunderstand,' she said. 'You can't see her because she's gone.'

'But ...'

'She disappeared. On Saturday night.'

Chapter Twenty-Three

'On Saturday night?' Charlie repeated stupidly. 'What time on Saturday night?'

The superintendent shrugged.

'I don't really know. She was sleeping in a wee box room up at the top of the house. I saw her heading up the stair maybe eight o'clock? There was not much entertainment for a wee thing like that here, and she was that weak I could not have asked her to work for her keep, not yet, anyway.' She made a face. 'My fear is that she heard my debate with the trustees, and felt she was not welcome.'

'Did anybody see her after that?'

'No, no one that's said anything to me.'

Charlie thought hard. Cuthbert Meston was presumably still alive at eight o'clock, or at least, he was not yet lying with his head in the horse trough.

'Do you know if anybody came to see her at all? All the time she was here?'

The superintendent frowned.

'A very angry young man came on Sunday morning. Not the kind we want round here. I made sure he was not let in.'

'Did you see what he looked like?'

'Small, sandy haired, blotchy red complexion. Looked like a man who works in a shop.' She flashed an apologetic look at Charlie. 'Not that I disapprove of men who work in shops, but it was the fact he was so angry made me bar him.'

'Angry with you? Angry with Minnie?'

'Not Minnie, I'm sure. Probably not with us when he arrived, but certainly with us by the time he left. I did not take to him.'

Alan, trying to deliver Minnie's belongings.

'Did Minnie know he had been here?'

'I don't believe so. She had gone by then, of course.'

Charlie had no idea whether Minnie would have wanted to see Alan or not. Maybe she would not want to see Alan when he was angry, anyway.

'Did anybody else call to see her? Or enquire after her? Or did anyone call in for anything, and she might have seen them?'

The superintendent frowned again, just touching on annoyance.

'Why on earth would you want to know that? Or why would your Bishop?'

'Just, from what you say, mistress, I wondered why Minnie would have left when she was comfortable here and weak for moving on. And that made me wonder if someone had taken her away, or if she had run away?'

'If someone took her away why not tell me?' The superintendent was huffy now. 'I was going to have to find her somewhere else anyway.'

'But you said she didn't know that. And I suppose it's just possible that someone took her away against her will, is it?'

'I suppose ...' She looked dubious.

'Or someone frightened her, causing her to run away?'

'Well ... I don't know what kind of establishment you think I run here. We're not used to people disappearing, never mind being taken away or running away.' Mrs. Gray sat back in her chair. 'Most of the inmates would be hard put to run anywhere, and the reason they're in here is that their families have put them here. No one's going to take anyone away. No one ... Well, not until now, anyway.'

'Would it be possible?' Charlie asked. 'I mean, could someone do it without being seen?'

She considered.

'As to that, well, it would be difficult. How would they know where she was? Or how to get there? There's a back stair and a front stair, but you've seen the front: it's in full view of the hall. The back goes up from the kitchen – that's the one she would use – and there's usually somebody in the kitchen or nearby.' She drummed her fingers on the table, staring past him for a moment, picturing the possibilities.

'Did she take her things?'

'She had only what she stood up in. No, I'd say she left of her own accord, even if she was somehow frightened into it.'

'Thank you, mistress. My master will be concerned – if you do happen to hear from Minnie, could you maybe send him a note?'

'I will. Yes, I will.'

Charlie rose to his feet, feeling he'd found out all he was going to for now. And it was growing late, if he was to report back to Bishop Skinner and get home in any good time.

'Who knew she was there?' the Bishop asked. He looked weary, and was snatching a moment while Dr. Seabury and Mr. Cooper were saying goodnight to Bishop Petrie.

'Alan the warehouseman. That's all I know, but there could have been others. The trustees of the place knew enough to tell the superintendent to get rid of her.'

The Bishop's mouth twisted in disgust.

'If they knew her circumstances, they could have told Meston. He's well enough known.'

'Or she could just have seen him out the window and been frightened, without him even knowing she was there,' Charlie suggested. 'We know he was in the area, even if we don't know why.'

'Perhaps tracking her down.'

'But what way would he do that, sir? He threw her out – I doubt he wanted her back.'

'Could she have taken something with her?'

'Not according to Alan, sir. He says Mr. Meston threw her straight out with nothing.'

Bishop Skinner tutted, half in disapproval, half in frustration.

'I don't know if this even helps us, Charlie.' He yawned. 'It's late: go you and take Dr. Seabury back to the inn and go home, and let's review the matter tomorrow. Monday ... four more days till Bishop Kilgour is due to arrive. Four more days to get this sorted out.'

Four more days, Charlie thought in the morning. Or three, and whatever bit of Friday we have before Bishop Kilgour gets here. If he doesn't do what Bishop Petrie and Dr. Seabury have done, and arrive early.

'Are you all right?' he asked Luzie in the kitchen. 'Not worried that someone else is going to – to do whatever Cuthbert Meston was going to do?'

'No!' said Luzie brightly. 'No, I'm not worried! It's an ordinary, busy day. And Cuthbert Meston's funeral is tomorrow, so I doubt any of the household will be out at all.'

'Aye, you're right. They'll be minding the body and receiving the mourners. I wonder if the Bishop will go?'

The Bishop had other things on his mind, however, when Charlie reached the Longacre house.

'Right, I'm awake this morning, Charlie. And we don't have long before Dr. Seabury arrives – if it stays fine I'll take him for another walk, I think. Take them both to see the qualified chapel.'

Charlie blinked at the Bishop, but Skinner shrugged.

'We all have to get on, Charlie, and it's a qualified chapel that Mr. Cooper ministers to in Edinburgh. One day the penal laws will be repealed, and there will be no need for these divisions and pretences. Now, where are we with Cuthbert Meston?'

'I don't know, sir. If Minnie – that's the missing girl – has anything to do with this, then I can't see how Dr. Seabury could have been the intended victim. The superintendent doesn't think that Minnie could have left unless of her own accord, but I wondered if she could have been frightened into going? Did she see Mr. Meston and think he was coming to see her? Or Alan Beith – was Sunday morning not the first time he had turned up? Had he frightened her with his anger? We just don't know, sir, and I canna see how we'll ever find out unless we find Minnie.'

Bishop Skinner sighed, and leaned back against his desk, arms folded. He stared at the floor.

'Maybe this is nothing at all to do with us. Maybe the closest we come to involvement in this was you finding the body outside this house.'

'Sorry, sir.'

The Bishop grinned.

'I don't suppose you set out to do it! But our contact with the brother, our concern about Minnie – those come from meeting the household because the body was here. Can it be that simple? Have I over-elaborated?'

Charlie shook his head.

'No, sir, for you've left out that Dr. Seabury met Mr. Meston on the boat, that someone told the magistrate about it, and that the magistrate then came here to see Dr. Seabury and Mr. Cooper. That's another connexion.'

'True ... And Minnie, quite separately – as far as we know – took refuge in a hospital just across the way. And then – here I go, complicating things again – then as far as we know the writer of that rather alarming letter about Dr. Seabury has come to Aberdeen – as has Bishop Petrie, of course, and as will Bishop Kilgour. Do you have the sense, Charlie, that things are converging on us? On Aberdeen, on this part of Aberdeen?'

And Charlie had not even mentioned Jem Hosie hanging around Longacre, or indeed – his heart thumped again when he thought of it - Cuthbert Meston threatening Luzie.

'It's beginning to feel a bit like that, sir, aye.'

'And I suppose what worries me is that it does all seem to revolve around Samuel Seabury – or perhaps Myles Cooper. And does that make him, then, the victim? The perpetrator? Or simply a very unlucky man?'

'Does an unlucky man make a good bishop, sir?' Charlie asked. Bishop Skinner made a face.

'I'm not sure. Cicero said that an unlucky man made a very bad general. So if the bishops could be seen as the generals of the church ... I think that is indeed a question for Bishop Petrie and Bishop Kilgour. They are much cleverer men than I am.'

Charlie privately doubted that, but then he had a high opinion of his master's intelligence. In fact, should he tell him about Luzie and Mr. Meston? That was something that did not revolve around Dr. Seabury. Perhaps it would help him.

He was just on the point of opening his mouth to speak, when there came a ferocious rattle at the risp downstairs.

'Heavens, that will be Dr. Seabury already. Myles always beats at the risp like a carpet – I believe he's frightened to stay too long in the street. Will you away and let them in, please, Charlie?'

Charlie bowed and headed off to the stairs. Whoever it was beat at the risp again, and he was tempted to call out that yes, he was coming: he could just picture an agitated Myles Cooper working away at the rattle, red in the face, while Dr. Seabury tried to calm him. At the foot of the stairs he met Jane, also hurrying to the door.

'Who on earth is that?' she asked. 'Have they no patience?'

'Probably Dr. Seabury and Mr. Cooper, miss,' Charlie said and passed her to do his duty.

'They're in an awful hurry,' said Jane. 'I hope there's nothing wrong.'

But when he opened the door, Jane suddenly vanished, and Charlie could see why. On the doorstep, in a state of high emotion and possibly drunk, was Jeremiah Hosie.

Chapter Twenty-Four

'No!'

Charlie heard the squeak as Jane closed the parlour door. He had stood back, thinking to allow Dr. Seabury in, and already Jem was in the hallway, flinging his hat and cane at Charlie and tossing his head in a most alarming manner. He always seemed to move more than was necessary, as if constantly catching his balance.

'Sir, can I help you?' he asked.

'I want to see the Bishop. I demand to see the Bishop. This is his house, is it not?'

Charlie had without thinking about it gone to stand with his back to the parlour door, just in case. Was this Jem's way of coming to ask for Jane's hand? Charlie did not think that the Bishop would be much impressed.

'I shall go and see if he is available, sir, if you don't mind waiting,' Charlie began, but before he could approach the stairs, Bishop Skinner appeared at the top of them.

'Dr. Seabury! Oh! Not Dr. Seabury.'

'Mr. Hosie, sir,' said Charlie helpfully. 'Mr. Meston's stepson.'

Jem Hosie pressed a hand to the silver braid on his black waistcoat, then spread his arms wide and bowed.

'Good day to you, Mr. Hosie,' said Bishop Skinner. 'How may I help? Is something the matter? I should have expected you to be attending your stepfather's coffin.'

'Matter? Indeed there is something the matter. Something

most grave.' Jem bared his teeth and scowled. He looked like a madman.

'Then perhaps we should step upstairs to discuss it in peace,' the Bishop suggested gently. 'Charlie, would you attend us in case we have need of you?'

Charlie nodded. He had done this before: clergy, of course, were often visited by people in need of comfort in various ways, and some of them could be dangerous. One look at Jem would make anyone think precautions were needed.

He followed the Bishop and Jem upstairs. Instead of taking their visitor into the cramped bookroom, the Bishop ushered Jem into the chapel, though whether this was to instil a greater sense of quietude or to give him more space to evade any violence, Charlie was not sure.

'Here, have a seat,' said Mr. Skinner, turning a chair in Jem's direction. 'I'll take this one, so, and then we are quite comfortable, I hope? How are things with your family? Are all the preparations in order? Can I help with anything?'

Bishop Skinner had a soothing voice and a kind face: it seemed to take the edge off Jem's agitation, but could not quell it completely. Jem sprawled on the chair, then sat up straight and folded one knee over the other. He did not seem quite to know what to do with his hands.

'I don't know how you can help. Minnie has gone.'

'Minnie ...' The Bishop pretended to be trying to remember.

'Minnie, our maid. She is gone.'

'Mr. Meston asked her to leave, I believe?'

'Threw her out!' Charlie thought Jem was going to spring from his seat, but instead he satisfied himself with a twitch of his head, ignoring the curl of hair that fell over his forehead. 'Threw her out into the snow.'

'And why was that?'

'Because she was with child!'

The Bishop allowed a silence to lie for a moment. Charlie wondered if he were waiting to see if Jem would confess an involvement, but nothing came of that.

'He threw her out on Friday night. She took refuge in a hospital not far from here, where Lodge Walk meets Queen Street.' As they knew. 'I went now to see her, for I had only just discovered where she was. And she is gone!'

'Gone whither? Did they know?' asked the Bishop innocently. There was always the chance that Jem had heard more than Charlie had discovered.

'She vanished the night that my stepfather was killed!'

'But where?'

'Nobody knows! But that very night – when he was walking the streets, up here, so close to where she was!' He pushed back the lock of hair at last, and shuddered as if a goose had walked over his grave. The Bishop nodded thoughtfully.

'I see. Are you suggesting that she killed him?'

For once Jem was struck dumb. Charlie could see, as he had not seen before, some clear intelligence working behind the hot, dark eyes.

'I should have liked to have seen revenge, certainly,' he said, less forthright than before. 'But to hear that Minnie had done it ... that would not be welcome. And in any case, how? She is tiny. She could no more have held my stepfather's head under the water than a mouse could.'

'Then someone else on her behalf, perhaps? Her father? Brother?'

But Jem was shaking his head.

'I never heard her speak of either. And she was from the country somewhere – how would they have known what had happened, and got here so fast?'

Charlie almost found himself nodding approval. It was a sensible point, more sensible than he would have expected. The Bishop, too, seemed impressed.

'Well, then,' he went on, 'what about the father of her child? He would seem, whoever he is, to be a prime candidate to take revenge.'

'As to that, who knows?' Jem shrugged. 'I had barely thought that she could have left the house long enough for such a thing to happen.'

So that might mean that the father was someone in the house, thought Charlie. But Jem seemed more confused by the question than anything.

'Have you any idea why your stepfather was here that night?' asked Bishop Skinner. 'I know it puzzled all of you at the time.'

'No idea,' said Jem. 'There's a small warehouse we sometimes supply along the street - Houstoun's - but I doubt he had been near it for months, and there was certainly no reason to be there late on a Saturday night. If he was not here to see Minnie, or to frighten her, what was he doing here?'

'Is there a chance - please, allow me the question, though it might well offend you - is there a chance that your stepfather was the father of Minnie's baby?'

That did make Jem sit up, so fast that he almost fell off the chair and windmilled his arms to recover.

'Him! With a servant? Never!' He struggled to compose himself, but Charlie was sure it was more laughter than distress he was trying to hide. 'He despised servants. Could barely tolerate them, only that he would not have known how to look after the house himself. They were hardly allowed to appear in his presence.' He drew in a long breath that flared his nostrils. 'He was an abominable, intolerant man.'

'Well,' said the Bishop, 'he must have had some good points.' No response from Jem. 'May I ask why you came here? I can no longer have a word with Mr. Meston, see if I can persuade him to amend his ways - nor do I think he would have listened to me if I had the chance. So what is it you want from me? How do you think I can help?'

'You can find Minnie,' said Jem, assured again. 'You're right, there is no fixing my stepfather now. But Minnie can be saved. Minnie and her child.'

'As to that,' said the Bishop, 'I suppose I can put the word around the town, see if one of the other clergy has come across her or knows of her fate. What is her surname?'

Jem's eyes flickered, and Charlie wondered if he had forgotten. But after a moment it came to him.

'Towie,' he said. 'Minnie Towie. From Portlethen way.' He named a village south of Aberdeen, but uncertainly, as if he doubted its existence.

'Then -' The Bishop broke off as the risp at the front door underwent another undeserved battering. 'That's surely Dr. Seabury now. Charlie, will you let him in?'

He must be feeing safe now. Charlie trotted downstairs again and opened the door to Dr. Seabury, waved ahead by an unctuous but urgent Myles Cooper. Charlie was still helping them with their coats when Bishop Skinner followed him downstairs with Jem.

'Jem Hosie, the stepson of that poor man found outside,' the Bishop made quick introductions, clearly not wishing to detain Jem. 'Mr. Hosie, Dr. Seabury and Mr. Cooper.'

Jem made his bow, as did the two clergy. If Jem cast a suspicious glance at their clerical dress, that was the only attention he paid them above the ordinary. It seemed he had not heard of Samuel Seabury, either from his stepfather or from the magistrate. Then who was it that had told the magistrate about the quarrel on the boat?

Bishop Skinner whisked Seabury and Cooper upstairs, leaving Charlie to see Jem off from the doorstep.

'I am most concerned about Minnie,' said Jem fervently, if confidentially. 'It really was my first reason for calling. You are not to think that it had anything to do with – with Miss Skinner.' He allowed his burning eyes to smoulder dreamily. Charlie had no idea what effect it had on young women, but it turned his stomach.

'But why are you so concerned about Minnie, sir?' Charlie thought he might as well ask. 'Do you think she's in some danger?'

'The danger of poverty? Cold, hunger?'

'Aye, I ken, but it just seems a bit ...'

Jem's gaze bored hard at him.

'You think I might be the father of her child, is that it?'

'Well, sir, you said she didna get out much ...'

'That I should sully myself with a servant, and then offer my heart to Miss Skinner? You thought me capable of that?'

Jem swept his coat about him, seized his hat and gloves, and swirled through the doorway like something demented. Charlie watched him for a moment: he paused in the middle of the street, an obstacle to passing carts, and turned his head from side to side, as if unsure which way to go. Home to question the others? A further search for Minnie? But home seemed to appeal more, or at least the direction of Broad Street. In a moment he had vanished into the entry.

So it was not just Cuthbert Meston that looked down on servants, then?

For all he seemed to despise his stepfather, he had a few things in common with him. Gazing after him towards Broad Street, Charlie prayed that one of them was not to be bullying Luzie.

It was when Charlie was returning to the stairs with the brandy that he noticed a folded piece of paper on the stone floor of the hall. He set the brandy tray on the hall table, and stooped to pick it up.

It was a wrapped letter, addressed to 'Bishop Skinner, Longacre', and, to judge from the state of it, it had not travelled far, or not in a carrier's pack, anyway. The corners were crisp and fresh, and the writing unblotched by rain or spillages. It must have been slipped under the door.

He laid it on the tray with the glasses, and headed upstairs to the Bishop's bookroom.

'What's that, Charlie?' asked the Bishop, poking the letter.

'I think it's just arrived, sir.'

'I didn't hear the risp.'

'No, just pushed under the door.'

The Bishop glanced at the others in the room, Dr. Seabury, Bishop Petrie, and Myles Cooper.

'Would anyone mind if I took a quick look at this? It's local, evidently, and I don't recognise the hand – it may be urgent.'

'Of course, John!' said Bishop Petrie at once.

'I'll go out on to the landing,' said Bishop Skinner. 'Come, Charlie, I may need to send a reply.'

He closed the bookroom door behind them, and slid a finger into the folds. The letter was unsealed, only tucked into itself to hold it closed. The Bishop flicked it open, turned it, and read quickly. There was not much to read.

'Oh, Charlie, not another one!'

'What is it, sir?'

Bishop Skinner laid out the letter for Charlie to read.

'The foreigner with his English friend is not fit to be a bishop, in America or anywhere else. If you consecrate, there will be consequences.'

Chapter Twenty-Five

'I should say it's not the same hand as the last note,' said Skinner, taking the letter back.

'Aye, and that was signed, sir. This person's not so keen to let us know who he is.'

'That's right ...' Skinner flipped the letter over, then looked more closely at the cover. There was little to be told from it. 'A local delivery, presumably. Just the street given, not the town.'

'That was my thought, too, sir. And fresh looking.'

'You didn't see anyone?'

'No, sir. I was in the kitchen.'

The Bishop tapped the now folded letter across his palm.

'Definitely not the same hand, though. Much more bold.' He thought for another few seconds. 'I'll have to ask Dr. Seabury about this one. After all, we discussed the one from Mr. Seller: it's only fair to give him the chance to comment on this one, too.'

'Will that not give him cause to think that he might be in danger?' Charlie had taken a moment to try to remember if this was one of the things he should not tell someone, but it was only Dr. Seabury he was not supposed to tell. The Bishop sighed.

'Mr. Cooper is convinced their lives are in danger every time they step into the street,' he said with a wry smile. 'I'm beginning to wonder if I'm protecting them unnecessarily. After all, like us here in Scotland, they've been through all kinds of hazard just to survive and get this far. Perhaps they are used to it.'

'I'm not sure a'body ever gets used to that kind of thing,' said

Charlie, more darkly than perhaps he had intended. The Bishop scrutinised him.

'Are you finding this a bit worrying, Charlie? Again, I assume because you've met with similar things before that you'll know how to deal with them, but perhaps I've ... I've relied too much on your strength?'

Charlie straightened, eager not to seem weak.

'Not at all, sir. All's well with me.' Unless Luzie's in danger, he wanted to add, but could not. But besides that, he did not want to let the Bishop and his family down.

'Well ...' said the Bishop. 'Well, I wonder if I should suggest a walk to them?'

'You might want to take a look outside, sir.'

The Bishop stepped into the chapel, and looked at the windows. It felt, Charlie thought, as if the house was floating upwards, as the soft, fat snowflakes fell steadily, silently, down.

'Oh.'

'I think it's set in for a whiley, too, sir.'

'It looks like it. I can't ask Bishop Petrie to go out in this, even in a chair. If he would even use a chair when a handcart is less extravagant.'

For a moment Charlie pictured Bishop Petrie careering through the snow in a handcart, smiling beneficently as he went. It did not seem wholly unlikely.

'Shall I tell Jean that everyone's in to dinner, then, sir?'

The Bishop sighed again, spellbound by the snow.

'Aye, you'd better. I hope she has enough in.'

'I'm sure she has, sir.'

The bookroom door opened on the landing, and in a moment Bishop Petrie, like a beatified mouse, appeared at the chapel door.

'Is everything all right, John?' he asked. 'You look worried.'

Bishop Skinner stirred himself.

'I had thought of taking our brother clergy to see the Qualifed Chapel,' he said, with a smile, 'but you see the weather! It would be hard to tell a qualified chapel from a Quaker meeting house in this.'

Bishop Petrie trotted over to peer short-sightedly through the window at the buildings beyond, blackened by contrast with the snow.

'Dearie me!' he said. 'I pray that all find shelter who need it out there. John, I think the good Lord is telling us to stay in and talk further with our American brother, a prospect that fills me with great joy.'

He smiled and nodded, and Bishop Skinner could do nothing but smile back: Bishop Petrie had that effect on people. In any case, no doubt the master would be pleased to have Bishop Petrie here to share his impressions of Dr. Seabury, even if he was reluctant to mention Cuthbert Meston's murder and the magistrate.

'Aye, Charlie, that'll be all for now,' said Bishop Skinner, resigning himself to his task. Charlie bowed and turned to go, leaving the bishops in the chapel - perhaps for a quick prayer before returning to their work.

If Monday had been spent at relative ease, with Mrs. Skinner taking her rest and the household quietly catching up on tasks while the master and his guests were out, Tuesday was much less calming. Charlie usually liked seeing the snow fall, finding it strange and magical in its silence, but today it was relentless. The light was not brighter than dusk all day, and Mrs. Skinner fretted about the quantity of candles and lamp oil they were using. Jane and Margaret gave up on their sewing, unable to see, and grew restless at the lack of employment. Johnnie and William were out at school, but already Mrs. Skinner was anxious about their return, as the snow piled high in the street outside. Charlie could see that there were some people about, including a couple of men trying to clear the snow as it fell, but he did not envy them, and he suspected that he would be sent to fetch the boys later. Any time he was called to the bookroom, the conversation there seemed more and more sporadic, almost surly. Everyone felt trapped.

Jean the maid did not seem to think this should be a barrier to finding the right ingredients for her dinner, though.

'Charlie, away out and see if your wifie has any cloves to this apple pie,' she said. 'The master's awful fond of a clove.'

'Well, I suppose,' said Charlie. It would at least give him the chance to call and see that Luzie was all right, her doorway cleared and so on. He pulled on coat and muffler and gloves, tying the muffler about his head as well as around his neck, trying to stretch it to cover his mouth and nose. It might not be far to home and Luzie's warehouse, but it was going to feel like an expedition to Kamchatka, he was sure.

He started by clearing the snow directly outside the door, then scraping away with his shovel towards where the men earlier had tried to maintain a path along the street. He thought of setting the shovel back inside the door before he set off, then thought better of it: it was a good prop, and he might need it at the other end.

The mouth of the street was like a cave under the buildings, dark and damp and ripe with the smell of those who had chosen, for want of anywhere better, to shelter there. Only a narrow opening at each end allowed in light and pedestrians: if Bishop Petrie had arrived in his hand cart at this moment, they would have had to widen the passage for him. Charlie was glad the little bishop was wrapped up safe and warm at the Skinners' house. The air was fugged with smoke from a couple of small fires, and the cooking of a piece of fish that should probably have been given a decent burial instead. Charlie gave a small coin to one or two of the beggars, and scrambled out on to Broad Street and the falling snow again.

He could barely see his own house across the street, but headed off in what he hoped was the right direction. After all, unless he happened on one of the lanies that led down to Ghost Row he would hit the wall at some point, then just work his way along until he found his own building. Assuming he could walk straight across the street in the first place.

There was more traffic here than there had been in Longacre, but still it was quiet for a weekday. A long cart laden with barrels had skidded sideways, the horses straining and slipping to haul it free. Charlie wielded his shovel here and there in an effort to help, but he and a couple of other men narrowly escaped injury when the cart suddenly slipped forward. They pulled each other out of the snow, laughing more with relief than anything, and Charlie slithered on across the street to where he could see Luzie standing at her door, watching the drama.

'What are you doing out in this?' she asked as soon as he was close enough. 'Apart from risking your life over that fool's cart?' She hugged him.

'Cloves for Jean,' he said, eager to get inside to the warmth. The cart had whacked his arm, and he knew it was going to hurt.

'Surely she could have done without? Is your arm all right?'

'It's grand. Are you just outside to laugh at us?'

Luzie half-smiled, then jerked her head towards the wall between shutter and door. For the first time, Charlie noticed black marks on it – writing.

'Dinna buy your guids here,' it said, sharp and dark. 'Muckit forren wummin.'

'When did that appear?' asked Charlie, a nasty feeling in his stomach.

'Some time this morn. I didna see till someone came in and told me it was there.'

'Then let's get it off there. What is it, charcoal?'

'That's what I thought,' she said, one finger hovering over the nearest letter without quite touching it. 'But I think it's paint of some kind.'

'Let's see if it'll scrub off. Have you hot water in the kitchen? I'll try this if you'll get me a poke of cloves for Jean.'

He scrubbed hard at the letters with a stiff brush and water with soap in it. The letters were persistent. Even with the wall soaking, he could still see, he thought, their outline. He sighed.

'I'd better get back,' said Charlie at last. 'Jean was already chopping the apples. I'll come back later if I can, though, and give them another go. At worst we can paint over it and put some words on the paint – "Best quality coffee here", or the like.'

'I'd like that.' She smiled. 'And I'd like fine to see you later, too!'

'We'll sort this out,' he said, more positive than he felt, and kissed her as a token of his return.

He shovelled snow away from the warehouse doorway before he left, knowing that the bruise on his arm would stiffen if he did not keep moving. His injuries were multiplying. The snow kept falling: it looked set to continue for days. There would be no shortage of shovelling to do.

No one else at the Skinner household wanted to venture out: it felt like an age ago that Dr. Seabury and Mr. Cooper had arrived that morning, and that Jem Hosie had appeared and gone again.

'I wonder if we should offer them a bed for the night?' Bishop Skinner asked Charlie after supper. 'I can't see Mr. Cooper wanting to walk back to the New Inn in this.'

Mrs. Skinner, part of the conversation, made a face.

'We'd have to give them John and William's room,' she said.

'The bed's gey small. I doubt they would both fit.'

'Maybe we should tell them that, and they'll find the inn more appealing,' said the Bishop with a grin. 'I know we should be hospitable, but I can't see Myles Cooper feeling we have done much for him if he ends up on the floor.'

'Well ... perhaps we should let them choose,' said Mrs. Skinner. 'What did Dr. Seabury say about that second letter?'

'He could tell me nothing,' said the Bishop. 'Quite different from the letter from Mr. Seller. Neither he nor Myles Cooper could think of anyone local they had sufficient contact with to produce that kind of response, though I think Mr. Cooper expects to discover animosity wherever he goes.'

'Are you going to tell the magistrate about it?'

'Ah, as to that,' said the Bishop, a little uncomfortable, 'I was grateful enough that the magistrate had not returned to question them about Cuthbert Meston – I hoped that they have again lost interest in Dr. Seabury. Telling them about the letter might revive their interest, and I cannot see that it would do enough good to balance that risk.'

Charlie was inclined to agree, and was glad enough when Dr. Seabury and Mr. Cooper decided to return to the inn rather than inconvenience the Skinners by staying overnight. He took them back to the inn in what was becoming a routine, then went quickly, shovel in hand, to pay the promised call on his wife. In the dark, the letters were definitely invisible.

'I still think a bit of white paint would be a nice touch,' said Luzie, greeting him with a hug. 'I like the idea of a sign like that. And if someone else painted on it again, we could just paint over it.'

Pleased that she was cheerful, Charlie assured her he would be home again soon, and headed back with the shovel to Longacre.

More snow had somehow appeared on the doorstep since Charlie had gone out: he wondered if it had slipped from the roof, as often happened when it was heavy. Something like a roll of it lay across the doorway, no doubt easy enough to kick his way through but Charlie had the shovel still, and swung it off his shoulder to dig quickly across the snow heap.

At once he hit something more solid than snow, even than compacted snow. Someone must have left something on the doorstep, and now it was covered. He crouched down to clear some snow with his gloved hand, and found a woolly cloth - someone's shawl.

But there was something about the firmness of the bundle that made him pause. In his mind came a picture of the beggars sheltering under the passage to Broad Street. Had one of them ventured out, only to meet their end? But why here, across the Bishop's doorstep?

Warily, he reached out and brushed away some more of the snow. Was this going to be someone he recognised? Someone to whom he had given occasional coins? Someone well kent in the neighbourhood?

But the face he uncovered was no one he had seen before. It was a girl, very small, dressed only in a gown and shawl. He did not know her, but he had a horrible feeling that he knew who she was.

Chapter Twenty-Six

'Could it be Minnie?' asked Bishop Skinner. He cast a last glance at the girl before he and Charlie left the chapel. Mrs. Skinner and Jane, aided by Jean, were attending to the corpse, tenderly, heedless of her identity.

'That was my first thought, sir,' said Charlie, 'but I never saw the girl. The description fits, but the description was really just "tiny".'

'And pregnant. No doubt they can tell us shortly, or the layer-out can, when she comes. She did say she wouldn't be long?'

'Her son did, sir - she's out at a birth.'

The Bishop frowned horribly.

'Why our door? Was she seeking help? Did we not hear her?'

It was a terrible thought, whoever the girl was.

'If she'd reached the risp you'd have heard it, sir,' said Charlie. But if he himself had been back, could he have heard her at the door even if she had not reached the risp? If he had not been delayed, could he have arrived before it was too late? If he had come straight back ... but then Luzie ... Even now he felt he should not have left her. But his obligations - his affections, even - were here, too.

The chapel door opened, and Jean appeared, carrying a bucket.

'Charlie, there's more hot water down the stair - can you fetch it and slop this out?'

'Aye, of course.'

'John?' Mrs. Skinner's voice came from the chapel. 'John, you'd better see this.'

Charlie was already halfway down the stairs. He hurried to fling the water out into the street, then to the kitchen to refill the bucket and back upstairs. The Bishop was in the chapel with the women, and the girl's body, naked from the waist up, lay on its front, as much decency as possible preserved in the circumstances. She was indeed tiny, ribs like the sand where the sea had ebbed, shoulder bones stark, hair thin and lying damp where the women had already begun to wash it.

And between those ribs, under the right shoulder blade, a horizontal, sagging wound, the edges clean as if one thrust of a sharp blade had been enough to finish her. There was little sign of blood, but over the back of a chair Charlie saw the girl's dress and shawl darkened and stained. He frowned.

'Weakened by that, as well as the cold and hunger, no doubt,' said the Bishop. 'I wonder if we could have saved her, even if we had heard her? But who would do such a thing? And who would dare to do it on our doorstep?'

But Charlie had seen the body more closely than Bishop Skinner had, outside in the snow.

'I dinna think she was alive when she reached us,' he said, then thought how strange that sounded. 'I mean, I think she was killed somewhere else and brought here, sir.'

'What?'

Charlie glanced uneasily at Mrs. Skinner and Jane, but it was hard for clergy ever to conceal the evils of the world from their families.

'There was no blood in the snow, and this would have bled, would it no, mistress?'

'It would, Charlie,' Mrs. Skinner confirmed. She laid a hand on the girl's shoulder, gently, as if trying to comfort her. 'But why? Why kill her, yes, but these things happen. Why bring her here, though? Was she still alive and someone hoped we might help?'

'Then why not rattle the risp, Mamma?' asked Jane sensibly. 'How could we know to help if we didn't know she was there?'

'Do either of you recognise her?' asked Bishop Skinner. 'Or Jean – do you know her?'

'I'm not acquainted with girls like that,' said Jean firmly.

'Jean! Don't make judgements,' said Mrs. Skinner. 'You don't know what this poor girl's life has been like. No, I don't recognise her, I'm afraid.'

'Jane?'

'No, Pappa. But she looks so pale and drawn: it might be hard to tell what she looked like alive.'

'True ...' The Bishop folded his arms, but his fingers still agitated. Too much to deal with all at once, Charlie thought. 'Who could we ask? We can hardly bother Mr. Meston or his household on the eve of his brother's funeral.'

'What about the warehouseman, Alan?' Charlie suggested. 'He would have known her, of course, and it would not be so difficult for him to come out.'

'Or the superintendent of the hospital - do you think she would recognise her? If it is her,' said the Bishop. 'Maybe that would be more convenient. And, I suppose,' he sighed, 'I'll have to tell the magistrate.'

He exchanged a look with Charlie.

It was not a happy look. If the magistrate found that someone else had been found murdered outside the Skinners' house, would he be back to question Dr. Seabury again? It was almost Wednesday already: two days before Bishop Kilgour arrived, two days in which they might have to hide things from Bishop Petrie. If the master wished that Dr. Seabury had never been tempted to leave America, he could be forgiven.

Charlie woke in darkness, not for the first time that night, picturing the pathetic corpse he had pulled from the snow, the wound in her upper back. By his best guess it was early morning, about an hour earlier than his usual waking time.

He slipped out of his warm bed and out of the house, hastily dressed, to reassure himself that no further damage had been done to the premises before Luzie woke. She was an energetic, early riser usually, but last night she had slept only fitfully, muttering from time to time. He told himself she was more angry than afraid but in truth he had never seen her so unsettled by something. He fetched the water and lit the fire to have her coffee ready for her.

'Will you be all right today?' he asked, once she taken the first reviving sips.

She nodded.

'It's Meston's funeral today. Surely none of them could do

anything on such a day?'

Cuthbert Meston's funeral, and still no idea who had murdered him, nor why. And now another death. He was not sure how Bishop Skinner felt, but it was Charlie's sense that it was time to sit down and think sensibly about the whole thing. It was not the sort of thing he was generally good at, but he thought that Bishop Skinner and Mrs. Skinner, and maybe Jane and possibly little Bishop Petrie, might together make a good deal of sense of the matter. And Dr. Seabury, if the Bishop was prepared to tell him his thoughts. But not Mr. Cooper. No, leave him in the dining room with the brandy bottle, and let those with a bit of wit sort the matter out.

He sighed. He was not sure that he could bring about such a conclave: he needed to do some of the thinking himself. After all, there were still some things he knew that he had not told the others.

He helped Luzie open up the warehouse and waited until the shop boy came in to help her before he left her. He was relieved to find Longacre free of corpses this morning, and hoped it would continue that way for some time to come. Glimpses of Meston's soaked corpse, the girl's miserable remains, flashed intermittently in his mind. Who could stab such a small, defenceless thing? What for? The father of her child, disposing of the evidence of his sin? Her existence seemed so fragile anyway, it hardly seemed worth the effort. Charlie felt a tear in his eye, and smeared it away with the heel of his glove. It was too cold to cry.

Coincidentally Mrs. Skinner was wiping the corner of her eye when he met her in the hallway.

'I've just sent a lad to fetch that superintendent from the hospital. It didn't seem right to ask even the warehouseman on the day of Cuthbert Meston's funeral – they'll be so busy. I just hope this poor woman can manage, and won't be too upset.'

'And is able to tell if it's her or not, mistress – I don't think Minnie was at the hospital for very long.'

'Aye, true, true,' Mrs. Skinner agreed. 'Well, whoever it is, she seems to be clean. I know that's an awful thing to say, but it's such a bother cleaning everything out, and at this time of year when it's so difficult to air things properly. Not even a flea, I should say.'

'So whoever she is, likely she wasn't living rough, would you say, mistress?'

Mrs. Skinner's look was sad, but realistic.

'No, I should say not. One more thing that makes Minnie the likely name. Poor child, poor child.'

Charlie was nearly finished his early morning chores when he heard a tentative rattle at the risp, and went to the door. Outside stood the superintendent from the hospital, the tails of her skirts wet with snow. Charlie at once let her in.

'Oh, it's you, of course!' said the woman. 'I wondered when the note came. I'm sorry I was delayed - one of our old ladies took a bit of a turn. I hope it was nothing urgent?'

Charlie ushered her into the parlour, where Mrs. Skinner was resting.

'Mrs. Gray, mistress. Would you like me to take her upstairs when you're ready?'

'That would be kind, Charlie. Mrs. Gray, I have a sorry task for you, for which I hope you will forgive me when we are not yet acquainted. Please, take a seat while I explain.'

Charlie stepped out to ask Jean to bring tea while Mrs. Skinner deftly prepared Mrs. Gray for the news, and for the task, should she agree. By the time Charlie came back, Mrs. Gray was bracing herself, hands tight in her skirts, and ready to accompany him up to the chapel.

'I have never been in an Episcopal chapel before, d'you know? How very interesting. Oh, and it is very pleasant!' she exclaimed, as Charlie led her in. Snowlight from the uncurtained windows lay bright across the plain room with its polished floor. Then her face fell as she saw the table, and the sheet, and the tiny form it hid.

The girl had not been left alone: the local woman who helped lay out the dead was with her, just finished her work. She nodded to the superintendent, clearly acquainted.

'Should I just lift ...'

'I'll help you, mistress. She looks gey peaceful, if that's your worry.'

'I don't even know if - if it's - oh. Oh, Minnie - yes, this is Minnie.'

'Do you ken her surname, mistress?' Charlie asked.

'No, I don't. There was so little time, and she was so weak, I hardly liked to press her with questions.'

'You kenned she was with child?' asked the laying-out woman.

'I did, yes.' Mrs. Gray sighed deeply. 'And she died just outside here? Last night?'

'Last night, aye,' said Charlie, 'but we dinna ken it was just here. Did you hear from her at all after she left? Or from a'body who might know where she was those couple days?'

Mrs. Gray screwed up her face in thought, though Charlie, from experience, thought she might have been trying to stop tears coming.

'A young man came yesterday, but he was looking for her – he seemed quite gentlemanly, then behaved very strangely when I told him she had disappeared. I don't know what it was about you, my dear,' she said to Minnie's body, 'but both the men who sought you had difficult tempers! Oh – is it possible that one of them killed her?' Her voice lost all volume, only a breath as the thought struck her. 'Could they have found her because of me? Because of us at the hospital?'

'I don't think so, mistress,' said Charlie firmly. 'You weren't able to tell them where she was, were you?'

'Well, no. No, I couldn't even have let anything slip, if I didn't know anything, could I?' She drew a deep breath, but it was not quite steady. 'But a murderer! At the hospital!'

'We don't know that,' said Charlie. 'In fact, they both seem to have cared for her, to some degree, so perhaps they were trying to protect her? Anyway,' he feared wandering too far down a speculative route. 'Anyway, we know who she is, now, and the master will see to it that she receives a decent burial, I'm sure.'

'May we – may we take her to the hospital?' The superintendent was hesitant at first, then firmer. 'I feel we let her down, you ken. Not that the trustees will like it, but – well, poor wee mite. How can they say no? And if they do –' Her lips pressed hard together, and she folded her arms firmly over her generously supported bosom.

And in that moment, Charlie realised that Mrs. Gray was much tougher than he had thought.

Chapter Twenty-Seven

Mrs. Skinner, acquainted with the verdict, saw Mrs. Gray off at the door, and turned to Charlie.

'Well, that answers that question, then, though we had all suspected it. Charlie, what on earth is happening? Does someone hate us? Or is there something more subtle here?'

'Mistress, please go and rest yourself again!' Charlie followed her into the parlour, and poured her a fresh cup of tea from the pot.

'I can rest my back,' said Mrs. Skinner, not unwilling to settle back on the sopha, 'but it's hard to rest my mind. Particularly when John is up half the night worrying over it like a dog with a bone. Is this anti-Episcopalian again? Anti-Jacobite? Has Dr. Seabury's arrival started all this, or was it going to happen anyway? And what has Cuthbert Meston to do with it, or his maid?'

'I was saying to myself this morning, mistress, that we needed to sit down and straighten everything out. Not that I want to presume.'

'No, it's a sensible idea. And before my husband sends for the magistrate, for that man was dead set against Dr. Seabury, and I could not see his reasoning. Or work out who told him that Dr. Seabury even existed, let alone argued with Cuthbert Meston on the boat.' She set down her empty cup, and folded her hands, businesslike, in her lap. 'So where should we start?'

Charlie shrugged: he had not seen himself leading this discussion.

'I suppose with Cuthbert Meston's murder. Either he was killed because he was Cuthbert Meston, or he was killed, as the

Bishop would have it, because he was mistaken for Dr. Seabury.'

'Or for Mr. Cooper.' She sighed. 'That I could understand.'

'Or, I suppose, randomly. But no one has said he was robbed.'

'No. No, I think it's probably one of the first two.'

'Now, there have been two letters telling the Bishops not to consecrate Dr. Seabury. But they don't really threaten his life. They just look hostile.'

'The second one in particular,' said Mrs. Skinner, nodding. 'In fact, you could almost take that one as a threat to his life. The consequences ...'

'The thing about the letters is that the second one was sent locally, and the writer of the first one is said to be in Aberdeen.'

'Ah, I see what you mean,' said Mrs. Skinner. 'You might think that having come from America, even if via England and Edinburgh, Dr. Seabury would have no particular enemies here, but in fact there are two.'

'That's – yes, that's what I meant.' Maybe they didn't need anyone else: Mrs. Skinner was quite clever enough to sort the whole thing out herself.

'We know who the first letter writer is – a Mr. Seller, wasn't it? Do we know where he is staying in Aberdeen?'

'No, mistress. I have a description of him from the carrier, that is all.'

'And we know nothing at all about the second writer, except that the style is terse and the hand more forceful.'

Charlie smiled.

'Aye, that's about it, mistress.'

'Well,' said Mrs. Skinner, with a wriggle of her clasped hands, 'that doesn't take us very far, does it?'

'Mr. Meston had no lantern when I found him, mistress.'

'Had he not? Why on earth not?' She pondered for a moment. 'Did his killer take it, having followed him secretly? Or was he accompanied by his killer who had a lantern, and therefore thought he wouldn't need one?'

'In either case, you'd think the killer would know if he had the right man, mistress.'

'Aye, that's true. But maybe he broke his lantern ... no, he would still take it home with him, wouldn't he, to be mended?'

'You'd think.'

'So, if his killer knew who he was ... this is a terrible conversation to be having, Charlie, is it no? A killer out there in Longacre, just outside our door?'

'I know, mistress. If you want to leave it –'

'I do not. I'd rather talk it out than sit and worry.'

Charlie gave a small bow. Mrs. Skinner went on.

'If his killer knew who he was, then it was someone who did not like Cuthbert Meston. That's difficult, too, for he was not an easy man.'

'That's true, mistress, but there are questions here, too. What was he doing up here in Longacre? Why had he been around Broad Street so much since he got back from Edinburgh? And also why was he in Edinburgh? Nobody seems to know.'

'Business, presumably.'

'Nothing he told his brother about, mistress.'

'Hm. Did he get on well with his brother, do you think?'

'I'd say so.' Charlie tried to think what his impressions had been. 'Mr. Stephen Meston seems a more affable man, I'd say. He was keen to show his brother in a good light when he was dead. He was out that evening, looking for Cuthbert Meston and wondering where Jem was, too – Jeremiah Hosie, Mr. Meston's stepson.'

Mrs. Skinner's face took on an odd expression.

'Oh, yes – I've heard a little about that young man. Quite the character, I hear.'

'Aye, mistress. So really, both of them were out and unaccounted for around the time that Cuthbert Meston was killed.'

'And what about this maid? Do you think Cuthbert Meston found out where she was, and followed her up here?'

'Well, maybe, mistress, though since he had thrown her out I canna see why he would be following her. But also, he came up to Broad Street just after he got back from Edinburgh, just after he'd thrown her out, before she would even have been up here. No, there was something else here he was after, or someone he was going to meet, or something he needed to do. And I doubt he managed to do it that first night, for he was back and looking purposeful twa-three times after that. I saw him myself, and so did Dr. Seabury and Mr. Cooper.'

And surely Luzie had not been the main target of that? There was no need to mention her, and worry Mrs. Skinner further.

'Oh, yes: back to Dr. Seabury and Mr. Cooper. And the quarrel on the boat.' She freed her fingers from each other and drummed them on the dark cloth of her skirts, making no sound. 'Do you think it's possible that Cuthbert Meston went home, considered the matter, and decided to pursue the quarrel further? Did he come up here looking for Dr. Seabury?'

'And then what, mistress?'

'Hm ... Do we know that they met on the boat? They had not encountered each other earlier in Edinburgh?'

'I have no idea, mistress. I never thought to ask. No, wait, he told Mr. Shand they had not met.'

'If this were a prolonged quarrel ... maybe with Myles Cooper instead then, for if you ask me, Charlie, that man is unstable ... then perhaps Mr. Meston came up here looking for them, and Myles and he fought ... what do you think?'

Charlie tried to picture it, frowned, and tried again.

'I think it could be, mistress. But I think Mr. Cooper would have had to be very lucky to get Mr. Meston face down in the trough like that, and hold him there. He doesna strike me as a gey strong man. And I'd swear he was awful, awful drunk.'

'No, true ... and though it has a degree of neatness to it, I suppose it would cause John a deal more problems than he has at the moment.' She sighed. 'Well, then, what about Jem Hosie? My husband said he was here yesterday, telling him all about how terrible his stepfather was and how he must have been involved in Minnie's disappearance. At least we know that Cuthbert Meston was not responsible for poor Minnie's death.'

'If a'body's unstable around here, mistress, it's Jeremiah Hosie,' said Charlie definitely, aware that this might help Jane at some future point. 'The man's wild.'

'Aye, so I hear,' said Mrs. Skinner thoughtfully. 'And not on good terms with his stepfather. Do you think he was the father of Minnie's child?'

'Four men in the house and the maid is expecting? You have to wonder, mistress, if one of them is, anyway.'

'That's true. There was no hint, when you talked with the household?'

'I didna feel they were telling me everything, but then why

would they?'

'Indeed. I just wondered if you had any impression.'

'They were all upset that Cuthbert Meston had thrown her out so suddenly, with only what she was standing up in. The warehouseman, Alan, said he had gathered her things to take to her when he found out where she was, but they wouldn't let him in.'

'At the hospital? Then that was one of the angry men Mrs. Gray spoke about. And the other, presumably, was Jem Hosie.'

'That seems to be right, aye.'

'The thing is,' said Mrs. Skinner, after a minute, 'if someone – say Jem – killed Cuthbert Meston because of what he had done to Minnie, throwing her out like that, then who killed Minnie, and why?'

'Oh.' Charlie had not thought of that.

'In fact, who killed Minnie and why anyway? She was so tiny, poor lass. What was she like, do you know? Fiery? Charming? Sweet? Bad-tempered? Bold?'

'I havena heard at all what she was like,' Charlie admitted. 'By the time she got to the hospital she was so weak I don't think she made much impression, except that she needed protection and help.'

'I just wonder ... I know it seems an odd thing to say, a horrible thing, but to look at her she hardly seems worth stabbing. Do you see what I mean? She could have been throttled or hit with a brick and that would have finished her. Who went to the trouble of taking out a blade, then having to clean it? There was nothing of her to stab.'

Charlie swallowed: it sort of made sense, but the mistress was right. It was horrible.

'But if she was a strong character, a bold girl – I don't mean bad, for she was not necessarily that – but if she was the kind of girl who talked back, or gossiped, or used her head and put two and two together – that's the kind of person it might be worth stabbing. Oh, my, Charlie, see where this is getting us? I'm becoming a terrible woman!'

Charlie wanted to say 'Well, you're a woman who puts two and two together, anyway,' but it was not his place. It might be awful, but he felt they were making some kind of progress.

'We need to think about why, having killed her, they brought her here,' he said.

'And that, from our point of view, is maybe the worst bit. Did someone want one of us – including Dr. Seabury and Mr. Cooper –

to be blamed for poor Minnie's death?'

'Maybe they wanted us to know she was dead, somehow.'

Mrs. Skinner shifted again on the sopha, trying to ease her back.

'She disappeared on Saturday night from the hospital, didn't she?'

'Aye, according to the superintendent, yes.'

'And she had not long been dead, according to the laying-out woman, when she was found. Though perhaps the snow can affect that – I'm not sure. But maybe not by much, and it was not snowing on Sunday or Monday.'

'I think I see where you're heading, mistress.'

'Aye, Charlie, that's a question. Where had she been, between Saturday night and Tuesday night?'

'If she had a friend she could go to, why had she not gone there first, and not to the hospital?' Charlie asked in turn.

'The superintendent told you she didn't think that Minnie could have been taken against her will, but she could have been lured out.'

'Or frightened out.'

'Aye, or frightened out. I'd swear she had not been sleeping rough: she was too clean. Did the child's father come to rescue her? But if so, why is she now dead?'

'We're away round in circles again, mistress. We dinna know enough.'

'But how do we find out more?'

And just at that moment, they heard the rattle of the risp.

Chapter Twenty-Eight

The woman on the doorstep was familiar to Charlie - Mrs Houstoun, the wife of the grocer at the other end of Longacre. She was short and bright, with a rosy face, hair so blonde it was almost white, bubbling in tight curls from under her bonnet, and a little gap between her front teeth that showed when she smiled, which was often. She was almost smiling now.

'Good day to you!' she said brightly.

'Mrs. Houstoun!' He bowed. He hoped she was not here to try to persuade Mrs. Skinner to change supplier for her tea and coffee: Luzie would not like that, but Mr. Houstoun was always keen to expand his range of customers. 'Are you wanting to see the mistress?'

'Oh, I don't want to disturb her - she should be resting! No, you might be able to help me.'

'If I can - do you want to step into the hall?'

'Who is it, Charlie?' Mrs. Skinner was disturbed after all. Charlie showed Mrs. Houstoun into the parlour. 'Oh, Mrs. Houstoun! Good day to you! You'll see I'm reclining in royal splendour here.'

'So you should be, Mrs. Skinner - don't even think of getting up! No, I was really just asking if you had seen our new maid?'

'I didn't know you had one!'

'Well,' Mrs. Houstoun jiggled awkwardly on her heels. 'She is very new, and maybe won't last, you ken? Particularly if she's this flighty.'

'What's her name, mistress?' asked Charlie, suddenly alert.

'Minnie. Minnie Towie.'

'Very small made? Mousy hair?'

'That's her!' Mrs. Houstoun beamed, then saw the look that passed between Charlie and Mrs. Skinner. 'Why? What has happened?'

'What made you come here?' asked Mrs. Skinner, not giving any more away just yet.

'Here? Nothing – I was working my way along the street. I've done all this side.'

'When did she disappear?'

'Last night, just before supper. I'd sent her out for candles, for we had run low, and she never came back.'

'Did you look for her then?'

Mrs. Houstoun squirmed.

'Look, you know something, do you not? Please tell me! I'm that worried about her!'

'You'd better take her upstairs, Charlie,' said Mrs. Skinner, and her tone made it very clear that Mrs. Houstoun should prepare herself for bad news. Mrs. Houstoun cast a frantic look at Mrs. Skinner, and allowed herself to be guided out of the room.

'What is it, Charlie? Please tell me!'

'Up in the chapel,' said Charlie, 'there's a girl ... but I'm awful sorry, Mrs. Houstoun. She's dead. We found her outside last night, in the snow.'

'Last night? Why did no one say ...?'

'We didn't know she was working for you,' Charlie explained. 'We weren't sure of her name until this morning. Here, let me take you upstairs, and we can make sure. It would be terrible to make a mistake.' But he was sure in his own mind there was no mistake. They were about to find out more about where Minnie had spent her last few days.

Indeed, when the sheet was pulled back Mrs. Houstoun took one look and burst into sobs, the first proper tears for the dead girl. Charlie waited patiently.

'Was it the cold?' she asked when she recovered. 'She had hardly anything when she came to us, but she refused all clothing, saying she would have her bag sent to her.'

'It was not the cold, mistress,' said Charlie. 'She was stabbed with a knife.'

'Oh!' Mrs. Houstoun covered her mouth with her hand, too

shocked to speak.

'Have you any idea who would do such a thing?' Charlie asked after a little.

'Me? No!' She took a moment to consider, and Charlie thought there was calculation behind her eyes. She would not want to be held responsible for someone in her household for such a short time, however struck she was by the death. Then she shook her head again. 'No! How could anyone? Why would anyone? Stabbed? Oh, poor wee lassie!' She laid a hand on Minnie's shoulder. If she believed in the old notion that a victim would bleed again if the murderer touched them, she was sure of her own innocence, anyway.

'Come away back down the stair,' said Charlie, suddenly sorry for her. 'No doubt the mistress will call for tea. You've had a shock.'

And no doubt the mistress will want a word, he added to himself, but he did not want to worry Mrs. Houstoun into flight – she looked edgy enough already. He hurried to the kitchen to fetch tea, and returned to the parlour, hoping that Mrs. Skinner would not dismiss him when he had served them.

'- been working for you?' Mrs. Skinner was saying as he entered the room.

'Only since last Saturday. We've been without a maid for several weeks, so when she ... she turned up,' Mrs. Houstoun pressed a very clean handkerchief to her blue eyes, allowing her to pause for a moment, 'it seemed so fortuitous!'

'She just turned up?' Mrs. Skinner queried. 'Did you know her?'

'Not at all! But I liked the look of her.'

Mrs. Skinner and Charlie exchanged glances over Mrs. Houstoun's head. That was not the recommended way to employ household staff. He could see the mistress was biting her lip to stop herself saying as much. Into the silence, Mrs. Houstoun continued, embarrassed.

'She chapped the shop door after we were closed. Quite a bit after we were closed, actually. I'd just – I was just away to my bed, and I checked the door, and there she was. She looked that cold and starved I could hardly leave her outside, could I? And we needed a maid.'

'And did you like her? Was she working well?'

'Oh, yes! She was canny, and clean, and quiet. My husband

hardly noticed her, which was the main thing.'

Charlie was not completely sure she had meant to let that slip. George Houstoun always looked a sedate, respectable man, but one never knew what went on inside people's homes.

'Did she say a'thing about herself? Where she came from? Why she was looking for work? Where she'd worked before?'

Mrs. Houstoun shook her head briskly, setting the white-fair curls bouncing.

'I just let her get on with her work, ken? There's always plenty to do, is there no?' She tried a bright smile at Mrs. Skinner, but it missed, slightly. Charlie had never known housework get in the way of a good gossip, anyway.

'She said nothing about being frightened of a'body? Hiding from a'body? Did she seem scared to go out?'

'No! Nothing the like of that. Well ...' She reconsidered. 'Maybe the last. I dinna think I sent her out on her own till last night: she came to the kirk with us on Sunday morning, but right enough, she was a bit uncertain about heading out on her own last night. She was a country girl, ken, and if I thought at all I put it down to not knowing her way about. But she was only to go to the candlemaker on North Street, so it wasna far.'

'So you've no idea why a'body would want her dead?'

'I canna believe a'body would want her dead. She was such a wee thing. How could she harm a'body?' She began to weep again, and Charlie, at a nod from Mrs. Skinner, poured her another cup of tea. The mistress had mentioned to him before that no one seemed to be able to drink and cry at the same time: no doubt a useful thing for a clergyman's wife to know.

Mrs. Houstoun did indeed seem to recover with the application of tea, and eventually stood, ready to go.

'Do you want me to make arrangements to have her taken back to our house today?' she asked. 'I mean, she wasna a member of your congregation – it canna be that convenient to have her there in your chapel.'

'Mrs. Gray at the hospital in Queen Street has already offered to have her buried from there,' said Mrs. Skinner gently. 'That is where she was, briefly, before she came to you.'

'At the hospital?' Mrs. Houstoun looked a little surprised. 'As a maid? I wonder why she left there - that would be a grand situation,

I'd have thought. I'll go and speak to Mrs. Gray and see if I can help her in some way.' Her curiosity, belated as it was, faded quickly as she gathered herself to go. Charlie saw her out, and returned to the parlour.

'Well,' said Mrs. Skinner, 'now we know where she was between Saturday and last night. If only all our questions could be answered so quickly and so completely. But what a way to employ staff!'

'Aye, mistress: no recommendation or a'thing.'

'Probably paid her very little, though, under those conditions,' remarked Mrs. Skinner, wisely. 'Well, at least she seemed to be comfortable there: she was clean, and clearly not as weak as she had been at the hospital. But we are still no nearer knowing who killed her, why, or why they brought her to our door. Or if that was even the same person – the one killing and the one bringing?'

'Aye, that's a question, mistress. And if she was off to the candlemaker in North Street – assuming she went where she was bid – that's in the opposite direction from here.'

'Which makes it look more deliberate still.' She frowned, as if trying to picture Minnie's movements last night. Could she have lost herself in the snow? She might not have known this part of the town well in easier circumstances. Mrs. Skinner seemed about to speak again, when the rattle of the risp once more interrupted them. Charlie went to the door.

Dr. Seabury and Mr. Cooper stood outside, eager as ever to begin the day's conversation with Bishop Skinner. Charlie thought Dr. Seabury seemed more relaxed as the week went on: as far as he was concerned, things must appear to be going well. Charlie wondered how he would feel if he knew all that was keeping Bishop Skinner awake just now.

He had barely begun to take their coats when Bishop Skinner appeared at the top of the stairs, and hurried down to greet them again.

'I'm afraid we have very sad news this morning,' he began.

'Not Bishop Petrie?' said Dr. Seabury, instantly anxious. Myles Cooper's shoulders had already shrunk, anticipating some kind of blow. Bishop Skinner frowned.

'No, not Bishop Petrie! He is in excellent health, as much as ever, and is awaiting you upstairs in the bookroom. No, it is the death of someone you met only briefly, but it is a sad case, nonetheless. That servant girl you saw being thrown out of Cuthbert Meston's house – she was found dead last night.'

'Oh, that is indeed sad,' Dr. Seabury agreed. He handed his gloves to Charlie and straightened his coat for the ascent of the stairs.

'I suppose she was out on the streets somewhere?' said Myles. 'It is a tragedy that no one could take her in, in her condition.'

'Oh, but she was taken in – she was staying at a woman's hospital not far from here,' Bishop Skinner explained. 'But she left there – of her own accord, it seems – on Saturday night.'

'Saturday night?' Dr. Seabury stopped on the stairs. 'That is a strange coincidence. Is that not the night that Mr. Meston was killed?'

'It is,' said Mr. Skinner. 'But she was a tiny thing, as you saw, so any thought that she might have tried to take some kind of revenge is highly improbably.'

'Some member of her family, then? The father of her child?'

'That is possible,' the Bishop agreed.

'And yet now she is dead – and the child, of course, too.'

'There is no chance that Meston killed her himself, before he was murdered?' asked Myles suddenly. 'He was such an angry man!'

'No, she died last night. She is resting in the chapel upstairs until her friends take her home – we shall say our prayers in the bookroom.' Now that he had broken the news, the Bishop seemed eager to move on with the day. Mrs. Skinner would have to tell him later all they had discovered. He ushered both the guests before him up the stair, then turned suddenly.

'Charlie,' he said, 'I wonder if I could ask you to do something.'

'Aye, sir, what's that?'

'Could you go to Cuthbert Meston's funeral? I should not like us to be unrepresented, but I have the feeling that Mr. Meston would not go to his rest easily if a bishop attended his burial.'

Charlie smiled.

'No, indeed, sir. Aye, I'll go.'

Chapter Twenty-Nine

'I'll come with you,' said Luzie, when Charlie returned home to don his best clothes. 'I am not enjoying my business today. I am looking out the door every five minutes to see if someone is painting words on my wall. If someone in that household is trying to harm my business, or me, I want to know.'

'I'm no sure that's the best reason to go to a funeral, my love,' said Charlie.

'Oh, I should not cause trouble,' she said. 'I shall know when I tell them my name whether they have done what was done.'

'And then what?'

'And then we shall see,' said Luzie ominously, and wrapped herself in her Sunday cloak as if she were strapping on her armour. Charlie bit his lip. He knew from experience there was nothing he could do to stop her, but he could not say he was looking forward to their morning. He prayed that the flat on the harbour would be so crowded with mourners that Luzie would get nowhere near Stephen Meston, or Jem, or even Alan.

It was indeed busy at the warehouse, but not, perhaps, as gloomy as many funerals. Charlie had the sense that a number of other merchants were attending the occasion to make sure that Cuthbert Meston was really on his way, and for a gossip.

Once again, before Luzie could even approach Stephen Meston or Jem, she was absorbed into a knot of merchants' wives who had secured a couple of benches by the kitchen fire and were taking full advantage of the grieving family's hospitality. It looked as if, for want of any female input in the household, or anyone to cook or bake, Stephen Meston had bought in copious quantities of hot baked goods, and perhaps in case they proved to be less than acceptable he had also provided an apparently endless supply of ale and wine. This early in the morning, such generosity was bound to stimulate conversation. Charlie wondered how many of the mourners would be able to stagger down the stairs for the burial when the time came. He did not want to find himself, for want of anyone better, carrying a corner of Cuthbert Meston's large coffin.

Stephen Meston himself was fretting about the kitchen, trying to make sure that everyone was attended to, that the carpenters knew where they were going for the kisting, that the minister (an alien in that household indeed, but indispensable today) was identified, greeted, and led, apologetically, to the dead room for the prayers. Normally a younger man in the family would ensure the guests were served, and Jem was about, sporadically serving pastries to elderly ladies, interrupting trade conversations with mocking asides, and sprawling in a chair with his hand to his forehead as if stricken by the most profound grief. Charlie wanted to shake him, and yet at the same time found himself feeling sorry for the lad. It was as if he had not been taught what to be, and was trying on endless variations of himself to see what might best fit. Charlie, a servant almost since he could remember, was glad of his own situation. He had never had the luxury of time and money to wonder who he was.

He eased his way politely between the merchants and the neighbours, and managed to catch Stephen Meston at a moment of stillness in the corner by the table, pouring himself a generous glass of wine. It smelled good, but then only the best would be appropriate for Cuthbert Meston's funeral – it was almost an advertisement for business. There was no possibility of a word with Stephen somewhere quiet, but no one was likely to overhear their conversation in the busy chatter around them.

'I've come on Bishop Skinner's behalf,' said Charlie. 'He wanted to pay his respects, but thought his presence here might make others uncomfortable.'

A look of relief did indeed pass over Stephen's face.

'Good of him, that's good of him,' he said. 'Please tell him I appreciated the thought.'

'I've also come with some news,' said Charlie, 'and I'm afraid it's not good news, even on such a day.'

'Oh?' Stephen was puzzled. His eyes flicked about the room, and Charlie thought he was probably checking to see that Jem was safely here.

'It's about your – the maid, Minnie.' He watched as Stephen's expression seemed suddenly to close.

'Is – is she all right?' Stephen asked after a moment. He took a sip of wine. 'Have you found her? Where did she go?' His voice, starting uncertainly, was growing in confidence, but something about the way he asked the questions made Charlie sure that Stephen Meston had known exactly where Minnie had been, at least until Saturday night. And why not, when both Jem and the warehouseman, Alan, had gone to see her there? So why should Stephen pretend he did not know?

Charlie pulled himself back from this train of thought to break his news.

'She's not all right, no. She was found dead last night.'

'Dead? Oh, no. But I thought she – didn't she find shelter, then? It has been so cold. If only I'd known ...' Shakily, he drained his glass, and refilled it.

'You'd have taken her back in?' Charlie tried to keep the surprise out of his voice. 'After your brother threw her out?' After his brother was dead, he added to himself.

Stephen Meston made a face.

'My brother was not so bad as all that. Not as bad as people thought him. Oh, he had a temper, aye, but he rarely bore a grudge, and he was rarely violent.'

Charlie nodded, as if agreeing that this made him a model amongst men.

'You think because he didna like your church – didna like any church, that he was not a good man. But he had his reasons.'

'Oh, aye?' Charlie made it encouraging, rather than cynical, he hoped.

'Aye, he did. See ... you're too young to remember. When would you have been born?'

'In the year '45, so they tell me.'

'Were you? Ill-starred enough.' Stephen stopped for a moment, as if he were sliding back in his own memory. He took another sip and cleared his throat. 'So aye, too young to remember those times, eh? And maybe too young to take sides?' They exchanged a wry smile at that: people might try to forget, but feelings still smouldered – and occasionally flared. 'I suppose with you working for an Episcopalian you'd be more on the side of the – of Charles Edward Stewart, but, well, my father's sympathies were with the Government. And he fought, and we lost him at Culloden.'

'I'm sorry,' said Charlie. Stephen nodded.

'I was five, so I barely remember him. But Cuthbert was nine, and he was devastated. He'd tried to follow our father to the battlefield, and he found his body. The way he told it, he found a priest praying over it. Maybe with the best of intentions – I can see that now that I'm older, of course – but the way my brother saw it, it was like corbie, pecking at the corpse. He couldna get the picture out of his head, and he never went into a church again – neither your kind nor his own. And he brought me up to do the same,' he added, with a slightly embarrassed shrug. 'And old habits are hard to break.'

'I can see that,' Charlie agreed. And after all, the man's soul was his own business – he had no call to explain himself to Charlie.

'Anyway,' said Stephen, waving his glass to punctuate his talk, 'when he met Mrs. Hosie, my late sister-in-law, it made him very sympathetic to poor Jem, who had lost his own father at the same age. They were close, then, those two.' He sighed, looking over to where Jem stood by the fire, one arm flung across the mantle, holding court with the merchants' wives. 'Cuthbert did so much for Jem. It broke his heart when they quarrelled, which they seemed to do more and more often. Jem does not see himself as a merchant,' he explained, smiling faintly.

'What does he see himself as?'

'As to that, I don't think even Jem knows. I hope he finds out soon, though.' He watched his step-nephew a little longer as he finished his wine, and as Charlie looked his expression changed from indulgent to something else – questioning? Concerned? But then Stephen shrugged it off, and turned back to Charlie. 'So my thanks and respects to your master the Bishop. Perhaps, if you tell him something of this, perhaps I might call on him some time?'

'I'm sure you'd always be welcome.'

'And Minnie – where is she? We could –' he looked around him at the flat filled with mourners. 'We could have her back here before the burial.' He refilled his glass. Charlie noted that he was growing more chatty with each glass, but he hoped he would stay coherent.

'As to that, I'm not actually sure,' said Charlie. 'She has been in the chapel where Mr. Meston lay, but friends are to claim her, I believe.' He took a breath, wondering if he should go further, but no harm could come to Minnie now. 'Two sets of friends, actually. Mrs. Gray, the superintendent of the women's hospital in Queen Street, offered to take her, but then her new employer also offered, so I'm not sure where she will go.'

'Her new employer?' Stephen looked startled.

'You might know her, or rather her husband. George Houstoun, a grocer in Longacre.'

'I know Houstoun, yes. We have sometimes supplied him ...' Stephen tailed off, a deep frown furrowing his face. 'Minnie was working there?'

'Since Saturday, apparently, aye.'

'Well, that's ... that's good. That she had somewhere, I mean. But then - I'm not sure I understand - but then how was it that she died out in the street? In the cold?'

'Oh, it wasna the cold that killed her, Mr. Meston. No, someone stabbed her.'

'Someone ... what?' The latest glass of wine lurched and almost spilled.

'Stabbed her. In the back. Then brought her and laid her in the snow, outside the Bishop's front door.'

'But why?'

'I'd like to know that myself,' said Charlie. 'I was wondering if you might have any idea.'

'Me? You're not suggesting that I might have - the night before my brother's funeral?' As if there was an acceptable night for murder, Charlie thought grimly. He had not really intended an accusation, but now they were on that road he pressed on.

'Where were you last night, then?'

'Well, I was here, of course!'

'Alone?'

'No!' Stephen stopped, and corrected himself. 'Well, not all the time. Alan, the warehouseman - he was here later on.'

'And Jem?'

Stephen winced.

'I believe he did get in some time. About three, maybe? But I was here all the time. I was - here all the time.' He spoke with emphasis, but Charlie had the impression he was trying to convince himself as much as Charlie. Had he really been here? And anyway, where had Jem and Alan been?

'Had you sent Alan out for something?' he asked. Stephen shook his head.

'No, he'd gone to see friends - they needed his help with something, he said, or obviously he wouldn't have gone out last night. Jem ... I have no idea.'

It was the answer Charlie had expected.

'Poor Minnie. Who would want to kill her?'

He reached out again for the bottle, and Charlie, noting his hand fumble, wondered if he should stop him from taking any more. He would want to be able to stand up at his brother's grave. But before he could speak, he felt someone touch his elbow, and heard a polite cough.

'Excuse me, Mr. Meston, may I have a word?'

It was Luzie. Charlie felt his heart jump. Stephen looked at her, clearly wondering if he had ever seen her before.

'My wife, Mr. Meston,' Charlie said reluctantly.

'Luzie Rob,' Luzie clarified. 'Trading as L. Rob. In Broad Street.'

Stephen's face drained of colour, and his jaw dropped. There was no doubt now he knew exactly who she was.

Chapter Thirty

'And what do you trade in?' Stephen Meston asked, after a moment.

'You know very well what I trade in, Mr. Meston,' said Luzie. She was keeping her voice down, for now. 'I trade in very much what you trade in. But better.'

'Really?' Stephen managed a polite little laugh. 'Better than ours? I must congratulate you, Mrs. Rob. You have set yourself a very high standard indeed.'

'Set it, and met it,' said Luzie. 'Your brother recognised that when he came and threatened to destroy my business if I would not supply him with coffee, because his customers – your customers – had told him mine was a far superior product. Now that he is dead, no doubt one of your household, or perhaps you yourself, inscribed those words into my shutters yesterday. I warn you, Mr. Meston, I have friends. They, and I, will not be cowed by your threats. It is not my business that will be destroyed, if anything like this happens again.'

Charlie found he was holding his breath. She was wonderful!

For a moment he thought perhaps Stephen Meston was going to agree: a hint of admiration passed over his face. But if he did admire her, he was also not going to allow her to continue.

'I think you'd better leave, now, Mrs. Rob. I have no idea what you are talking about, and we would not want people to think you had come to my brother's funeral to show him any disrespect, would we?'

'You might not,' said Luzie. 'But I think there are a few here who would sympathise with me. Quite a few. But you're right in one thing, Mr. Meston – it is time for me to leave. You have been warned.'

And with her head held high, she turned, and made her way to the door. Charlie managed not to give Stephen Meston a backward glance as he followed her.

Out on the quay, Luzie paced sharply away from view of the flat, then stopped abruptly. Charlie caught her arm: she was shaking.

'Do you think that will work?' she said.

'If it doesna, nothing will,' said Charlie at once. 'You were terrifying!'

She laughed, a little breathless, then looked past him.

'Oh, no,' she said, 'he's sent the stepson to follow us.'

Charlie turned to find Jem Hosie, a little unsteady, almost caught up with them. He stepped in front of Luzie protectively, but Jem said,

'Wait! Please, I'd only just seen you were here when you were leaving. I wanted to talk to you.'

'On your uncle's behalf?' asked Charlie cautiously. Jem frowned and shook his head.

'Why would I be speaking for him? I wanted to ask for news of Miss Skinner – Miss Jane. Is she well?'

Charlie and Luzie glanced at each other. Jem misunderstood.

'She is unwell! My angel – what is the matter? Let me go to her!'

He was on the point of rushing past them, and Charlie had to put an arm across his chest to stop him.

'No! There's nothing wrong with Miss Skinner. Nothing except the upset of some bad news, which will, I fear, be worse for you. A death, of someone you know.'

'Someone I know? And Miss Skinner knows too? Not, I hope, her friend Miss ... um ...'

'No, no friend of Miss Skinner's. Your old maid, Minnie.'

'Minnie? Minnie is dead?' He put his hands to his brows, eyes gaping. 'How do you know? What has happened?'

'I've already told your uncle. She was found in Longacre last night, in the snow.'

'Sleeping in the street?' Jem narrowed his eyes, suddenly looking like a boy playing at being a man. He would not often, Charlie thought, have come across someone of his acquaintance sleeping in the street.

'No,' he said. 'When she left the women's hospital, she found work.'

'Did she? Then she was safe! Oh, but wait – then how is she dead? Was it the baby?' This was accompanied by an embarrassed glance at Luzie.

'It was not the baby,' Charlie reassured him. Then he made sure he was watching Jem carefully. 'She found work with a Mrs. Houstoun, a groceryman's wife in Longacre.' But Jem gave no reaction, nothing like his uncle Stephen. 'Your stepfather apparently had some dealings with him from time to time.' This time Jem made a face, but it was his automatic response to mention of his stepfather, Charlie reckoned. The Houstouns meant nothing to him.

'Was she safe there, then?'

'I believe so, but she ventured out –'

'Into the cold! The poor lass!'

'It was not the cold that killed her,' said Charlie, patiently. 'Someone stabbed her.'

Jem stared at him, his jaw loose, his fists twitching. For a moment Charlie thought Jem was going to punch him. Then the young man sagged from the top down, and fainted in a heap on the slushy stone of the quay.

'Oh, for goodness' sake!' Luzie added a few expressive words in Dutch as she crouched beside Jem, tapping at his jaw to rouse him. She was similarly brisk with their own children, but it seemed to work. And here it had some success, too, for in only a moment or two Jem was sitting up, groaning, and rubbing his elbow which he seemed to have knocked in the fall. Luzie sat back and stood up, brushing dirty snow from her skirts.

'What happened?' Jem asked.

'You fainted when I told you that Minnie had been stabbed,' said Charlie helpfully. He wondered if it would have the same effect, but this time Jem scrambled, not without elegance, to his feet, and contemplated the damage to his black coat and breeches. His lips were pressed tightly together, and he said nothing. With the kind of deliberation that only happens when someone is concentrating very hard on staying upright, he took a few steps towards a bollard, and propped himself carefully against it. Then,

'That is terrible,' he pronounced.

Charlie nodded.

'It's a tragedy, right enough,' he agreed.

'Who did it?'

'No idea.'

'Well, who is going to find out? They must be punished! Oh!' he gasped, running a hand through his hair to render it wilder than ever, then looking rather green. 'Oh, tell Miss Skinner she must not venture out! It is not safe! My stepfather and now Minnie, both in Longacre – she must not go out at all! Unless I am there to protect her!'

'I'll make sure she stays safe,' said Charlie, though high on his list for that would be keeping Jeremiah Hosie well away from her. But it had not occurred to him until now that perhaps the Skinners were in some kind of danger. Perhaps the Bishop was right – everything seemed to be centring on them, and that might not be a safe thing, whatever he did to try to protect them. From Jem or anyone else.

'You'd better get back in to your stepfather's funeral now, or you might miss the burial. Is that the minister?' He nodded at a skinny creature with a nose as thin as a blade, making his uncertain way along the quay towards them, looking up at the buildings as if he was not sure where he was going. Jem stared at him.

'No, the minister's already in. I doubt my uncle would have called in two: it was hard enough to find one that would do the job.'

But the thin man did enter by the warehouse door, and vanished from sight. Jem shrugged.

'Some other fellow come to make sure the old man's dead.'

'Have you and your stepfather never got on?' asked Charlie, remembering what Stephen Meston had said. Jem pursed his lips.

'We maybe did. But then he grew more and more stern, more prone to bad temper.'

'But he still gave you money, supported you.'

Jem was dismissive.

'My mother's money, no doubt.'

'Your mother must have been a wealthy woman!'

'Oh, she was! She was ...' But he looked suddenly unsure, as if he was beginning to wonder just how much he had been spending of his stepfather's money. 'I'd better get in,' he said. Then, with a kind of uncomfortable pride, 'Stephen asked me to take my share of bearing the coffin.'

'Just right,' said Charlie. 'That's just the right thing. You'll do it well.'

Jem turned at last to go back in, and just at that there came a yell from the warehouse doorway.

'Out you go! I'll no have you here!'

To their surprise, the thin man they had just been watching stumbled out of the building, staggered to catch his balance, then with a yelp of distress fled the way he had come. Stephen Meston appeared, watching him go, swaying a little against the doorpost.

'He must have been a minister, then,' said Jem. 'Or asking for charity.'

'We'd better go. Get your uncle some tea before the burial, eh?' Charlie suggested. Jem looked at him blankly for a moment, then back at his uncle.

'Oh! Oh, aye, that's an idea. Thank you. My best greetings to Miss Skinner.'

'I'll tell her,' Charlie agreed.

He and Luzie climbed the hill, arm in arm, back up to the Castlegate. They walked slowly.

'What an extraordinary household,' said Luzie. 'I feel quite exhausted.'

'Aye, I'm the same,' Charlie said. 'I nearly feel as if I've been in a fight.'

'You're very good to Jem.'

'I sort of feel sorry for him,' said Charlie. 'I mean, he's as mad as can be, but he might yet grow out of it, if he's taken in hand.'

'By you?'

'A servant?' He grinned back at her. 'I doubt it. But while he's pals with me because of Jane Skinner, I can maybe do something for him. Pass on my years of wisdom, ken?'

'Aye, right,' said Luzie, squeezing his arm. 'I suppose even a small amount will help, eh?'

They laughed together as they reached Luzie's warehouse. A quick inspection showed no more damage to the shutters, but of course the household were all now at the funeral. As it was daylight, too, with plenty of people about that might see someone up to something, Charlie was not sure it proved anything, but Luzie nodded, as if she had made her point. She unlocked the door and went inside, and Charlie headed on to Longacre and the Skinners' house, hoping he could shake off his fatigue to be of some use for the rest of the day. It was not even dinner time yet, and he felt as if he could sleep for a week.

He slipped up to the chapel first, and found, as he had expected, that Minnie's body had been removed. Jane was rearranging the furniture, so it could not have long happened. She greeted Charlie with a smile as he went to help her.

'Mrs. Gray won, in case you were wondering. She and Mrs. Houstoun had a polite wrangle in the parlour, but it was clear Mrs. Houstoun was really only doing her duty, and Mrs. Gray actually cared for the poor girl.'

'I'm glad,' said Charlie. 'Oh, miss, Mr. Hosie sends his best greetings, and I promised to tell you.'

Jane's nose wrinkled.

'Oh, I suppose it's Mr. Meston's funeral today. Poor Jem: he might have been at odds with his stepfather, but no doubt he'll miss him. And he might have to do some work now.'

'That might be the making of him,' said Charlie. 'Has anything else happened while I've been out?'

'It's been one of those weeks, hasn't it? You'd think you couldn't turn your back but there would be something new. But I'm not sure that anything is – apart from the departure of the body of a murdered girl from the chapel. Did you go to Mr. Meston's burial?'

Charlie cleared his throat, a little embarrassed.

'We were asked to leave before then,' he said, then realised the Bishop had entered the chapel just in time to hear him say it.

'You were thrown out of a funeral? Charlie!' The Bishop's eyebrows rose high. 'I'm shocked! What did you do?'

'Oh ...' Charlie remembered that he had not told the Bishop about Luzie's quarrel with the Mestons. 'Stephen Meston had had too much to drink. We weren't the only ones. A fellow who came after us barely lasted two minutes.'

'I'm sorry I didn't go,' said the Bishop. 'But I'm sure Stephen Meston was upset, and that is probably why he overindulged. It is a very sad day for him, all the more that no one knows yet who was responsible. What are we to do, Charlie? Two people found dead outside in the street, and no notion who killed them. I pray most fervently that somehow, somehow, with God's help we can sort all this out before Bishop Kilgour arrives on Friday.'

Chapter Thirty-One

'Have you sent for the magistrate, sir?' asked Charlie. The Bishop clicked his fingers.

'I knew there was something I'd forgotten. Between Mrs. Gray and Mrs. Houstoun, and Mrs. Skinner telling me all that had happened this morning, and then Bishop Petrie's dog being sick in the dining room, and talking with Dr. Seabury ... but those are excuses. Charlie, would you go then and tell him about Minnie, and where she is now? No doubt he will want to talk to us but he will probably want to see her first.'

Charlie did not want to go anywhere near the magistrate: the man had given him the chills, never mind that he might want to talk to Charlie about Cuthbert Meston and Luzie. But he bowed obediently, considered that his best clothes, which he was still wearing, might impress the magistrate with a sense of his respectability, and headed for the stairs. But even as he reached the bottom step, there was a sharp rap at the door. When he opened it, he realised he would not have to go after all. On the doorstep were Robert Shand, the magistrate, and his grinning henchman.

'I wish to communicate once more with Dr. Seabury,' said Mr. Shand. His voice was almost metallic: it hurt Charlie's ears.

'Of course, sir. Please step into the parlour and I shall see if Dr. Seabury is available.'

'I expect him to be so,' said Shand, shrugging off his coat and allowing Charlie to catch it.

'He's here again, sir,' said Charlie upstairs. 'Looking for Dr.

Seabury.'

'Oh, goodness! Come back downstairs with me, Charlie, and fetch wine. Don't be too efficient: I'll see if I can palm him off without having to disturb the others.'

Yet he hurried down the stairs himself, and Charlie, as he followed, heard him at the parlour door.

'Mr. Shand! You have pre-empted me: I was about to send my man to fetch you.'

'Oh, aye?'

'You'll have heard about the girl found last night?'

'I have. A girl, I believe, not unknown to Dr. Seabury.' His tone was grim.

'As to that, I am not so sure,' said the Bishop. 'He believed he had once glimpsed her, but that is all. Can I offer you some wine against the cold morning? If we are to have a good conversation about this you'll want to be comfortable.'

Grudgingly, Mr. Shand sat on a hard chair. There was something of the sterner reaches of the Kirk about him, Charlie thought, and headed for the kitchen.

Mr. Shand's dim henchman had not followed him into the house, but had been sent off on an errand. He would not be bothering Jean while Charlie attended to the guests. As he returned to the parlour, he could hear the magistrate's clipped tones.

'... took an inordinate time to think of sending to my office, Bishop. I hear the child's body was found yesterday evening.'

'It was – too late in the evening to be bothering you, I thought,' said the Bishop humbly. 'Forgive me if I misconstrued. And then, this morning, people came to identify her.'

'What people?' Mr. Shand ignored Charlie as he placed the tray on the table, and poured wine for both men. He then stood back against the wall, making himself invisible till needed, like any good servant.

'No doubt you will find out very quickly,' said the Bishop. 'She had latterly worked for Mrs. Houstoun, the grocer's wife here in Longacre.'

'I heard she had worked for Cuthbert Meston.'

'Only until last Friday, as I understand it,' said the master. 'It's all quite complicated, I believe. She left the Mestons', then found a temporary refuge at the women's hospital on Queen Street –'

'But that is a respectable house!' It was the closest thing to emotion that Mr. Shand had shown, beyond sour irritation.

'It is, and I'm sure that if it had not been a crisis Mrs. Gray would have abided by the conventions of the place. I believe she has spoken with the trustees. The girl stayed there only one night, then secured a place with Mrs. Houstoun.'

Mr. Shand frowned, lifted his glass and took so tiny a sip from it that it hardly seemed worth the effort.

'Yet you sent word to the Meston household this morning.'

So that was where his information had come from. Charlie was surprised that Stephen Meston had been sober enough to think of sending anyone to the magistrate, or that he had thought it so urgent he must not have waited until after his brother's burial.

'Yes, indeed. I thought it only courteous, as at least two members of that household had been concerned for the girl's safety.'

'Because she had been seen in this area, not far from this house, not far from where Dr. Seabury has been staying.'

'Really?' Charlie marvelled at how calmly the Bishop took that. 'Is that what they said?'

'Why else should they be concerned for a girl they had thrown out?'

'Well, because it was Cuthbert Meston who threw her out, not the rest of them,' said the Bishop mildly. 'The others, as I understand it, were shocked, and worried about her. And with Cuthbert Meston dead, they went looking for her.'

'Dr. Seabury, as I understand it, was there when the girl was thrown out and took some interest in the matter. I should prefer to speak with him.' Mr. Shand's narrow lips closed on the words, and Bishop Skinner sighed.

'Very well. Charlie, will you fetch Dr. Seabury, please?'

Charlie was happy to leave Mr. Shand, and trotted upstairs to the bookroom.

'Dr. Seabury, Bishop Skinner would like a word in the parlour, please, sir.'

'Oh!' Dr. Seabury glanced at Myles Cooper, who, as usual, took on the look of a hunted mouse.

'Is something the matter, Charlie?' asked Bishop Petrie. He was in the chair next to the fire, his lapdog tucked into a blanket on his knee. If Cooper was a hunted mouse, Bishop Petrie was a happy little vole in its nest. Charlie gave his head a little shake.

'No, sir, I don't believe so. Bishop Skinner has a visitor he would like Dr. Seabury to meet.' He was rather proud of that, which was essentially true.

'Well, Charlie, if there is anything I can do to help, anything at all, you know ...' Bishop Petrie fixed Charlie with his bright gaze, and Charlie had the impression that however clever he had been, Bishop Petrie had a clear idea that something was going on. He sighed. He knew it would be easier if Bishop Skinner just accepted defeat and confided in Bishop Petrie.

Down in the parlour, the conversation was relatively short. Robert Shand seemed be so sure that Dr. Seabury had something to do with Minnie's death that in fact he could think of no questions to ask that would advance his cause, going over and over again the brief and only moment when Dr. Seabury had actually seen Minnie.

'Sir, I am doing my best to help here,' said Seabury at last, frustrated with the repetition, 'but in all honesty I only saw her for a few seconds, and that in light that was not the best. She was flung from the doorway, she fell in the snow, I approached her to see if she was all right, and she ran away, up a narrow alley.'

'And what about your quarrel with Mr. Meston?'

'Mr. Meston was probably not even aware that we were there. The door was slammed almost before Minnie had hit the ground. If it even was Minnie. For all I know,' said Seabury, allowing a little anger to show through, 'Cuthbert Meston could have thrown a dozen girls from his door that night, and I only saw the one.'

'Don't be ridiculous, Dr. Seabury,' said Robert Shand through tight lips. 'Why would he throw out a dozen girls? What are you implying about Mr. Meston's household?'

'Nothing! I was just trying to make the point that I only saw a girl being thrown from Mr. Meston's doorway, that I don't really know who she was but on the balance of probability she was this poor child Minnie, but that was the only time I saw her!'

'Why did she take refuge only a couple of streets away from where you were staying? Where you were visiting, too?'

'I don't know! I didn't know she had until today. I don't know this town – I have never been here until last Friday.'

'But you had met Mr. Meston in Edinburgh.'

'Not to my knowledge, no.'

'But you quarrelled with him on the boat. Don't tell me, Dr. Seabury, that you are in the habit of picking quarrels with complete strangers.'

'I didn't pick a quarrel with him. He noticed that we were clergy, and verbally attacked us.'

'I find that most unlikely, Dr. Seabury. Mr. Meston was a prominent merchant in this town.'

'Noted,' Bishop Skinner put in gently, 'for his uncontrolled temper, it has to be said.'

'But towards a stranger? On a boat?' As if that made it more unlikely.

'Perhaps he had had a bad day,' said Bishop Skinner.

'No doubt caused by his meeting you!' The magistrate returned to Dr. Seabury.

And so the conversation turned about, once or twice more, until Mr. Shand seemed to grow bored, and stood to leave.

Bishop Skinner and Dr. Seabury stopped to recover their breaths before returning to the bookroom.

'I am so sorry, Bishop, that all this should have pursued me from the moment I set foot in your town,' said Dr. Seabury. 'The letter from that man representing William Smith, Mr. Meston dead, and now this poor girl!'

The Bishop managed a smile.

'I should rather apologise to you, Dr. Seabury! You've not had a pleasant time of it – more testing than perhaps anyone had intended. And speaking of testing, we had better, if you are ready, return upstairs – if perhaps Charlie would bring some tea? I feel in need of reviving!'

But upstairs, Bishop Petrie was stirring from his cosy chair.

'It's Hepzibah – she needs a little walk, I'm afraid. I shan't be long.'

'Charlie, would you perhaps ...?' asked Bishop Skinner, but Bishop Petrie was determined.

'I shan't put anyone else to any trouble!' he said. 'I won't hear of it!' And so they waited, smiling patiently, as Bishop Petrie organised himself and gathered up the lapdog's lead. They waited again while they heard his light footsteps patter down the stairs, and the front door open and close. Then, collectively, they let out the breaths they had been holding.

'What I don't understand,' said Bishop Skinner, 'is how the magistrate got your name, Dr. Seabury? How did his office attach you to all this in the first place? How did they know you had quarrelled with Cuthbert Meston on the boat? How did they know you were there when Minnie was thrown out? It makes no sense to me whatsoever. You tell me you had never met Cuthbert Meston before that journey, yet he and his household seem determined to do you harm!'

'Perhaps because I am a clergyman ...' began Dr. Seabury uncertainly, but he was interrupted by a noise from Myles Cooper that could only be described as a wail.

'It was I! It was I! All this is my fault!'

Chapter Thirty-Two

'Your fault, Myles?' Samuel Seabury was surprised. 'How could anything make it your fault? Unless you did know Mr. Meston before - had you met him in Edinburgh?'

'No!' Myles' pale hands flapped. 'No, I never saw him until the boat, though the name was familiar ... Though of course we did not hear his name then.'

'Then what is it? How can any of this be your fault?'

'I went to the magistrate!' Myles' hands rose to shoulder level like a couple of overweight birds, then sank at once to lock with each other again. 'I went to the magistrate's clerk the morning after we arrived. I wanted him to know how terribly Mr. Meston had behaved towards you. I told him how horrible he had been. And he seemed inclined to disbelieve me, so I added that we had seen him throwing his maid out of the house.'

'We did, yes,' said Dr. Seabury. 'But -'

'I wanted to make us look better,' said Myles bitterly, 'so I told him we had remonstrated with Cuthbert Meston. That he had sworn at us and chased us away.'

'Oh, goodness, Myles!' said Dr. Seabury. 'I can see your intentions were good, but -'

'And now they will charge you with murder, and it will all be my fault! My fault!' Myles almost sobbed. But he drew breath, trying to steady himself. 'But the worst of it is, Samuel - the worst of it is there is more!'

'Why, what else did you do?' asked Bishop Skinner, seeing

that Dr. Seabury could not bring himself to ask. Charlie felt sorry for Dr. Seabury: Myles was his friend, and was financing him – yet he could not have been an easy man to like.

'When you went to ask about accommodation,' said Myles, still talking to Dr. Seabury, 'a man came up and asked me if I knew you – asked if I could point you out.'

'Oh, dear,' said Dr. Seabury. 'And you said you didn't, I suppose?'

'No, I said I did,' said Myles. 'Of course I said I did. I was not going to deny you!'

'Well, and I am not Christ,' Dr. Seabury pointed out reasonably, in the circumstances. 'So if you did not, as you say, deny me, what did you do?'

'I pointed you out,' said Myles at once. 'Only, you see, I didn't. I pointed to Cuthbert Meston instead.'

There was a moment of awful silence. Charlie looked across at Bishop Skinner. His eyebrows had risen on his high forehead, and Charlie could almost swear he was nodding to himself. More evidence, of course, that Dr. Seabury had been the intended victim. Which meant that he might still be in danger.

Bishop Skinner cleared his throat.

'Do you know anything about this man, Mr. Cooper? Did he give you his name? Give you any indication of his purpose?'

'No, nothing like that, not at all,' said Myles.

'Well, then, what did he look like?'

'I'm not sure ...'

'Was he a gentleman? A tradesman? Someone learned?'

'Learned, I'd say,' Myles decided, with a growing sense of importance.

'Taller than you? Shorter? Did you have to look up to his face?'

'No! No, across, really.'

'Did you feel he was older than you, or younger, or about the same?'

'Older,' said Myles, more confident now. 'Definitely older. His hair was grey and his face was wrinkled.'

'What about his voice? Was it Scottish? Maybe even from Edinburgh?'

'No, not from Edinburgh. More like what we hear here,

though not quite. But Scottish, yes, definitely.'

'Lean? Stout? In between?'

'That's harder,' said Myles. 'It was a cold night, and we were all wearing thick coats or cloaks.'

'What had he, a coat or a cloak?'

'A coat, I believe. And a good solid black hat. Or at least dark-coloured, with a widish brim. Expensive, I remember thinking. He was a respectable man – but one never knows, you know. He could have been up to anything. Which is why –'

'Why you told him Cuthbert Meston was me. And now, oh, my dear Myles, now Cuthbert Meston is dead.'

Myles turned the colour of yesterday's snow, and Charlie thought he might burst into tears. It seemed the full implications of his actions had not previously struck him.

'Oh. Oh, my.' His lower lip wobbled unattractively.

'The thought had occurred to me,' said Bishop Skinner, 'but Mr. Cooper was not to know. But anyway, what was your impression? Was he stout or lean?'

'I – I don't know!' Myles was distinctly unsettled now. 'I don't remember!'

'Well ... was it easy to look round him? Could you see Dr. Seabury and Mr. Meston easily, without having to shift to left and right? I'm assuming you were facing them when this man appeared.'

'Yes, yes, I was watching most carefully in case anything happened to Samuel ...'

'You worry too much, Myles,' said Dr. Seabury, shaking his head.

'Worry too much? But look what's happened! If I hadn't worried too much it could have been you outside there, dead in the horse trough!'

'Stout or lean?' Bishop Skinner persisted, softening it with a smile.

'I don't know! Lean. Lean, he must have been lean. I remember thinking how thin his nose was, and his shoulders – they were very narrow. He was lean.'

'Thank you, Mr. Cooper.'

A thin nose. Something, somewhere in Charlie's head a bell was ringing. A thin nose ... He thought of Jem Hosie – he was lean enough, certainly, with a nose that could be described as thin. But he would not have been deceived when Myles pointed out his stepfather in place of Dr. Seabury, and why would he have been looking for Dr. Seabury anyway? How would he even have heard of him?

Jem Hosie, fainting in the snow that morning, down by the quay. And a thin man, approaching the Meston warehouse as if unsure – a thin, Charlie would have said respectable man, older than Myles, with grey hair under his hat brim. His widish hat brim. Could it possibly have been the same man? Looking, still, for Samuel Seabury?

But that was not quite what had been niggling at him. What was it? He thought back over the conversation just now ... back to Bishop Petrie leaving ... to Robert Shand leaving ...

'The thing is, Bishop, I cannot see why anyone in Aberdeen should want to wish me harm! Wish to prevent me being consecrated, perhaps, should your decision go that way, but wish to kill me? It seems extreme.'

'I agree, Dr. Seabury, and yet there we have two people dead. What is it, Charlie?'

'Sir, the thin man, with the thin nose. I think he was at the Meston warehouse this morning. He was the one that Stephen Meston threw out after we left.'

'Oh, yes? But does that help –'

'Sir – sorry, sir. But I've just realised where I've heard that description before. The man who sent the letter to you from Inverugie – Mr. Seller. The carrier said he was older, respectable, and thin – thin with a nose "like a wee sail on his face to catch the wind", that's what he said. And he said that Mr. Seller was in Aberdeen.'

He had the uncomfortable experience, for a moment, of being the exact focus of every thought in the room. Then Bishop Skinner sat back, and tapped his chin thoughtfully.

'There we are, then. I think, Charlie, it's time we tried to find Mr. William Seller.'

Fortunately it was Wednesday. The Peterhead carrier – and Charlie knew the timetables of several of the carriers, being well used to helping Luzie deliver her goods to them for onward transport –

came into Aberdeen on Saturdays, left on Mondays, reappeared on Wednesdays and left again on Thursdays. Charlie would be able to catch him at the inn on the Castlegate just about now. He hoped that his helpfulness with the muddy cart two days ago would encourage the carrier to answer a few more questions about Mr. Seller.

Certainly the man did not look entirely hostile when Charlie appeared, and accepted the parcel of coffee for a Peterhead grocer that Charlie had thought to collect from Luzie on his way. He sniffed the package.

'Aye, the auld nag aye has a spring in her step when she smells this stuff on the cart!' he said, almost cheerfully. 'I'd best bring it into the inn for the night, mind. We dinna want to keep all the animals in the stables awake till all hours.'

'See, remember last time I saw you I was asking about yon man Seller?' Charlie thought he might as well make a start while the carrier was in a good mood.

'Oh, aye. What now?'

'I was wondering if there was a'thing else you could tell me about him? Where he might be staying in Aberdeen? What he does for a living?'

'You're gey interested in him for a man you havena met,' grumbled the carrier, but he considered, tossing the coffee gently from hand to hand to help him think. 'I believe he was a teacher when he was younger. He still teaches whiles, now I mind it – if a lad is aiming for one of the colleges and needs a wee bittie help with the exams and all.'

'Did he go to one of the colleges himself?' There were two universities in Aberdeen, Marischal College and King's College: Bishop Skinner was a graduate of Marischal, the one that sat at the back of Longacre.

'I believe he did ... maybe he comes in to stay with one of his pals from that time? Ken they're always gey close, they students.'

'I suppose. And if he was a teacher ...' University students, if they were not gentlemen, went on to be teachers, clergy, sometimes doctors ... did that help? Where could Charlie even begin to look?

'I canna mind ...' The carrier screwed up his face terribly, as if squeezing out some half-lost fragment of information. 'Did he say something about a hospital?'

'The Infirmary?'

'I dinna ken. He didna say infirmary, onywyes. Hospital was the word.'

Like the women's hospital where Minnie had taken refuge. Not all hospitals were infirmaries. Hospitals ... Charlie closed his eyes, and in his imagination ran along some of the streets of Aberdeen. Hospitals – oh!

'Could it have been Robert Gordon's Hospital? Ken, the poor boys' school?'

'A school and a hospital – d'you know, it might just have been that?' The carrier thought for a moment, then nodded. 'It was that, I believe. Someone he knew there. A teacher, like himself.'

'Thank you!' said Charlie, bouncing on his toes to be gone. 'Thank you!'

'Aye, well,' said the carrier after him as he skipped from the stable yard, 'you can wash my cart again next time it needs it!'

Robert Gordon's Hospital was a charitable institution for the education of the promising poor of the town. Set in its own grounds, it was home to, Charlie thought, a couple of dozen lads identifiable by their uniforms – tailed coats, yellow buttons and blue woollen bonnets - on the occasions when they were permitted to march through the gates and attend the town kirk. Charlie vaguely knew the master by sight, but now he thought about it, it was an elderly assistant he had in mind, one who stooped along at the back of the short procession and kept an eye on the stragglers. He would be closer to the age of the mysterious Mr. Seller, and might well have been one of his colleagues at King's or Marischal.

An enquiry at the gate gave him a name, and also an address – outside the school grounds, and along a lane to a cottage that overlooked the hospital's pleasant gardens. There was nothing as sophisticated as a risp, so Charlie rapped on the weathered wood of the door. In a moment, an elderly maid answered.

'I'm looking for a Mr. Figgis,' said Charlie with a polite smile. 'Is this his cottage?'

'It is, sir,' said the maid. 'Who shall I say?'

'I'm here from Bishop John Skinner, in Longacre.'

There was a sudden scrape from within, as if someone had pushed their chair back in alarm. Charlie said quickly,

'It's actually a Mr. Seller I'm seeking. A Mr. William Seller.'

From the dim hallway emerged a figure, tallish, graceful, and very thin. Even in the poor light Charlie could see how fine his nose was, the merest slice.

'Mr. William Seller? I am he. What is the Bishop's will?'

Chapter Thirty-Three

'Good day to you, sir,' said Charlie. 'Bishop John Skinner presents his compliments, and asks if you would be kind enough to visit him at his house in Longacre.'

'Longacre? Where's that?' The man's voice was as thin as the rest of him, thin and rather sharp.

'Off the Broadgate,' came a voice from inside the house. The elderly assistant master Charlie had remembered appeared, stooped but smiling. 'I warned you not to toy with bishops, Will – now you are summoned by one!'

'It may be a matter of the greatest gravity, Archie,' said Mr. Seller, but Charlie thought he looked worried. While the maid helped Seller into his coat and the friend Archie teased him with the ease of old acquaintance, Charlie took the chance to give Seller a good look over. He did not seem strong enough to hold Cuthbert Meston's head down in an icy horse trough, though he might have been more wiry than he appeared. Physically, he could easily have killed Minnie. But in his heart, was he a killer? Charlie was not sure. The one thing he did know was that this was certainly the man he had seen only this morning, being thrown out of the Meston flat. It was one question answered. But what had he been doing there?

With the assistance of Archie, who had a key, they were able to take a short cut through the Hospital grounds with their serried trees, over which the school building, modestly domed, maintained a watchful eye. At Schoolhill Archie bade William Seller farewell and good luck, and Charlie led him up the Kirkgate to Broad Street and into Longacre. Mr. Seller looked dubious at the dark passageway, and relieved when they emerged into the decent street beyond – if he were trying to pretend that he had never been here before, Charlie thought it was convincing.

With Mr. Seller established in splendid isolation in the parlour, Charlie went to fetch Bishop Skinner.

'Mr. Seller, sir, in the parlour.'

'Already, Charlie?' Bishop Skinner sat up in surprise. 'Well done!' He glanced at the clock on the mantel. 'There should be time before supper. He spoke softly, for Bishop Petrie and his lapdog were dozing by the fire. 'Dr. Seabury and Mr. Cooper did not, I think, expect you to return with him so quickly – they have returned to the inn for a rest. I believe Mr. Cooper has not been sleeping well. But let us go and attend to this matter.'

'Seller, did you say?' Bishop Petrie was not as dozy as he had seemed – even the lapdog pricked up her ears. 'Not the man who wrote to our brother Kilgour about Dr. Seabury?'

'Ah,' said Bishop Skinner, 'As it happens, yes. I believe so, anyway.'

'I thought you had satisfied yourself on that point, John,' said Petrie, mildly. 'That the man he mentioned, Dr. Smith, was a jealous troublemaker, ambitious to be the first American bishop himself.'

'Well, I –'

'Surely you have not summoned him all the way from Inverugie?' Bishop Petrie seemed not to hear Bishop Skinner. 'That is remarkably thorough of you!'

'But I thought –'

'Or is there more to this than meets the eye, John? Charlie seems to have been very busy these last few days, and you yourself have a grey look about you, and I am convinced that this cannot all be put down to concern over Dr. Seabury's possible consecration, nor even to anxiety for your wife in her present condition. I know you, John – remember our long conversations before your own consecration? I know you will always try to do your best. But it is important to remember that you do not have to be alone doing your best – and the decision over Dr. Seabury will be better taken by all of us not only with God's direction, but also with all the information we have at our disposal – shared between us.'

Bishop Skinner's head had sunk further and further as

Bishop Petrie had spoken. By the end he looked so despondent that the lapdog dropped down from Bishop Petrie's lap and went to place a paw on Bishop Skinner's knee. Charlie knew how she felt, but he was glad it had come to this. Bishop Petrie was always brighter than people supposed.

Bishop Petrie waited patiently. Bishop Skinner wriggled his shoulders.

'I cannot explain it all to you now,' he said. 'Not with Mr. Seller waiting downstairs. Can I say for now that a man is dead, that the magistrate has had his attention drawn inadvertently to Dr. Seabury in connexion with the death, but that I think there is a chance the man was killed by someone thinking that he was Dr. Seabury? And as Mr. Seller had seemed to know something about a threat to Dr. Seabury, and as Charlie discovered that Mr. Seller was in fact in Aberdeen, it seemed to make sense to meet him and ask him why he sent that letter, and what he knows?'

Bishop Petrie gave a little nod, as if he had expected as much.

'And you thought, no doubt, to have the whole matter cleared up before Bishop Kilgour and I even appeared, so as not to worry us! And then I appeared early – oh, dear, I am sorry, John!'

'You are always welcome, Bishop,' said Bishop Skinner sincerely.

'Then allow me to help,' said Bishop Petrie. 'Allow me to join you in your meeting with Mr. Seller. Bishop Kilgour sent me a copy of his letter, you know. I should be very interested to meet the man himself.'

'I should be grateful for any help, sir,' said Bishop Skinner. Then he added with a grin, 'Any at all! I am confounded by this matter – any answers we discover only provoke more questions!'

'Then let us go and examine this curious person,' said Bishop Petrie.

Reminiscent of Robert Shand, the magistrate, earlier, William Seller was seated on a hard chair, back straight, feet together, hands folded on his lap. Unlike Robert Shand, however, the moment he saw the two bishops, he sprang to his feet.

'Mr. Seller,' said Charlie, presenting him. 'Bishop Petrie, and Bishop Skinner, sir.'

'My lords,' said Mr. Seller, breathless, but Bishop Petrie

interrupted him.

'No lords here, sir, just bishops.'

'Please sit down, sir,' added Bishop Skinner. 'Thank you for coming to see us.'

'I am honoured if I can be of any assistance,' Mr. Seller assured him.

'And we'll be delighted. Are you the William Seller of Inverugie, who took the trouble to send a letter to Bishop Kilgour in Peterhead, concerning a Dr. Samuel Seabury?'

'I am, sir. Bishop.'

'Bishop Kilgour forwarded to both of us a copy of the letter,' said Bishop Skinner. 'I wonder if you would be good enough to explain again how you came to write it?'

'Well, it was a curious thing,' said Seller, not at all reluctant to tell his story. 'I was pleased to receive, quite unexpectedly, a letter from an acquaintance in London. We had been at school together, here in Aberdeen. At the Grammar School. I progressed to King's College, to my good fortune, while he went south to be, I believe, a merchant, in his uncle's business in Chelsea, near London.' He sounded impressed – Charlie guessed that Mr. Seller had never travelled so far himself. 'And out of the blue he wrote to me in Inverugie. He had remembered that I was an Episcopalian – a reason for our friendship in those benighted days – and he was kind enough to assume that I might be acquainted with Bishop Kilgour. Well, of course, I know Bishop Kilgour by sight, and the matter my old friend described seemed serious enough that I felt I could indeed take the liberty of writing to Bishop Kilgour on the subject, though the connexion was tenuous enough – my school friend's cousin's brother. This Samuel Seabury seemed guaranteed to do harm not only to the reputation of you three gentlemen who were asked to consecrate him, but to the whole church, both here and in America. And when relations with England are so delicately balanced, this seemed to me too much to risk.'

'So you sent the letter,' said Bishop Skinner. Charlie glanced at Bishop Petrie, who appeared to be focussed on scratching the ears of his lapdog, but Charlie was absolutely sure that not a word of the conversation escaped him. Much of this must be new to him: he was soaking it in. 'And did you attempt to follow it up with any further action?'

'Further action?' Mr. Seller was puzzled.

'Did you, for example, intend to pay a visit to Bishop Kilgour?'

'No, I should not presume so much!'

Bishop Skinner nodded.

'Then did you, perhaps, send another letter? To him, or to either of us?'

'Another letter?' Mr. Seller shook his head. 'Again, I should have thought that presumptuous. I had given over the information I had received. It would not be my place to see that anything was done about it. That would have looked as though I did not trust Bishop Kilgour.'

'So this, then,' Bishop Skinner produced a paper from his pocket, 'is unfamiliar to you?'

He spread the paper before Mr. Seller. Charlie could see it was the second, anonymous, letter with its brusque message. Mr. Seller read it quickly, and made an odd little squeak of alarm.

'Entirely unfamiliar! I have never seen it before – nor, I believe, is the hand known to me. This – this is a threat!'

'It certainly looks like one, yes.' Bishop Skinner stood and laid the paper on the parlour table, then leaned against the back of a chair. 'So you came here to Aberdeen to meet Dr. Seabury, then?' asked Bishop Skinner. 'Perhaps to make sure in that way that the information had been received, and was used?'

'No, not really,' said William Seller. 'In fact, I don't know how you knew I was here.' He gave a little shrug, as though acknowledging that bishops moved in ways it was not his place to understand. 'I was to visit my friend at Gordon's Hospital, and as I set off I received word from a friend in Edinburgh that Dr. Seabury was on his way here. As I was near the harbour, I went to enquire, and found a man who knew Seabury by sight and pointed him out to me. But it was late in the evening: Seabury appeared to be staying with friends by the quay and, satisfied that I at least knew where he was, I let him be and carried on to my friend's house for supper. And there I left it – that would have been Friday night – for we were much engaged until this morning, when I thought I should call on him. I had nothing to say to him, I admit, but I was curious to meet a man whose ambition had driven him from New York to London to Edinburgh to Aberdeen. But alas, it seems that I had interrupted a family funeral. And perhaps his friends there had come to realise what like of a man he was, too for at the very mention of the word 'clergyman', I was shown the door in a very forthright manner. Very forthright indeed,' he repeated, unconsciously rubbing his arm. Charlie thought it must be where Stephen Meston had grabbed him to propel him through the door.

'So it was Samuel Seabury you were looking for at the quay this morning?'

'It was, sir, aye, indeed.'

'And you know nothing of the family you called on there?'

'Nothing - nothing at all. They seemed to be merchants, perhaps?'

'They are, yes,' said Bishop Skinner.

'Then you too have tracked Dr. Seabury down! Or has he been already to trouble you to pursue his goal?'

Bishop Skinner cleared his throat, glanced at Bishop Petrie for support, and leaned forward, elbows on his knees.

'Mr. Seller, what if I were to tell you that Bishop Kilgour knows Dr. William Smith of old? Knows his reputation, at any rate. And that all of the ambition and manipulation and deviousness which Dr. Smith lays at Samuel Seabury's door is, in fact, his own?'

Chapter Thirty-Four

'His - his own?' Mr. Seller frowned. 'But surely not! My friend, my old school friend, he was quite sure ...'

'I fear he has been tricked,' said Bishop Petrie gently. 'Or misled. There has been plenty of time since Samuel Seabury's arrival in England for Bishop Kilgour, knowing this occasion might arise, to correspond with friends in America and with the other clergy of Connecticut. There is no doubt that they are in full support of Dr. Seabury, and that Dr. Smith is - oh, dear - not well-regarded except by a small coterie of friends.'

'And I, like a fool, was flattered into believing it all! Oh, this makes me most cross! Most cross!' His pale face pinkened, and his knees rose so that his feet stood on tiptoe. 'I must beg your forgiveness, Bishop Skinner, and Bishop Petrie, and I must write to Bishop Kilgour straight away, and oh! But I should apologise to Dr. Seabury, too! For he is the one to whom I in my pride and vanity have done the most damage! What if you had not known? What if you had believed me? Is - tell me, is he a good man? Will he be consecrated?'

'As to the second, I cannot yet say,' said Bishop Skinner carefully. 'But as to the first, I think I am convinced that yes, he is a good man.' He met Bishop Petrie's eye. Bishop Petrie gave a little nod.

'Then I must indeed make reparation,' Mr. Seller continued. 'Can you tell me where I might find him? Or how I might send him a message?'

'Of course - we can arrange that. If you'd like to write it now

I can be sure it reaches him,' said Bishop Skinner.

Or you can meet him yourself, Charlie thought, if you stay much longer. But he was not sure that Mr. Seller would be able to face that last indignity. Instead Charlie fetched pen and ink from the bureau in the corner, and brought paper to the parlour table. As he arranged it, Bishop Skinner asked, almost casually,

'By the way, where were you on Saturday night?'

'With my friend at Gordon's Hospital. The boys have an early supper on Saturdays and we supped with the master in his apartments.'

'And last night?'

'Last night?' Mr. Seller blinked at the odd questions, but he was not going to hold back, not if he could restore himself in their eyes. 'Last night we supped with the boys in their hall, then retired again to the master's lodgings. It was a most instructive and pleasant evening.' He sighed.

'And you were nowhere near here?'

'Sir,' said Mr. Seller, 'I did not even know this street existed until today!'

Mr. Seller, not at all satisfied with the reliability of his own judgement any more, left as soon as he had written the note, barely waiting to scatter sand over the wet ink before he was on his feet. Charlie had been offered as his escort back to the cottage behind Gordon's Hospital, and he had gratefully accepted. At the mouth of Longacre they met Dr. Seabury and Mr. Cooper heading in the opposite direction with a lantern of their own: Dr. Seabury gave Charlie a surprised wave, and Charlie bowed and continued. Mr. Cooper, by contrast, stared at Mr. Seller as his usual hunted look settled on his face. He had recognised, no doubt, the man he had misdirected down at the harbour.

By the time Charlie returned, Jean was already heaping the supper into lidded dishes for carrying to the table.

'Och, I'm right glad to see you, Charlie. Is this you working here another twa-three minutes afore you're off some place else again?'

Charlie thought it would be best to make a joke of it.

'Aye, I thought I would drop in and see how you were getting on. Will I help you take a few of these dishes in, then?'

'Since you're here,' said Jean, barely mollified.

Jean, with her one arm, could not lift any of the dishes once they were full, so of course Charlie carried them in to the dining room, as he always – or almost always – did. Bishop Petrie was right: Charlie had been busy this week, and poor Jean had been left to cope. He hoped he would be able to make it up to her when all this was done – whenever that might be.

Bishop Skinner had evidently found the opportunity to give Bishop Petrie more details about all that had been happening: when Charlie went to tell the household that supper was ready, he found Myles Cooper lamenting again his many sins, his misguided contact with the magistrate's office, his misidentification of Cuthbert Meston as Samuel Seabury. Everyone else looked a little weary of his confessions, but Bishop Petrie was sitting forward, absorbing all the details. Charlie prayed his involvement would move matters on now. He thought Bishop Skinner looked a little relieved, with his burden at least shared.

As supper progressed, it became clear that in fact there had been a general exchange of information while he had been out. Dr. Seabury withdrew from his pocket, on several occasions, Mr. Seller's abject apology for assisting, however innocently, in maligning him.

'He should not have jumped to conclusions!' Myles Cooper wagged a finger sternly.

'Nevertheless he is innocent, and thought only to save the reputation of the Church,' said Seabury, not for the first time. Bishop Petrie nodded approval again, but Seabury continued. 'And also, if this is the man who you thought might have mistaken Mr. Meston for me –' something like a sob emerged from Myles – 'then surely I am at no risk now? In fact, there was never a physical threat?'

Charlie, topping up glasses discreetly, was not sure that Dr. Seabury should look so pleased at that – if he had not been the intended victim, then questions arose once more as to his innocence of the killing. But then, he thought to himself, did that not in itself prove Dr. Seabury's innocence? If he had instinctively wanted to defend himself against accusations that were true, he would surely maintain this mistaken identity theory. After all, he could hardly kill someone else mistaking him for himself. Charlie imagined that suicides were rarely cases of mistaken identity.

But he had forgotten something.

'My dear,' said Mrs. Skinner, as involved in the debate as ever, 'have you not told Dr. Seabury about the second letter?'

'Oh!'

'What second letter?' asked Myles at once. 'Who offers a new threat?'

'Shall I fetch it, sir?' Charlie asked, pausing in his pouring.

'Not at all, Charlie, I shall run along.'

Bishop Skinner was back in moments with the second, the anonymous, letter he had left in the parlour.

'It was a local delivery,' he explained, handing it to Dr. Seabury. 'It was pushed under the door.'

Dr. Seabury took it, and read it, lips pressed taut. Then, as if trying to make sense of it, he read it again, aloud.

'The foreigner with his English friend is not fit to be a bishop, in America or anywhere else. If you consecrate, there will be consequences.'

Myles yelped.

'That is a real threat! A genuine one! That is proof that Samuel is the intended target! Have you shown this to the magistrate?'

'Have you any idea,' said Bishop Petrie, 'who could have sent this? Is it, do you think, the work of your acquaintance, Dr. Smith?'

Dr. Seabury set the letter down delicately on the table, as if it had thorns.

'This is not, I think, Dr. Smith's style. He is too confident of his own virtues to try something anonymously.'

'Someone who supports him?'

'Someone local here? But who?' He sat back in his chair, one hand toying with the stem of his wine glass. It looked tiny and fragile in his fingers. 'The way he used Mr. Seller is much more what I would expect of Dr. Smith. An innocent man made to think he is doing the right thing, on the basis of good reports of Dr. Smith and insinuations about his opponent. This,' he touched the edge of the letter with one wary fingernail, 'is too ... too violent for Dr. Smith.'

'It must be someone local,' said Myles. 'Someone who knows me, too! His English friend! We are both in danger!'

'Could it be someone local, in fact?' asked Dr. Seabury. 'I mean, someone unconnected with Dr. Smith – someone who does not know us personally but for more ... political reasons might want to prevent any consecration here?'

'As to that ...' Bishop Skinner looked to his wife, and then to Bishop Petrie. 'No doubt there would be those who might find something to object to.'

'Our brother Bishop Rose, in Fife,' said Bishop Petrie with a sigh.

'Bishop Charles Rose? I have heard of him, of course. But why should he object?' asked Dr. Seabury, alarmed.

'Bishop Rose is more Jacobite than the Jacobites!' said Bishop Skinner with a smile.

'But with sad reason, too,' added Bishop Petrie. 'Maybe you have heard of Robert Lyon? A priest of our church, and a good friend of Bishop Rose – in fact, intended to marry his sister. The rebellion did not end well for him, I'm afraid.'

'But I am no Englishman,' protested Dr. Seabury. 'I may have been on the Government side in our own war, but that, surely, is not relevant here?'

'It is enough for Bishop Rose, I'm afraid, that you were ordained in England originally. But our brother Rose would not send anonymous threats – or any threats, come to that. I should think that if there is to be a consecration, Bishop Rose will simply send his apologies and say that a sudden ague has made travel impossible that day.'

'I – I see.' Dr. Seabury's gaze fell once again on the letter. 'Then if that is the worst you can think of ... who would have sent this? And what do they mean, consequences? And do they hate me, or what I stand for, or the thought of me as a Bishop, or the thought of a bishop for the American church?'

'It does seem more personal than that,' said Mrs. Skinner, who could not see the letter clearly from where she sat, but had obviously digested it. '"Not fit to be a bishop" – that sounds as if there is some reverence for the episcopal state, at least.'

'But do they mean he is not fit because of his character, or because, for example, he was ordained in England? It's still not clear,' her husband objected.

'I believe that I detect in it some animosity against the church, madam,' said Bishop Petrie. 'As if they suspected we could not manage our own affairs. But I agree, there is something personal about that point.'

Dr. Seabury sighed.

'You will be wishing we had never come here, Bishop Skinner. We have brought nothing but trouble to your house.'

Bishop Skinner smiled.

'It's hardly your fault, Dr. Seabury. We shall resolve this, no doubt, by some means and by God's help.'

'Charlie, will you see to the parlour fire, please?' asked Mrs. Skinner. 'We'll come in shortly.'

'Aye, mistress.'

He took a couple of the emptied dishes with him, and when he had left them in the kitchen he slipped back to the parlour. All was cosy, but he had not had the chance to tidy after Mr. Seller's visit. The pen, ink, sand and paper were all still on the table. He tucked them back into the bureau in the corner, straightened the table cloth, and picked up another piece of used paper that lay beside the lamp. The lamp had not been lit, so he pushed the paper into his pocket while he fetched a spill from the mantelpiece and lit it at the fire. Then he straightened the chairs, made sure that there was a comfortable cushion on the sopha for Mrs. Skinner, and nodded. All was trig, and the brandy decanter and glasses were ready on the sideboard. He hoped that Myles Cooper would not overindulge this evening, for it took twice as long to escort him back to the inn when he and Dr. Seabury had to support him between them. And if Mr. Cooper would only consider - he would be much less vulnerable to a killer if he were only sober enough to run away.

Chapter Thirty-Five

But he returned Dr. Seabury and Myles, unsteady but generally moving independently, to the inn without incident. Snow was falling again as he checked the Skinners' front door and glanced about Longacre, just in case. No bodies – it was a strange thing to be relieved about.

Luzie was taking stock in the warehouse when he reached home, but she paused in her counting to greet him.

'All well?' she asked.

'As well as it can be, I suppose, in the state we're in. That thin man, the one we saw thrown out by Stephen Meston, that was the man that sent the letter warning that Dr. Seabury would not be right as bishop and the Connecticut clergy wouldn't support him.'

'That man? What is he doing in Aberdeen?'

Charlie explained, as best he could, and at the same time shifted some sacks and barrels to help Luzie get to all her stock. It was not a large warehouse, but the goods were magical – all those scents, the shapes of seeds and beans and bark and root, the thoughts of how far they had travelled to reach Scotland. And how Luzie could distinguish between each, smelling the variation between shipments and origins, picking out the very best: he was tremendously proud of her.

'Any bother today?' he asked.

'None at all, with them all at the funeral. Or drunk,' she added.

'Well, that's something.'

'In fact, good sales today,' she went on, 'and one or two new orders. I think I may have benefitted from the Meston warehouse being closed.'

'It's an ill wind,' Charlie agreed, though the thought made him slightly uncomfortable.

'You're still in your best clothes from this morning,' she remarked. She herself had exchanged her Sunday bell hoops for pocket ones, much easier for manoeuvring about the warehouse. 'I'd best brush them down when you're in your nightshirt.'

'Aye, I don't want to be doing any more work in these if I can help it.'

Back in the kitchen, supper was already laid out. He pulled off his coat and waistcoat at Luzie's gesture, and handed them over for brushing.

'You ken I cannot sit down to eat if I can see work to be done!' she said with a grin.

'Then I'll hide my legs under the table until you've eaten your supper,' he said, 'and you can brush my breeches later.'

The food was cold anyway, bread and cheese and ale, so he waited for her, cutting some thick slices of the bread and cheese for each of them.

'You've a bit of paper in here,' said Luzie, checking his pockets.

'Oh, I shouldna! I picked that up in the parlour. What is it, anyway?'

Luzie, being Luzie, sniffed it before reading the direction.

'It's a wrapper from a letter. "Bishop Skinner, Longacre." Interesting,' she said.

'Oh! I ken what that's from. Here, I'd better take it back in the morning, in case he wants to show it to the magistrate.'

'That? What would the magistrate need to see that for?'

'It's the wrapper from another letter,' said Charlie. Luzie folded the coat and waistcoat and laid them on a kist, then sat down with him. She poured out ale into two cups. 'A letter threatening "consequences" if Samuel Seabury is consecrated bishop.'

'Another one? From the same man?'

'No – he denies it, and the hand is very different. But it's local, as you see.'

'I saw that, aye. So who did send it?'

'We dinna ken. It's no signed.'

'Interesting.'

Charlie swallowed a bite of bread and cheese.

'You said that when you sniffed the letter. Go on, then: what does it smell of? A special scent from a grand lady who's husband was murdered by the Jacobites?'

She grinned back at him.

'I havena had much opportunity to sniff grand ladies,' she said, 'though I daresay it would be an experience. But no: I'd say that letter's spent a bit of time in a warehouse not unlike mine.'

'Not unlike yours?'

'Aye, but not mine. The coffee is different, though the spices are very similar.'

'Luzie! Are you sure?' He had not noticed any smell himself, but then he was not Luzie.

'Oh, aye. It's quite distinct – I think there's maybe even a wee bit of clove dust in the folds.'

'Coffee, but not yours ... anyone else's that you can say?'

She wriggled on the bench, frowning.

'You'll not think I'm making it up?'

'Of course not. Why would I think that?'

'Because I'm almost certain it's the coffee that the Meston warehouse stocks. Almost certain – in fact, let's say I'm certain. After all, I only smelled it this morning.'

'Well ...' Charlie's head was spinning. If the Mestons had sent this – if Stephen Meston had, then what did it mean? He had shown no great animosity to Episcopalians. What was he up to? 'The magistrate will never believe this.'

Luzie shrugged.

'Then if it's useful information, make use of it yourself. Tell Bishop Skinner. I'll take an oath, if he wants me to.'

'From Meston's warehouse ...' He believed Luzie completely, but it still did not make sense. 'I'm going to have to sleep on this. I'll tell the Bishop in the morning, anyway.'

'Well,' she said, 'I'm glad you don't feel the need to run across and tell him now. Just when I've got you back for the night.'

And that was Wednesday, he thought to himself on the edge of sleep. A day full of incident, but a day closer to Bishop Kilgour's arrival, and it felt as if they were no closer at all to finding out who had killed Cuthbert Meston and Minnie, and whether or not Dr. Seabury was involved. At least Charlie was not on his own here, as he had been once before: Bishop Skinner and Bishop Petrie, not to mention Mrs. Skinner, were all much more capable than he was. But there were things he could contribute, he knew. Between them, maybe they would work it all out.

But what he really wanted to know, since it involved the threats Cuthbert Meston had made against Luzie and her business, was what it was about Broad Street and Longacre that had drawn all the incidents here. Could it be coincidence? Cuthbert Meston took the trouble to come up here even when he was tired from his journey from Edinburgh. He died here the following night - with no lantern. Minnie sought shelter only a street away, found work at the end of the street, and then was left on the Skinners' doorstep. Jem and Alan had come looking here for Minnie. Jem was often seen lingering about Longacre in the hope of seeing Jane Skinner - at least, that was what he said. Dr. Seabury and Mr. Cooper had taken a place in the inn only a few minutes' walk away. In fact, the only person he could think of attached to the matter who had nothing to do with Longacre at all was Mr. Seller. Did the matter really revolve around the Skinner household and the arrival of Dr. Seabury? Or was Cuthbert Meston the real focus?

The faces of Meston, and Seabury, and Myles, revolved slowly in his mind's eye, more and more slowly, until at last they faded away, and he slept.

Thursday's first impressions were, for most people, good. There was a hard frost on the new snow, which made moving about, on foot or with wheels, a bit easier. Dawn was late, of course, but the day was as bright as anyone could expect of the eleventh of November. It lifted Charlie's spirits a little, before he considered the implications. A good heavy fall of snow might have delayed Bishop Kilgour: this weather would help him on his way.

Some of the neighbours had had to work at the pump before Charlie reached it, to melt the solid ice inside. It was work that some of them enjoyed, standing in the snow with hot stones forming a little cone of heat around the pipes, waiting for the gurgle and crack that told them they were not working in vain. Charlie stamped his feet as he waited his turn. The horse trough was still frozen hard, but mercifully seemed this morning to contain nothing but water. And he could see Johnnie Skinner sent out to sweep the doorstep before he went to school, and there were no corpses there, either. Maybe the day was not a bad one, after all.

He took the water home, broke his fast with coffee, and kissed goodbye to Luzie before heading back to Longacre to start work there. In his pocket he carried the letter wrapper: he wondered what Bishop Skinner would say to Luzie's information. Would it help at all?

'She's quite sure?' asked Bishop Skinner. He had reunited the letter and its wrapper, and laid them out on his desk in the bookroom. His question was not distrustful: he knew Luzie.

'She says so. She was only down at Meston's warehouse yesterday morning, sir, so she had a clear memory of it.'

'Of course, for the funeral.' Bishop Skinner rose, and leaned against the desk. 'What do you think, Bishop Petrie?'

'I have not had the pleasure of meeting any of the household,' said Arthur Petrie, once again cuddled into the chair by the fire, 'but from what you said, I should have thought this letter derived more from the dead brother than from the living one. But what about the stepson? Could he have done such a thing?'

Bishop Skinner looked at Charlie.

'You have met him more often than I have. What do you think, Charlie?'

'The style would appeal to him,' said Charlie at once. There was something quite dramatic about the letter. 'But I think Jem Hosie is wrapped up in what he thinks of his family, and in being a young man who has not yet found a purpose in life. I doubt he has thought over-much about bishops and the like.'

'Interesting - thank you, Charlie.' Bishop Skinner pondered. 'I suppose Mrs. Rob would not, being in the same business, have a sample of Stephen Meston's handwriting about her warehouse, at all?'

'I'd be surprised, sir, they don't do much business between them.'

'So nothing of Cuthbert Meston either, then. And certainly not Jem Hosie's.' He thought for another moment. 'I know you said your attendance at the funeral ended badly, Charlie, but if you went back down there to the Meston warehouse, do you think any of them would help you identify the hand?'

'I doubt it, sir,' said Charlie. 'Not for a few days, at least. Stephen Meston was in his cups but I think he'd just seen a bittie too much of me recently.'

'I see. That's unfortunate.'

'Aye, sir. I'm sorry.'

'It's more likely my fault,' said Bishop Skinner. 'I'm too eager to get this matter sorted out. You'd think they would be, too, though I suppose they don't see our questions as a means to that end.'

'It's quite a busy wee street, is it no?' said Bishop Petrie. 'Longacre, I mean. I've never glanced out the window but there was at least two or three people up and down, about their business. You'd think maybe somebody would have seen something, if not when your Mr. Meston was killed - that was near the middle of the night, was it no?'

'Aye, sir, and no lantern,' said Charlie, unable to resist mentioning his puzzle.

'In the dark, of course. But the girl - Minnie, is it? Poor soul - she was left outside much earlier in the day. Did no one see what happened? Did no one wonder at someone dumping a bundle outside someone's door, and leaving?'

'It's true,' said Bishop Skinner. 'I don't believe anyone has really asked the neighbours what they saw. That's a good idea: even after dark, at this time of year, there are usually plenty of people about. Right! How do we go about this? Charlie, what do you think?'

I think, said Charlie to himself, that Jean will be laying the table for dinner on her own again today.

'Aye, sir, I could make a start. Straight away if you please.'

'You might as well, Charlie. They'll talk to you.'

They would indeed. He just hoped that at least one of them would say something useful.

Chapter Thirty-Six

Bodsy Bowers, the school teacher, would just be preparing for his pupils coming. The architect down at the end was a bit too grand for Charlie – he might have to ask Mrs. Skinner to talk to his wife, as a better tactic. Mrs. Houstoun must not have seen anything, or she would not have been looking for Minnie the next day. Charlie was still pondering where else to start as he left the house, and almost immediately noticed a familiar figure propped in a doorway across the street. It was Jeremiah Hosie.

'You'll catch your death waiting here the whole time,' he said as he approached. Jem looked frozen, but he still struck a fine attitude.

'My devotion keeps me warm,' he said. 'Is she well? Is she safe? Has she asked for me?'

'She is well and safe, Mr. Hosie, aye. I hope Mr. Meston's burial went off all right?'

Jem tutted.

'As well as you could expect, with no one fit to stand up straight.'

'Including, maybe, yourself?'

'Oh, the time out in the fresh air talking with you and Mrs. Rob refreshed me. I was the only one upright, I promise you, except for the minister, and he ran off home as soon as the corpse left the house.'

'Did your uncle say a'thing about the fellow he threw out?'

It took Jem a moment to remember.

'Oh, him, the skinny one. No, he said nothing. I doubt he remembered. I only pray that poor Minnie's funeral arrangements will be more dignified. As she deserved.'

'That'll be tomorrow or Saturday, no doubt,' said Charlie. He would like to go, if Bishop Kilgour's arrival permitted. 'Speaking of Minnie, Mr. Hosie - you're around Longacre a lot, for good reason, obviously. But you must by now be familiar with some of the local residents, are you not?'

'I suppose,' said Jem, not particularly interested. 'There is only one house that captivates my attention.'

'I know, but an observant young man like you - you'll notice things, as you're standing here, won't you?'

'Hm.' Jem considered. 'Maybe. Why do you ask?'

'Well, I don't suppose you were here when your stepfather was killed -'

'No, indeed!' said Jem quickly.

'But if you were hereabouts earlier that evening, did you see anyone behaving oddly? Anything out of place?'

'Let's see ...' Jem applied his mind to the matter. 'Saturday night. I was not here all of the evening, you know. I went to supper at a friend's house. So I must have left here ... about eight, perhaps?'

Charlie had not found Cuthbert Meston until after eleven.

'Did you maybe come back later?'

'No.' Jem tossed his head. 'No, I did not.'

'I daresay you stayed late at your friends'.' He must have done, for he had not returned to the Meston warehouse when Charlie was down there, and he had been missed.

'It was a good evening, yes.'

'Before you left here,' said Charlie, 'did you see anything then?'

Jem stared at the ground for a moment, as if he might see an answer there. He had shoved his hands into his oxters, and Charlie could see that his fingers were squirming. He waited, like a man expecting a hen's egg to hatch.

'I saw my stepfather earlier,' he said at last. 'I thought he was looking for me, so I hid. He's been up and about here a few times since he came back from Edinburgh. I knew right well he would not approve of my deep affection and respect for Miss Skinner, so I thought either my uncle or Alan must have clyped on me, and he was up here to catch me lingering about the place. Each time I've hidden, but he kept coming back. The strange thing was ...' He frowned, and his fingers flexed again, 'Aye, it was strange.'

'What was?' asked Charlie.

'Well, over the last few years, see, he'd have come after me if he thought I was up to something he didn't like. It was as if he'd lost all trust in me, and all patience with me. As if he thought I could take no responsibility for myself. But, see, each time he did that, I knew fine what mood he was in – rank fury, usually, before he'd grab me by the ear and drag me out of some howff. For example.'

'And so what was different this time? These times?'

'He had no look of fury about him at all. Maybe he was just tired, or something, but no, he did not look angry. He looked, if anything, worried.'

'But you never found out what he might have been worried about?'

'No, because someone went and killed him.' For the first time since Cuthbert Meston had died, Charlie thought Jem actually regretted his loss. Not for the first time, Charlie felt sorry for the lad. A bad time to lose a parent, just when you were not getting on. He tried to make his voice gentle, the way Bishop Skinner could.

'Have you any notion, Mr. Hosie, who might have done that? Who killed him? Or even,' he said after the least pause, 'who killed Minnie?'

Jem rearranged himself against the doorway, looking past Charlie. It seemed his attention was on the horse trough, and then, reluctantly, on the step of the Skinners' house. Imagining, or remembering? If he had only seen something, some time, that might help ...

'I was here on Tuesday night,' said Jem, as if he had only just worked it out. 'The night before the burial. I could not bear being at home a second longer – I had to get out.'

'And you came up here?'

'As usual.' Jem puffed out a dismissive sound, mocking himself. 'I was here ... I walked a little, for it was biting cold. I went out to Broad Street and walked past the college, and down one of the lanes to North Street. Don't ask me which one: they all smell the same to me,' he said, with a tilt of his head as if challenging Charlie to defend the less salubrious quarters off the Gallowgate. 'I came along

North Street then to the end of Longacre. I was going to walk to Queen Street and then round, but I felt I needed to be back here – Miss Skinner might have needed me. But then I didn't ...' He hesitated, and Charlie did not push him. 'There was a man with a bundle. At least, I thought it was a man, but he – or she – was not large, and they were well happed up in a cloak and muffler. And it was dark.'

'What about him? Or her?'

'I can't say.' Jem's face was screwed into a frown, but it was not so much the over-dramatic scowl he was accustomed to. He was genuinely puzzled. 'There was something about him. I didn't want to be near him. He had the bundle over his shoulder, and he stamped off through the snow into Longacre. I stooped to fix the top of my boot – it didn't need fixing, but I felt stupid wandering ten paces towards the mouth of Longacre then stopping and turning, so I pretended ... I watched him walk up Longacre, out of the corner of my eye, but as I say it was dark, and something about him meant I didn't want to linger. I carried on into Queen Street, and all the way along it and out into Broad Street again. And then I looked into Longacre to see if the fellow was still there, but I could see no sign of him. So I came back and stood here for ten or twelve minutes. But I was not easy, and in the end I went home.' He shivered, and Charlie thought it was genuine.

'But you couldna see much of the man – or woman?'

'Not much at all. I mean, I don't even know what he was doing or where he was going, but I did not like the look of him.'

Charlie swallowed. Nor did he, really, but the right place ... the right time ...

'This bundle – what was it like?'

'It cannot have been awful heavy. He had it just over his shoulder – the way you would carry a coil of rope, maybe. But it was not a coil – it was long and thin, if you see what I mean.'

'Well ... could it have been Minnie?'

Whatever Jem had thought the man was up to, it was clear that this possibility had really not occurred to him.

'Minnie! Alive ...?'

'Of course no. Unless she was stunned. But it seems anyway she was not killed on the doorstep over there – there was hardly any blood. She was killed somewhere else. Could this fellow have been bringing her from her place of death to the Bishop's doorstep?'

For a moment he thought Jem was about to faint again, but after a wobble the young man steadied himself.

'I don't – I don't know. I'd have said ... I don't know. She was tiny. There was nothing of her. Maybe it was, aye.'

Charlie swallowed hard. He wished he did not have to think too closely about this.

'Did you see him picking her up, when you were in Queen Street?'

Jem thought hard.

'No, I don't believe I did. He was crossing the street and he stopped to shift the bundle a bit, but I'm sure he was already carrying it when I first caught sight of him. Or her. A strong woman could have picked Minnie up, easily.'

'I don't suppose you saw any blood in the snow?'

'Blood?'

'She was stabbed, remember?'

'Aye, but blood?' said Jem. 'Mind where the slaughterhouse is?'

'Oh.'

'That's about where he was heading from.'

'Well, that would certainly have been convenient for him.' Charlie sighed.

'I'm going to go and warm up somewhere,' said Jem, pushing himself away from the doorway. 'Tell Miss Skinner she has only to summon me if she has need of me. I'll be here at once. But I'd be no good to her frozen to the wall.'

Jem was away before Charlie had a chance to agree. Maybe the lad was beginning to see sense.

Charlie looked about Longacre. He had barely started on the neighbours, but he felt it was time to go back and report to Bishop Skinner and the others. No doubt Dr. Seabury and Mr. Cooper would be there by now, too. Was there anyone else he should talk to now, before he went in again?

'Good day to you – Charlie, is it not?'

He turned and saw a familiar figure in a prim blue coat, buff waistcoat and cloak with a crisp black hat on his powdered curls. The rough red face was smiling just a little, but tinged with solemnity.

'Mr. Houstoun, good day!' Charlie bowed. He had not

thought to speak to Mr. Houstoun, having pushed Mrs. Houstoun down his list of priorities.

'I should like to convey my – er, my regrets to your master, Charlie,' said Mr. Houstoun. 'When I discovered that our maid – though she had not been with us more than five minutes – had been found dead on Mr. Skinner's doorstep – well, I could not imagine anything worse. A dreadful thing, altogether.'

'Aye, sir, very sad indeed.'

'Sad – yes, of course. It was sad. My wife was very distressed at her loss - it is so hard to keep servants, is it no?'

As a servant himself, Charlie did not think it was his place to make a response to that.

'Had she mentioned to you any fear of going out and about, sir?'

'I dinna think so,' said Mr. Houstoun. 'She came to the kirk with us, of course, on the Sabbath, and I saw no cause for concern then. But maids are my wife's business, so I doubt she would have said a'thing to me.' He raised his chin, as if establishing the distance between him and the lowliness of his household. Charlie thought he would not find out much more here about Minnie's last days.

'It's a bad thing when there are two corpuses found in the street within the course of a week, eh, Mr. Houstoun? I wondered, as one of the well-established men of the neighbourhood, if you had seen or heard of a'thing strange? A'body behaving oddly, say, about the place?'

He was sure Mr. Houstoun would consider himself about that kind of thing, but after only a moment's thought Mr. Houstoun had an answer for him.

'I'll tell you who's been acting gey peculiar about the place this last wee whilie,' he said, 'and I'm surprised the magistrate has no taken him in already to query him. For he seems to me the obvious man to have killed yon Cuthbert Meston.'

'Oh, aye, sir? Who's that, then?'

'His stepson, of course. Jeremiah Hosie.'

Chapter Thirty-Seven

'What have you seen him do, exactly, sir?'

'He's hanging around all the time - never out of the place.' He glanced around, as if suddenly aware that in fact Jem was not there at that moment. He cleared his throat. 'Watching, where he has no right to be watching.'

'I think,' said Charlie carefully, not wanting to bring Jane Skinner into it, 'he might be courting.'

'Courting! As if any respectable father would allow an approach from that laddie! Though I suppose he'll have money now,' he added thoughtfully. 'Aye, and maybe that'll teach him some responsibility. Or make him worse. Ha!'

'I think someone told me that his stepfather was one of your suppliers? That Cuthbert Meston's warehouse sold you coffee, and such?'

George Houstoun ground out his throat again, and Charlie thought a less upright man would have spat into the snow.

'Aye, he did, from time to time,' he admitted. He coughed this time. Charlie hoped he was not coming down with something. 'Coffee, and such, as you say. A – a good respectable business man, aye. Though he never to my knowledge darkened the door of the Kirk, nor indeed any other religious establishment – not even your master's, I gather.'

'So I've heard, sir, aye.'

'Well – well. The tea was of excellent quality, all the same. The coffee – I've heard tell there's better in town, now, but I've no idea where to find it. I doubt Cuthbert Meston would have told me, even if he had been alive.' He chuckled, almost, then seemed to think it inappropriate.

'Were you at his burial yesterday?'

'No, no. Trading with a man is one thing. Attending his burial when he's a godless individual is another. Did – did Mr. Skinner attend?'

'No, sir, he did not.'

'Probably very wise. Still, that tea ... I wonder now if we could perhaps approach Mr. Stephen Meston?' He tapped the end of his cane on the ground for a moment, then seemed to realise that he had been thinking out loud. 'Good tea is hard to come by. Please to tell your master what I have said – it was a most regrettable incident.'

For which, Charlie noted, he had carefully not apologised, nor taken any explicit responsibility. Nor had he referred to Mr. Skinner as 'Bishop'. Charlie bowed, and grinned to himself as he headed back across the street to the Skinner house, glancing back to see Mr. Houstoun's fastidious pacing down towards his own home and warehouse. He did not seem to be aware of Charlie's connexion with L. Rob's warehouse, and Charlie was not going to enlighten him.

'Jem Hosie?' asked Bishop Petrie. Dr. Seabury and Mr. Cooper had not yet arrived, and the two bishops were closeted cosily in the bookroom, with some of Luzie's good coffee and a plate of sweetmeats. The lapdog jumped down and went to investigate Charlie's boots, as if they might, from having been close to Jem Hosie, yield some clue. She was disappointed.

'Cuthbert Meston's stepson,' Bishop Skinner reminded him.

'Were they on good terms?'

'No, not really,' said Bishop Skinner sorrowfully.

'I think it was his age, sir,' added Charlie. 'He's awful young.'

'I have seen him lingering outside in the street,' Bishop Skinner admitted. 'Quite often, recently. In that respect, George Houstoun is quite right.'

'Thing is, sir, he says he wasna there the night his stepfather was killed – well, he was earlier, but left about eight. He'd seen Cuthbert Meston there twa-three times that day – I'd seen them both there myself at one point – but he says he thought his stepfather was after him to ...' he paused, trying to avoid mentioning that the object of Jem's affections was Jane Skinner, 'to fetch him back home, and so he fled. I did see him run to the other end of Longacre and disappear down a lanie one time on Saturday, when Cuthbert Meston was coming in at this end.'

'Why would he flee his stepfather?' asked Bishop Petrie.

'I daresay they did not quite agree on how the young man should be spending his time,' said Bishop Skinner. 'Jem Hosie is always rather finely dressed, and often, I should say, drunk. No doubt on his stepfather's money.'

'Aye, I fear so, sir. But there's more.'

'Oh, aye? Then tell, Charlie! Though as I've said before, every time we learn something new about this matter, it raises more questions than it answers.'

'Well, sir, the night that Minnie was killed – Tuesday – Jem Hosie says he was here.' And he went on to tell the two bishops about the figure Jem had seen, carrying a bundle that might just have been Minnie.

'But from outside the slaughterhouse? That's no use,' said Bishop Skinner at once. 'There is always blood about that place. We'll never know if he killed her there or not.'

'Does it matter?' asked Bishop Petrie. 'We know she was killed somewhere in that direction – which, if I am not mistaken, is near where her mistress Mrs. Houstoun sent her for – was it candles? Lamp oil? Anyway, we knew she had been sent in that direction, and if this man was indeed carrying her back from there into Longacre, we can, I suppose, assume that she was killed somewhere about there. We don't need to know exactly where, do we?'

'I don't suppose it would have been one of the slaughtermen, would it, sir?' asked Charlie suddenly. 'I mean, they're awful handy with their knives, and all. And they're terrible drinkers.'

'Do you mean that whoever did it then brought her here, randomly, just to avoid the connexion with the slaughterhouse?'

'I suppose.'

'Well, anything is possible,' said Bishop Skinner dubiously. Charlie felt himself flush.

'It does mean that the two deaths are just coincidental,' put in Bishop Petrie, clicking his fingers to bring his lapdog back to him. Hepzibah obeyed. 'And that would be odd, the two deaths from the same household in the one week, in the same area, and the body left here when this household was already linked with the first death. So I'm afraid, Charlie, I can see your reasoning but I don't quite believe it works.'

'Aye, sir. Well, I had to say it.'

'Of course you did, Charlie. We need all our thoughts and fears and theories out on the table, don't we, John?'

'Oh, that we do,' said Bishop Skinner fervently. 'Who knows, one of them might actually lead us to the solution!'

'If the two deaths are linked,' Bishop Petrie continued placidly, 'then there must be a limited number of people likely to have carried them out, surely?'

'You mean Samuel Seabury and Myles Cooper?' asked Bishop Skinner.

'Not at all - don't be so gloomy, John!' said Bishop Petrie. 'I am not at all convinced that Dr. Seabury is a heartless killer - or even a desperate one, as this killer might well have been. I admit I may be wrong, but surely there are other possibilities? This Jem Hosie, for one.'

'Aye, that's true,' said Bishop Skinner. 'And presumably the other members of his household. His brother Stephen - perhaps to inherit the rest of the business?'

'There's Alan, the warehouseman,' said Charlie helpfully. 'Alan Beith. He's a quiet fellow, and he says that Meston was a good master, but he didna look that happy any time I've seen him.'

'Was he the one who came with them to fetch the body?'

'Aye, sir. Like I say, quiet.'

'I barely recollect what he looked like.'

'Sandy, small. Quiet.'

Bishop Skinner smiled.

'I'll remember him from that.'

Charlie smiled back.

'What about people he might have crossed in his business dealings?' asked Bishop Petrie. 'I am curious as to why he was spending so much time up in this part of the town, and late at night, too. He was a grocer, was he not?'

'Wholesale, mostly, I believe,' said Bishop Skinner. 'He would have supplied some of the local grocers. He was one of the kind who specialise in the Dutch trade - spices, teas, coffees, that kind of thing. Expensive, and high quality.'

'Forgive me, Charlie, but is that not what Mrs. Rob does? High quality Dutch trade?'

Charlie felt himself set, like glue. His mouth did not seem to want to work.

'Charlie?' asked Bishop Skinner.

'Aye, sir,' he managed at last.

'Did she have any business dealings with Mr. Meston?' asked Bishop Petrie.

'Not ... not as such, sir,' said Charlie, though it was hard to get his jaw to move.

'Not as such? Didn't she like him? As I understand it, merchants have to get on – or rather, they are able to pretend friendship to further business. What did she think of him?'

'She didna like him at all, sir,' said Charlie miserably. He knew he was going to have to tell them.

'What was the matter?'

'He came to her warehouse last Friday night, while I was here, and he threatened her, sir. He said his customers had told him her coffee was better than his, and if she didna sell him her coffee – him and no one else, mind – he would see to it that her business was destroyed.'

'Charlie!' Bishop Skinner was horrified. 'Why did you not say?'

'I imagine,' said Bishop Petrie after a moment, 'that Charlie did not want to fall under suspicion of Cuthbert Meston's murder. Is that not the case, Charlie?'

'It is, aye, sir,' said Charlie. He could not look at either of them.

'You did find the body, Charlie. And you found poor little Minnie.'

'Sir,' Charlie groaned. As if they needed to remind him.

'I believe Charlie has been exceptionally unlucky in this,' said Bishop Petrie. 'But even had he wished to take some kind of revenge on Cuthbert Meston, that would hardly extend to Minnie. Had Mr. Meston ever threatened Mrs. Rob before?'

'No, sir. In fact, she had no idea he even knew of her existence. She knew of him, of course – the small fish always know where the big fish are.'

'Of course.' He managed to look up to see that Bishop Petrie was smiling. 'And this was on Friday night? The night – if I am right – that Mr. Meston returned from Edinburgh, tired and weary, and still set off into the night to come up here?'

'That's right,' said Bishop Skinner. 'But surely he didn't come up here to threaten – forgive me, Charlie – a minor competitor?'

Charlie nodded to show he knew what his master meant. It made no sense to him, either, and he took no offence at the Bishop's words.

'That's my thought, too, sir. That he was here for something else, and just took the chance. I mean, Luzie has no connexion in Edinburgh, not that would cause that kind of hurry, I'd have thought.'

'Did he leave it at that? The one threat?' asked Bishop Skinner, concerned more, Charlie was sure, for his welfare than for blaming him for Meston's death.

'He had little chance to repeat it, I suppose, if he died the next evening,' said Bishop Petrie.

'Aye,' said Charlie, 'when I saw him hereabouts so much on the Saturday, I did wonder what he was up to –'

'Which is why, no doubt, you noticed him and his stepson and what they were doing outside,' said Bishop Petrie.

'I suppose so, sir. But no, Cuthbert Meston did not go back to see my wife. But there was something, sir, after he died.' He described the damage to the front of Luzie's warehouse, and, tentatively, told them how upset she had been.

'I mean, sir, it didna take that much to remove it, but it wasna nice, sir. Luzie had enough to deal with during the Dutch wars: she was scared it would all crop up again.'

'I can understand that,' said Bishop Skinner. 'But I wonder why they bothered? Cuthbert Meston was lying there ready for burial, and – who? His brother? His stepson? His warehouseman? Someone comes up to this part of town – again – and does that to the warehouse of a competitor they have not previously taken under their notice? It makes little sense.'

'Oh, I think there is one way it makes sense, John,' said Bishop Petrie. 'Someone, in Cuthbert Meston's household or not, is trying to have Charlie blamed for Meston's death.'

Chapter Thirty-Eight

'By making it look as if he has a motive to attack Meston, you mean?' Bishop Skinner clarified. 'To divert attention from the real killer?'

Charlie shivered.

'That means it is someone from the Meston household, does it no, sir?'

'That seemed most likely in any case, did it not?' asked Bishop Petrie. 'Two from the same household are killed – it's the clearest place to look for the killer, and a very good reason why the killer might want to take matters out of the household and point to someone else.'

Bishop Skinner sighed.

'And then there's the second letter,' he said. 'Mrs. Rob is convinced it came from a spice warehouse, and I believe her. The spice warehouse most closely connected with all this is, of course, the Meston warehouse. I think we need to know if that is Cuthbert Meston's hand, or was it written by someone else there? And if it is Cuthbert Meston's hand, where was it in the days between his death, or whenever he wrote it, and the moment it was pushed under our door here?'

'You want me to go back down there, sir?' said Charlie, reluctantly.

'I know what you said earlier, Charlie, but perhaps, with the burial over, things will be less tense. You might find that tempers have eased, and you'll find out more.'

'And you have something specific to ask,' added Bishop Petrie. 'That should make it easier.'

Charlie tried not to let his feelings show. Never mind whether or not they were your master, there was nothing like clergy for persuading you into things you didn't necessarily want to do. He wondered if it was something they taught you at the universities.

'Aye, sir. But if it's all the same I'd better help Jean with the dinner preparations afore I go.'

'Jean? Oh, of course,' said Bishop Skinner. 'And Jane and Margaret can give her a hand, too.'

But it was Charlie who had to bring in the coal, of course, and take it up to the various hearths, and Charlie who had to get the dining table sorted out and polished and the chairs properly placed around it, and Charlie who had to refill the decanters, and Charlie who hurried out to the pump to refill the water buckets when one of them was tipped. Or perhaps, he thought to himself, he was putting off the moment when he would have to go down to the harbour again. Stephen Meston would surely not welcome him. Yet if one of that household was trying to make Charlie look responsible for the killings, then Charlie was very keen to prevent them.

Mrs. Skinner was resting in the parlour as Charlie quietly refilled the pastille burners – not a heavy job but a tricky one that Jean worried about in case the pretty burners fell and broke. He thought she was asleep, but in a moment she opened her eyes and gave him a concerned frown.

'My husband says Luzie's been having trouble at her warehouse. Why didn't you say, Charlie?'

'I didn't want to worry a'body,' said Charlie. 'And then, with Mr. Meston dead, I thought it was over, anyway.'

'Luzie must have been dreadfully worried,' said Mrs. Skinner. 'I wish you'd said. I could have gone and sat with her, or something, surely, to make her feel safer.'

'She'd have said you should be resting, mistress! And not making yourself anxious.'

'Aye, well, I suppose. But Jane or Margaret could have gone.'

And what if Jem was the one damaging the warehouse? With Jane there? What would have happened then? Charlie found it hard to imagine.

'Maybe best not, mistress,' he said. 'Luzie has the shop boy with her, and I think she's prepared for any further, um, insult.'

'Well, if you think it best, Charlie. And with Cuthbert Meston gone, surely things will calm down. His brother never struck me as anywhere near as bad-tempered and ambitious.'

Charlie was trying to think of an answer to that when he heard the master's light step on the stair, and the front door open. In a moment the hall was full of the sounds of Dr. Seabury and Mr. Cooper, arriving and shedding their outerwear. Before Charlie could go and help, Myles Cooper's delighted tones rang out.

'And I have the most delicious piece of scandal, just arrived this morning in a letter from a friend of mine in Edinburgh!'

'Oh, not another one,' murmured Mrs. Skinner, pulling her shawl over her face, then emerging again. 'I wish he would not: it makes me feel clarty just to listen to him.'

'The Reverend Aristotle Cummins.' Myles' voice found doors no challenge, when he was in good form. 'A clergyman of my acquaintance, I might add – though perhaps not an acquaintance I should now wish to claim! He died a month ago, and the contents of his will have been made public now, of course. He was a very wealthy man.'

'Some bequests to worthy charities, no doubt?' They could just hear Bishop Skinner's suggestion. Mrs. Skinner shook her head sharply.

'That would not be scandal.'

'The bulk of his substantial fortune, all to a son no one ever knew he had! The acknowledged son, in fact, of someone else entirely!'

'Oh, good heavens,' grumbled Mrs. Skinner, as Charlie went to help the Bishop with the guests. 'Tell them, if they ask, that I am asleep. He is almost better drunk than in a mood such as this.'

She pulled the shawl back over her face again, and settled down. Charlie left the parlour quietly and tidied the guests' gloves and hats, then turned to fetch the brandy.

'Not gone yet, Charlie?' asked Bishop Skinner, about to follow Seabury and Myles upstairs.

'Just away to go now, sir, once I've the brandy up the stair.'

'Good man. Thank you.'

Charlie sighed. Mrs. Skinner was right: the arrival of Myles Cooper made leaving the house much more appealing this morning.

Thursday – by this time tomorrow Bishop Kilgour might well be with them, if he started early, or broke his journey in Ellon overnight. Five possible killers, Charlie thought, beating the path once again down to the harbour. Stephen Meston, Jeremiah Hosie, Alan the warehouseman, Samuel Seabury, Myles Cooper. And himself, he supposed, though at least he knew he had not killed either Meston or Minnie. Six possible killers. Or six more likely killers, because of the connexion between the two victims. Possible killers – well, they were endless.

The day was bright, the sky glancing blue, and the ground had frozen hard again, the beaten snow on top of it bound into uncomfortable ridges and furrows, cart tracks and boot marks. It would be good travelling weather for Bishop Kilgour: he would make good time. But at least Bishop Petrie knew what was going on now: he would defend what Bishop Skinner had been doing, no doubt: he would make sure that Bishop Kilgour was not too cross. Charlie had never seen Bishop Kilgour cross, but he had a feeling it might be an unpleasant experience. Bishop Kilgour had a great air of authority about him, and his wrath, without doubt, would be mighty. Would he think that Dr. Seabury was guilty? Would he refuse consecration? Charlie could not imagine how Dr. Seabury might be feeling: he had come so far and waited so long, and now, perhaps, because of the death of someone he had not even met until last Friday, all his hopes would be dashed.

But for now he had to think about the Meston household, about Stephen, and Jem, and Alan. Three possible, maybe likely, killers. And he was off to visit them.

What if they trapped him? What if they realised he thought one of them might be a killer, and killed him as well? He felt stupid – the idea had not even occurred to him till now, that he might be walking into danger. He was sure Bishops Petrie and Skinner had not thought of it either, or they would never have asked him to go back. They probably thought that in broad daylight, on the busy quayside, no one would dare ... But what if they did?

But his feet kept walking, obediently, down the hill and round the corner. And when he reached the warehouse, he had to admit that it did not look as dangerous as he might have imagined.

For one thing, it had the air of a building only just open for business. Alan, squinting in the sunlight, was opening the creaking shutters as though he expected them to fall on his head at any moment. Stephen, in his shirt and waistcoat, his neck cloth loose, stood in the doorway looking like a man who had spent five days on a rough sea. The whole place smelled, even from the outside, stale and nasty, like a badly-run howff in the worst part of town.

As Charlie hesitated, Stephen, clearly not recognising him, waved a limp hand.

'Good day to you! We're a little late this morning, but almost ready for business, as you see! How can I be of assistance?'

The effort at briskness seemed for a moment to have been too much for him: he swayed and clutched at the doorway with one hand, at his mouth with the other. But the moment passed, and he straightened, favouring Charlie with a ghastly smile. It faded when he realised who Charlie was.

'You again! Did I not send you away yesterday?'

'If you want to be accurate,' said Charlie, not feeling particularly threatened, 'you sent my wife away and I went too. Before that you and I were having a good wee chat.'

'Were we?' Stephen frowned. 'I suppose you'd better come in.' He turned in the doorway, and had second thoughts. 'Actually, outside is better. I dinna want to look at the kitchen just now. Have you found me a maid? Because it's getting urgent.'

'No, I havena,' said Charlie, 'and to be honest until we know what happened to Minnie, I doubt there's a girl desperate enough for work that you'd get her to come here. Not a respectable one, anyway.'

Stephen glanced past Charlie at Alan, now sweeping slowly along the outside of the warehouse. Alan looked up and met his employer's eye. Charlie wondered if between them they had been hoping for a maid who was not that respectable. He would definitely not be suggesting the position to anyone of his acquaintance.

'So if you havena found us a maid, why are you back here again?' Stephen asked, propping himself against the wall. The cold did not seem to be bothering him.

'This came to my master's house,' said Charlie, pulling the anonymous letter from his waistcoat pocket, 'and we wondered if either of you knew the hand?'

Stephen frowned at the wrapper, and Alan, just reaching them with his brush, stopped to look.

'That's the master's hand,' said Alan at once. 'I mean, Mr. Cuthbert Meston.'

'Is that right?' Charlie asked Stephen.

'It is – that's my brother's hand. But ... when did it come to you?'

'Well,' said Charlie, 'after he was dead.'

'Then someone must have taken it for him.'

'Well, I doubt it was his ghost,' said Charlie irresistibly. Stephen shuddered, and Alan turned pale.

'Could Minnie have – I mean, would Minnie maybe have taken it to you?'

'I doubt it,' said Stephen Meston shortly. Alan's mouth shut abruptly. Charlie eyed him, but Stephen went on. 'What was the letter about? Can you say?'

'It was anonymous, and threatened Dr. Seabury.'

'My brother and the clergy! If his ghost does walk it will be because I brought a minister into the house for the kisting.' Stephen was looking queasy again. 'But why would he threaten Dr. Seabury? It seems more trouble than it is worth, surely?'

'Not for Dr. Seabury, I think,' said Charlie. 'It's no a small matter for him. No with twa murders on the doorstep, one a bloody corpus, and the magistrate giving him some awful canny looks.'

'Excuse me –' Stephen's words were muffled as he almost ran to the quayside. The splatter of his spew echoed around the stone walls. Charlie ignored it as best he could, and turned to Alan.

'You were the father of Minnie's child, were you no?'

Alan had not taken his eyes from Stephen Meston.

'I was,' he said.

Chapter Thirty-Nine

'Do the others know? Mr. Stephen Meston and Mr. Hosie?'

'I suppose,' said Alan, bleakly. 'Mr. Cuthbert Meston knew right well.'

'Even when he threw her out?'

'Aye, of course.'

'He didna think to make you marry her? If you'd been quick you might not even have had to pay the fine for antenuptial fornication, if that was what was worrying him.'

'In the kirk? I doubt it bothered him much - and it would have been us paying it anyway, I daresay, not him. And as for making me marry her ...'

'Aye?'

'I wanted to marry her. I'd asked her to marry me long afore this, and she'd said yes, and all. But when I went to ask Mr. Cuthbert for permission, he said no.'

'Why on earth would he say no?'

'He didna want married servants. Said their minds werena on the job, they had other priorities.' He pronounced the word as if he were echoing Mr. Meston's enunciation, sharp and somehow unpleasant.

'And you didn't want to leave his employ?'

'Leave? Aye, well, I might. I'd thought of it many's the time. But he'd no give me a character, nor her either. No, we had no choice, when it came down to it. I'd have left in a mintie, and taken Minnie with me, if I'd thought he wouldn't poison every other merchant in the town against me just out of spite for putting him out. And it's the only trade I know, ken? I've been here since I was a lad. I should have gone years ago, but then Minnie started and I couldna leave her. Yon Cuthbert Meston,' he said, an eye still on the brother, and spat generously into the snow. 'You might as well be a slave.'

A sudden vision of Samuel Seabury crossed Charlie's mind. He wanted to think more about what Alan had said, but time was short.

'Stephen Meston, is he as bad?' he asked quickly, listening for Stephen's returning footsteps. But there was more retching going on instead. Alan thought about it.

'No,' he said at last, 'he's no. Och, no, he's no. No so ambitious, ken, nor as cruel. But somewhere in there there's the same hard streak, all the same. It just doesna come out quite so often. That's what I think, anyway.'

'Then maybe things will improve for you,' said Charlie, noticing that Stephen was starting to wipe his mouth.

'Aye,' said Alan bitterly, 'maybe they will. But there's no Minnie to share it with.'

'Minnie?' Stephen had reached them. 'Has there been any word yet of who killed her?'

'No, sir. I suppose the thinking is that it's the same person who killed Mr. Cuthbert Meston, otherwise it would be a mighty coincidence.'

'Did you say that to me yesterday?' Stephen screwed up his face, anxious.

'I don't believe I did, no.'

'But did you say - or did I dream it? - that Minnie was working in George Houstoun's household?'

'What?' Alan's face was a picture of surprise. 'Is that a fact?'

'That I did say, aye,' said Charlie. 'Mrs. Houstoun told us she was working there from Saturday night until her death.'

'So that's where she was!' said Alan, shaking his head as if in wonder. 'No doubt she would have sent word when she was ready. The Houstouns, eh?'

'Aye,' said Stephen, 'I thought, when I remembered it this morning, that I must have dreamed it. That's ... But how did she die on the street, then?'

'She was sent out on an errand, and never came back,' said

Charlie. 'Someone may have seen her killer carry her into Longacre and lay her by Bishop Skinner's front door – that is where she was found, of course, but not where she was killed.'

Stephen rubbed his face, as if it would help him think, and cleared his throat. Charlie tried not to stand downwind of him, for he was in serious need of a wash.

'Has Houstoun any idea who might have attacked her?' Stephen asked carefully.

'I dinna ken that a'body's asked him,' said Charlie diplomatically. It was probably not the moment to say that George Houstoun was pointing the finger at Stephen's nephew Jem.

'And has anybody asked him what he was doing himself that evening?' asked Stephen. Charlie blinked at the change of direction.

'You mean you think George Houstoun might have –'

'He's an odd fellow, as I remember him,' said Stephen. 'Full of himself and of the Kirk. Did he know that Minnie was with child? I couldna see that going down well with him. Not at all.'

'But presumably he would just throw her out again,' said Charlie, through a wave of pity at the thought of poor Minnie, cast out twice in a week. 'He wouldna go to the trouble of taking her out in the street and stabbing her, would he?'

'Would he not?' said Stephen darkly. 'Are you sure? He's an awful strict, straitlaced kind of a man. Though he could hold his nose and buy tea from us even when he didn't approve of Cuthbert not going to church.'

'So trade was good between this warehouse and his shop?' Charlie asked. He felt he was not getting a clear picture of their relationship.

'It was, once,' said Stephen. 'But we have not supplied them this long time.'

'Could Mr. Cuthbert Meston have been in Longacre trying to get that trade back?' Charlie asked. 'We still don't know, I think, why he spent so much time in Longacre and Broad Street on Friday and Saturday.'

'I doubt it was for the sake of selling bohea to George Houstoun,' said Stephen, blunt in his assessment.

'Are you sure, sir?' Alan asked, a little diffidently.

'I don't believe we'd sold them anything for months,' said Stephen. 'Why do you ask?'

'Something Mr. Meston said on Friday evening, sir. At the time I didna hear him properly, and of course I didna question. But now you're saying "Houstoun", it's making me think that was what he was saying.'

'Saying when? Or where?'

'He was taking a few bags of spices out – cloves, and mace, I think it was. Small enough to put in his pockets. Samples, like, or a wee bit more generous than samples.'

'On Friday evening?'

'Aye, sir. Just afore he went out again. After he came back from Edinburgh, of course.'

'Of course. But he said Houstoun?'

'Like I say, I didna hear properly and I thought he was saying something about a house. I thought to myself – the way you do – that if it was important he'd say it again, but he was more muttering to himself than anything else. But as I say, now you say it, it could have been Houstoun.'

'Maybe some mutual friend in Edinburgh wanted him to try the trade again?' Charlie suggested.

'Still, straight away on his return?' said Stephen. 'He was tired from the journey. Surely that could have waited until the next day?'

'And maybe that was what Mr. Houstoun said, too,' said Charlie, with growing excitement. 'And that was why he was back on the Saturday!'

'You could be right ...' Stephen frowned, thinking it through. 'I'm still surprised he'd want to court Houstoun's business again, but I suppose it's possible. And he was in a good mood – for him – on Saturday morning. Almost as if he were looking forward to something. And in my brother's books, the only thing really worth looking forward to was a good deal. Hm, yes, maybe you have it, Charlie!'

'Did he take a lantern with him?' Charlie asked suddenly. Stephen blinked.

'Yes, when he came back. Why would he not?'

'So you've a lantern missing?'

'I suppose we must have.' Stephen steadied himself on the doorpost and looked back into the hallway beyond, where the household's lanterns hung on a row of nails. 'No, nothing missing,' he said.

'That's good, then,' said Charlie, but he noted it in his mind. 'The only thing, though, sir, if Mr. Cuthbert Meston really did visit the Houstouns on Saturday – or even Friday – is to wonder why Mr. Houstoun has not come forward and said so?'

'Maybe he has not even realised it might be helpful,' Stephen suggested. 'Maybe it's time to go to the magistrate, and pass it on.'

'Even if it's only a possibility, sir?' asked Alan anxiously. 'I couldna swear to it that that was what he said when he took those spices.'

'Aye, well, even possibilities need to be followed up sometimes,' said Stephen.

'I could tell my master,' said Charlie. It seemed to him that it would be useful to know what was happening, and if he left this in the hands of the Meston household he could easily lose track of the information. And the bishops would want to know about this, no doubt of that. Then he remembered the reason he had revisited the Meston warehouse, and decided to make sure of that information, too.

'So this letter,' he said, waving the wrapper written in Cuthbert Meston's decisive hand. 'You've no recollection of seeing this before, either of you?'

'I think if I'd seen my brother writing to a bishop I would have remembered it,' said Stephen with half a smile. 'And I never have.'

'Alan?'

'Not a bit of it. It's the kind of thing he'd likely have sent me out with, anyway,' said Alan, 'to save money on a messenger. Particularly when it was that local. And I've never delivered anything to your master's house, before or after Mr. Cuthbert's death.'

Which presumably left Jem, Charlie thought, as he climbed back up Marischal Street with one hand on the railings to save himself from slipping. He should have asked Jem when he saw him that morning, but he had not had the letter with him then. But why would Jem hold on to a letter like that, and deliver it after his stepfather's death? Of course, Jem might not have known what was in the letter – might have agreed to deliver it on Friday or Saturday and forgotten, then found it in his pocket later and decided to fulfil his stepfather's request, even though it might be too late.

But that scarcely made sense. If Jem had a letter to deliver to the Skinner household, he would have done it directly, in his best coat and polished buttons and in person - any excuse, in the hope of catching sight of Jane. He would certainly not have forgotten about it.

Could Minnie have had the letter? Could she have had it in a pocket when she was thrown out of the house at the quay, and found it later, and decided to deliver it? That would have been particularly dutiful of her, Charlie thought, carrying out the wishes of an employer who not only was already dead but who had thrown you out of his house into a snowy night. But perhaps Minnie had been that kind of person. He should have asked Alan when he had the chance - what kind of person was Minnie? They had been wondering, after all. Mrs. Gray had had no great impression of her as she had been in such a bad state when she had stayed at the hospital. Maybe he could ask Mrs. Houstoun. And then he could ask Mr. Houstoun if he had killed his wife's new maid. Charlie snorted to himself as he reached the Castlegate, and tramped through the brown slushy puddles across to Lodge Walk, and along the lanies back into Longacre, careful to avoid the rubbish half-hidden by the latest snowfalls. At least in winter the lanies smelled less. At the front door of the Skinners' house, he scraped his feet with great care before going inside, to take his latest news to the clergy.

Chapter Forty

'No, they're away out in this fine weather,' said Mrs. Skinner, with a longing look through the parlour window at the sunshine outside. 'Not for long, though: they're coming back to their dinner. Bishop Petrie went with them, so they can't even have gone far.'

'Aye, but in which direction, mistress?'

Mrs. Skinner shrugged.

'As to that, who knows? Bishop Petrie aye likes to take a look at the sea when he's in Aberdeen, but that might not be today.'

'Oh, well, I'll go and see if Jean needs help with the dinner.'

'Did you find out anything interesting?' Mrs. Skinner was not going to let him go that easily, not if he could alleviate the boredom of resting. 'You went back down to the Meston warehouse, did you not?'

'I did, but there were things I realised afterwards I should have asked. Like what kind of a lassie Minnie was, and suchlike.'

'Of course. Well, what did you get, though? My husband said you'd taken down the wrapper of that second letter. Did they know the hand?'

Charlie nodded.

'Aye, it was Mr. Cuthbert Meston's hand.'

Mrs. Skinner made a face.

'Well, that makes sense as regards the contents, but how did it get here, days after the man was dead?'

'Mr. Stephen Meston and Alan the warehouseman swore they had never seen it before. Jem Hosie was not there, but I don't believe it could have been him.'

'Because he was on bad terms with his stepfather?'

'Because ... because I don't think he would have left it so long, nor pushed it under the door and left.'

'Because he wants to court Jane?'

Charlie felt his eyebrows shoot up, giving him away.

'I didna think you knew ...'

'John doesn't know, or I don't think he does. Jane told me herself, though I had suspected something of the kind. He's around Longacre so much, and always seems to be staring at this house – it was growing quite unnerving!'

'Oh, aye, good. I mean, good that you know, mistress.'

'And what you say makes sense. He would no doubt have seen it as an excuse to chap the door and get inside, if he could.'

'That's my thought, mistress. Then I wondered if maybe Minnie pushed it under the door? If she'd been given it to deliver, and forgotten about it when she was thrown out, then found it later? I mean, it would be good of her to do it for a master who had thrown her out, but – well, that was when I remembered I hadna asked the Meston people what like of a lass she was.'

Mrs. Skinner tapped her fingers together.

'I don't think it could have been Minnie, Charlie.'

'It arrived before she was dead, I believe.'

'It might have, but think about it. About the first thing Cuthbert Meston seems to have done when he arrived back from Edinburgh is to find out that Minnie is with child, and throw her out. Did he have time to give her a letter before that? After all, he had only met Dr. Seabury on the boat.'

'Oh.' Charlie was dismayed. 'Aye, you're right. It couldna have been Minnie. In that case, I have no notion who it was at all.'

'He seems to have spent so much time hereabouts on Saturday – maybe he gave it to someone to deliver, and it was mislaid? Or something like that. And whoever it was, they were embarrassed at having left it, so did not knock at the door.'

'He probably said not to knock at the door, mistress. After all, he hadna signed the letter: he would not want his messenger seen.'

'Oh, true.' She pondered, then sighed. 'Well, anything else? My husband said that George Houstoun, who I always thought was a pompous old gossip, believes that Jem Hosie is responsible for the killings. What do you think?'

'Och, I dinna think so,' said Charlie. 'He's gey full of himself and his doings – he'd likely have challenged his stepfather to a duel, or the like. And I couldna see him stabbing wee Minnie. Though depositing her on our doorstep – that might be a gesture that would be more like him.'

'I think George Houstoun should find something better to do with his time,' said Mrs. Skinner. 'I'm half surprised he hasn't taken to sitting at his own doorstep with a spindle and a shawl wrapped round his head, claiking with the other old women.'

'Stephen Meston thought that Mr. Houstoun might have done the killings, mistress.'

'Did he?' Mrs. Skinner was richly surprised, and took a moment to consider the idea. 'I heard he was not on good terms with Mr. Meston – Mr. Cuthbert Meston – but then who was? I hadn't George Houstoun down as a man who could hold someone's head down in a horse trough. I'd have thought he wouldn't want to get his hands dirty, touching a godless individual like Cuthbert Meston.'

'And then there's Minnie, mistress.'

'Well, yes! Did he know she was with child? He would not have put up with that, I'm quite sure. But to stab her? When he could just throw her out and be pleased with himself?'

'That's about what I said, mistress. But then, it seems that Mr. Cuthbert Meston headed out on Friday evening with a pocket full of large samples of spices, as if maybe he was going to do business with someone. They were wondering if someone in Edinburgh had suggested he begin trading again with Mr. Houstoun, and he set off up here to open negotiations.'

'That late at night? As soon as he was home?'

'Well, aye, mistress. That might be why he went back the next day again, because it was too late on Friday.'

'That would be very keen, for Meston. A lot of effort to put in to trading with someone he professed not to like, and who did not like him. That's almost more like Jem and his courting.'

Charlie laughed.

'Not like Mr. Meston at all, from all I hear.'

'No, indeed. Hm. Charlie, I feel weary of lying on this sopha, and in need of exercise. Will you escort me to see my good neighbour Mrs. Houstoun? I believe we shall find her at home, and it will be an opportunity to see if she needs any help with the funeral arrangements for poor Minnie.'

'Are you sure, mistress? It's slippy enough outside ...'

'I can see from here that the sun has cleared a good bit of the street, and we are not going far. I'll be careful, I promise! Will you get Jean to fetch my cloak and bonnet? The sun is shining, and I long to be out in it!'

She did have the good sense to lean on Charlie's arm as they picked their way through the snow and down Longacre, and Charlie made sure they did not rush. It was awkward with her hoops bouncing against his legs, but at least Mrs. Skinner was well happed up against the cold and could afford to take a moment or two to make sure she did not slip or fall, and it was not long until they reached the small but would-be smart grocery shop where George Houstoun plied his trade. Inside the shop, which, like Luzie's, would have been the parlour if this had still been an ordinary ground floor flat, George Houstoun was in charge behind the counter. All the goods were in immaculate order on shelves and in sacks. Charlie thought Luzie would approve, and wondered why she did not trade with Houstoun. He shrugged to himself: there could be several reasons, none of them relevant to the current matter.

'Good day to you, Mr. Houstoun!'

'Oh ... Mrs. Skinner. It's a whiley since we've seen you in the shop.'

'True, true - and I do like your tea. Perhaps I could take an ounce of it while I'm here? But it's your wife I've come to see. I thought I should find her here, in the shop.'

'A shop is no place for a woman,' said Houstoun, with a humouring smile.

'Oh! Then is she within?'

George Houstoun's hands were already weighing out a packet of tea even as he himself was frowning.

'Aye, I believe she's in the kitchen. It's nothing serious, is it?'

'Why would it be serious? I'm just calling on a neighbour for a news.' Mrs. Skinner beamed. 'And to find out if there's anything I can do to help in the matter of your maid.'

'Aye, well,' said Houstoun, more forthcoming now, 'it's true that funerals are expensive businesses, and any contribution ...'

'Lovely,' said Mrs. Skinner. 'Thank you so much. Charlie, can you take the tea, and we'll go through?'

Without a parlour, Mrs. Houstoun was obliged to entertain any visitors in the kitchen at the back of the flat. While the Skinners' kitchen had a window, even if it only looked out on the wall of the college, the Houstouns' kitchen had no natural light at all, and they squinted into smoky half-light to find Mrs. Houstoun scrubbing vegetables in a bucket at the table.

'Oh! Mrs. Skinner!' Embarrassed at being caught at such a menial task, Mrs. Houstoun dropped a neep into the bucket with a splash. Then she picked up the bucket, set it down again, and wiped her muddy hands on her apron.

'May I sit, Mrs. Houstoun?' asked Mrs. Skinner. 'My poor feet are so tired!'

'Of course! Of course. Here, take this seat.'

'Charlie, help me, will you?'

Pretending to be more frail than he hoped she was really feeling, Mrs. Skinner leaned on Charlie's arm and eased herself down into the room's good chair, and sighed with relief.

'Can I get you some tea, Mrs. Skinner?' Mrs. Houstoun asked. She had worked out where to hide the shameful bucket, and wiped the table clean. Now she untied her muddy apron, flung it over the back of a chair and hovered anxiously. Charlie could see her eyes darting about the room, making sure that everything else was clean and respectable. It was: even the cover on the box bed was as neat as if it had been pressed that morning, the lamps trimmed, the pewter plates gleaming. The flat did not seem large, and Charlie was surprised. He had always thought of Mr. Houstoun as a prosperous man, but perhaps he did not see the need for spending money on space.

In a moment the tea was brewing, and Mrs. Houstoun sat opposite Mrs. Skinner, an anxious smile on her pink and white face. Charlie made himself invisible as possible in the corner of the room, ready to help if required.

'What can I do for you, Mrs. Skinner? Is it something about poor Minnie? Mrs. Gray has her, you see – she has much more room than we do, of course – but I'm helping her with the funeral. It's tomorrow.'

'Yes, indeed, and I hope to be able to be there at least for the kisting.'

'Have you any idea - has anybody worked out at all - what happened? Why she was killed? Who killed her?'

'Your husband suspects Jeremiah Hosie, did you know?'

'Jeremiah Hosie?' There was an unexpected quiver in Mrs. Houstoun's light voice. She cleared her throat. 'That's Cuthbert Meston's stepson, is it no?'

'That's right.' Mrs. Skinner hesitated. 'He's been seen in Longacre quite a bit, recently. I don't know if you've noticed?'

Mrs. Houstoun shook her head quickly.

'No, no, I'm not sure I have.'

'More up our end than down here,' Mrs. Skinner reassured her. 'I don't know if he's really guilty or not, but it does look awkward for him.'

'Why is that? Oh, the tea.' Mrs. Houstoun plucked the teapot from the table, and just about managed, with shaking hands, to fill two cups. She passed one to Mrs. Skinner, and sat again in her own seat, on the edge of it. Mrs. Skinner tipped a glance at Charlie and met his eye. Mrs. Houstoun was growing less easy by the minute.

'Well, the two people who died, Mr. Meston and Minnie, were from the same household. An odd coincidence, you might think, unless it was someone from that household, or well known to that household, that killed them both.' She had been looking away from Mrs. Houstoun during this, down at her tea. So it was Charlie who was the first to notice that huge, shining tears were coursing down Mrs. Houstoun's sweet pink face.

Chapter Forty-One

Beyond the kitchen door, in the shop along the passageway, they could hear voices. George Houstoun was busy with customers. Mrs. Skinner, looking up from her tea cup, noted Mrs. Houstoun's tears in silence. Charlie waited to see what would happen next.

'Is it Jem?' she asked quietly, at last.

'Jem? No!' Mrs. Houstoun almost choked at the thought. 'No, not Jem. He's only a boy.'

'Then,' said Mrs. Skinner, and took another breath, 'then Cuthbert Meston?'

'And I can't even grieve properly.' Mrs. Houstoun pulled out a serviceable handkerchief from somewhere, and wiped her face, careful not to rub it too hard.

'Oh, my dear,' said Mrs. Skinner, and laid a hand on Mrs. Houstoun's knee. 'That's terrible for you.'

Charlie was glad she could speak at all. He was stunned. And yet, when he thought about it, it made perfect sense. What was the one thing that would make a normal man leave his house, even exhausted after a journey, and tramp off through the snow to see someone at night? What would make him go back the next day if he had been unsuccessful? Not a possible customer for a few samples of spices, no. A woman, though ... They should really have thought of it before. But then, Cuthbert Meston did not seem to be the kind of man who much sought the company of the fair sex.

Mrs. Houstoun was certainly pretty, with that curly blonde hair and those blue eyes. He could see why Cuthbert Meston, long widowed, might have taken an interest in her. But what on earth did she see in him?

'How long have you ...' Mrs. Skinner tailed off, but her tone was understanding.

'Nearly two years,' said Mrs. Houstoun with a sob. 'I mean, obviously we can't see each other very often, so it's not ... Anyway, aye, two years this December.'

'And when did you last see him?'

'Saturday night.'

Charlie's spine tingled. A step closer?

'The night he died?'

Mrs. Houstoun nodded and sniffed.

'He tried to see me on Friday night - he'd been away in Edinburgh - but my husband was at home, and he couldna. So he managed to meet me in the street on Saturday, and arranged to come on Saturday evening. See, my husband often goes to meet his friends on a Saturday evening, so it's always been our - our chance.' Another sob caught her throat, and she put a hand to her breast. 'I ken fine it was wrong, Mrs. Skinner. But my husband ... makes me so unhappy.'

'Did he know about Cuthbert, do you think?' asked Mrs. Skinner. It was no time to go into the morals of the matter.

'No! No, not at all. If he'd known - well, he'd have killed me, I'm sure!' Then she realised what she had said.

'Killed you? Or killed Cuthbert?' Mrs. Skinner asked gently.

'No, no, I'm sure he would never kill Cuthbert. Never. I mean ... Cuthbert was much bigger than he is. Surely he couldn't have ...?' She glanced anxiously at the kitchen door, but the voices in the shop continued, quite at ease, it seemed. Charlie was surprised they were not affected by the tension emanating from the kitchen.

'No, well, I'm sure you're right, my dear,' said Mrs. Skinner. 'You've probably kept everything very discreet.' She squeezed Mrs. Houstoun's hand. 'But you may well be able to help to discover who was responsible for his death - you'd like that, wouldn't you? To make sure that - that the problem is solved?'

'The problem?' Mrs. Houstoun squeaked, then put her hand to her mouth. 'The problem is that he is gone! That cannot be solved.'

'No, no, you're quite right, that was not what I meant at all. I did not mean to cause you more distress. But if you could help to bring his killer to justice, would you not wish to do so?'

Mrs. Houstoun blinked hard again at the word 'killer'. She thought for a moment.

'I should not want people to know that – that he came here.'

'Of course you wouldn't, and I don't know that anyone needs to know that. This little talk is just between us, aye?'

'Aye ... Then yes, I'd like whoever did it to be punished. When I think of it – holding his poor head down in the cold water like that! Who could do such a thing?'

'A strong person, clearly,' Mrs. Skinner replied, a little more brisk. 'Now, if you will, tell me, as you may well have been the last person to see him alive – did he say or do anything that might lead us to his killer? Was he afraid of someone? Or concerned about something he had done, or that someone else had done?'

'He said nothing about being afraid,' said Mrs. Houstoun slowly. 'He was full of his visit to Edinburgh – he'd been there near two weeks, and we'd missed each other.'

'Did he bring you anything?'

'No - he brought some spices from his warehouse, in case my husband walked in and wondered why he was there.'

The generous samples, Charlie thought, that Alan had seen him take from the warehouse. All very well if George Houstoun had walked in on his wife and her lover when matters had not gone too far.

'Very sensible,' said Mrs. Skinner, with a twitch at the corner of her mouth that Charlie recognised as a suppressed laugh. 'Did he tell you what he had been doing in Edinburgh, then?'

'I think he told me most of it, aye. He was all agitated about it, you ken, and he couldna find Jem, so he had to tell someone.'

'Can you tell us?'

Mrs. Houstoun hesitated, pursing her rosebud lips.

'Did he not tell Jem?'

'Had he told Jem when he told you?'

'No, I just said ... oh, and then ...'

'That's right. So you see, I should think someone has to tell Jem, whatever it is, don't you?'

Mrs. Houstoun heaved a sigh that seemed too large for her little body, then glanced once more at the kitchen door. George Houstoun appeared to be holding forth in the shop – they could hear his voice quite clearly. As long as he stayed there ...

'Well,' said Mrs. Houstoun, 'it's like this. A few weeks ago, Cuthbert had a letter from a lawyer in Edinburgh. Nobody he had heard of before. And it was about Jem - see, Jem's not of age yet, and for his mother's money and all Cuthbert was Jem's curator bonis, of course. So the lawyer had written to Cuthbert, and asked him to go down to meet him in person.'

'I understand, yes. but what about?'

'Well, that's what confused Cuthbert at first. It was about the death of a clergyman, a minister, ken?'

Mrs. Skinner nodded.

'And the minister had left a will. He was rich - came from a wealthy family. And he'd never married, I think, or at least he had no children. No legitimate children.'

'Right ...' Mrs. Skinner encouraged her. It was not clear whether Mrs. Houstoun was reluctant to tell the story, or was trying to find her way to a clear path through complicated details. She took another breath, and went on.

'Now, Cuthbert's wife, Mrs. Hosie, she had told Cuthbert she was a widow, that Mr. Hosie had died when Jem was a baby. It made Cuthbert awful sorry for the lad. He was gey fond of Jem, for all Jem's foolery recently. He could drive Cuthbert mad, ken? Lads that age ...'

'Aye, of course. Difficult age,' said Mrs. Skinner obediently. 'But Mrs. Hosie - was she a widow, then?'

'Well, as it turns out, no, she wasna. And Jem was the son of this minister. And the minister had confessed everything in his will, and left his whole estate to Jem, to be looked after by Cuthbert till Jem came of age, of course.'

'A minister,' said Mrs. Skinner. 'Jem's father a minister.'

'A minister who left his lover with an unacknowledged child for twenty years,' said Mrs. Houstoun, suddenly sharp. 'Now Cuthbert had no love for the church anyway - you'll maybe ken that, being a Bishop's wife and all. He wanted to talk to Jem, to let him know his good fortune, to talk over - with Jem nearly being of age - what to do with the money, to tell him never to trust a clergyman, though I daresay he'd told him that before. He was - he barely knew what to do, I can tell you, Mrs. Skinner. All that money - and Cuthbert liked money, of course. All that money, from a minister. Proof that they were not to be trusted, while at the same time - well, all that money! To his own stepson! And of course, all the questions about Mrs. Hosie, and why she had never told him, and he had trusted her and loved her and taken her son in without even knowing that he was – was the bastard son of a wealthy minister – I can tell you, Cuthbert was fair guddled that night. He didna ken what to think, or where to turn.'

'Jem will have to know, of course,' said Mrs. Skinner.

'But who will be his curator now? He's another year off full age,' said Mrs. Houstoun knowledgeably.

'Maybe Stephen Meston?'

'Aye ... aye, maybe. Maybe so. He's nowhere near as clever as Cuthbert, but I suppose he could manage.'

'I'm sure he could. But he'll need to write to the lawyer in Edinburgh and sort things out there, as well as with some lawyer here. No doubt he'll have thought of that, anyway, with Cuthbert dead.' Mrs. Skinner pondered. 'Will you tell him?'

'No! No, I've never had any dealings with Stephen Meston. What would he think? And a woman and all!'

'My husband might go and have a word, if you like.'

'Oh, yes! Yes, that would be best. I don't think Stephen has the same dread of clergy as Cuthbert had. Aye, he would listen to Mr. Skinner, right enough, I'm sure he would.'

The hint of a smile touched her face, the sign of a lifted responsibility. But Mrs. Skinner was not quite finished.

'Tell me, did Mr. Meston make any mention to you of an American clergyman he met on the boat? A Samuel Seabury? Or a Myles Cooper?'

The smile vanished, and Mrs. Houstoun turned scarlet.

'The ones he quarrelled with?'

'That's the ones, I believe, yes.'

'No doubt it was because of all he had just learned, but he did not take to those two fellows at all. When he learned that one was like to be – is it consected, you say? Consected as a bishop – and he had less love for bishops than he had for real ministers, anyway – he was just scandalised at the whole idea. In fact, he wrote a note he said he was going to drop in to your house – now, why your house?'

'Because it was to my husband and his fellow bishops that Dr. Seabury was applying for conse – for consecting,' said Mrs. Skinner.

'Aye, that's it. They were Episcopalians, not Papists. That's right. So he dashed off a note and he said he would leave it in to your house on his way home that night, but he forgot it. He was that bewildered, my poor lamb ...'

Anything less like a poor lamb than Cuthbert Meston Charlie could barely imagine. But lying helpless in that horse trough, with his head under the icy water ... maybe so. Maybe there was pity there to be felt.

'So you left the note in under the door?'

'I did, the first chance I had. I didna want anybody to know it was me: I hid it in one of the spice sacks in the shop, and then took it across when my husband wasna looking.' She seemed quite pleased with herself for this subterfuge - a duty done to her dead lover, anyway.

'Well, I mustn't keep you any longer,' said Mrs. Skinner, looking to Charlie to help her up from her chair. 'But here's a thing - did Mr. Meston see Minnie when he was here? Did he know she was working for you?'

'Why would that matter?' asked Mrs. Houstoun, clearly baffled. 'No, she appeared after he had left. He went early, in case George came back. But what has Minnie to do with Cuthbert?'

'Ah, well ...' Mrs. Skinner had no intention of saying. 'Oh, and before I go, do you know the name of the lawyer who met Mr. Meston in Edinburgh?'

'No, I don't believe he said,' said Mrs. Houstoun. 'But I do remember the name of the clergyman, for it was an odd one. It was the Rev. Aristotle Cummins.'

Chapter Forty-Two

'A woman! Why did we not think of that? So obvious.' Bishop Skinner slapped the dining table. The children had all left to go about their various businesses, and Mrs. Skinner had gone to rest after telling the bulk of her tale, and delegating the remainder to Charlie. Charlie had been invited to sit with the men at the dining table still, and to take a glass of wine, but he had declined and stood behind Jane Skinner's chair near the foot of the table, half in the company and half not. The dark little dining room with its oak panelling was cosy, the fire in the fireplace a cherry glow, and Charlie feared that if he did sit down, never mind taste the wine, he would be asleep in seconds.

'Let he who is without sin cast the first stone,' said Myles Cooper in tight-lipped piety. 'Not that I ever thought Cuthbert Meston was without sin. Certainly not.'

'Correct me if I'm wrong,' said Dr. Seabury, 'but does this not mean that I am, and never have been the killer's intended victim?'

That, Charlie saw, brought back the hunted look in Myles' pale eyes.

'How do you mean?' he asked, and took a gulp of wine. As usual, he was already a little excitable with it.

'I believe you are right, Dr. Seabury,' said Bishop Petrie, slipping the best part of the beef Charlie had served him down his lapdog's waiting jaws. 'The first letter was obviously from William Seller, who was at Gordon's Hospital in the company of at least two others on the occasions of both killings. He could not have murdered either victim. Then the second letter is clearly from Cuthbert Meston – his hand has been identified, we know it lay somewhere near spices for a while, and then we know who delivered it, when and why.'

'But how does that prove that Samuel is not in danger?' asked Myles querulously.

'It may not prove that he is not in danger – who in this world can say that they are not?' said Bishop Petrie with a smile. 'But it does prove that the author of the second letter did not kill Cuthbert Meston mistaking him for Dr. Seabury. The one person who could not possibly make that mistake would be Cuthbert Meston himself.'

'Oh. Oh, yes,' said Myles, a little reluctant.

'Then what about George Houstoun?' asked Bishop Skinner. 'If he knew about his wife and Cuthbert Meston –'

'She swore he did not, sir,' said Charlie. 'Said he would have killed her if he had known. It may have been wishful thinking, though – it's been going on for two years come December. You'd think he might have suspected something by now.'

'Hm.' The married men at the table, Bishop Skinner and Dr. Seabury (though he was widowed) met each other's eye and frowned. Charlie reconsidered – he had no suspicion that Mrs. Skinner would ever be unfaithful to her husband, but if she were she would be clever about it. Was Mrs. Houstoun that clever? Perhaps not, but then sometimes men – and women – could be blind to things they did not wish to see.

'So maybe George Houstoun,' said Bishop Skinner thoughtfully. Bishop Petrie, who had never married, slipped another piece of food to the lap dog and nodded.

'Then Mrs. Skinner said that Mrs. Houstoun knew what Cuthbert Meston was so concerned about that night. Go on, Charlie, tell us what it was. Was it something he learned in Edinburgh, right enough?'

'It was, aye,' said Charlie. 'A lawyer wrote him to tell him several things that seem to have shocked him. Jeremiah Hosie is illegitimate, for one.'

'Really? And he had no idea?'

'I believe not, sir.' Mrs. Hosie must have been good at secrets, too. 'His mother had had to bring up the child only with the support of her own family, I gather, so put it out that she was a widow.'

'Poor Mr. Hosie. That will be a shock, indeed, beside which

the others cannot have been so great, surely.'

'Aye, well,' said Charlie. 'Jeremiah's father died recently, acknowledged the whole thing at last, and left Jem all his money. And Cuthbert Meston was his curator – is it curator bonis?'

'The one looking after his goods till he comes of age, yes,' said Bishop Petrie, smiling at Dr. Seabury for whom the term was probably an unfamiliar one. 'A kind of trustee, in Scots law. So now Cuthbert has charge of the money. Or he did ...'

'That's an interesting turn,' agreed Bishop Skinner. 'And perhaps, in some respects, a rather more pleasant shock. But did you say there was a third shock?'

'Aye, sir. You ken Mr. Meston's attitude to the church?'

'Oh, michty – I fear I know what is coming!' said Dr. Seabury. 'Please do not say that the dead father was a clergyman!'

'I'm afraid so, sir.'

There was a shocked silence. Clergymen were human, too, of course, but for a child not to be acknowledged – for the mother to be abandoned – that was shameful. Then Myles, alert for gossip as always, leaned forward.

'A clergyman in Edinburgh? Since the lawyer was there.'

'I believe so, sir.' Charlie cleared his throat, and hoped he was not mistaken. 'His name, I believe, was the Reverend Aristotle Cummins.'

'Cummins! I knew it!' Myles slapped the table, and made the glasses jump.

'Myles!' Dr. Seabury admonished him.

'But you remember the letter I had yesterday! It was the very story!'

'You said you knew the man,' Bishop Skinner remembered.

'I did, and I cannot say I am the least surprised! Aristotle Cummins – as rich as Croesus, and I'd say has never had to do a thing in his life that he did not wish to. Remember, Samuel, I told you about the time I met him at the coffee house?'

'Oh. Oh, that Mr. Cummins.' Dr. Seabury had clearly not been terribly impressed by the story.

'That's the one. Bought me dinner – best food I've had since I came to Scotland. Nothing out of the ordinary to him, of course – that's the way he lives! Lived, I should say,' he added suddenly, and his shoulders hunched again as he reflected on what he had said. 'Of course Mrs. Skinner's table ...'

'Oh, most clergy can't run to that kind of luxury, can we?' Bishop Skinner said lightly. 'We all know that.'

'But perhaps we should be careful about this,' said Bishop Petrie, and Bishop Skinner nodded. Charlie frowned.

'Why's that, sir? As Bishop Skinner says, the money gives us a whole new angle.'

'Quite right, Charlie, and it may even be the right one. But if the magistrate gets to hear that Mr. Cooper, as Dr. Seabury's friend, has yet another connexion with the Meston household –'

'But I had no idea!' Myles protested.

'And even if he had ...' Dr. Seabury struggled with the logic, 'how would knowing that Cuthbert Meston was to oversee his stepson's new fortune drive either of us to murder him?'

Bishop Skinner nodded again.

'It is a tortuous path, certainly.'

'Nevertheless,' said Bishop Petrie gently, 'I think it best if the magistrate does not know of your acquaintance with Jeremiah Hosie's father. Who knows what the man might deduce from that? Perhaps that you had expectations from Mr. Cummins yourself, and wanted Jeremiah never to know of his father's bequest, or of his father, indeed. Had Cuthbert Meston told anyone else of this matter?'

'It seems not, sir,' said Charlie. 'He had been seeking Mr. Hosie, and from what Mrs. Houstoun said the story came out because of his frustration in not finding Jem. Certainly Mr. Stephen Meston and Alan the warehouseman seemed to have no idea why Cuthbert Meston was looking for Jem that night, except to bring him home and stop him wasting all his money.'

'I cannot see that this changes a'thing,' said Dr. Seabury. He drew out his handkerchief, mercifully clean, and waved it in emphasis. 'I agree we should not mention Aristotle Cummins to the magistrate: it is nothing to do with us, and it will, in any case, harm Mr. Hosie's reputation, to be discovered a bastard.'

'Though a rich bastard,' Myles put in, then subsided, embarrassed again.

'But surely, the key piece of information here is that Cuthbert Meston was seeing this Mrs. Houstoun, a married woman, and whatever she says this is a small town like any other small town, and – how long did you say this had been going on, Charlie?'

'Two years come December, she said.'

'Two years,' Dr. Seabury repeated. 'How, I ask you, could he not know?'

'But had he only just found out, do you think?' asked Bishop Skinner, 'or was this, if you know what I mean, a slow boil?'

'As to that, who knows? Does it even matter?'

'I like to know why people do things,' said Bishop Skinner.

'People are so very interesting, aren't they?' Bishop Petrie beamed at him. 'I don't know this George Houstoun. What is he like?'

'Charlie, you've probably met him more than I have,' said Bishop Skinner. 'What do you think of him?'

'A very upright man, sir, but no very keen on Episcopalians.'

'Another one!' cried Myles, looking martyred.

'Nor anybody who is not an adherent of the Kirk. So he had his reservations about Mr. Meston, too.'

'Reservations would not be enough to kill someone,' said Bishop Skinner.

'But it would add to his resentment if the man was his wife's lover, all the same,' Dr. Seabury added.

'Of course. So go on, Charlie.'

'He's - well, he looks down on most people, I think, sir. Without much reason, that I can see - he's not the best grocer in this part of town, and his shop is a humble enough place, though well kept. I hear he doesna spend a shilling where sixpence would do, and he keeps - or believes he keeps - a tight rein on his wife and the household.'

'Likes to be thought very respectable?' suggested Bishop Skinner.

'Aye, sir. I think that's where the pride comes in. He's never put a foot wrong as far as the kirk goes, and I think he believes everyone else a sinner.'

'Well, we are,' said Bishop Petrie. 'As Mr. Cooper so helpfully reminded us earlier of Our Lord's words, "Let he who is without sin cast the first stone". Knowing, of course, that no one was. Alas!'

'But you think that George Houstoun would have been there with the stone in his hand?' asked Bishop Skinner.

'I believe he would, sir.'

'Then how was it that he took in Minnie? Did he not know that she was expecting a child?'

'That I don't know, sir. It was Mrs. Houstoun took the girl in, and I'm not even sure that she knew.'

'But they knew that she had been working for Cuthbert Meston, presumably? That he had thrown her out?'

'Of course,' said Dr. Seabury. 'That might explain her death, too. What did Cuthbert Meston say when he found out his rejected maid was now working for his lover?'

'Oh, aye, that's a good question!' Myles poured himself another glass, and Samuel Seabury gave it a dejected look.

'See, the thing is, sir, I dinna believe that the Houstouns knew of the connexion at all.'

'Really?' Bishop Skinner exclaimed.

'No, sir. See, apparently Cuthbert Meston left the Houstouns' flat before Minnie arrived on Saturday night. He was gone. And to go by what Mrs. Houstoun says, Minnie never mentioned the Mestons. She had no idea there was a link between the two at all.'

'She never asked where Minnie had come from?'

'No, sir. See ... if Minnie priced herself cheap enough, an employer who wanted to economise would never ask questions.'

'Never get a character from a past employer?' Myles was astonished. 'And let them into your house? Sleeping there? Cooking your food?'

'Aye, sir, it's not the way things should be run. But then, there are servants who are desperate enough for anything with an old employer, and this could be their escape.'

'But they could find themselves in all kinds of awful situations!' It was Dr. Seabury's turn to be appalled.

'They can,' agreed Bishop Skinner, 'and they do. It is not a happy thought. But for a girl in Minnie's position, as Charlie says, such a situation may have been her only hope.'

Was it better than slavery? Charlie could see the question behind Dr. Seabury's eyes. Surely it must be. But perhaps not by much.

Chapter Forty-Three

After dinner, the men retreated to the parlour. There was no sign of Mrs. Skinner, and Jean in the kitchen, washing the dishes in a one-handed clatter, told him that the mistress had retired to her bed for an hour or two.

'She was that exhausted after the march you took her on this morn! I dinna ken what made you think of such a daft thing. You're an awful fool.'

There was no point in arguing. Charlie went back to the parlour with the brandy, praying that Mrs. Skinner and her child would be all right.

'You'll want more conversation, I suppose,' Dr. Seabury was saying. Myles, the gossipy letter about Aristotle Cummins pressed against his ample stomach, had already fallen asleep across the sopha.

'On the contrary, Dr. Seabury,' said Bishop Skinner. 'With Bishop Kilgour arriving tomorrow – if the weather suits – I would suggest a rest today. Not that he is a fearful interrogator! I should not want you to dread his arrival. But he will want to talk, and to listen, and to pray with you, and with us. And you have done almost nothing but those things since your arrival.'

'And the day is still fine,' added Bishop Petrie, patting his lapdog. 'I shall be taking my little friend here out for her walk. If you wish to accompany me you would be very welcome.'

'And I should like to go and speak with George Houstoun,' said Bishop Skinner. 'I have done little in this matter except to sit here like a spider in its web, and expect people to bring me information – even to my own wife! So now I shall go and see if I can find out anything for myself. Charlie, will you come with me?'

'Aye, sir.'

'Then perhaps we shall leave Mr. Cooper here to recuperate from his dinner, and see what we can find out.'

The cold hit harder after their time in the cosy dining room, pinching their cheeks and trying to nibble inside their gloves. Outside in the street, Charlie caught sight of Jem in his usual doorway. Jem straightened when he saw Bishop Skinner, as though he might come straight over and ask him for Jane's hand, but then he slumped back against the doorpost. Charlie felt sorry for the lad. If he kept on this way, his heart was most likely to be broken.

It was growing dark now, though, and perhaps Jem would soon be away home. Charlie wondered just how Mrs. Skinner was going to ensure that Jem learned of his mixed fortunes. Did Jem already know or suspect that he was a bastard? It would be a shock if he did not. It would not prevent him from working in the family grocery warehouse, but the stigma was such that they might well lose custom. Once he knew, could he keep it hidden? Charlie remembered Dr. Seabury's comments about small towns. No, that was not likely.

The lamps were still on in George Houstoun's little shop, but inside there seemed to be an after-dinner quiet. Charlie had his hand on the door when the Bishop called him back, in a whisper.

'Wait! I want to think. I have not the aptitude for conversation that my wife has.'

'Then we'd better decide what we want to ask him, sir.'

'What we want to ask him? I'm not even sure I've decided what I think happened. Let me see ...' The Bishop pressed his gloved fingers into his high brow, as if squeezing his thoughts into shape. 'Our thesis is that George Houstoun –' he stopped, suddenly fearing being overheard. He went on more quietly. 'That George Houstoun found out that Cuthbert Meston had seduced his wife, and consequently killed him – perhaps met him in Longacre as they were both going home on Saturday night, and, as I say, killed him.'

'Did he take him by surprise, sir, or did he challenge him?'

'Good question, Charlie. I don't know.'

'Did he happen upon him, or go out looking for him?'

'Surely he must have happened upon him. How would he know when Meston would be there? Even if he believed that Meston was visiting his wife when he was out, he would not know when he might leave.'

'Houstoun might have been waiting in the street for Meston to leave,' Charlie suggested.

'It was an awful cold night to be waiting outside!'

'Jem does it, sir.'

'Yes – why does Jem do that?'

Charlie shrugged, and said nothing. He regretted mentioning the lad.

'Anyway,' said Bishop Skinner, 'Jem is a young man. George Houstoun must be about our age – he could even be in his fifties.'

'Perhaps his wrath kept him warm, sir.'

Bishop Skinner gave him a look, and then grinned.

'Why is this so much more daunting than trying to work out if God means someone to be a bishop or not? I know: let's pray.'

In the middle of the street, with neighbours trotting past about their business, the Bishop bowed his head and Charlie did the same.

'Lord, we pray for guidance in all our doings, and for success in our endeavours. Be with us as we seek justice and resolution here. And grant us a safe return home afterwards,' he added, a little quickly. 'Amen.'

'Amen,' said Charlie, with feeling.

'Right,' said Bishop Skinner, 'let's go.'

He reached out a long hand for the door, and in they went.

George Houstoun, as trig as a freshly groomed cat, was behind the counter, weighing tea into packets. He looked up with a genial smile, probably granted to every customer, then started in surprise when he recognised Bishop Skinner. For a moment he did not seem to know what to do. Then the genial smile reasserted itself, though Charlie noted a certain wariness in Houstoun's eyes. Because he had something to hide? Or just because there was an Episcopal Bishop on his premises?

'Good day to you, Mr. Skinner,' he said, stumbling a little over the name. Charlie wondered if he called the Bishop something else entirely behind his back. 'How may I be of assistance?'

'I think some of that fine tea would be excellent,' said the Bishop, 'though of course my wife deals with that kind of thing. But it does smell delicious. I shall mention it to her.' The Bishop, too, sounded perfectly calm and cheerful, a neighbour paying an ordinary visit to a neighbour. But Charlie could see his gloved fingers tangled nervously behind his back. Another thing he had learned in his dealings with clergy: serenity on the surface concealed just as much anxiety in them as it did in anyone else, and sometimes more. With the possible exception of Bishop Petrie, who seemed serene all the way through.

'I was so sorry to discover the sad fate of your new maid,' Bishop Skinner went on. 'Minnie, was it not?'

'I believe so. I barely knew her,' said George Houstoun, but allowed himself a mournful little sigh, all the same. 'I told your man here to convey my regret to you that she was found on your doorstep. It was good of you to take her in to your – chapel.' He could not seem to help making a face. 'She seemed a decent, likeable girl, came to the kirk with us on Sunday and so on.'

'Where had she come from? Was she new to the town? I don't believe I had seen her before.'

'I've no idea. My wife deals with the staff,' said Houstoun grandly, though Charlie knew they had had no staff for a while till Minnie turned up – and now, presumably, had none again. Houstoun made it sound like a regiment.

'A country girl, perhaps, lost. She was very lucky to find your household when she did, it seems to me.'

'Aye, a lass on her own like that – terrible things can happen!' said George Houstoun, then remembered that indeed they had. He cleared his throat roughly. 'Still, I should not have liked to think of her sleeping out in the cold, or worse. At least her last few days were spent in comfort and respectability.'

'Indeed: a blessing for her, and for you, as her benefactor,' said the Bishop smoothly. 'Were you here on – wasn't it Saturday night when she arrived?'

'No, I wasna,' said Houstoun. Charlie was watching him carefully but he saw no sign of agitation at the thought of Saturday night. 'Most Saturday nights I go out to meet some of my fellow merchants in a private parlour in the New Inn, to talk over the business of the week. I went out as usual at six, and when I returned at ... well, it was past twelve, I believe, for there was a deal of business to discuss.' He nodded to himself, but he had reddened a little.

'Though we would have stopped at midnight, for the Sabbath. And there the lass was, or at least my wife said she was, for she had already retired for the night. I did not see her till next day, when she prepared the fire and so on for the day.'

'Did you by any chance see anything on your way home that night that ... I don't know, anything out of place, that might have frightened her?'

'On Saturday night? No, I did not: it was quiet and calm, nothing going on at all. I think she probably just lost her way. By that time of the night even Jem Hosie had found a home to go to,' he added spitefully.

For the moment the Bishop ignored the name.

'And how was she for the rest of her time with you?'

'Like I said, I had little enough to do with her. She seemed to give satisfaction, which is all that was required, really. She was mostly in the house. We lost our last maid a whilie ago, and I daresay there was work that needed to be done to catch up, and that would have kept her gey busy. Let me see – when did I see her go out at all? For she would have had to go through the shop here, and I would have seen her – unless I was occupied with a customer and missed her. She was an awful small wee creature,' he said, and for a moment he seemed touched by genuine sorrow.

'She was here on Monday,' Charlie thought it might be time to help. 'Would she have sent the laundry out for you?'

'That's it! That's when I saw her!' George Houstoun clicked his fingers. 'The laundry. She comes out with two bundles bigger than herself – she had to drag the second one, and I was hoping that no customer would come in and fall over the bundles, or over her. That would not create a good impression, would it?' He gave a little chuckle. 'I watched her haul them outside, and then she must have been out there with the laundry woman for a whilie, getting them on to the cart.' No indication, Charlie noted, that George Houstoun might have given poor little Minnie a hand with the heavy bundles.

'Ah, and that was what happened next,' said Houstoun, fitting memories together, 'because she was a whilie, as I say, and I went to the door to make sure the laundry cart was not blocking it or spoiling the view of the stock. But the cart was away, and I looked about for the lass, and there she was, talking with – now, did I no tell you? She was talking with yon shilpit individual, Jem Hosie.'

'She met him?'

'I doubt she knew him,' said George Houstoun, 'for where would she have met him? He was just at his usual, bothering people in the street, watching where he has no right to be watching, no doubt making sure no one in the neighbourhood had seen what he was up to on Saturday night - oh!'

'What is it, Mr. Houstoun?' asked the Bishop, after a moment.

'I - I've said to your man here that I thought Jem Hosie was the likeliest fellow to have killed his stepfather. What if he thought our maid had seen him do it?'

Chapter Forty-Four

'Do you believe him, sir?' asked Charlie when they were far enough from the shop not to be heard. 'I mean, the bit about Minnie being killed because she saw who murdered Mr. Meston – that sort of makes sense. But he seems dead keen that Jem did it.'

'As to that, I'm not sure,' said the Bishop. He stopped and looked about him. The various lamps about the street lit it reasonably well at this hour. 'I see Jem has gone, for now. If he's right, and Jem did kill his stepfather, and thought he had been seen, he might well have come looking for Minnie. Minnie would have known them both and been able to identify them to the magistrate. All Jem would have had to do, once he had found that Minnie was working at Houstoun's, was to wait until she was sent out on her own, and follow her, presumably.'

'But then to leave her on your doorstep, sir?'

'Why not? He seems a strange enough young man.' The Bishop sighed. 'I don't know. To go by his own account, Mr. Houstoun was out from six to past midnight on Saturday, at his meeting. You found Cuthbert Meston's body just after eleven, was it not?'

'Aye, sir, thereabouts.'

'Then I'd like to know if he really was at his meeting, or if he was out in the street waiting for his wife's lover.'

'I could go and ask at the inn, sir.'

'That's a good start, yes. Do that, would you? And then, I suppose, we need to talk to Jem Hosie.'

Charlie knew the staff at the New Inn moderately well, and had seen a good deal of them recently in all his escorting of Dr. Seabury and Mr. Cooper. Thinking back to that Saturday night, when he had first almost carried Myles Cooper back there, he remembered that Jockie Watson had been on duty, so Jockie was the first person he looked for.

'A meeting?' Jockie asked, a bit puzzled. 'What kind of a meeting, like?'

'Local merchants, apparently. They take a private parlour each Saturday to discuss business. Not very grand, I'd say,' he added, thinking of George Houstoun's level in society.

'A private parlour? Och, aye, that'd be the club.'

'A club?'

'Best takings of the week, from that club!' said Jockie with enthusiasm. 'They near drink the place dry!'

'A drinking club? Wait, now,' said Charlie, 'do you ken the names of any of the members?'

'Oh, aye, most of them. They've been coming for years. All gey respectable when they arrive, ken, and then the drinking starts. The wonder is that they're all in the kirk in the morn, and all. The Lord must have blessed them with gey strong stomachs.'

'Is George Houstoun among them?'

'He is, aye. He was one of the founding members, as I recall it. He's here most weeks.'

'Was he here last Saturday?'

Jockie laughed out loud.

'Aye, he was, for I had to throw them out in the end! He was the last to go - after midnight, and the guests were complaining about the singing from the parlour, see. I gathered him up and shoved him out the door, and wondered if he'd get home all right, for it was a cold night.'

'Had he left the parlour before that, do you know?'

'I doubt it,' said Jockie. 'He was there every time I went in with more drink. There's a grand big cludgie in yon parlour, in its ain closet, so there's no need for them to go anywhere. Anyway, off he went, still singing, and the way he was walking it would have taken him three times the distance to get home as it ought to. I heard tell the next day he was in the kirk just as usual, so I stopped worrying.'

'Definitely after midnight?'

'Aye, sir. And by the sound of things, in such a state that if he did kill anybody, it would have been by accident.'

'I'd never have thought it of him,' said the Bishop, 'behaving like that. Well, he could not have killed Cuthbert Meston, anyway. And I'm less surprised, now, to find he has no idea about what his wife was up to. His Saturday nights must be blanks for him.'

'Should we look for Jem Hosie now, sir?'

The Bishop glanced at the clock in his bookroom.

'If we can find him ... I know it's not far off supper time, but, well, it's Friday tomorrow. Bishop Kilgour will arrive.'

'And Minnie's funeral, too, sir.'

'Come on, then.' The Bishop pushed himself away from his desk. 'Let's go and see where he is.'

Jem had not returned to his doorway since they had come back from George Houstoun's shop.

'Could he have gone home?' asked Bishop Skinner.

'Maybe, sir. But he comes and goes so much, I wonder if there's somewhere hereabouts he takes shelter when he needs a break from his vigil?'

'His vigil?'

Charlie hoped the darkness hid his embarrassment.

'I mean it looks a bit like a vigil, does it no, sir? There all hours.'

'There all hours and yet just when his stepfather is murdered, in plain sight of his accustomed place, he is gone. Very convenient.'

'Why do you think he might have done it, sir?'

'He was on bad terms with his stepfather, was he not? Perhaps it was just a quarrel taken too far.'

'I'd have thought then that he would have been the kind to give himself up, like a character in a story, all tragic.'

'Hm, maybe you're right. But –'

'Oh, sir, there's Mr. Mennie at the well. He takes an interest in what's going on – he might ken where Jem has gone.'

Mr. Mennie was drawing a bucket of water, and looking about even as he pumped, maybe for someone to gossip with. His eyes lit up when he saw Charlie approach.

'Aye, fit like, Charlie?'

'Nae bad,' Charlie acknowledged. 'That for your supper, or are you ready for the morn already?'

'Supper,' said Mennie shortly. 'A late supper, by the time this lot boils. Is yon your master out and about at this hour? Are you taking him somewhere for his supper?'

'No – well, maybe. I was just wondering – ken that lad that stand over in yon doorway all day?'

'Aye – and I ken who he is now. He's Cuthbert Meston's stepson, and George Houstoun at the end of the road will have nothing but that that lad killed Meston. They were aye quarrelling, ken?'

'Is that so? Michty,' said Charlie. 'Tell me, when the lad's no here, is there some place local he goes to warm up?'

'As it happens, I ken that and all,' said Mennie, looking smug. 'For I've seen him twa-three times in yon howff on the Ghost Row.'

'Down yonder? Why for?'

'To warm up, like you say.'

'Oh, well,' Charlie shrugged. 'Thanks. I hope your supper's no too late.'

'Ach,' said Mennie, and went on pumping, though Charlie was conscious of his eyes on Charlie's back as he returned to the Bishop.

'There's a howff on the Ghost Row,' he began.

'I know there is. Is that where Jem goes?'

'Aye.' Charlie wriggled. 'I'd best go alone, do you think, sir?'

Bishop Skinner gave him a look.

'No,' he said, 'I'll come too. I've been in a howff before. And, well, I'd like to see what the lad says for myself.'

'Well, sir, if you're sure ...'

'Come on, or we'll never be done.'

The main problem with the Bishop and the howff was that the Bishop was a tall man, and the howff had apparently been built for goblins. Even Charlie had to stoop to get through the door, then nearly fell down three uneven steps to where the floor was, well below street level. He put out their lantern, but immediately wished he had not, for the air inside the place was black fug from tobacco smoke, fire smoke, and probably centuries of inadequate cleaning. He felt the

Bishop's hand on his shoulder.

'Just in case we lose each other,' said Bishop Skinner, but Charlie thought he heard a laugh in the voice.

It was hard to tell how large the place was. Charlie stumbled into a table, and bounced off it on to a stool which nearly floored him. Then a pair of shiny boots lay across his path, and he would have tripped over them, too, if someone had not put out a hand to steady him. It was Jem.

'What are you doing in here, Charlie?' he asked, waving the stem of a long-arched clay pipe. 'Is this where you come to drink away the ills of the day?'

Charlie felt his way to a free stool beside Jem, and looked back to see the Bishop was also drawing a chair across to join them. Jem's eyes gleamed in the mottled light as he recognised Charlie's companion: Charlie's own eyes were starting to sting with the smoke. Jem stood, awkwardly – he was a tall man himself. He bowed.

'Good evening to you, sir,' Jem said. 'Can I invite you to join me in a jug of claret? It is – not at all undrinkable.'

Jem himself was evidence of that. He seemed to have drunk a moderate amount already.

'Thank you,' said the Bishop. 'But if you'll order it, please allow me to pay.'

'You are very kind, sir,' said Jem, and stopped a passing serving man, who goggled when he took in the howff's latest customer.

'What brings you here, Mr. Hosie?' Charlie asked. 'I'd have thought to find you in the New Inn, or its like.'

'Never!' said Jem extravagantly, almost knocking the jug of claret from the serving man's hands. He steadied himself, handed out glasses, and laid the claret on the table by Jem's elbow, then left. 'This is life! That serving man - he's an old soldier, deaf in one ear from the guns, half the fingers missing on his left hand. Over there? Smugglers, bringing in brandy from France. Never say I told you,' he added, one finger pressed against his lips, eyebrows wild and high. 'And – and ... well, just take it from me. Life.' He slumped back in his seat, then seemed to remember who his companions were, and made the effort to sit straight again. 'Not that I don't appreciate the more ... um, respectable guests at the New Inn, too.' His dark eyes flitted towards the Bishop and away again. 'But what brings you here?'

'A question, Mr. Hosie, if we may,' the Bishop began, smiling to reassure him as if he were calming an edgy horse. 'A name - I'd like to know if it's familiar to you.'

'Go on, then, sir?'

'Aristotle Cummins,' said the Bishop monumentally.

'Who?'

It was clear at once that the name meant absolutely nothing to Jem. The Bishop, clearly a little let down, frowned and said,

'Forgive me, for I intend no impertinence -'

'Of course, not at all, sir.' Jem still looked confused, as if he thought he had failed some kind of test.

'What is your financial situation? I'm sure it cannot be confidential, for you know that the mothers of many young ladies of your acquaintance almost certainly discuss it already!'

Oh, no, thought Charlie. The Bishop is making a joke, but that is not the way that Jem is going to take it.

Jem sat up even straighter.

'My late mother had money of her own, sir, which my stepfather holds - held - for me until I reach my majority. And I believe - I have been told - that my stepfather himself was to make mention of me in his will. I am to have a share in his warehouse and business. I can, with some little application, support a wife, when I reach my majority, sir.'

Charlie's heart went out to the lad. He thought that Bishop Skinner was enquiring on his own behalf, with reference to Jane, surely. But Bishop Skinner, who had not entered into such negotiations for either daughter before, was oblivious to Jem's agony. Instead, skipping down the list of questions he wanted to ask, he moved brightly to the next one.

'Last Monday, did you meet your stepfather's erstwhile maid, Minnie, in Longacre?'

They expected him to say no, either to deny it because it was suspicious, or to deny it because it was George Houstoun's fantasy.

'Aye, sir, I did. I spoke to Minnie outside George Houstoun's shop.'

Chapter Forty-Five

'You did?' The Bishop was startled. 'So you knew where she was? Where she had taken refuge?'

'Well ...' Jem began to look uneasy. 'Well, I sort of did, yes.'

'But you seemed surprised when I told you!' said Charlie, unable to help himself. 'As if you hadn't known where she was.'

'I ... I met her there by accident. I mean. I was in the street, waiting –' He broke off, with a glance at Bishop Skinner. 'I was in Longacre, and I thought I recognised her in the distance. She was bringing bundles out of George Houstoun's house.' He gave a little laugh, though his face remained serious. 'At that distance, it wasn't so much her I recognised, as her determination. The bundles were nearly as big as she was, but she had no help, except the laundry woman joining to swing them up on to the cart. She dragged them out of the shop all on her own. Typical Minnie! She would never ask for help. She was just so ...'

'Thrawn?' suggested Bishop Skinner, without smiling.

'Not thrawn exactly,' said Jem, his head on one side to analyse the finer points of meaning. 'Stubborn, aye.' A step kinder than thrawn, Charlie thought.

'Why did you not say before where she was? That you had seen her?'

'Who would I have told? And why?' Jem asked, reasonably. 'I suppose I might have said something to Alan, or to my step-uncle. But I've barely seen them. And anyway ... anyway, I thought I could protect her.'

'Then she knew she was in danger?'

'Oh, aye,' said Jem ominously, 'she knew. She knew well enough.'

He looked miserable now, and Charlie was sure it was not an act. Bishop Skinner said nothing, and Charlie took the hint, keeping silent. Sometimes it was the best way to get someone to talk, just saying nothing, and waiting. The muffled noise of the howff rose and fell about them before Jem began again.

'I was angry my stepfather had thrown her out, into the snow, with no warning. I thought he was the danger. When she vanished from the women's hospital, the night he died ... I couldn't work it out. Had she seen him, maybe from a window, and thought he was coming after her? Maybe he was, indeed. Or had she – well, I knew she couldn't have killed him, not on her own. I mean, I said she was stubborn, but she could not possibly have weighed him down the way he died, in that horse trough. He could have flicked her off him like a flea. I wondered if someone had killed him to avenge her, but as far as I knew she had no family in the town and no friends of the kind who might do such a thing.'

'The father of her child?'

'Aye, maybe,' said Jem, nodding. 'That occurred to me. I don't know what like of a man he is, though. And it doesn't explain why Minnie is dead, does it?'

He was brighter than even Charlie had given him credit for: he had at least done some reasoning, here. The Bishop looked at Charlie, then back at Jem.

'But then you spoke with her, did you not? Outside George Houstoun's shop?'

'I did. I ran over when I realised who it was. I was that pleased to see her alive and well, even if she was working for that scooneral, Houstoun.'

'And what did she say?'

'She tried to ignore me, at first. She pretended not to hear me, then she sort of looked through me, as if she had never seen me before. Stubborn! But I'm determined, too. When the laundry woman had left, she had nothing to look at but me, and I kept saying her name, until at last she gave in.

'I asked her if she was working for George Houstoun, and she said she was. I said to her now my stepfather was dead, would she not come back and work for us? I said I knew she was expecting a child, but that we would look after her. At that she gave a laugh, and I wondered if she thought my uncle might be nearly as bad as my stepfather – well, he can snap at times, but honestly, he's a much easier man to live with. And I said that if that was what she was worried about, I would protect her.

'"From what?" she said. "And how?" I said I could stand up to my uncle perfectly well, and I would take her side. But Minnie just gave another of those hollow laughs. "You cannot protect me from a murderer," she said.

'Like a fool, I asked her what she meant. She looked about her, to see who might be overhearing us, and drew me over towards the wall of Houstoun's shop. I had nearly to bend double to hear her, for she kept her voice very low.

'"Listen," she said, "see Saturday night? I ken fine what happened to the master."

'"You do?" I said. "Then what was it?"

'"I'm no telling you," she said. "I'm keeping quiet, and then he canna fault me for a'thing. But if you think I'll ever go back to yon warehouse, you're wrong. I'll never darken its doors again."'

Perhaps Jem did have a career before him as an actor – Charlie had never heard Minnie speak, nor seen her alive, but he felt he had seen and heard her now.

'Did she mean ...' said the Bishop. But Jem had not finished.

'"I'm going back in here, now," she said, pointing to George Houstoun's shop, "And if you see me again you just pretend you never knew me. And I'll do the same. Stay well away, if you think there's a'thing you can do to protect me." And she laughed again, and it made the hairs stand up on the back of my neck. Then she went to go back into the shop, and then she stopped, tapping her hand on the doorpost as though she was trying to make a decision. Then she looked back, and just muttered, gey quick, "It was a man well kent to me and to you," and then she went inside, fast, and I never saw her again.'

'A man well kent to both of you,' the Bishop repeated, after a long sip of his claret. 'Who do you think she meant?'

'I supposed,' said Jem, and his face was bleak, 'that she meant either Alan the warehouseman, or my uncle Stephen. And I don't want her to have meant either of them. For if she did, and if one of them killed my stepfather – then I can only imagine that the same man came back up here and stabbed Minnie. Just because he knew – whichever of them it was – that she had seen them kill my stepfather.'

There was a horrid little silence in their particular corner of the noisy howff. Charlie felt sick, and by the look on his face, so did Jem.

'I don't like to ask you this,' said the Bishop at last, after several sips of claret, 'but did you get any impression at all that – an impression of which one it was she meant?'

But Jem shook his head sharply.

'No, not at all. I've been over it in my mind, and sometimes I think she meant Uncle Stephen, and sometimes I think she meant Alan. And because of that, I don't think she gave any hint of one or the other. She was too scared. And I said I would protect her ... I hadn't a hope,' he finished bitterly.

'No wonder ...' Charlie stopped.

'What's that, Charlie?' asked the Bishop.

'I was just away to say the funeral cannot have been easy for you, Mr. Hosie.' No wonder Jem had been drunk, before he had even heard that Minnie was dead.

'I've been trying to stay away. I know it's cowardice,' said Jem, 'but I cannot work out in my head which of them it was, and it's unbearable to be there with them. And yet ... and yet if it's Alan I should warn Uncle Stephen. And if it's Uncle Stephen, I should probably tell Alan. I don't know what to do!'

'Look,' said Bishop Skinner, 'we're trying to sort this out ourselves.'

'But why would you?'

'Well, because it seemed for some time as if it was all centred on us – on Dr. Seabury, who is visiting us, and his friend Mr. Cooper. Your stepfather quarrelled with them on the boat from Edinburgh, and saw to it that a very hostile anonymous letter was sent about them that arrived after his death. And he was murdered almost outside my house, and then Minnie's body was left outside the front door. The magistrate, at least, finds it all quite suspicious.'

Jem was wide-eyed.

'I see ... That – that's why you were at my stepfather's funeral, is it?'

'Aye,' said Charlie, 'that was one reason, anyway.'

'Neither you nor Mr. Stephen Meston seemed to know what business Mr. Cuthbert Meston might have around Longacre,' the Bishop went on, 'and so we wondered if it was in fact something to do with us and our business. We even thought –' he caught Charlie's eye, 'well, I even thought, for some time, that he had been killed in error, and Dr. Seabury, who is of much the same build, might have been the intended victim.'

'That's – my, no wonder you were worried!' Jem shook his head. 'What a guddle. And all my stepfather's fault. I suppose ...'

'Why do you think either Alan or your uncle would have killed your stepfather, though?' the Bishop asked.

'Why not?' asked Jem simply. 'He was a hard master, and not easy on his own brother, either. He made both of them work hard, and gave neither of them much freedom. He brought up Uncle Stephen himself, after their father's death, and told him what to do and how to behave. So it might just have been a bid for freedom, or sudden anger, or ...'

'Would either of them have done it because of his treatment of Minnie?' the Bishop asked.

'Do you mean was either of them the father of Minnie's child? Or just generally?'

'Either.'

'Well, no, I don't think so. I mean, we all tried to look after Minnie. She was just so tiny – she looked as if she needed looking after. She always said she didn't! Chased us away if we tried to help too much.' He laughed, then turned sombre. 'But she did need looking after in the end, and none of us was there.'

Well, if Minnie was right, one of them had been there, hadn't they? thought Charlie. But it seemed that Jem could not quite accept yet that of the two men he had lived with for so many years, one was a double murderer.

'So anyway,' Jem pulled himself up in his seat again, 'I think it's best if I just don't go home for a whilie, find somewhere else to stay, until I work out what I should do. I need to clear my head, try to work things out.'

'You could come and stay with us,' said Bishop Skinner. 'There's not a great deal of room, but you'd be safe there – and I doubt your uncle would think to look for you there!'

Charlie watched as Jem took in this offer. He could almost

see the thoughts in Jem's mind - proximity to Jane Skinner, offered to him on a plate, with a perfect excuse! Surely he would take the chance with both hands? But then something else seemed to occur to him, and he straightened his back, and faced the Bishop in as grown-up a manner as he could manage.

'Thank you, sir, it is a kind offer. But I shall not trouble you: I have friends I can impose upon, and perhaps it is best if I remove myself from the scene of the drama as far as possible.'

'Then at least, Mr. Hosie, tell me where you might be reached if need be - and for my own peace of mind.'

'I'll send word as soon as I am settled,' Jem promised. He seemed about to rise and set off, then paused.

'But tell me, sir, if you will - you mentioned a name earlier. Is it another clergyman my father threatened? Who is Aristotle Cummins?'

Chapter Forty-Six

'He was a clergyman, yes,' said Bishop Skinner after a moment. 'It was concerning him that your stepfather paid his visit to Edinburgh.'

'Oh?' Jem did not seem very interested in Edinburgh. 'Unusual – I daresay he had taken in some bond or other and was seeking payment, otherwise I don't see how he might have fallen into business with a clergyman. Only money would make my stepfather travel so far – travel is expensive, you know!'

For a fleeting moment, Charlie caught Cuthbert Meston's face and voice in Jem's words. He would make a skilled actor, certainly. Then Jem frowned, even as he collected the shoulders of his coat around him.

'I doubt the business is finished, though,' he said.

The Bishop paused again.

'What makes you say that?'

'Oh, only that a letter came for my stepfather after his death, with Edinburgh on the wrapper. I saw my Uncle Stephen pay for it when it arrived, so I suppose he's carrying it on. Another year or so,' he sighed, 'and I expect I shall have to involve myself in such things, too.'

Bishop Skinner stood, and belatedly remembered to bow his head under the low ceiling. A lesser man would have sworn at the knock he gave himself.

Outside in the frozen street, Charlie could feel the odours of the howff linger about him – he would have some explaining to do to

Luzie, when he managed to get home. He stopped to sort out the lantern as the Bishop and Jem turned ahead of him to bid each other farewell.

'Are you sure you have somewhere safe to go?' the Bishop asked. 'Have you no light?'

'I can find my way, and I shall be quite safe,' said Jem, 'thank you, sir. I shall let you know where I have gone – and I should be much obliged if you would be good enough to let me know if you find anything out.' He gave a little nod, as though to approve his own grown-up demeanour. Then it broke. 'I wish I could have protected her!' he gasped. 'How could I have let her die?'

'You must not blame yourself, Mr. Hosie,' said the Bishop gently. 'Stronger forces were at work, I think. And she is at peace now.'

'I pray so,' muttered Jem, on the verge of tears. Then he dashed the back of his hand across his eyes, and straightened once more. 'I shall bid you good evening, sir: it is a cold night to be lingering. And God's blessing on your searches.'

'Thank you, Mr. Hosie. Take care of yourself.'

They turned in different directions, the Bishop and Charlie up towards Broad Street and Jem further down the dark lane where the howff lay.

'I hope he finds safety,' said the Bishop, glancing after him. Already he could barely be seen in the darkness.

'I'm sure he has friends to go to, sir,' said Charlie, though on what he could base this he had no idea. Jem seemed the kind who needed an audience, though Charlie had never seen him with people of his own age. As long as he did not go home to the warehouse on the quay, though, he was likely to be all right.

'I suppose we must go home for supper,' said the Bishop, 'though I should like fine to go and find out what is in that letter from Edinburgh that was sent to Cuthbert Meston. Do you think that Stephen Meston now knows all the story of Aristotle Cummins and Jem?'

'It seems likely, sir,' said Charlie, 'though it may be that Mr. Meston had other business in Edinburgh and the letter was to do with it. But what difference would it make if he does know, sir? It might be that he is appointed Jem Hosie's curator in place of Cuthbert

Meston, I suppose.'

'Aye, someone will have to be, anyway, until he is of age. But I wonder ... Cuthbert Meston did not know what the story was until he went to Edinburgh, and when he came back, from all I can gather, he had no intention of telling anyone until he was able to talk to Jeremiah and tell him about it. By your account of what Mrs. Houstoun said, the news fairly burst out of him, did it not?'

They had reached the mouth of Longacre. Charlie peered down the street to the far end, where he could just see the lamp outside the Houstouns' shuttered shop.

'That was the impression I had, sir, yes.'

'So he did not tell Stephen, for he had not told Stephen when he left Mrs. Houstoun's flat, and he never left Longacre alive.'

'Unless it was Stephen who killed him, though, sir.'

'Yes, unless it was. Which is what I'm coming to: what if he did meet Stephen, and told him? Stephen would know, then, that he had not told Jeremiah, and so if Stephen killed Cuthbert, and kept it quiet, where would the money go? If he took on the role of Jeremiah's curator, it's possible that Stephen could cream off quite a bit before Jem came of age, would you think?'

'Stephen would have to think a bit fast for that, would he no, sir?' Faster than me, anyway, Charlie thought. The Bishop frowned, disappointed.

'Ah, yes, Jem said the letter came after Cuthbert Meston's death. Stephen could only have found out about the business from Cuthbert ... unless he didn't count telling his brother when he told Mrs. Houstoun?'

'It's possible, sir,' said Charlie, opening the front door for the Bishop to go in first, 'but it's not the impression I got.'

'Yet Minnie said someone they both knew ... Do you think Jem could have been right, that Stephen just lost his temper and wanted his freedom? Thank you.'

Charlie took Bishop Skinner's coat and hat, and laid them on the hall stand. The house was never over-warm, but coming in from the frosty night he could feel his cheeks tingle.

'If his temper is anything like his brother's, it wouldna surprise me, sir. And someone said to me – oh, it was Alan – that Stephen was a better man than Cuthbert, but that he still had a hard streak. He was certainly not in a good mood at the funeral.'

'Funerals ... It's Minnie's funeral tomorrow, is it not?'

'I believe so, sir.'

'I wonder what time Bishop Kilgour will arrive? That frost will help speed him here ... on any other occasion I should be delighted, but now I find myself hoping for any slight, harmless delay.'

'And you wanted to see Stephen Meston, too, did you no, sir?'

'I did ... I don't think I can reasonably call after supper. That's not a time to chap on anyone's door and expect a welcome, I should say. And then I want to go to Minnie's funeral – or if Bishop Kilgour has already arrived, I'd like you to go.'

'Can I make a suggestion, sir?'

'Of course, Charlie. And we'd better see if supper is ready, or Jean will think we don't appreciate her.'

'It's on those lines, sir, my suggestion.'

'In that case, go on!'

'Just to ask if Miss Jane and Miss Margaret could help Jean tomorrow, sir? She's already saying I'm not doing enough, and she's been left to fetch and carry and all that she struggles with.'

'Of course – I'll tell Jane to make sure the two of them are ready and willing first thing in the morning.' He sighed. 'Is there anything else we can do tonight, Charlie? Anything to further our case?'

'I canna think of a'thing, sir.'

'Then I'd better tell everyone what we've found out, and see what they say. This time tomorrow Bishop Kilgour will be here: if this is not settled, he will never agree to a consecration. Not while there is any doubt hanging over Dr. Seabury's head.'

'But surely,' said Dr. Seabury at the supper table, a little desperately, 'surely, again, that exonerates me? Minnie said that the killer was someone she and Jem knew – well, I did not know Minnie, and I'm sure she would not even have recognised me if I had been there.'

'Aristotle Cummins' natural son!' Myles was still enjoying the gossip. 'Oh, he was always a close one. Who's to say his son has not inherited his talent for deception? Keeping a bastard hidden all these years!'

Charlie thought of Jem's cleverness in imitating Minnie and his stepfather, a kind of deception, an act. And he was certainly acting a great deal of the time, with his dramatic gestures and poses. Was he really deceptive, too?

Bishop Skinner must have heard his thoughts.

'We only have Jem Hosie's word for it that Minnie said that. Yet,' he went on, 'it does seem probable. We've said it before - two people from the same household murdered - you want to look first at the other members of that household.'

'Did Jem Hosie know that Alan was the father of the bairn?' asked Bishop Petrie. 'Could there have been some jealousy there?'

Bishop Skinner looked at Charlie, serving second helpings of broth, who shook his head.

'I dinna think so, sir. I mean, I dinna think he knew. Jem was fond of Minnie, to judge by all he said and did, but I didna see any sign he thought he was competing for her.'

'I'd agree,' said Bishop Skinner. 'I'd have said he was fond of her as an elder brother might be - and devastated by his inability to protect her. If you ask me, I'd say his heart lies elsewhere, for he seems the kind to pretend to himself a romantic attachment to someone like Minnie, someone he saw as vulnerable, if he were not committed elsewhere.'

Around the table, Mrs. Skinner, Jane, and Charlie, avoided each other's eyes with great care.

'Where is Jem Hosie now? Has he gone home to confront his uncle, or their warehouseman?' Bishop Petrie asked, concerned.

'He has gone to stay with friends. He said he would send me word when he was settled, so that I could tell him if anything happens.'

'So if what you say is true,' said Dr. Seabury, 'and of course it does seem sensible, that the killer was connected with both Cuthbert Meston and Minnie, and that that seems to point to Stephen Meston or to the warehouseman - what is his name again?'

'Alan - um, what's his surname, Charlie?'

'Beith, sir.'

'Alan Beith, then,' said Dr. Seabury with a smile for Charlie. 'What do we know about these two men? Is one more likely than the other? I confess I should very much like not to have this hanging over me, when the magistrate has not even said what he thinks!'

'Quite right - we need to clear this up,' agreed Bishop Petrie. 'And the sooner the better. John, what do you know?'

'I have only met them briefly – Stephen Meston a little more than the warehouseman. Charlie, you have been there a few times, now. What do you say?'

'Alan is quiet and a little surly, though I have only met him since Cuthbert Meston threw his sweetheart out of the house so I may not have seen him fairly, sir. Mr. Stephen Meston is very anxious to tell me what a good man his brother was, despite his temper, and to justify his dislike or distrust of the clergy – of all persuasions. But he has a temper, too, when he's taken drink, and Alan says he has a hard streak in him. What Stephen Meston thinks of Alan I have no idea: he has barely mentioned him. Oh – well, there was one very small detail, sir. Stephen Meston told me that on the night before Cuthbert Meston's funeral, Alan had to go out to see friends who needed his help. He made it clear that otherwise, of course, Alan would not have gone out – he was making the comparison with Jem Hosie, who had gone out drinking, I believe. He made Alan out to be a dutiful, respectable young man, as if that behaviour was exactly what he would expect from him. Alan resented the way Cuthbert Meston treated him – and treated Stephen, too. He said that Meston would not let him and Minnie marry, as married servants did not regard their employer as their first priority. He called it slavery, sir.' This time Charlie did not meet Dr. Seabury's eye, but he heard the word echo a little around the table.

'Slaves have been known to kill their masters,' said Dr. Seabury quietly.

Charlie made sure he helped Jean clear everything up after supper, though he felt dead on his feet. At last he bade her good night, received her usual monosyllabic answer, and headed off into the freezing night, locking the front door behind him and giving it a little proprietorial pat. He turned to go home.

Even before he reached the passage out to Broad Street, he smelled smoke on the air. When he came to the mouth of it, he could see clearly where it was coming from.

Smoke was pouring from the doorway of Luzie's warehouse.

Charlie ran.

Chapter Forty-Seven

In a moment he saw that Luzie, along with the children from upstairs, were safely out in the street. The children were in their nightclothes. As Charlie ran he dragged off his coat and when he reached them, he flung it around their shoulders, then hurried to his wife. Luzie had no need of cover. She was in the midst of the action, directing neighbours to scoop snow from the street edges and fling it in through the warehouse door.

'Charlie!' she cried when she saw him. 'Look what they have done now!'

'You mean this was deliberate?' Charlie's hands and feet carried on to help with the snow gathering, while his mind tried to take this in. The Meston household, still trying to destroy Luzie's business? What had she done to attract such hostility?

'I've hose for the bairns,' a plump woman announced, efficiently heading off to warm the children's feet.

'Is everyone out?' Charlie shouted.

'Aye, aye,' came various voices, some resigned, some frightened. Plenty had brought buckets and were scooping snow from further along the street, bringing it back to fling into the eye-watering depths of the warehouse. He noticed a few barrels and sacks in the middle of the street: presumably Luzie had managed to drag a few things out before she had to give up.

But even as he joined in the firefighting, it became apparent that the fire was diminishing, the tumbling smoke began to drift and thin, its stench slowly replaced by an unappealing mixture of cold tea and coffee, and soggy cinnamon, and whatever had been picked up with the snow. The neighbours who had helped, blackened faces hopeful but wary, gathered a few more buckets and threw the contents through the doorway, then stopped to cough. Luzie, more concerned for her stock than for her own safety, plunged inside, and began tossing out into the street bits of broken, charred wood that would serve as nothing more than kindling. Before going to help her, Charlie turned to thank everyone there in the street, clutching their buckets, their hands and arms soaked with snow and water. There were even those who had come through from Longacre, like Bodsy Bowers and George Houstoun, though he suspected that in the latter's case it had been more curiosity than an eagerness to help that had stopped him. All those who had been close to the work were smoky, sooty and bright-eyed with exertion. Even Bodsy had a grubby neckcloth, and Mr. Houstoun seemed almost to have come prepared in an older suit of clothes than Charlie had seen him wear before. Charlie grinned to himself as he nevertheless thanked the grocer for his help and received a prim nod in acknowledgement. After all, the man had himself described standing and watching as his tiny maid had lugged out laundry bundles almost as big as herself, and had not mentioned even considering giving her a hand.

He looked about at the remaining spectators. The woman from upstairs was ushering the children back into the building, now more anxious to get them back to bed than about potential conflagration. She glanced back at him, and whisked the coat off their backs and into Charlie's hands.

'You're a good man, Mr. Rob,' she said with a grin. 'Now mind you keep an eye and don't let it take again!' Then she was back with the bairns and their snow-encrusted hose.

He smiled back, and continued his survey of the people in the street. He had heard, once, that people who set fire to things can never resist the temptation to stay and watch them burn. But no matter how carefully he scanned the crowd, he could not see Stephen Meston, nor Alan Beith, nor even Jem Hosie. But any one of them, had he been there, could have vanished before he had had the chance to look.

He followed Luzie into the warehouse to find she had lit a lamp, and was already sweeping the floor. Only a little of the stock, fortunately, seemed to be damaged.

'They pushed a rag through a crack in the shutters, and lit it,' she said briskly. 'Most of the stock was over this side of the room, praise be to Heaven. But I have a sack of coffee beans that is – well, over-roasted.'

They looked at each other, and burst out laughing. And then Luzie's laughter turned to tears, and Charlie took her in his arms, and she sobbed and sobbed into his waistcoat until she could sob no more. A few tears slid down his own sooty cheeks: it had been a scramble in his head from the moment he first scented the smoke until now. He would have to sit down with a mug of ale, and try to take everything in.

'We'll have to lock the door,' he said at last, holding her now a little away from him.

'Aye,' she agreed, 'though the place will stink. Can you help me bring in what's in the street?' She gave a final sniff, wiped her eyes on her apron, and led him back outside. Now almost everyone had dispersed, and between them they dragged and rolled the barrels and sacks that had been pulled clear back into the warehouse. Then Charlie locked and bolted the door, and they abandoned the shop for the night and retreated to the kitchen with its cosy box bed, though they left the shop door open, to hear if the fire took again. Charlie was torn between simply falling into the bed, and washing and talking first. But Luzie was still edgy, and it was clear that sleep was not the best option for now. She poured two cups of ale, and they sat together, side by side on the bench by the table.

'You're sure it was deliberate?' asked Charlie, though the image of the rag in the shutters was still clear in his mind.

'Oh, aye, yes,' said Luzie. 'I saw the rag myself when I looked outside. There must have been oil on it, or something – I think I smelled lard. Good quality lard, too – what a waste!'

They laughed a little again at that.

'You've made some dangerous enemies, my love,' said Charlie, 'to waste lard like that.'

'The Mestons, aye. Well, Stephen Meston.'

'Did you see him? Or Alan, or Jem?'

She scowled.

'No, I did not! They would have been far away by the time I found the rag.'

'But the fire must have taken quickly,' said Charlie, 'for

otherwise someone on the street would have seen it and called you outside.'

Luzie shrugged.

'Maybe you're right. I haven't had much time to think. When I saw the fire, I just assumed it was them. I mean, who else has taken the trouble to threaten me?'

'No, you're right, my dear,' he agreed. 'I just wondered - they must have moved fast, with people still out in the street. And I ken Jem is not at home yet, nor was intending to go home ...' He stopped. He had not considered Jem to be a possible fire raiser until the words were out of his own mouth. He liked Jem - or at least felt for him. He had no wish to accuse him. Could he have done this? On behalf of his stepfather's business?

No, he was sure Jem would do no such thing. Jem had an intensity that could almost be felt, burning behind his eyes. He was too wrapped up in the story of his stepfather's death and then Minnie's murder, and the possible involvement of his step-uncle or Alan Beith. Charlie would have been surprised if anything else had even occurred to him this evening.

But Stephen Meston, or Alan Beith at his orders ...

He drained his ale mug.

'You go on to bed, my love. I'll see you later.'

'Where are you going, Charlie?' He knew from her face she was making a very shrewd guess.

'Never mind - I'll be back late, probably. Dinna worry. It'll be all right.'

Those words beat in his head in time with his footsteps as he made his way, lantern-lit, back along Broad Street towards the Castlegate. It'll be all right. What did he mean? What did Luzie think he meant? Was either of them right?

The frost was hard, the air sharp as he drew it into his throat. The blood pumped in his temples as he smelled smoke from his own clothing, felt again Luzie's sobbing against his chest. Then the salt spray tempered the cold as once again he slithered his way down to the harbour, and the warehouse by the quay. It was all very well for the Bishop to say that it was late to be calling on people, but that was for a polite visit, a social call. A social call was not what Charlie had in mind.

No courteous rattle at the risp, either, he thought, as he surveyed the front of the building briefly. A light where he knew the kitchen to be, edging about the closed shutters. Nothing elsewhere. With luck he'd catch them finishing their supper - Stephen and Alan at least. If Jem was there ... then that posed more questions about Jem. Allowing himself no further time to reconsider, Charlie set his lantern down, stepped smartly forward and hammered on the door.

It took a moment for the response to come, and he had his fist raised to batter again, when he heard footsteps on the stairs inside.

'Is that you, Jem?' came Stephen Meston's voice, answering at least one of Charlie's questions. There was the sound of bolts being slid back. 'Time you started coming home at a more reasonable hour, my lad.'

The door opened and Stephen, peering round it, caught sight of Charlie.

'What, again?' he asked, and made to close the door. But Charlie was ready, and shoved forward as hard as he could. The door, and Stephen, fell backwards, and Charlie was in, though he had to catch the newel post to save himself from tumbling, too.

'Leave my wife alone!' he shouted, as soon as he had breath. 'If you come near her warehouse or her once more, I'll – I'll see your own business ruined!'

'What are you on about?' Stephen demanded. 'Is that the woman at the funeral? Is she no your wife?'

'She is, as you well know.' Charlie's fists were twitching. He was not a man who fought readily, but just now he did not much feel like holding back. The least thing Stephen might say could end in a punch right in his stupid face. Charlie was breathing hard, and Stephen, sensibly, looked nervous.

'I – I don't know what you're talking about,' he said, and it was clear he was trying his best to sound calming, conciliatory. He was not a fighting man, either. 'I'm really sorry, but I've no idea.'

'You need a hand, here, sir?' Alan's voice came from behind Charlie – he must have tiptoed down the stair to join them. Charlie turned so that he could see them both. Two against one, said some reasonable voice in Charlie's mind. Maybe not so sensible, even if Stephen did not look much use in a fight, even if Alan was small and, usually, insignificant. Just now he had a bit of a fixed look in his eye, and Charlie briefly wondered if he had underestimated him. Then he paused, and sniffed.

'What now?' asked Stephen, watching him. 'What do you smell? Is it the supper? We're no managing the cooking awful well, since Minnie ...'

It was true, there was a nasty odour of over-cooked kale about the place, and some kind of gravy that had perhaps been around too long. But there was, apart from Charlie's own clothing, no smell of smoke.

And they would have smelled of smoke, or whichever of them had lit the fire. The way it had been set, and the way they would have had to linger a little if they were not to be thought guilty, they would have been in the billows as the fire took. And there was no smell.

Charlie caught his breath, and made himself unclench his fists, relax his jaw.

'Where were you both this evening?'

Stephen turned white. Alan's jaw dropped, as Stephen demanded,

'Is it Jem? Where is he? Is he all right?'

'We've both been here all evening,' added Alan. Then, his freckled face grim, he glanced at Stephen and asked, 'What's Mr. Jem done now?'

Chapter Forty-Eight

'You're sure you havena been out?'

'We've been here since dinner. We had work to catch up on in the warehouse – you ken, with the funeral and all we're behind, and a cargo had come in from the Hook ... we've been working at it all day. We only stopped to make something to eat.' The look that briefly passed over both their faces told Charlie even more about the quality of the cooking. 'We could have done with Jem here giving us a hand.' Stephen's face had not yet recovered its colour. 'Tell me he's all right? Tell me – for now with my brother and poor Minnie, I begin to fear your arrival.'

'Oh!' Charlie had been slow to realise why Stephen looked so shocked. 'No, as far as I know Mr. Hosie is fine – I mean, I know nothing of any harm that has come to him. No, someone set fire to my wife's warehouse. And after the threats ... well, I thought it must be one of you.'

'Set fire to her warehouse? All that fine coffee? That's terrible!' Stephen seemed genuinely distressed at the thought. Alan looked more thoughtful.

'Threats?' he asked. 'What was that, then?'

Charlie shook his head a little to clear it. He had not expected to have to explain what had happened.

'Mr. Cuthbert Meston called in to my wife's warehouse last Friday night, told her his customers had complained that his coffee was not as good as hers, and demanded she ensure that he was supplied with her coffee. When she refused, he threatened to destroy her business.'

Alan's pale eyebrows wriggled, taking it in.

'Well, aye, I ken what he was like. But he's dead, ken?'

'Aye, indeed,' Charlie agreed, 'but since then there's been things written on her shutters after dark. Threats, d'you see? And when she challenged Mr. Meston here about it at Mr. Cuthbert Meston's funeral, he seemed to know something about it.'

'I did?' said Stephen.

'She certainly thought so,' said Charlie.

'I remember her coming and being angry,' said Stephen, frowning. 'She was that raist with me, but I'm not sure I remember why.' He rubbed at his forehead. 'Was that it? She thought I'd written threats on her shutters?'

'Are you saying you didn't?'

'Well, I am, aye,' said Stephen. 'I mean, I've hardly had time for myself, these last few days. Why would I take the time to go to – is she up by Longacre as well? I think I remember the place ... why would I go up there and threaten someone I barely knew? Anyway, our coffee's good – someone has to have the best, I suppose, and this time it isn't us. It's still good.'

Charlie glared at him, examining his face minutely. Then his hands – you could tell a lot from people's hands. And all he saw in Stephen's hands was anxious tension, and all he saw in Stephen's face was confusion, and honesty, and a deep desire to be believed. Charlie sagged against the wall. What should he do now? What would Luzie want him to do? She would not want him to punch the wrong man, that was certain. He glanced round at Alan, grumpily protective of his employer. He was not the right man either, Charlie was sure of it. So now what?

Luzie would just want him to go home now. But before he did, there was another question in Charlie's head – what, now that he was here, would Bishop Skinner want him to do?

'Listen,' he said, trying to sound now like someone who had not just beaten at their front door with a view to throwing a few punches, 'listen, have you had any more ideas of what Mr. Cuthbert was doing in Edinburgh?'

'What has that to do with your wife's warehouse?' asked Stephen, not at all convinced.

'Well ... he came back from Edinburgh and then went up to

Broad Street and threatened her. Maybe he was doing business in Edinburgh and my wife's name came up?'

'He was not doing business in Edinburgh,' said Stephen, now a little sulky. 'Not that kind of business.'

'How do you know?'

Stephen did not answer at once. Charlie knew he should wait, but it had been a long evening.

'Jem said a letter had come from Edinburgh since your brother's death, a letter addressed to him.'

'I didn't see ...'

'He said you paid for it.'

'Oh, that letter.' This time Charlie was not convinced, but it barely mattered. Stephen went on. 'It was from some lawyer. Cuthbert must have met him in Edinburgh when he went down – I mean, that seemed to be why he had gone down. There was not much to the letter – I can show you, if you insist, but it looked as if it was a matter of an inheritance. Och, look, here – come upstairs and I'll show you the thing.'

He must have had the letter in his room, for he disappeared for a moment leaving Charlie and Alan, still hovering protectively, in the kitchen.

'Did you know about yon letter?' Charlie asked. Alan shrugged, but he was still hostile.

'I dinna even know about it now. I've never seen nor heard of it. So has a'body found out yet who killed them? Who killed my bonnie Minnie?'

'I've no idea. I'm just a servant, ken.'

'Oh, aye.' Alan was dismissive. 'Aye, we're no here to have minds of our own, are we?'

Charlie tried a conciliatory smile, but Alan had turned away to poke at the fire. The room was not over-warm, and the remains of their supper still lay on dishes on the table, congealing unattractively.

'Here,' said Stephen, coming back into the room. 'Take a look for yourself. I canna see that it has anything to do with anything.'

The letter was indeed short, and the lawyer's black, sloping hand was fairly clear.

'You will by now no doubt have informed your young Charge of his good Fortune in the Legacy from Mr. Cummins. I trust we will have the Pleasure of meeting him in the near Future either here or, if it please you, in Aberdeen, to discuss further the Arrangements concerning the Legacy until his coming of full Age.'

'Who is this Mr. Cummins?' Charlie asked, handing the letter back to Stephen. Stephen shook his head.

'I've never heard of him. You'd have to ask Jem – but I doubt Jem knew this was coming. He's never mentioned any expectations except for his mother's own money. I suppose this could be a godfather? Some relative of his mother's, perhaps? I've never heard the name before.'

'Was your brother Mr. Hosie's legal guardian?'

'Aye, he was. I don't know who would be now.' It did not seem to have occurred to him, even, that he himself might have that role.

'And does Mr. Hosie yet know of this?'

'I've barely seen him since the letter came. There was the funeral – it did not seem the time. I need to speak to him, though, and to write to this lawyer and explain ... doubtless they'll appoint someone else.'

In any case, Charlie thought to himself as he trudged back up Marischal Street again, it did not look as if Stephen would have had the opportunity to take the money without Jem knowing, nor even that the idea had occurred to him. The letter had simply arrived at a busy time and required thinking about, and Stephen had not yet had the chance to do that.

The bell of the Town Kirk grated a little, then swung into action. Charlie counted the chimes – midnight. It was Friday. Minnie's funeral, and the arrival of Bishop Kilgour. Who had set fire to Luzie's warehouse? He was sure it was not Stephen Meston nor Alan Beith. Could it have been Jem? He did not even know where Jem was tonight. Someone else entirely? That thought would not comfort Luzie. Oh, Luzie ... Charlie, tired though he was, put a touch more speed to his stride, and headed home to be with his wife.

Charlie did not sleep well: the lingering aroma of heavily scented smoke in the house made its way into his dreams, and from Luzie's restlessness beside him he was sure she was similarly affected. Nevertheless, they rose at their usual time in the morning, bleary-eyed and mostly wordless, and went about their early duties with as much enthusiasm as automata. If Charlie had been less tired himself, he might have been more amazed at Luzie's uncharacteristic lack of energy. As it was it made perfect sense to him.

And today was a day when he needed his wits about him, he thought reluctantly as he made his way over to Longacre. Today was the day that Bishop Kilgour was to arrive, the day that Bishop Skinner hoped they would at last piece together what had happened, so that they could concentrate on the important matter of Samuel Seabury. Bishop Kilgour was a busy man: apart from all the other considerations, he would not want to be kept waiting while they dealt with death and destruction.

'I've had word from Mrs. Gray,' said Bishop Skinner, almost as soon as Charlie had appeared. 'Minnie's funeral is to be early: one of her old women is on a decline and needs her attention, and besides, she does not think that there will be many people to mourn poor Minnie. I had wanted you to go, but I think I shall attend, too. Mrs. Skinner is very fatigued today so Jane will come in her stead, to sit with the women. Margaret can help Jean in the kitchen.'

Charlie did not see that that would placate Jean very much. She tolerated Jane, as a sensible girl, but Margaret she regarded as flighty and too young for reason. But he nodded, knowing he would have to go and break the news to Jean anyway. At least he would not have to linger long.

'It's a disgrace,' muttered Jean predictably. 'Not a hand's turn of work have you done about the place since yon American arrived.'

Charlie could not help glancing at the buckets of coal he had brought in that morning, which he would now take upstairs, nor at the barrel he had already filled with water for the day. There was little point. He did his best to smile apologetically, and left Jean to it.

'I sent a note to Stephen Meston,' Mrs. Gray said when she admitted them, in person, at the women's hospital in Queen Street. 'I don't know if they can come or not, but I thought I should.'

'Mr. Hosie said he hoped to be here,' Bishop Skinner reassured her.

'I think the warehouseman will probably come if he can,' Charlie added. Mrs. Gray seemed pleased.

'I don't like to think of her friendless at the last. But the Houstouns are here, anyway – they have provided much of the food,' she admitted.

The room where they had laid out Minnie's tiny body was lined about the walls with all the benches and chairs the house could provide, and about a dozen of them were already occupied by the old women for whom this hospital was home. Most were solemnly aware of the occasion, but one or two were gossiping more loudly than was the custom at a funeral. Charlie thought that Minnie probably would not mind.

Mrs. Houstoun was busying herself helping Mrs. Gray serve the funeral meats, and her husband George Houstoun stood by the fireplace proprietorially in a fine black coat and buff waistcoat, presiding over the hospitality. He must have expected Bishop Skinner to appear for he had his best customer's smile ready, and something like it, empty and more patronising, for Jane Skinner. Charlie noted his well-polished buckles and smiled to himself. George Houstoun always took every opportunity to be well turned-out.

Except last night, at the fire, Charlie thought suddenly. An old suit of clothes, Charlie had noticed. Now, why would he wear an old suit?

Unless he knew in advance that there was going to be smoke and dirt, of course.

Unless it had been George Houstoun who had set the fire.

Chapter Forty-Nine

When he caught George Houstoun's eye he was sure. Houstoun had never before found it difficult to meet the gaze of someone as lowly in his eyes as Charlie. Now he tried looking past him, at his chin, at his hair, at his feet ... Charlie looked away then, too. Time enough later to sort out that particular matter – though now that he had thought of it, it made sense. George Houstoun had never thought much of women in business, and Luzie had refused to sell him her fine coffee. No wonder Houstoun was resentful – and no wonder Stephen Meston had looked bewildered.

'What's the matter, Charlie?' asked Jane Skinner quietly, waiting as her father paid his respects to the corpse.

'I think it would take too long to explain just now, Miss,' said Charlie, 'and it has nothing to do with Minnie or Cuthbert Meston's death, so I think I'd better leave it till later.'

'I'm going to ask Mrs. Gray if there's anything I can do to help,' said Jane. 'Coming?'

'Aye, of course.'

There was not, honestly, much to do. It allowed Mrs. Gray to disappear to tend to her patient for the best part of the morning as the mourners sat about, eating shortbread and listening to the two old women by the window talking about their grandsons. At nine Stephen Meston arrived, with Alan Beith, and they went at once to pay their respects to Minnie. One or two of the old women perked up and paid a little more attention with two comparatively young men in the room. Before Bishop Skinner could speak with either of them, they had been found seats amongst the women and absorbed into the conversation. George Houstoun smirked, then caught Charlie's eye again by accident. He looked away hurriedly.

Bishop Skinner came over to Charlie.

'Tell me again what you found out last night?'

Charlie went over all that had happened at the Meston warehouse, not that it was much. Bishop Skinner looked at the two men, one at a time, covertly over Charlie's shoulder.

'So did you take any impression that either of them might be guilty?'

Charlie puffed out in frustration and shook his head.

'I have no idea, sir. And, to be honest ... we only have Jem Hosie's word that Minnie said anything about two men they both knew. Except ...'

'Go on?'

'Except they said he had taken a lantern with him. And all their lanterns were there, at home.'

'You reckon that – what, someone automatically took it home?'

'It's the only thing that makes sense, I think, sir,' said Charlie.

'Aye, that's true enough,' said the Bishop after a moment. 'So what if it was Jem Hosie, then? And we don't even know where he's gone, though I daresay he'll turn up here before too long.'

'Will he, though, sir?' said Charlie.

'What do you mean?'

'I mean, he told us last night he wasna going home.' Charlie sighed. He knew he had misread people before, believed them innocent when they were anything but. Now he knew he had to give Jem a closer examination than he had wanted to before. 'He told us he wasna going home, but if I had been Jem and guilty, I'd have taken my chance and left the town. If he set off last night, he could be miles away by now.'

'That ...' Bishop Skinner paused, thinking through the implications. 'Then – if they don't catch him – he would not hang. And perhaps he may have had his reasons, with his stepfather. But murder is still a sin as well as a crime, and there is Minnie to consider.'

'It's only ... I'm only thinking of all the possibilities, sir,' said Charlie apologetically. The thought of Jem killing Minnie was still a disturbing one – could he really see the lad doing it? If Minnie threatened him in some way – if Minnie had seen him, not Stephen or Alan, kill Cuthbert Meston?

'Aye, well, that would be right,' agreed Bishop Skinner. 'All three of them ... all three of them knew both Cuthbert Meston and Minnie. But which of them could have done it? Shall we ever discover the truth?'

'Och, sir,' said Charlie, suddenly anxious at his master's desperate face, 'surely we will! It might not be in time for Bishop Kilgour coming, mind you.'

At that, Bishop Skinner gave something like a grin.

'I'm losing all hope of that, Charlie!' He clapped Charlie on the shoulder, but his expression was still worried. He glanced around the room. 'And still no Jem.'

But it was not one of the Meston household that noticed his look. It was George Houstoun, by the fireplace, still trying to look as if he were in charge, and in fact appearing more anxious by the moment.

Bishop Skinner moved away to talk with one lonely looking, elderly lady, and Charlie, moving as if he had no particular purpose, shifted over to talk to Jane, who was tolerating Mrs. Houstoun's chatter.

'May I have a word, Miss?' he asked.

'Of course, Charlie!' Jane managed not to look too pleased to have an excuse to leave Mrs. Houstoun. They moved away, towards the door to the hallway. 'What is it?'

'I'm sorry to draw you from your conversation,' he said, 'but I could do with knowing what you know of the Houstouns?'

'Don't in the least worry about the conversation, Charlie, as I suspect you know! But why do you want to know about them? She talks too much, but I think it may be because she is not very happy. He does not look happy, either, but in his case I think it may be his own fault.'

'How do you mean, miss?' He was inclined to agree, but he wanted to hear what she had to say. She was her mother's daughter, quick and thoughtful.

'He sets himself and those around him such high standards, and of course no one meets them, so he is perpetually disappointed. And he seems to despise all women, which makes it difficult when he has married one. He will not allow her to be a helpmeet in his business, and as they have no children she has no business of her own, and instead gossips about other people's. It is very sad.' She paused. 'Is that what you wanted to hear?'

'Aye, I suppose. I mean, thank you, miss. If Mr. Houstoun were to be slighted by a woman - say, a woman in his line of business, what do you think he would do?'

'Oh!' Jane gave him a sharp look. 'What has happened, Charlie? Is Luzie all right?'

'Aye, aye, she's fine. There was a wee bit of a fire last night, but no one was hurt.'

'And Mr. Houstoun set it?'

'That's my belief, aye.'

'Hm. Well, I can't say I'd be completely surprised.'

'And what if he took against another person in his line of business? Maybe was slighted by him – in his business and personally?'

'And this time I believe you mean Cuthbert Meston, do you not? I know you and my father went to speak to him about Minnie, at least.'

'Aye, that was who I had in mind. I thought we had ruled him out because he was so drunk the night of Mr. Meston's death, and because of what Minnie said. But now, after what happened with Luzie's warehouse ... well, I'm no so sure.'

He could not help glancing over once again at George Houstoun, and saw that the man had been watching them. His heart skipped – he prayed he had not inadvertently put Jane Skinner in any danger.

Mrs. Gray appeared at the top of the stairs, frowned, and hurried down to them.

'Has the minister not arrived yet?'

'No, madam,' said Jane. 'No sign of him. I believe that the carpenter is waiting in the kitchen.'

'Then the poor lass is not even kisted? Where's the minister?'

'Perhaps he has been delayed,' said Jane. 'You know what it's like for clergy. Oh, perhaps this is him now?'

The risp rattled, and Mrs. Gray hastened to the door. But when she opened it, it was Jem Hosie who swept inside, bowed elaborately, then saw Jane and froze, almost mid-bow.

'Miss Skinner!' The words slithered breathlessly from his lips, and he bowed again, much more awkwardly. 'I ... I wasn't expecting ...'

'Good day to you, Mr. Hosie.' Jane curtseyed precisely.

'We are gathered in the parlour here,' said Mrs. Gray, oblivious, guiding Jem in to make his respects. Jane and Charlie stayed at the doorway, Jane looking a little dismayed. But at least, Charlie thought, Jem had not taken the chance to run while he had it. Did that mean he was not guilty? Or that he was confident of not being suspected?

'So what for is the wee lassie dead?' came a creaky, penetrating voice. It was one of Mrs. Gray's old women, the one that Bishop Skinner had gone to speak to. Conversation in the parlour, which had ebbed and flowed again at the arrival of Jem, drained away completely. Charlie stepped softly back into the room, sensing that the tension in the place had risen even higher. Mr. Houstoun looked as uncomfortable as he had earlier, but now Alan Beith and Jem were exchanging odd looks. Mrs. Houstoun stood, one hand to her breast, little rosebud mouth gaping, eyes wide. Stephen Meston stared about him for a moment, then rose unsteadily to his feet. Everyone turned to look at him. What was to come? A confession? An accusation? As wary as Charlie, Bishop Skinner glanced about for Jane, then for Charlie. Charlie nodded, to show he was ready for whatever the Bishop wanted him to do. But before anyone could do anything, the old woman went on.

'I mean, was it the bairn, or what?'

George Houstoun was surprised into speech.

'The bairn? What are you talking about?'

'She was expecting, was she no?'

'She was.' It was Alan Beith, growling.

'What do you know about it, man?' Houstoun demanded. 'What are you doing here anyway, Meston? This is my maid that died. I didn't have you as one of those men who goes about to strangers' funerals for the food and drink.'

'She was our maid before she was yours, Houstoun,' said Stephen, and he sounded weary. Jem was watching him like a cat at a mousehole. Houstoun was clearly taken aback.

'She left you? Did she tire of labouring in such a Godless house?'

'My brother threw her out, because she was with child.'

'Then it's true?' George Houstoun's jaw wobbled briefly, then he scanned the room for his wife. 'Did you know this? Did you know you had taken a fallen woman into our home?'

'I – I didn't know she had worked for – for Mr. Meston.'

'That's not what I asked you, woman! You don't have much to do – the least you could do is to make sure that we have respectable servants!'

'If you'd let me pay them properly we might be able to have them!' Mrs. Houstoun retorted, then covered her mouth, shocked at her own boldness. But Mrs. Gray hurried over to her.

'Mrs. Houstoun, please, and Mr. Houstoun – remember where you are, both of you.'

'I will not be spoken to like that,' said Mr. Houstoun. 'And I will not remain at this – this event. The burial of a woman so far fallen from grace? No wonder the minister is not here!'

'I'm sure he is on his way,' said Bishop Skinner suddenly. 'After all, our Lord lowered himself to eat with sinners. And when it comes down to it, can any of us cast the first stone?' His voice was mild, but firm. George Houstoun worked his jaw, lost for an answer. Bishop Skinner, taking advantage, addressed the woman who had asked.

'This girl was murdered, mistress. And it's my belief that she was murdered because she saw who killed Cuthbert Meston over in Longacre last week.'

Jem nodded.

'I agree with Bishop Skinner,' he announced boldly, then glanced at Jane. 'He must be right.' He went to stand by the Bishop, emphasising his support.

Mrs. Houstoun sat down suddenly, and stared hard at the floor.

'Well, I hope you're not accusing me,' George Houstoun almost shouted. 'I had no reason to kill Meston.'

'Mr. Houstoun!' snapped Mrs. Gray. She laid a kindly hand on Minnie's shoulder as she lay, a silent witness to this unseemly squabble. 'Be good enough to keep to your word, and leave this house.'

'I shall!' But he still hesitated a moment, as if afraid of what might be said in his absence.

'Don't let him go like that!' Stephen Meston made a lunge for the door, to block Houstoun's way. 'What if he did kill them both?'

'If he knew that Minnie had seen him kill Cuthbert Meston,' said Bishop Skinner, 'and she was in his house, why did he wait until Tuesday to kill her? He had every opportunity to do it before that, and stop her from talking.'

'I don't hold with bishops,' said Houstoun, 'but for once you're speaking sense.'

'You're very kind, sir,' said Bishop Skinner with a smile. 'No, I don't believe you killed either of them. But the murderer is in this room, nevertheless.'

A shiver ran up Charlie's spine. Was the Bishop guessing, in the hope of chasing out the guilty man? Beside him he felt Jane clutch at his sleeve, equally anxious.

Alan Beith got slowly to his feet.

'It's Jem, is it no?'

'Me?' Jem's dark eyes widened. 'What?'

'You never got on with your stepfather, did you?' Alan said. 'Go on, Mr. Jem, admit it. Think of the fine speech you could make from the scaffold.'

'What?' Jem was struggling to speak. Alan laughed, but it was bitter.

'And as for Minnie, you kenned she loved me more than you. You were aye jealous.'

'Wha - what?'

'Oh, I don't think that makes sense,' said Jane Skinner, stepping forward. 'No, that's wrong.'

Jem turned and stared at her in wonder.

'Jane?' The Bishop looked at her too, surprised. Then he looked at Jem, and light dawned. And then he looked again at Alan Beith.

'I think perhaps, Alan, you are clutching at straws - is that not so?'

Alan drew breath, paused, then shouted,

'Look out! He has a knife!'

He sprang for Jem while the room erupted in screams. Charlie shoved Jane back towards the door, away from Alan. There was a knife, indeed: light flashed on the blade. The Bishop staggered, clutching the table as Jem tumbled against him and fell, with a grunt, to the floor.

Charlie lunged and seized Alan. He had a tight grip on Alan's arms, forced behind his back. The knife fell with a soft, scarlet thud on to the boards. Bishop Skinner stepped back, astonished, but Jane knelt quickly beside Jem, touched the wound with featherlight fingers. Charlie could see her face, but he hoped that Jem had not seen that brief moment when she recognised there was no chance of survival. But Jane quickly shifted to a smile, and brushed Jem's long hair back. Jem looked up into her eyes, and for a moment his own face lit up, happiness blazing. Then the light faded, and was gone.

Chapter Fifty

'I am a fool,' said Bishop Skinner, his elbows on his knees. 'Such a fool. I provoked that attack – and now poor Jem ...'

Jane Skinner, her face still blotchy, gave her father a hug, but had no words.

'Did you know which of them had done it? How did you know?' asked Myles Cooper eagerly.

'I didn't,' said the Bishop. 'I hoped that if I said I knew, something might give one of them away.'

'Charlie knew, though, didn't you?' said Jane. Everyone turned to look at him, and he felt his face turn scarlet. He had to clear his throat.

'I thought I did, maybe ...'

'Why was that, then, Charlie?' asked Bishop Petrie.

'Well ... Jem Hosie said it had to be Stephen or Alan, though we had no proof that Minnie had actually told him that. I thought it had to be Jem or Alan, really, because Stephen hardly knew his way round this part of the town. I didna want it to be Jem, but I had to think about that, all the same. But Alan was aye telling me reasons why Stephen or Jem might have done it. Jem didna get on with his stepfather, and Stephen was a hard man, and the like. As if he knew well that suspicion would fall on the household, and he wanted to make sure it missed him. It made me wonder more about him. And he was the most likely person to know where Minnie was. And he was out the night Minnie died – I mean, they were all out and all over the place the night Cuthbert Meston died, but Jem and Alan were out the night Minnie died – but Alan was the one who had gone to the trouble of having an excuse for being out. I doubt if they look for his friends who needed his help, they'll no find them.'

He stopped, still red in the face, and stared at the floor, hoping they would not ask him anything more.

'He said,' put in Robert Strang, the magistrate, 'that he was defending the Bishop from Mr. Hosie, who had a knife.' He was, as usual, perched on an upright chair with his limbs arranged as neatly as a statue. 'But there was no other knife, was there? Only his own. And when I told him that, of course, it all came out, for he was going to be tried for Mr. Hosie's murder, anyway. He resented Cuthbert Meston's treatment of Minnie, and of himself, and it culminated when Meston threw Minnie out. But when he told Minnie what he had done, thinking she would be pleased, he realised he had made a mistake. I don't know that she had seen him, as she apparently told Mr. Hosie. But she knew, nevertheless. And she was not going to hide a murderer, even if he was the father of her child. A man of unsteady temper.' He pursed his lips, and eyed Myles Cooper and Samuel Seabury. 'All this going on outside your door here, Mr. Skinner, and yet in the end it had nothing to do with you, or your guests.'

'No. It might all have happened somewhere else had it not been for the Houstouns. And perhaps for Jem's ...' he glanced at Jane, 'for Jem's frequent appearance in Longacre. All the fankle of Jem and anonymous letters and threats to Luzie Rob's warehouse – involving George Houstoun again - that must have given Alan the idea of leaving poor Minnie outside our door, too, to reinforce the whole idea.'

'And of course you, Mr. Cooper, very helpfully told us of Meston's quarrel with Dr. Seabury – which in the end was also irrelevant,' added the magistrate with precision. Myles shrank into himself and wriggled his shoulders.

'I was trying to be helpful,' he pouted.

'Of course you were, Myles,' said Dr. Seabury, though he could not quite suppress a sigh. 'It was good of you.'

At last the magistrate gathered himself up neatly and declared that he had no need to trouble them longer for now. His hefty helper had already dragged Alan Beith off with a look of great enthusiasm, and as soon as Mr. Strang had gone the entire house seemed to breathe a sigh of relief.

But no sooner had they thought of stirring than there was a sound of carriage wheels in Longacre, and they drew to a halt just outside Bishop Skinner's front door.

'Oh, heavens,' he said, without having to rise from his chair. 'Bishop Kilgour.'

And it was.

'Brother Skinner! John! Good to see you looking so well and content,' Bishop Kilgour began. 'And Brother Petrie! Why did you not come to stay with us in Peterhead? I am convinced the waters would have done you the world of good. Yet still ... I am pleased to find you as well as you are. Now, then – this gentleman must be Samuel Seabury, the much-journeyed American. Good day to you, good day to you!'

After dinner, after supper, and all the following morning the tubby little whirlwind that was Robert Kilgour was closeted with Dr. Seabury and Bishops Skinner and Petrie in the bookroom, while Myles Cooper irritated his hosts by sleeping, drinking, relaying more Edinburgh gossip, and pacing nervously up and down the parlour like an expectant father awaiting his infant's first cry. Jane Skinner, still a little red-eyed, insisted on accompanying Charlie when he took Bishop Petrie's lap dog out for a walk. She had said little since yesterday morning, but he was pleased enough to have her company.

'I canna be out for long, miss,' Charlie explained. 'Jean's at her wits' end.'

'With the preparations? I know. I'll help, too, as soon as we get back. And it still might all come to nothing, of course ...'

'I hear, by the way, that Minnie was safely buried in the end.'

'What a funeral, Charlie – but thank you for telling me. Poor little Minnie.'

When they returned, Mrs. Skinner, from her seat in the kitchen, was directing operations, with shopping lists, and instructions to Jean, and orders for her daughters, and a stiff piece of paper for a fan which she agitated before her forehead. Jean was stacking freshly baked food on racks in the pantry with one-handed efficiency.

'Any word, Mamma?' Jane asked. Bishop Petrie's dog, wisely, retreated under the chair.

'Nothing yet, no. I have the invitations written, though: the minute we hear, if it's yes, Charlie, you'll have to run out and deliver the lot. Johnnie can help you. Jane, can you wash those vegetables? Margaret, have you looked over the table linen? Have we enough decent napkins - the large ones?'

'My dear!'

It was Bishop Skinner at the kitchen door. Everyone stopped what they were doing, and turned towards him. He had rarely had such an expectant audience.

'Yes, John?'

'Bishop Kilgour has said yes. There will be a consecration tomorrow!'

The smell of polish in the chapel upstairs was almost overwhelming, but as the Episcopalians of the town arrived, chatting excitedly, it was at last drowned by the competing scents of wig powder and rosewater. Charlie, in his best suit of clothes again, stood ready to admit the congregation, while Johnnie Skinner showed them to their seats. William Seller, whose concerned letter had almost prevented everything, had received an invitation and arrived, nervous, accompanied by his old friend from the school.

'Are you quite sure?' he said for the third time to Charlie. 'I am to be admitted?'

'Aye, sir: Bishop Skinner and Dr. Seabury asked specially.'

'Praise the Lord!' murmured the thin man, and headed up the stairs in wonder.

'Charlie!' Bishop Skinner called from the top of the stairs, 'we have no chair ready! Can you fetch up one from the dining room?'

'Aye, sir.'

He made for the stairs, and met Dr. Seabury, lingering nervous on the landing. Unexpectedly, he put out a hand to Charlie to stop him.

'Aye, sir? Can I help at all?'

'Slavery, Charlie,' said Dr. Seabury.

'What, sir?'

'This business - I have talked it over with the bishops, Charlie. The girl, Minnie, and Alan - they were no better than slaves, were they?'

'Not really, sir, no. I see what you meant about not being able to leave, even if you're supposed to be free.'

'But when I say no better than slaves ...' He frowned, as if he could not quite articulate his thoughts. 'That shows, I suppose, that I do not think slaves well treated.'

'That's what people think, sir, I suppose.'

'I am resolved, after all I have seen here, to treat my slaves better,' said Seabury. 'To free them - particularly as things are now in America - to free them might place them in danger. And it would be seen as eccentric, I believe. But I can treat them much better than I do. I resolve to do so.' He nodded, firmly, but seemed to have forgotten that Charlie was there. Charlie bowed, and turned away. It was, he supposed, a step in the right direction. Good treatment was the main thing, for slave or free - or for anybody.

A chair. Charlie hurried down into the dining room, laid and ready for the dinner that was to follow. He hesitated. Was there a particular chair he should take? But there was little distinction between the dining chairs. He seized the nearest, and carried it quickly upstairs to the chapel, setting it beside the small, plain table with its white cloth that served as a Communion table.

And it was not much later when he watched from his place, standing by the door of the chapel with half a dozen others who could not find a seat, as Samuel Seabury, placed on the chair by the guiding hand of Bishop Kilgour, had the hands of all the bishops laid on his head, and the prayers of consecration said over him, and having sat as Samuel Seabury, he arose as the first Bishop of Connecticut.

Myles Cooper, looking after Bishop Petrie's lap dog in the front row, wiped a tear from his eye. Charlie breathed out in relief, and Mrs. Skinner, seated at the other side of the chapel, saw him and grinned. And all three bishops - all four now - were grinning, too. It was done.

A note:

Samuel Seabury, clergyman of Connecticut, did indeed sail to England in 1783 to ask for consecration as the first Bishop of the Anglican Church in America, and was indeed turned down, after many delays, because he could not take the oath of allegiance to King George III. This was ironic, as he had actually been a loyalist in the war. He then travelled to Scotland and asked the bishops there to consecrate him, which they did on 14th November, 1784.

Bishops Kilgour, Petrie and Skinner were real, as was Myles Cooper. William Seller did indeed send the letter to Bishop Kilgour, raising concerns which Seabury managed to allay: he had the full support of the Connecticut clergy. Sellar's letter, along with some of the correspondence between the Bishops regarding Seabury (and from Seabury later, including his joking reference to becoming 'Bishop of America'), is held in the National Records of Scotland (www.nrscotland.gov.uk). A brief summary of the history of the Scottish Episcopal Church, including this complicated period, can be found at www.episcopalhistory.org.

The chapel in which Seabury was consecrated no longer exists, though there is a plaque in Marischal College, Aberdeen, to mark its approximate site. Bishop John Skinner, who later became Primus (or head bishop) of the Scottish church (as did his son William later still), built a new chapel beside his house and then, later, founded what is now St. Andrew's Cathedral in King Street, Aberdeen. There Seabury and Skinner are further commemorated. One aisle has a ceiling decorated with the shields of the (then) forty-eight states of America, and at its consecration in the 1930s the American ambassador, Joseph Kennedy, attended, along with his son John. There are still strong links between St. Andrew's, Aberdeen, and the Episcopal Church in America, particularly in Connecticut.

Married women at this stage in Scottish history (and for much longer) were known by their maiden names, so that Seabury in his letters refers to Bishop Skinner's wife as Mrs. Robertson, and Luzie would have been known as Mrs. Gheertzoon. But for the purposes of clarity to a modern audience I've taken the liberty of changing this to more familiar usage.

John Smith, city architect, was a young lad who lived with his father in Longacre – he later worked with Prince Albert on the building of Balmoral Castle. Bodsy Bowers the teacher was also a real person.

Roughly nothing else in this book actually happened!

Scots words in this book (though many are also in use elsewhere)

Behouchie - bottom
Canny - wise or knowing
Chap - knock (on a door)
Claik - gossip
Clart - muck
Cludgie - chamber pot
Clype - tell tales
Corpus - corpse
Curator bonis (Latin Scots law) - lit. carer for goods, one who oversees an estate for a minor or legally incapacitated person
Dominie - schoolmaster
Fankle - fuss
Fit like? - How are you? (mainly north-east)
Fou - drunk
Gey - very
Guddle - confuse / confusion
Happed - wrapped, warmly dressed
Howff - rough pub
Kist - box or chest
Kisting - placing a body in its coffin, usually attended with prayers
Lanie, whilie, etc. - the diminutive is a particular North-East habit
Mintie - minute
Neep - turnip or swede
Nervish - nervous
Oxters - armpits
Pech - pant, gasp
Quine - woman (see Norwegian kvinne, if you're into that kind of thing)
Raist - angry
Risp - a twisted iron bar with an iron loop around it, rattled in place of a door knocker.
Scaffie - refuse collector
Scooneral - scoundrel
Skyrie - bright, glaring
Shilpit - starved or drawn-looking, unimpressive
Tappit hen - a kind of lidded jug, a Scottish quart measure
Thrawn - stubborn

Trashtrie – useless or worthless rubbish
Trig – neat and tidy
Ull-fashent - nosy
Wainished-like - thin
Wheen – a great quantity

About the Author

Lexie Conyngham is a historian living in the shadow of the Highlands. Her historical crime novels are born of a life amidst Scotland's old cities, ancient universities and hidden-away aristocratic estates, but she has written since the day she found out that people were allowed to do such a thing. Beyond teaching and research, her days are spent with wool, wild allotments and a wee bit of whisky.

We hope you've enjoyed this instalment. Reviews are important to authors, so it would be lovely if you could post a review where you bought it! Here are a few handy links …

Visit our website at www.lexieconyngham.co.uk. There are several free Murray of Letho short stories, Murray's World Tour of Edinburgh, and the chance to follow Lexie Conyngham's meandering thoughts on writing, gardening and knitting, at www.murrayofletho.blogspot.co.uk. You can also follow Lexie, should such a thing appeal, on Facebook, Pinterest or Instagram.

Finally! If you'd like to be kept up to date with Lexie and her writing, please join our mailing list at: contact@kellascatpress.co.uk. There's a quarterly newsletter, often with a short story attached, and fair warning of any new books coming out.

Murray of Letho

We first meet Charles Murray when he's a student at St. Andrews University in Fife in 1802, resisting his father's attempts to force him home to the family estate to learn how it's run. Pushed into involvement in the investigation of a professor's death, he solves his first murder before taking up a post as tutor to Lord Scoggie. This series takes us around Georgian Scotland as well as India, Italy and Norway (so far!), in the company of Murray, his manservant Robbins, his father's old friend Blair, the enigmatic Mary, and other members of his occasionally shambolic household.

Death in a Scarlet Gown

The Status of Murder (a novella)

Knowledge of Sins Past

Service of the Heir: An Edinburgh Murder

An Abandoned Woman

Fellowship with Demons

The Tender Herb: A Murder in Mughal India

Death of an Officer's Lady

Out of a Dark Reflection

A Dark Night at Midsummer (a novella)

Slow Death by Quicksilver

Thicker than Water

A Deficit of Bones

The Dead Chase

Shroud for a Sinner

Hippolyta Napier

Hippolyta Napier is only nineteen when she arrives in Ballater, on Deeside, in 1829, the new wife of the local doctor. Blessed with a love of animals, a talent for painting, a helpless instinct for hospitality, and insatiable curiosity, Hippolyta finds her feet in her new home and role in society, making friends and enemies as she goes. Ballater may be small but it attracts great numbers of visitors, so the issues of the time, politics, slavery, medical advances, all affect the locals. Hippolyta, despite her loving husband and their friend Durris, the sheriff's officer, manages to involve herself in all kinds of dangerous adventures in her efforts to solve every mystery that presents itself.

A Knife in Darkness

Death of a False Physician

A Murderous Game

The Thankless Child

A Lochgorm Lament

The Corrupted Blood

Orkneyinga Murders

Orkney, c.1050 A.D.: Thorfinn Sigurdarson, Earl of Orkney, rules from the Brough of Birsay on the western edges of these islands. Ketal Gunnarson is his man, representing his interests in any part of his extended realm. When Sigri, a childhood friend of Ketil's, finds a dead man on her land, Ketil, despite his distrust of islands, is commissioned to investigate. Sigrid, though she has quite enough to do, decides he cannot manage on his own, and insists on helping – which Ketil might or might not appreciate.

Tomb for an Eagle

A Wolf at the Gate

Dragon in the Snow

The Bear at Midnight

Other books by Lexie Conyngham:

Windhorse Burning

'I'm not mad, for a start, and I'm about as far from violent as you can get.'
When Toby's mother, Tibet activist Susan Hepplewhite, dies, he is determined to honour her memory. He finds her diaries and decides to have them translated into English. But his mother had a secret, and she was not the only one: Toby's decision will lead to obsession and murder.

The War, The Bones, and Dr. Cowie

Far from the London Blitz, Marian Cowie is reluctantly resting in rural Aberdeenshire when a German 'plane crashes nearby. An airman goes missing, and old bones are revealed. Marian is sure she could solve the mystery if only the villagers would stop telling her useless stories – but then the crisis comes, and Marian finds the stories may have a use after all.

Jail Fever

It's the year 2000, and millennium paranoia is everywhere.
Eliot is a bad-tempered merchant with a shady past, feeling under the weather.
Catriona is an archaeologist at a student dig, when she finds something unexpected.
Tom is a microbiologist, investigating a new and terrible disease with a stigma.
Together, their knowledge could save thousands of lives – but someone does not want them to …

The Slaughter of Leith Hall

'See, Charlie, it might be near twenty years since Culloden, but there's plenty hard feelings still amongst the Jacobites, and no so far under the skin, ken?'
Charlie Rob has never thought of politics, nor strayed far from his

Aberdeenshire birthplace. But when John Leith of Leith Hall takes him under his wing, his life changes completely. Soon he is far from home, dealing with conspiracy and murder, and lost in a desperate hunt for justice.

Thrawn Thoughts and Blithe Bits **and** ***Quite Useful in Minor Emergencies***

Two collections of short stories, some featuring characters from the series, some not; some seen before, some not; some long, some very short. Find a whole new dimension to car theft, the life history of an unfortunate Victorian rebel, a problem with dragons and a problem with draugens, and what happens when you advertise that you've found somebody's leg.

Printed in Great Britain
by Amazon

87815559R00192